ONE SHILLING. (7)

I0685311

ON THE QUEEN'S SERVICE,

A TALE OF MANY LANDS.

"KICK THOSE PISTOLS OVER TOWARDS THE WINDOW! KICK THEM OVER, OR, YOU DIE ON THE INSTANT!"

LONDON: HOGARTH HOUSE, BOUVERIE STREET, FLEET STREET, E.C.

ON THE QUEEN'S SERVICE,

A TALE OF MANY LANDS.

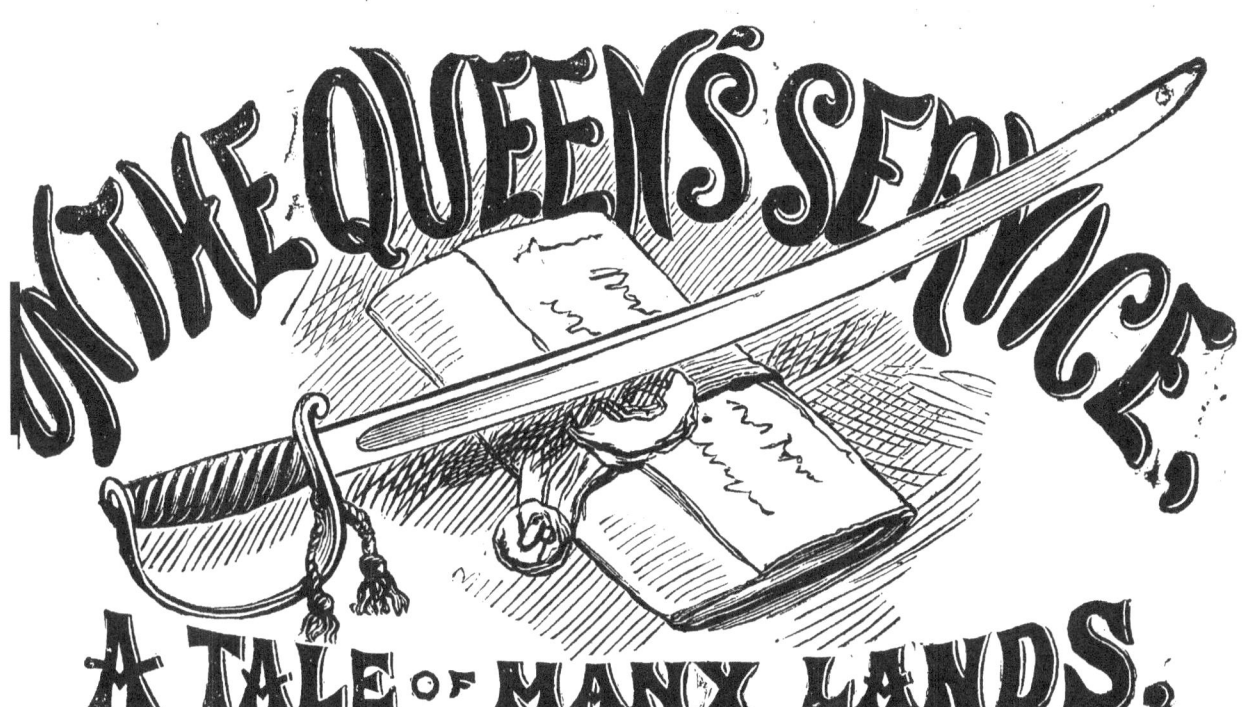

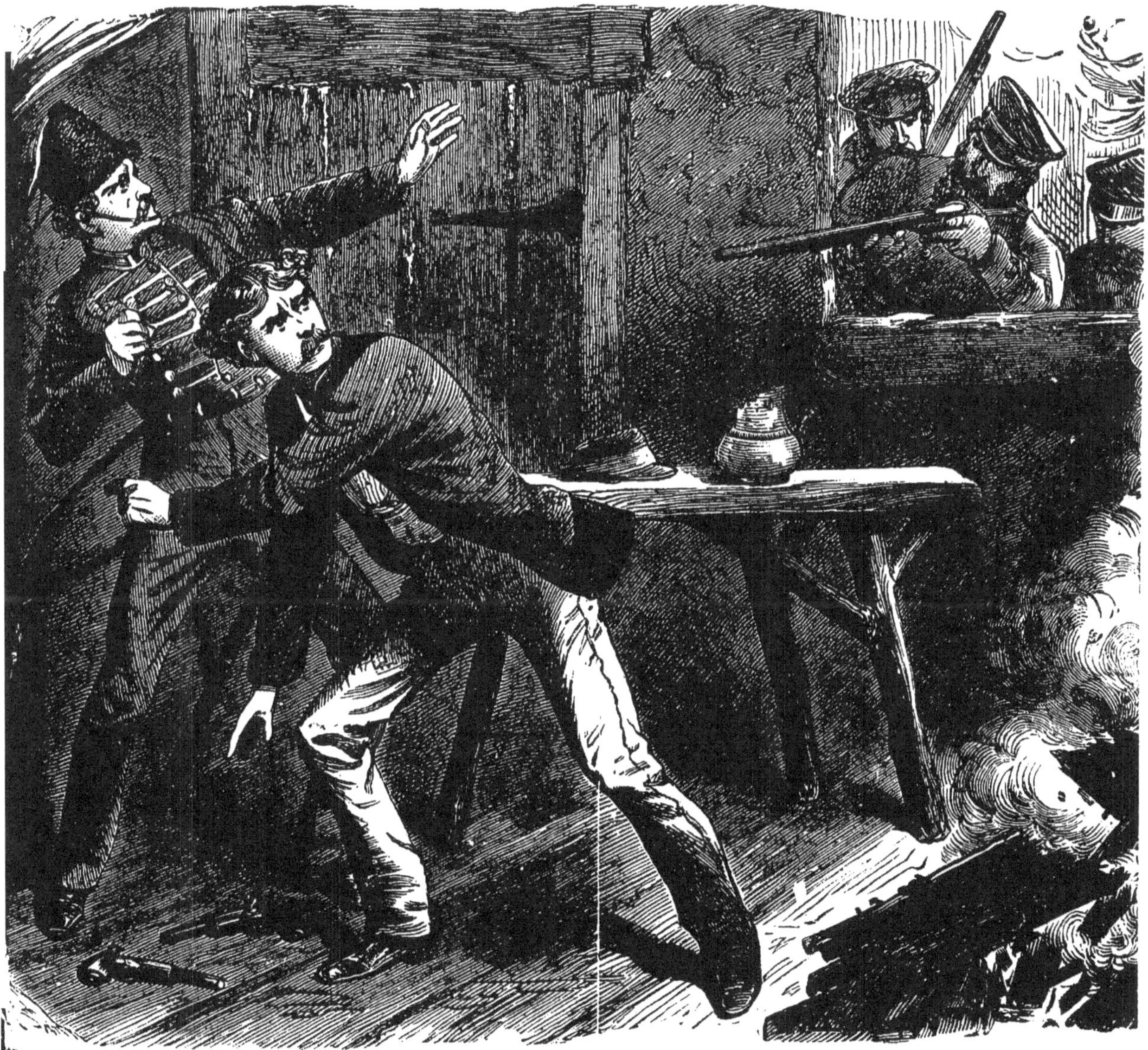

KICK THOSE PISTOLS OVER TOWARDS THE WINDOWS; KICK THEM OVER, OR, YOU DIE ON THE INSTANT."

No. 1

ON THE QUEEN'S SERVICE:

A TALE OF MANY LANDS.

———◦◦◦———

By J. J. G. Bradley.

Author of "Through a Thousand Perils," "That Rascal Jack," "The Cruise of the Alabama,"
"The King of the Conjurors," &c., &c., &c.

———◦◦◦———

CHAPTER I.

IN WHICH I VENTURE TO INTRODUCE MYSELF TO MY READERS.

THE year 1855 was the most breathlessly exciting of any that have distinguished the present century, with the sole exception of 1815, the year of Waterloo.

Napoleon's reign of a hundred days I recollect nothing of, for the simple reason, perhaps, that I was not born for a considerable time after; but inasmuch as 1855 was pregnant with the most romantic, adventurous, and startling events of my life, its every event has become indelibly engraven on my memory.

A few words will explain the reason of this. The year 1855 was the second of the Crimean war, and from its January to its December I was engaged in the arduous and hazardous duties of a Queen's Messenger.

The narration of all my adventures during that comparatively brief period of my forty-five years' experience of things mundane would fill many a bulky tome, but as a serial tale must have its limits, I will try to pack the most sensational and exciting into considerably shorter compass.

This must be my excuse for not dwelling upon my birth and parentage—childhood and schoolhood.

My readers can feel no interest in knowing who I was the son of, or at what age I cut my teeth—suffice it, therefore, to say, that at the period my tale opens I was just about the age to combat and surmount the many obstacles that would naturally lie in my path—namely, twenty-five.

I was enjoying myself very much at a ball at the Countess of Cleveland's, when a large, blue enveloped, official-looking letter, bearing the Royal arms on a great splatch of red wax, was put in my hands by a gorgeously liveried footman, who seemed to be duly impressed with the importance of the missive of which he was the bearer.

I was not dancing at the time, and recognising the stamp of the Foreign-office, and that the envelope was furthermore marked "On Her Majesty's Service," I made my way to an obscure corner of the card-room, and read the official communication at my leisure.

Now this did not take me very long to do, for though the letter was written on a large page of foolscap, it simply contained short but imperative instructions to present myself before Her Majesty's Principal Secretary of State for Foreign Affairs, at five o'clock on the following evening, and to hold myself in readiness to proceed forthwith to Con-

stantinople, by way of Mont Cenis, Turin, Milan, Trieste, and the Adriatic.

A nice route this to take in the second week of January!

I cursed my ill-luck for five minutes, and at the end of that time coming to the sensible conclusion that, as the future was disagreeable, I had best plunge heart and mind into the enjoyment of the present, I returned to the ball-room, and danced and drank champagne alternately until the brilliant assembly broke up.

I did not sleep any the less soundly that night because on the succeeding one I might be crossing over from Dover to Calais in a January gale.

The next day, at noon, I bade farewell to my kind friend, the Earl, of whose hospitable mansion I had been an inmate since Christmas Eve—caught the up-express at Didcot half an hour later, and at five o'clock, p.m., to the very minute, I put in an appearance at the Foreign-office.

I and the Chief Secretary of State knew each other very well, and his first greeting, as I entered his luxuriously furnished office, was—

"Ah Dunbar, I'm deuced sorry, 'pon honour, that I can't despatch you to Paris, Vienna, Rome, Florence, or some such earthly Paradise at this infernal time of the year, but urgent affairs of State—you know the hackneyed expression—demand that you go elsewhere. Let me see, you speak Russian and Turkish, I think?"

"Don't know a word of either language, my lord."

"Oh you don't mean that," exclaimed the Foreign Secretary, with a slight elevation of his thick, bushy eyebrows. "I thought you were one of our best linguists?"

"Well, my lord, I speak French, German, Spanish, Portuguese, and Italian, and have a tolerable smattering of Danish, Swedish, and Polish. I certainly think that gives me some claim to the title of linguist," I replied.

"Ah, well, yes—so it does, certainly; but you see with the exception of French, the other seven tongues are at a complete discount just at present. Yet never mind, my boy, the upper classes all over Europe speak French, and I don't suppose you will have much to do with the lower ones. Besides you are the best man I can lay my hands on just at present. Do you know the hour at which the tidal boat leaves Dover for the Continent?"

"Two o'clock in the morning, my lord."

"Not for nine hours!"—well, it can't be helped. Were you to take a special steamer across, you would not get to Paris much ahead, if at all, of the tidal express?"

"I query if I should arrive there so soon," I rejoined.

"No, I really don't think you would. Now, my friend, stay not an instant in Paris. Take a special train, if no express is on the point of starting, straight away for Dijon and Macon, and from thence to St. Michelle. How you will cross Mont Cenis this awful weather I leave you to solve; but, whatever the danger, it must be done. If four horses won't drag your diligence through the snow, have a dozen; if a dozen don't suffice, hire a score; money is no object. Do you follow me, Dunbar?"

"Closely, my lord," I replied, with a nod of the head.

"Arrived at Turin, you take train again to Milan, from thence to the Quadrilateral and Trieste. Don't follow the Venice route: 'tis shorter, I know, but there may be obstacles that you wot not of in the way. From Trieste you proceed by a steamer of the Austrian Lloyds direct to the City of the Sultan, where you will give this despatch into the hands of the British Admiral, whose fleet lies off Pera, and this one to the Sultan Abdul Medjid."

"My lord, it shall be done," I said, as I put the two despatches in the breast-pocket of my coat.

"On returning to the Admiral's ship," continued the Foreign Secretary, "you will hold yourself entirely at his service. You may have to proceed with further despatches to the commanders of the British army before Sebastopol, and from them very probably to the warrior prince and prophet Schamyl, in the far-off Caucasus."

Again I bowed. I rather liked the idea of the e further journeys as they would be over a *terra incognita* to me.

"Now," said the Foreign Secretary, "I have one more instruction to give you, and it is this: you will travel armed to the teeth, and defend your despatches with your life, for their loss may lose England the Crimean War. Travel night and day, sleep, even in your diligence, with one eye open, for perils will beset every inch of your way—perils the magnitude of which you cannot guess. At the pay-office you will draw a thousand pounds to cover your expenses to Constantinople. There you can draw more if needful from the British Ambassador, Lord Stratford de Redcliffe. And now, good bye, my boy, and may Heaven prosper your mission!"

To my surprise the noble lord not only shook hands with me—but actually wrung my hand as though he were bidding me an eternal farewell — then half pushed me from him, and ten minutes later I found myself proceeding up gaslit Pall Mall, scarce certain whether I was on my head or my heels.

I soon shook myself together, however, and forthwith buying a despatch-bag having three brass locks thereon, I drove straight to my favourite hotel.

CHAPTER II.

IN WHICH I AM FAIRLY EN ROUTE.

THE first thing I did, on gaining my hotel, was to secure a bed and sitting room opening into each other, and then to order a thoroughly substantial dinner to be sent up to me without loss of time.

Whilst it was preparing I stowed away my important papers in my new despatch-bag, locked each one of the three locks very carefully, and secured the three brahma keys around my neck inside my shirt.

Then I wrote on a parchment label, "Lieut. Harry Dunbar, H. M. 57th Regiment, Hotel Byzance,

Grande Rue de Pera, Constantinople," and tied it around the handle of the bag.

This was simply an innocent ruse on my part, for it was not advisable to let the character in which I travelled be generally known. The travelling bag of a simple lieutenant in a marching regiment might not be considered worth the stealing, but the despatch-bag of a Queen's Messenger would—hence the precaution.

Having packed up a portmanteau and labelled it in like manner, I sat down to my dinner and enjoyed it much, taking my time over it and making the most of it, as not knowing when I should have leisure for another.

After I had finished I looked at my watch.

It was exactly a quarter to seven o'clock.

I rang for the things to be cleared away, and, telling the waiter to have a hansom cab at the door exactly at eleven o'clock, and to call me at five minutes to the hour—I went to bed, and a few minutes later was sound asleep.

I was awakened, not by the waiter thumping at one of the doors, both of which I could have sworn I had locked, but by some one moving about my room.

"Who the devil's there? speak or I fire. I've a revolver in my hand—so look out," I said, plucking the weapon I had named from under my pillow as I spoke, and pointing at the darkness, for I could see nothing else.

"Pardon, zare, pardon; put away ze pistol. I'm in erreur. I've mistake ze room. I come home from opera and mistake ze room. Isn't this number dirty-tree?" exclaimed a voice, the owner of which seemed to be rather nervous, to say the least of it.

"No, this is number forty-five," I answered, "Where are you? Oh I see. Lucky for you that you are no burglar, my friend, for I'm a dead shot That way for the door. Good night," and by the time that I had finished speaking, the intruder, whoever he might have been, was out of the room.

I struck a light instantly, and took a peep to see that my despatch-bag was all right.

Yes, there it was on the chair by my bedside with my clothes heaped on top of it.

Then I went to look at my doors.

The folding ones opening into the sitting-room were tightly locked, and bolted on the inside as well. The one communicating with the passage was closed, but not locked.

I tried to lock it, but could not. I pulled out the key, not without difficulty, for it was bent. I looked in the keyhole, and saw a coil of twisted wire.

My door had been forced—devil a doubt of it There was the fact staring me in the face, and this discovery utterly precluded the possibility of my going to bed again.

On looking at my watch, however, I was greatly comforted by the discovery that it was twenty minutes to eleven. I therefore began to dress, and the instant that the waiter tapped at my door I surprised him by walking forth all ready equipped for my journey.

I said nothing to him concerning what had happened—it would have answered no useful purpose to have done so. Had a man entered my room and attempted my very life I dared not have stayed to prosecute or to have given evidence, so I tossed off a liqueur glass of the best French brandy, paid my score, and springing into my cab, bade my Jehu drive me to the London Bridge Railway station with all speed; for in those days stations at Charing Cross, Cannon-street, Ludgate-hill, and the Mansion House were undreamt of.

Arrived at the station, I secured the window seat

with my back to the engine in a first-class carriage, and had hardly shaken myself into a comfortable position when three other passengers entered and filled up that department of the carriage that was next the platform.

Presently a fifth came in, and seeing the near department full, essayed to open the door that led to the further one, old-fashioned first-class carriages generally being divided into two by a door in the middle.

Finding it locked he appealed to the guard to open it, who, however, politely informed him that the whole department had been secured by an old titled lady who preferred travelling alone.

On this the applicant left the carriage grumbling, and found a seat somewhere else.

A second later the guard slammed to the door, raised his whistle to his lips, blew it, and the engine giving a shrill response, we steamed out of the station.

CHAPTER III.

THREE PLEASANT FELLOW-PASSENGERS.

IN those days the London and Dover tidal trains stopped only at one station *en route*, namely Ashford.

That station was about half-way between the Metropolis and Dover, and was reached after a run of about an hour.

After my four hours' sound sleep at the hotel I could not again manage to woo slumber.

As events turned out this was a fortunate coincidence.

My three companions seemed most gentlemanly men. They were dressed in the best form and the two who after awhile began to converse, were evidently possessed of a most liberal education.

The third passenger remained silent, and, wrapped up in a heavily-furred coat and railway rug, with a soft silk cap drawn over his ears, seemed to desire nothing so much as to be left alone to his reflections.

This was the same case with myself, for I had many important things to think of, and some abstruse calculations to make, and yet I could not help now and then listening to what I may call the brilliant conversation of the two talkers, who were discoursing on all the topics of the day in turn, with a clearness and a lucidity that showed them to be deeply read in European politics.

Fancying once or twice by the glances that one or the other cast on me in turn, that they wanted to draw me into the debate, I closed my eyes and pretended to be asleep—a state of being I might ultimately have relapsed into, had not the conversation changed just as I got to my third or fourth drowsy nod.

"He is asleep at last," said one in a whisper.

"Wait, he will be sounder in another five or ten minutes," remarked the other debater in the same low tone.

Then a third voice with a decidedly foreign accent said, "Remember ze ole laddy in ze next compartmong—and zat Monsieur has pistol revolvers."

Where had I heard that cracked yet hoarse voice before?

Though toned down now to a murmur I the next instant knew that it pertained to the individual who had entered my bedroom at "The Golden Cross," an hour and a half previously, evidently by forcing my door.

Then I knew as certainly as though the fact had been written in letters of fire before my eyes—that my three fellow-travellers were emissaries of Russia, and that they were there for the sole object of robbing me of my despatches, to obtain which they would doubtless not scruple to murder me.

At the same instant it recurred to my memory that since the outbreak of the Crimean War no less than three Royal Messengers had mysteriously disappeared between London and Trieste.

Two were supposed to have perished amid the snows of Mont Cenis, which no railway tunnel pierced in those days, while the third was presumed to have gone down in the Sablonière packet when that vessel foundered off Corfu in the autumn gales.

Now I began to suspect, with a chill of undefinable horror, that they had all been murdered by Russian assassins, and that a similar fate menaced myself.

Opposed to three strong men—and I could tell that they were such—I should have no chance of getting the upper hand in a struggle, waged within the narrow confines of a first-class railway carriage.

Added to this, my revolver—though I had made great capital of it on the occasion of an unknown intruder entering my bedroom at the Golden Cross—was in reality unloaded.

I had powder, bullets, and caps, about my person, and in the ordinary course of events, I should have charged my deadly little pea-shooter whilst crossing the Channel in the mail steamer.

That I should have any use for such a weapon in traversing the fertile county of Kent, in the first-class carriage of an express train, I hadn't the slightest suspicion.

My danger was, therefore, imminent, for we were about midway between London and Ashford and it would still take a good half-hour to reach that station.

From the old lady in the adjoining division I could expect no assistance, but by way of screams, and they would avail little in a fast train, rushing on through a howling and boisterous January midnight, at the rate of forty miles an hour at the very least.

There were no means of communication between travellers and guards in those days, so that clearly my charming fellow-passengers had time to murder me, pitch me out of the window, and clear away all traces of the struggle, ere the train drew up at Ashford; and, if they took the extra precaution of murdering and getting rid of the old lady as well, they could step quietly out of the train, and aboard the mail packet at Dover, carrying my personal belongings as part and parcel of their own baggage, and not the slightest danger, risk, or suspicion, would attach to them.

Suddenly it occurred to me that my revolver, unloaded though it was, might yet have some effect if pointed at their heads with the assurance that individually and severally, I would blow their brains out.

Thrusting my right hand inside my great coat, I grasped the stock, as it protruded from the breast pocket of my shooting-jacket underneath, and then slightly opened my eyes to note the position of affairs.

Horror of horrors! the very quivering of my eyelids and what I deemed to have been the concealed movement of my right hand must have been noted, for my intention had been anticipated, three revolvers were levelled at my head.

"Move your right hand but by an inch, my friend, and you never move it more," said the wretch who sat opposite to me, with a diabolical leer.

"Monsieur vill see ze necessitee of giving up hee's despatch-bag, vidout noise or nonsense," said the bearded baboon, who alone out of the three could not talk English without a foreign accent.

"By Heaven, he'd better, or we'll soon pepper all noise and nonsense out of him," growled the man who sat on my left, and the cold muzzle of whose pistol touched my very ear.

"What does this mean, gentlemen?" I exclaimed, affecting to misunderstand them. "If this is a joke allow me to inform you that 'tis a very sorry one."

"Joke? You'll find that it's no joke, young gentleman, if you d n't comply with our demands, and that right speedily, too. Our patience is not quite so long as our pistol barrels. Your despatch-bag is under your seat; haul it forth and give it to us," said one of the men.

"Despatch-bag? I don't understand you," I rejoined; "I am but a subaltern in an infantry regiment proceeding to the seat of war. I've only my personal luggage with me."

"That's false, for you are a Queen's Messenger, travelling with most important despatches to the Sultan and the allied admirals and generals in the East. These despatches we must and will have, whether you choose to die in their defence or no," said my left-hand companion.

"But as murdering you will be quite a superfluous labour under the circumstances, inasmuch as we only want your papers, you may quietly leave the train—the door of the carriage is unlocked," remarked the tall man who sat opposite to me.

"Leave the carriage! Why the train is dashing on at the rate of forty miles an hour—to do so would be almost certain death," I replied, still trying to gain time.

"To remain will be quite certain death and a leaving of the carriage as well. Come, deliver up the bag, and then essay the leap. Why handcuffed prisoners have leapt out of a train whilst at full speed, and escaped all injury," said the last speaker, impatiently.

Thereupon he who spoke English with a foreign accent turned the handle, and threw wide open the door of the carriage.

A gust of wind swept in, together with a tempest of blinding sleet and snow.

"Zare, von goot spring and you roll down ze embankmong on to snow heap soft as fedder bed. Zen just as we's on board ze mail pakket-bot and getting out ob sight ob ze Got-tam English shore, you reach som out-ob-ze-way lillie roadside station and telegraph to have us arrested when too late, ah! ah!" and the man-baboon up in the corner grinned like a hyena.

All this while, however, I was trying with my feet, concealed in a great measure as they were by the railway rug that was thrown across my knees, to kick my precious despatch-bag out of the open carriage door.

Had I succeeded in doing so I should at once have sprung out after it, but I was detected in the act, and the baboon, as I had mentally designated him, sprang forward to clutch the end of the bag as it just worked itself out from underneath the rug.

But, regardless of the levelled pistols of his two companions I gave him a terrific facer that sent him spinning out through the door, and a terrible scream the next instant rose to the leaden heavens as the rushing train tore off doubtless one or other of his limbs.

Then I myself was dashed back upon my portmanteau, in the corner next to the door, by a blow from a pistol-butt upon the forehead, and whilst the fellow who delivered it possessed himself of my despatch-bag, the right forefinger of his companion sought the trigger of his revolver, and I knew by the keen, steady glance he cast along the barrel that he was about to shoot me.

I tried to murmur a prayer, for I verily thought that the last minute of my life had arrived, but suddenly a clear, manly voice shouted—

"Recover your weapon, ruffian, or you are a dead man."

CHAPTER IV

A PLEASANTER PASSENGER STILL.

LOOKING up, I saw that the door of communication between the two compartments of the carriage had been noiselessly opened, and in the aperture stood a tall, elegantly formed, and handsome young man of about my own age, whose outstretched right hand held a revolver within an inch of the fellow's head who had been so coolly and deliberately taking aim at me.

I saw that the wretch was cowed, and hoping to overawe his companion also, if I could do no more, I promptly plucked my own revolver from my pocket and menaced him in turn.

"Restore me my bag or I blow your brains out!" I said, as coolly as my excitement would let me.

The bag was dropped and kicked under my seat instantly.

"Now choose between three things, and choose quickly," I continued. "Be shot dead—leap out of the carriage, as you advised me to do just now—or wait until we arrive at Ashford, and be delivered over to the police, to stand your trial for attempted robbery and murder."

Almost before I had finished the ruffian and coward, albeit a loaded revolver lay on the cushions ready to his hand, crept to the open carriage door, and, with a yell, leapt out into the darkness.

The instant he had done so I turned to my gallant rescuer, and said—

"I owe my life to you, but before I endeavour to express all my gratitude, will you give the rascal whom you are covering with your revolver the same option of three divers fates that I have just given his companion?"

"Oh, no objection on earth," he rejoined, with a laugh, "but the beggar had best make his spring quickly, or I shall have some difficulty in resisting the temptation of a running shot, I shall 'pon honour."

The man heard and took the hint. A hop, a skip, and a desperate leap, and he was gone.

"Clear away, by George, that's better luck than he deserved, 'pon honour it is. Suppose we shut the door and have the window up. I find it chilly, don't you?" and as he spoke, the stranger returned his revolver to his pocket, shut the carriage-door, though it required great strength, and no little courage to do so at the rate at which we were travelling, and then seating himself opposite to me, proffered me his cigar-case.

I must say that the coolness and nonchalance of this young man, after so terrible and unprecedented an episode of railway travelling, perfectly took me aback.

I began to stammer forth my thanks, however.

But he promptly shut me up with—

"My dear sir, pray don't: surely it is possible to render a trifling assistance to a fellow-traveller, without such profuse expressions of gratitude. You were embarrassed, and I assisted you out of your embarrassment, that is all. Now take a weed, do, and think no more about it. What sort of weather do you think we are going to have, eh?"

"Abominable," I replied, "but I really must, despite your chivalrous disclaimer——"

"Of carrying bad cigars—yes, just so," he said interrupting me. "These are prime fellows, I assure you. I bought them in New York a fortnight ago, at a guinea each."

"Do I owe my life to an American gentleman?" I asked.

"No, I have only been travelling in the States, that's all. I went there after doing Iceland, Greenland, and a lot of other lands too numerous to mention."

"You are, indeed, a famous traveller," I remarked, as I illumined one of his cigars and puffed it into a dull red glow. "Where may you be journeying now?"

"Oh I'm taking a trifling spin at present to the City of the Sultan, by way of Paris, Dijon, Macon, St. Michelle, Mont Cenis, Turin, Milan, the Quadrilateral, Trieste, and the Adriatic. From thence curiosity may lead me onward to see something of the Crimean War, and from there I may very probably proceed to the Caucasus, whose warlike people I have read much of, and would like to make a personal acquaintance with. From the Caucasus I may go straight on across Asia to our British possessions in Hindostan, from thence visit Australia, and when I arrive there if I find any expedition fitting out for the South Pole, which I am given to understand there may be, why I shall join it."

The magnitude of his intended journey and the fact that its first dozen stages or so were identical with the route I myself had to travel, nearly took my breath away.

I told him the latter fact forthwith.

"Capital!" he rejoined, "for we can be travelling companions."

"Scarcely," said I, "for doubtless you travel for pleasure and information, and so journeying intend to stop for awhile at each point of interest; I on the other hand must traverse my marked-out route with the rapidity of the eagle, and like him keep my eyes ever fixed on my goal."

"Ah, and so I love to travel; what you regard as a duty I regard as a pleasure. My only delight in travelling is the rapid annihilation of space. Besides the ground we shall on this occasion traverse in company I have already traversed a score of times at the least," exclaimed my companion jubilantly.

"Why you must have spent three-fourths of your life on the road," I made reply, more and more amazed.

"You guess infinitely short of the reality. I've spent nine-tenths of my life in travel. As a youth I travelled for enjoyment; since I have grown to be a man I have travelled to conquer an all-devouring grief."

"Do you find in such flittings to and fro a satisfactory cure for such grief?" I asked.

"I find it a sedative but not a cure," he made answer; "but I have hitherto roamed over the world alone. With your cheerful companionship I might succeed better."

"I fear you wouldn't enjoy it in the least at the price you would have to pay for it, my dear sir," I answered, with a smile. "A Royal Messenger has to rough it, I can assure you—no weather and no danger dare stop him in his course—often he daren't stay even to sleep for weary days and nights in succession, and, added to that, we have often to spend a thousand pounds on a journey which a private traveller could accomplish with the utmost comfort for fifty."

"Oh, believe me, expense is no object," said the stranger, "and the greater the hardships I meet with en route the better I shall be delighted. On reaching Paris—if I telegraph from Calais—an old servant will meet me at the terminus station of the Chemin de Fer du Nord with a couple of thousand pounds in gold and notes. Come, say that we are comrades and friends, at least for that short spin to the City of the Sultan, the Crimea, and the Caucasus, and I'll be eternally your debtor."

"Nonsense, I shall be eternally yours," I rejoined. "I accede to your request, since you will dare all that comes in your way, with the greatest pleasure in life."

We shook hands vehemently upon the compact.

We had hardly done so when we slackened speed, and an instant later drew up at Ashford station.

CHAPTER V.

THE FACE AT THE WINDOW-PANE.

AT the railway buffet we drank to our future friendship and pleasant companionship. Then entered our carriage again, and "hey-presto," no sooner had we done so, than away we once more steamed Doverwards at our old rate of headlong speed.

My companion talked incessantly—and agreeably too—so that I had to play the rôle of listener, which suited me admirably, Queen's Messengers not being in general very communicative people.

Suddenly, however, my fellow-passenger stopped abruptly in the middle of a sentence, and his face blanching to a deadly pallor, whilst his eyes seemed to be half starting out of his head, he pointed with a long lean forefinger to the window of the carriage.

Glancing round in reply to this mute appeal, I saw a face of even a more deathly white than his own, noseless and eyeless, but with a horrible gash crossing the narrow forehead, pressed against the glass.

The hideous object retained its position there for a second, and then seemed to be whirled away by the wind into the darkness.

My companion touched my arm, saying—"That is the face of the man with the foreign accent, whom you hurled headlong out of the carriage."

"I know it is," I said. "I recognised the fellow in an instant—I thought he had fallen on the line and that the train had gone over him; but instead of that, he must have caught one of the bright brass handles in falling, and have maintained himself on the footboard."

"Good God! can you for an instant believe that that face belonged to a living man?" asked my companion, whose name I had ascertained by-the-bye to be Louis Foucarte; "why, it was eyeless and noseless, added to which no man could live for three minutes with that awful gash in his forehead. I saw the white brains oozing out through a fissure in the frontal bone. No, it was an apparition that we both beheld."

"I noticed all that you did, but I tried to convince myself that 'twas some hallucination of vision; that the drifting sleet and snow, and the glow of a great red lamp that is affixed to the side of the third carriage back, gave the horrible aspect to a face that might reasonably have been cut and gashed to some extent," I said.

"But you don't think so, on calm reflection?"

"No, I confess I do not," I replied, somewhat reluctantly; "for though many people still believe in apparitions, very few in this sceptical nineteenth century like openly to own to that belief."

"Come, I'm glad that you believe in the supernatural, because I myself have such firm faith therein—Heaven knows I have cause."

He gave a kind of involuntary shiver, and then continued—

"You, in your rapid journeys to and fro through Europe, must, upon one or more occasions, have had practical proof of the truth of the supernatural. Suppose we beguile the remainder of the journey by each relating an actual experience?"

"With all my heart," I replied. "Who shall begin?"

"I would rather that you would, if agreeable, but first take a drop of brandy out of my flask."

"Thanks—I will—and whilst I am narrating an actual experience you must excuse my loading my revolver, for if that face appears at the carriage window again, be it man or devil's, I shall let fly at it."

Having thus expressed my intentions, I began the narrative of an adventure that had happened to me three years previously, on the very line of route that we were now to follow.

CHAPTER VI.

THE MARSEILLES MERCHANT AND HIS VALISE.

IN the winter of 1851—I recollect the year, because it was that of the first Great Exhibition (Prince Albert and Sir Joseph Paxton's) —I had occasion to travel through the South of France, charged with a diplomatic mission from high authorities in England, to one of the Italian Grand Duchies.

The nature of this trust was of sufficient delicacy and importance to induce me to take as companion of my journey a friend (also a messenger in the service) on whom I could place implicit reliance, and to whom I might look with some faith for hearty co-operation.

This was an old school chum who had been my fag at Eton, and who, four years after we had parted as boys, was associated with me in the service to which our inclinations had eventually and mutually prompted us.

I must explain here, in order to be properly understood, that our friendship had never from its earliest date been characterised by any remarkable sympathy or interchange of sentiments. We were not Damon and Pythias, and had never sworn eternal fidelity, or promised that neither should survive the other's decease.

No, we were capital friends, excellent companions, but as unlike in tastes as we were in appearance.

Thus, whilst my whilom fag had grown to be a noble-looking young man of twenty, I was simply what you see, only deducting forty-eight months from my age, and, had not old fellowship been of sufficient inducement to select him as a *compagnon de voyage*, his strength, presence of mind, and courage, would alone have suggested to me that Jack Leslie should share my somewhat perilous mission.

I had managed, with considerable adroitness, to obtain leave of absence for him at the precise time for which my journey had been arranged, and late in the month of December we were ascending the lower spurs of the Alps, with the snowy slopes of Mont Cenis, seeming to lead up to the very sky, about a couple of leagues in our front.

Our travelling carriage was a type of its kind. It surely must have been manufactured by Noah out of the ruins of the ark; and within its dusky recesses you must imagine Jack Leslie and myself, huddled in opposite corners, be-furred and be-wrapped in an attempt at defiance of the frost, which obscured the windows and glistened on the surface of our rugs.

The road was so rough, however, that we were compelled to keep our faces uncovered, fearing for our heads against malicious corners of the windows; and when we could brush the frosty steam from the glasses the prospect of the country, new to us both then, seemed terribly barren and depressing.

"Is there much more of this?" asked Jack in grumpish tones, "because I'm being shaken like a nut in its shell, and there's no getting any sleep in this beastly old jolting rack-on-wheels."

"I'm extensively contused myself, as the police always describe a black eye delivered to one of the force," replied I, in very *staccato* tones, for the road was more than usually rutty at this juncture; "but as far as I can see, I fancy there is better ground a-head, and then we may get a little sleep."

"What's the time? How bitter the cold is! And *how* I wish the rotten thing didn't roll so!" exclaimed Jack.

"It wants four hours of daylight, old fellow."

"Four hundred thousand fiends!" commenced Jack, angrily, when the clattering of the glass windows and the ricketty panelling of the coach ceased, and in a moment more we were smoothly travelling over a good high road.

Weary as we were, the dull rumbling of the liberated voiture was as the murmuring of bees that invited to sleep, and in a few minutes we had forgotten the world and the weather in a deep, heavy slumber.

In this slumber I dreamed a dream, and the fashion of it was as follows:—

"It appeared to be a lovely night in summer, and I was travelling over a *route* which I had never seen before, and I felt myself transported back to the date of thirty years from 1851—in other words, since I was only twenty-two at the time of my dream, to just eight years before my birth.

"These details may seem absurd or *bizarre*, but must be told for the proper understanding of my story.

"Though I was unacquainted with the road over which I passed, a thousand national signs convinced me that I was in Savoy, and when my dream developed and became more vivid I found that I was journeying by means of an antique posting chariot, and that I had a companion seated opposite to me.

"This (how I knew it who shall tell?) was a rich merchant of Marseilles, who was seeking Modena and the confines of the Grand Duchy for the purpose of commercial negotiation.

"I must assure you here parenthetically that, though this was but a dream, the minuteness with which every detail was impressed on my mind was in itself remarkable.

"The merchant was a clean-shaven, ruddy, jovial, man of perhaps forty-five years of age. After the fashion of his compatriots of Marseilles he was given to a considerable display of chains, rings, and other matters of portable and ornamental jewellery, while by his side rested *a valise bound in steel and protected by three neat-looking locks.*

"At certain joltings of the vehicle the comfortable sounds of tinkling metal and rustling paper suggested that the said valise was primed with good gold pieces and rich store of notes on the banks of Genoa and Turin.

"In the course of a friendly conversation the merchant admitted with much freedom of trust that there were some three thousand pounds in gold, and more than fifteen thousand pounds in notes and bills lying in the valise.

"He did not seem oppressed by the knowledge that this valuable trust was in the keeping of only himself, nor did it occur to him that such an unusual temptation might convert a carriage companion into a robber.

"On the contrary he was quite at his ease, and gaily drew my attention to the beauties of the scenery through which we were moving. He chatted about the chateaus, the forests, the villages, &c., in hearty fashion and unwearying voice, his cheerfulness seeming to add to the brightness of the prospect, glowing beneath the summer sun.

"On a sudden, without a twilight warning, darkness profound and horrible fell on us.

"The wind rose and whistled chilly through the open windows of the carriage.

"In attempting to close them heavy drops of rain or sleet beat upon our hands, and a pale flash of lightning was followed at no long interval by the hoarse muttering of distant thunder.

"The rain now fell in torrents, and a gush of wind which I shall never forget blew open the doors of the decayed chariot, which instantly stopped.

"My eyes, now becoming accustomed to the darkness, rested, at this dreadful moment, on the faces of a man and a woman, both of whom stood at the door of the chariot, their stony eyes glaring through the gloom at us.

"I shudder whilst I recall the fiendish features of this ghastly pair. Swollen with passion and quivering with hate and malice, they seemed to be of that hideous order of the enemies of man which the Arabian fables have called Ghouls.

"I was petrified and spell-bound to my seat.

"At this moment the man, with a satanic grin, pointed his livid claw to the female, and then to the valise, which lay, as I have stated, by the merchant's side.

"Instantly, with a ferocious cry, the hag thrust her head into the carriage, and, after extracting the valise, directed, in her turn, the attention of the male figure to the jewellery, so fatally conspicuous on the chest and fingers of my companion.

"Their bony hands fell on their prey, who remained as one dead; and like horrible vampires they dug their talons into his chest; and, greedy of appropriating, each to itself, the treasures of his flesh and blood, began to rip the body asunder.

"At this sickening spectacle I closed my eyes, but the spattering of hot blood on my face and a horrible crackling sound compelled me to look again, and I saw these demons rending the unhappy man's limbs from the trunk, amidst an infernal accompaniment of laughter.

"From the dead man's clothing they next pillaged his chains and rings, which the female attached to her own livid and hateful neck and fingers.

"Then the male made a sign to our postillion (who all this time had remained an indifferent spectator of these atrocities, expressing no compunction, but merely whistling a hunting tune), to descend from the saddle and assist them.

"The wretch, whose utter apathy was even more abhorrent to me than the ferocity of the two murderers, obeyed at once, and still whistling his accursed tune helped to ransack the valise.

"This was soon accomplished, and the trio then occupied themselves in disposing of their prey.

"The money was transferred to a short sack, and suspended over the shoulders of the female, while the other wretches dragged the dismembered trunk to the base of a large stone cross which stood at the junction of the four roads at which the carriage had been stopped.

"Lifting up the square stone which formed the base of this monument, they flung the mangled body of the merchant, together with the broken valise, into a shallow pit beneath it, which seemed to have been dug in anticipation of its contents.

"This over the trio broke into a parody of the Burial Service, and at its profane conclusion they uttered a yell of delight.

"Simultaneously with the echoes it induced came a deafening peal of thunder, the lightning ran snakily along the earth, and the three wretches fell to the ground and disappeared in the pitchy darkness which enveloped the scene—of which no trace remained save that in my ears still seemed to sound the low whistling of the imperturbable postillion."

The next moment I awoke.

It was still night, and Jack Leslie was lying asleep in his corner of the carriage.

Staggered as I was by the horrible impression left by my dream I did not awake my friend, as I rather dreaded to encounter his inevitable chaff when I gave a reason for the pallor and terror that I knew must be plainly visible on my face.

I touched my repeater—it struck three quarters after three o'clock. There were, therefore, three hours of darkness still to be accounted for—by sleep if possible, or by conversation should Jack Leslie awake and feel inclined to talk.

Candidly, I did not care to coax back slumber, and I was beginning to make up my mind to awake my companion, when, with a violent start, which I could feel through all the swaying of the vehicle, he awoke of his own accord, with a face white as the dead, and nervously clutching my shoulder, looked into my countenance anxiously.

"You're all right then, Harry, old fellow. Thank God for that! Whew!" he exclaimed, and subsided.

"What is it?" asked I hastily.

"Nothing, old man. I was dreaming, that's all. What's the time now?"

I told him, and he expressed his surprise.

I began to speak, but he said quietly—

"Don't talk to me just yet, Harry. I—I—I'm not quite awake yet—I am not, indeed."

So we travelled on in silence for some minutes—slowly now, for the road had again become heavy.

The air was quite still, and suddenly I caught the sound of a low whistling.

I rubbed my eyes. Could I be dreaming again?

No, for there was Jack Leslie opposite to me as before—but how changed! He was livid, and his eyes seemed to be starting out of his head.

"Listen!" he cried hoarsely, "listen! My God! Do you hear it? Do you hear that whistling?"

He held up his hand for silence; but I heard it also, even as I had heard it in my dream.

IT WAS THE HUNTING TUNE OF THE POSTILLION.

"Jack!" I cried breathlessly. "Do—do *you* recognise that air?"

"Recognise it?" answered he shudderingly, "I should think I do. Listen once more."

Again we heard our postillion at his hunting song.

Then gradually I began to perceive the mysterious sympathy between us.

Hitherto, I had taken all Jack had said as part of my own thoughts, I had seen no remarkable affinity betwixt *his* recognition of the air and *mine*.

Before I could speak with a view to investigate this marvellous concurrence of thoughts, my friend leapt up with a cry of horror, and ejaculated, as he pointed out of the window nearest to him—

"The four roads! The stone! The cross!"

I looked in the direction of his finger; there it was, the whole scene, complete in every detail—the story of my awful dream.

"Jack!" I cried, "this horrible place, that cross! do you recognise them also?"

"I saw them," he replied, "in a dream just now! Under that stone lies the mangled body of the Marseilles merchant! Horrible!"

Our dreams had been identical.

When we had passed the hateful spot, we spoke more freely; *in no single feature had Jack's dream differed from mine*, and we were dreaming, thought for thought, at the same moment of time.

It was useless to divert either mind from the conviction that the cross roads and their monument had been the scene and receptacle of a cold-blooded murder and its victim, and, with this impression fresh upon us, we determined to investigate the spot on the first opportunity that offered.

Before, however, a plan had occurred to either of us, the carriage stopped for the "relay" at a miserable little *auberge*, which evidently served as a post-house for travellers.

We leapt out at once, and were proceeding towards the light which advanced from the porta, when we were suddenly rooted to the spot with surprise.

"Look, Jack!" I whispered. "Look!"

"THE WOMAN!" said my friend, shuddering— "*The Woman of our dream!*"

There was no mistaking the repulsive, the only half-human, features of the hag as she approached us, with the lantern dimly gleaming through the wintry gloom.

It *was* the old murderess of the cross-roads.

The postillion whistled his *air-de-chasse.*

"Manners, Stephano!" croaked the old woman, with a multitude of bows to us. "Manners! where is your politeness that you whistle before gentlemen?"

"Right as always, Madre Gaston," replied the postillion, with a grin. "Always right! but—force of habit, you know—who better? 'Tis an old tune, and I whistle without thinking. A thousand pardons to these gentlemen, and to you."

I looked at the postillion.

He was a very aged man—perhaps, indeed, as much as seventy-five years old—and I could not help remarking that he looked very infirm for such an occupation."

"Bad habit again," he chuckled, clearly reading my thoughts, and in his way replying to them. "I was born on horseback, I verily believe, and I shall doubtless die in the saddle, with a crack of my whip for a requiem, and to the last—to the last, mind you—whistling my favourite air—aye, to the last."

Jack Leslie, keeping his eyes fixed on the old man, added quickly—

"*Struck by lightning besides—in certain cross-roads, at the foot of a solitary stone cross!*"

The postillion seemed petrified at this unexpected conclusion to his speech—his arms fell to his sides— his eyes glared on us, but he did not speak.

The old woman, with a yell of terror, sank to the earth and buried her face in her withered hands.

I rushed up to her and picked up the lantern ere it was extinguished.

This movement on my part aroused the postillion.

"Gaston! Gaston!" he shouted. "Help! Help!"

An instant more and Jack had seized the old villain in his powerful grasp, and, while I was binding the old woman's wrists with my silk pocket handkerchief, another old man came running up from the post-house uttering cries of alarm.

THE TRIO OF THE CROSS-ROADS WAS NOW COM-PLETE.

Urged on by this additional evidence I secured the new comer, who was the husband of the foul hag, and within five minutes from our stoppage at the *auberge* we were masters of the ground—having easily captured at a *coup* the villainous actors in the tragedy which had formed the subject of our double dream.

So far we had proceeded, when to our unutterable delight the sound of carriage wheels was heard.

Almost immediately there arrived upon the scene a travelling chariot conveying no less important a dignitary than the Alcaldé of Mentoné—who, in great annoyance at the non-production of the post-horses which should have been awaiting him as a "relay," grumbled loudly at the usurpers—*c'est à dire*, ourselves—and threatened us with the law.

"It is the law that *we* seek, Senor Alcaldé," cried Jack Leslie. "Your authority is needed here."

The magistrate unrolled himself, like a mummy from its swathings, and descended.

I need not recount his surprise, and at first expostulations, at our detention of the three people on the evidence of a mere dream.

We stuck to the point, however, and cross-examined the trio so closely that their confused replies aroused at last the worthy Alcaldé's suspicions.

His mounted escort was at hand, and a portion of these conveyed the gang to prison.

Not to prolong my story to undue length, the criminals confessed to the murder and robbery of a Marseilles merchant, who, it was then remembered, had disappeared many years before in a mysterious manner in the neighbourhood.

The cross at the junction of the four roads was uprooted, and beneath it lay, partly covered by the fragments of a decayed, steel-bound leather valise the whitened bones of the murdered man.

The old couple and the postillion were executed at Turin three days after they had pleaded guilty.

There, that has been my first and last experience, until to-night, of anything in the nature of apparitions or clairvoyance.

I lighted a fresh cigar, and urged my companion to give me confidence for confidence.

He apparently made a violent effort to master some very strong emotions which I was of course a stranger to, but apparently he failed, for presently he said:—

"I cannot do it—not now at least—my tale is a far more terrible one than yours; perhaps by daylight I shall feel bolder—indeed I am sure to. But see, I need not be making excuses, for the question of time would alone have prevented my relating my horrible experiences. Look yonder are the heights of Dover."

Foucarte was right—we had, indeed, annihilated space. Five minutes later we were lying alongside the mail packet.

CHAPTER VII.

ANOTHER STAGE ON OUR ROUTE EASTWARDS.

WE had a rough journey across Channel that night. The sea rolled mountains high, and once or twice completely swept our decks of everything that was not secured.

The passage should have taken eighty minutes, but instead of that nearly two hours elapsed ere we sighted the red light on Calais Pier, which it took another half hour to reach.

Had it not been for my earnest solicitations I verily believe the captain—bluff manly-looking sailor though he was—would have put back to Dover before he was well out of sight of its lights— but there being only male passengers aboard, all of whom backed me up, he continued his journey, on my assuring him that, sink or swim, I must touch French shore ere daybreak.

Once or twice, I know, I made up my mind that we never should reach it—for one paddle-box was dashed to pieces by a heavy sea, and for a minute or so we thought the paddle-wheel was damaged also.

Happily we were mistaken. Had its revolution been obstructed we should have lain at the mercy of the sea, which would have made short work of us indeed.

As it was, however, after nearly three hours of deadly peril we got alongside Calais Pier, and ten minutes later we were in the train again, and *en route* for Paris.

It was still pitch dark, but by the time we reached Montreuil the pale grey light of early dawn made the surrounding flat uninteresting landscape visible, and, just as the thousand and one church bells were ringing for eleven o'clock mass, the day being Sunday, we steamed into the magnificent station of the Chemin-de-Fer-du-Nord at Paris.

CHAPTER VIII.

MYSTERIOUS OCCURRENCES AT THE PARIS RAILWAY STATION.

NOW, I had observed my companion Louis Foucarte send a telegram from Calais on to Paris, and I had naturally pretty accurately guessed its nature.

I was unprepared, however, for the appearance upon the railway platform of a gorgeously liveried, or I suppose I should say uniformed, chasseur—who wore a cocked hat with a plume of green feathers in it—whose breast was covered with gold lace, whose nether person was encased in a pair of top-boots of the most formidable proportions and resplendent polish, and who lastly and to all appearance hurriedly, came up to the window of our carriage and handed to my companion a Russian-leather bag which seemed to be heavy.

"Is all well?" asked Foucarte of this man.

"All is well, Monsieur," was the reply, accompanied by a kind of salute, performed quickly with the left hand.

The man spoke in French, but with a most strange accent. True a Norman or a Breton speaks French very peculiarly, but this man to my mind had a more strange accentuation still.

Besides, although the custom was still maintained in Hungary and Italy, household chasseurs arrayed in resplendent uniforms had gone out of fashion in France with the Bourbons, and had fallen into desuetude even before then.

My astonishment was increased when the chasseur designated my travelling companion as "my lord," and "your excellency" by turns.

I noticed that he whom I alone knew as Louis Foucarte, tried to check this mode of address, but the old chasseur was deaf as a post, and blind as an owl, and failed to catch either frowns or mutterings.

Then Louis Foucarte undid his travelling portmanteau, and gave to the old man an ill-tied-up brown paper parcel thereout.

In process of being handed from one to the other, it came partly unfastened, and whilst a portion of what was unmistakably female dress became revealed, something fell to the bottom of the carriage.

This something Louis Foucarte picked hastily up, crumpled out of shape in his hand and thrust into the open palm of the chasseur, not so skilfully however, as to prevent my remarking that it was an old lady's false front of iron-grey hair.

Foucarte then dismissed the chasseur, apparently with a handsome gratuity, and proceeding to the refreshment bouffet we made a hearty breakfast, and next taking a voiture, drove straight away to the Great Southern station in the opposite suburbs of Paris.

We arrived there in ample time to catch the train for Dijon; so we, as the Americans say, "liquored-up," laid in a stock of sandwiches and a pâté-de-foie-gras in case we should hunger on the road, and then chose our carriage and our seats at our leisure.

Now for the past ten minutes I had observed that three well-dressed men seemed to be dodging us everywhere, more apparently with the object of attracting my companion's attention than anything else.

Once or twice in passing them he seemed to give them a meaning glance, which they did not appear to understand, and upon one occasion when the elder of the three seemed as though coming forward to speak, he uttered what sounded very like an oath, in an unknown tongue, and the stranger, as if in direct reply thereto, shrugged his shoulders, turned on his heel, and rejoined his two companions.

After we had taken our seats, and the guard had locked us in, these three men passed close by our carriage-door twice, as though expecting that Foucarte would now certainly address them, or give them some kind of instructions.

But he only frowned—I caught him distinctly doing that—and the next instant we shot out of the station.

But a stranger incident occurred as we were just moving away, for six French cocked-hatted and sword-girt gendarmes rushed on to the platform, and pouncing on the three men who had so repeatedly attracted my attention, handcuffed them with the greatest celerity.

I instantly glanced round at my companion, and noticed that his face had turned white as marble.

I made no remark at the time, however, and away we steamed, leaving the suburbs of Paris in something less than a quarter of an hour behind us.

Then I could keep silence no longer.

"Monsieur Foucarte," I said, "I owe you my life, and deeply grateful I am to you for your preservation of it, I do assure you. There is, however, something most mysterious and unfathomable about your position, your tastes, and your general conduct, and although such trifles would concern me but little, were you my companion in a mere pleasure trip, placed as I am—the bearer of important despatches, the safe delivery of which may change the fate of Europe—I cannot be too circumspect in my choice of companions. Therefore if we are to continue the journey together, you must open your heart to me, and let light in upon my mental darkness."

"What has made you grow suddenly suspicious of me?" asked Louis Foucarte, very calmly.

"Firstly, hearing you addressed by a title; secondly, by your passing a female disguise into the hands of your old chasseur; thirdly, by the fact of your evidently knowing those three men who were arrested by French gendarmes just as we steamed out of the station," I replied.

"What if I refuse to explain matters, monsieur?"

"Then we will part the best of all possible friends at Dijon."

My companion then, after what appeared to be a terrible inner struggle, broke out with—

"I see I must tell you my history—of the curse that haunts me. In no other way can I divert your very natural suspicions. Well so be it. 'Tis broad daylight now, and I have no dread. Nay, don't seek to prevent me—I shall be happier when I have made of some one a confidant."

And forthwith he commenced the following truly horrible narrative.

CHAPTER IX.

THE STORY OF A FATHER'S CURSE.

YOU have doubtless long ago arrived at the conclusion that I am French. You are right—I am.

"My father gained rank and riches in the army of the first Napoleon. At Marengo he began his military career by beating the *pas de charge* on a little brass drum—he ended it leading a *corps d'armée* at Waterloo in the capacity of General of Division.

"His Imperial master had also made him a Count, and given him a chateau and a large estate near Marseilles, which Louis XVIII. or his successors never thought of depriving him of.

"At Waterloo my father received a wound which incapacitated him from taking part in any future campaigns; but, however he might have regretted this had Napoleon remained on the throne, as things turned out he took a grim satisfaction in the fact, for he would as soon have drawn sword in defence of the kingdom of his Satanic Majesty as in that of a Bourbon or an Orleanist monarch.

"I shall never forget when, arrived at the age of fifteen, I expressed a desire to go to the military school of St. Cyr, in order finally to obtain a commission in the army, the rage the poor old gentleman fell into—finally declaring with an oath that rather than see me swear allegiance to an old woman like Louis Philippe he would follow me to the grave.

"Of course I had to bend to his imperious will, and the honourable profession of a soldier being closed against me, I determined to travel in pursuit of pleasure over the whole world, which my father at length gave a reluctant consent to my doing, supplying me with abundant means to gratify my whim comfortably.

"For five years I was continually on the wing—ever remaining more than a week in one place.

"In those five years I traversed the five continents of the world through and through, in every direction.

"I was in India when I received an imperative summons from my father to return home without an instant's delay.

"Six weeks later I was in his presence.

"He told me that he had sent for me in order at length to gratify the darling wish of my heart—a Bonaparte was again supreme ruler of France, and would doubtless soon be Emperor. The army required to be loyally officered, and I might obtain a commission for asking.

"Now, during my five years' wanderings I had contracted as great a detestation for the army as before setting out I had felt an affection for such a life. I had grown to look upon military servitude as little better than penal servitude, and in India I had contracted a deep affection for a young lady of English birth, whom I was anxious to return to in all haste and marry.

"I had flattered myself that my father would have approved of my choice and settled upon me a handsome income.

"On the contrary, directly I expressed my reluctance to embrace a military career he heaped upon me every kind of invective, told me I was a rascally Orleanist, and ordered me from his presence, never to return to it more.

"My temper being as hot as his own we parted in mutual anger. The next day his notary called on me at 'The Golden Bee,' the village hostelry, and told me that my father would never see me more, but that he would allow me eighteen thousand francs a year as long as I never came within a hundred miles of the Chateau Marengo, as my father had baptised his residence.

"I sullenly agreed to the terms, and pocketing my first half-year's allowance I started that very day back to India, and six months later I returned to France with my fair young English wife, and took up my abode at Bordeaux where we lived happily for some months.

"At length, however, for the purpose of increasing my income, I indulged in speculations which turned out disastrously. In six weeks I lost just as many thousand francs, the result being that for the ensuing four months my income would be nil.

"Satisfied that by this time my father's anger towards me must have passed away, I resolved to pay him a visit, and at its conclusion lay my difficulties before him.

"I did the one, but not the other, for directly my father set eyes on me he became a veritable madman. He cursed me in the presence of all the servants, told me that I had broken my word, and that not another sou would he give me were I starving at his gates; then he ordered his menials to turn me out of doors, declaring with horrible profanity that I should never look upon his face again.

"He was obeyed by all but one man, a chasseur whose life he had saved in one of the Peninsular battles, many years ago, when with other Spanish prisoners he was about to be put to death by order of Massena, and who ever since had been his most faithful and devoted follower.

"This old man begged hard that I might be forgiven, for he had danced me on his knee when a child, and been my constant out-door companion and protector. I do believe, in fact, that he even loved me more than my stern parent did.

"His entreaties, however, were of no avail, and the other servants, who were new ones and unknown to me, felt no hesitation in obeying my father's commands.

"Out of the villa I was forced, but not until exasperated at such treatment I had vowed with a terrible oath that even made my fierce father shudder as it reached his ears, that I would look upon his face again even if I could not do so until the time came when I should behold it within a coffin.

"The old courier, Gaspero Zarco he was called, ran after me to bid me farewell, and thrust a slender purse into my hand, which I was bound to accept because I did not know but what my young wife was starving. I did so with tears in my eyes.

"And my wife did starve, for on my return to Bordeaux I was arrested and thrown into prison for debt.

"When I came out of it I found that my wife was dead and buried. I visited her grave, and kneeling beside it I cursed—aye, bitterly cursed—the author of my being.

"From the grave I went straight away to the humble lodging I had taken, and the first person I encountered on entering it was my father's chasseur, Gaspero Zarco.

"'My father is dead!' I exclaimed. 'I see it in your face.'

"And Gaspero told me that I was right in my surmise, for he had breathed his last two days previously.

"'Then,' said I, with a reckless burst of laughter, for the death of my sweet young wife—a death that he could have prevented—had very nearly turned my brain, 'the time has come for me to keep my oath. Nor heaven nor hell can prevent my gazing upon his accursed face now.'

"Gaspero tried to bring me to a more proper state of feeling—vain the attempt. We rode night and day towards the Chateau Marengo—I, at every place where we stopped for relays of horses, drinking off a tumbler full of raw spirit as though it had been water.

"It wanted five minutes to a close, hot, sultry summer's midnight when we rode up to the closed gates of the Chateau Marengo.

"The chasseur sprang to the ground, and threw them open.

"Without waiting for him to remount, I set spurs to my foaming and panting horse, and dashed up the carriage drive at a gallop, reeling in the saddle as I rode, for I was as drunk as drunk could be.

"Arrived at the great hall-door I dismounted, and hammered away at it with the butt of my riding whip.

"It was quickly opened by a crowd of startled-looking servants, many of whom, I saw, recognised me.

"'I am come to keep my oath. I am come to look upon my father's face,' I exclaimed, staggering across the hall. They all made way for me as though I was plague-stricken.

"'Come! come!' I said, with a reckless laugh, 'in which room does the old man lie? Give me a light and tell me.'

"Still they hesitated—they deemed me mad.

"'A light, a light,' I shouted. 'I am master now, and will be obeyed, or I will bundle all of you out of

"RECOVER YOUR WEAPON, RUFFIAN, OR YOU ARE A DEAD MAN."

No. 2.

doors as you bundled me at his orders only six months ago. Now will you give me a light, and tell me the room where he lies?'

"'The oak chamber, monsieur,' said one, handing me a candle. 'Shall any of us attend you?'

"'No,' I said, with an oath. 'Stand back all of you.'

"Light in hand I proceeded up the old oaken staircase three steps at a time, whistling a gay opera tune.

"Then I traversed the long gloomy corridors, and with a burst of reckless laughter threw open the door of a room—the door of the oak chamber.

"It was a large and sombre apartment, lighted by a vast oriel window. Through this window—one casement of which I noticed to be open—the full moon shone brightly upon a dark oaken coffin that lay upon two tressels, well within the pale unearthly light.

"I steadied myself with difficulty, put on, as well as my drunkenness would allow, a mock tragic attitude and manner, and burst out with—

"'Now, unnatural and cruel father, from a debtors prison and from the grave of my wife—whose murderer thou art—I am come to keep my oath. Nor heaven nor hell can hinder me from looking upon thy face now.'

"Scarcely had the sacrilegious and terrible words quitted my lips when my eyes, getting accustomed to the gloom that pervaded the apartment, spite of the moon and candle alike, perceived some black and hateful-looking object perched on the edge of the coffin.

"I approached it, but in my haste very nearly fell over the coffin-lid which lay upon the floor.

"Affrighted apparently by the noise, the accursed-looking object, with the red gleaming eyes, uttered a hoarse croak, and slowly and lazily spread out a pair of dusky pinions that must have measured at least six feet from tip to tip.

"Then I saw that it was a monstrous raven.

"Its long yellow beak was gore-clotted, as were its head and breast. The creature was evidently too gorged to move. It could only flap its wings again and renew its horrible creaking, as though thereby disputing my right to enter the room.

"Unheedful of its remonstrances, however, I advanced, considerably sobered now, and holding my candle aloft took a peep inside the coffin.

"Good God! how can I describe the horror I experienced when I saw a vast bloody wound where my father's face had been? The raven had pecked and pecked it out of all resemblance to humanity. Hell, or else a higher power, had interfered to prevent the fulfilment of my impious and terrible oath.

"I never attended my father's funeral, for I was a raving lunatic for many a long week after.

"At length, thanks to the skilfulness of my doctor, and the tender, almost motherly, attention of old Gaspero Zarco, I recovered my reason, and ultimately my health.

"Then I found that, my father having died intestate, I was the heir of both his real estates and personal wealth.

"But I at once made Gaspero Zarco my steward, for the Chateau Marengo I would not have passed another night in for all the wealth of Christendom.

"From that hour to this I have travelled, travelled, travelled, week after week, month after month, year after year, but my father's faceless ghost seems to follow me everywhere, with the ghastly raven fluttering above his head.

"Yes, I have seen him in Indian jungles, in the Australian bush, in American backwoods, on Peruvian pampas, in Canadian wilds, aye, and even in London parks. In fact, I'm a being accursed, haunted, doomed. Knowing all this, will you still accept me as your comrade?"

"I will," I said, grasping him warmly by the hand, "and, what is more, I will soon make a changed man of you. I suppose the old chasseur who awaited the arrival of our train on the platform of the Chemin-de-fer-du-Nord was Gaspero Zarco. Eh! am I right?"

"He it was. I knew that he would be in Paris on special business, and so I telegraphed to him."

"After that all my previous suspicions are, of course, scattered to the winds," I said.

"Suspicions! What did you take me for, then?"

"Truth to speak, I for a minute or two fancied you might be a Russian spy," I rejoined.

"What! I, who saved your life from Russian spies?"

"There are spies and spies," was all I could answer.

"Ah yes, true, but had I been what you thought me, I should assuredly not have taken other spies' work off their hands. Oh, dear no. But now that you have heard my history you know different—do you not?"

"I do, indeed, and so there is no need to refer to that terrible tale again. Try and forget it, my friend. I will do all I can to teach you how. We shall be a month in each other's society at any rate."

"Very well, then, let us attack our pâté de fois gras and some brandy," said Louis Foucarte.

To this proposition I had not the slightest objection, and managed to make a very good meal.

Scarcely had we cleared the pâté, and the flask of brandy when we arrived at Dijon.

CHAPTER X.

IN THIS CHAPTER WE REACH MONT CENIS.

THAT same evening, at dusk, we reached St. Michelle, and here the railway terminating (for a tunnel right through Mont Cenis, thus connecting Italy with France, was at that time only dreamed of), I engaged as light a carriage as I could obtain, and had four strong and well-bred horses harnessed thereto.

With their help I fondly hoped that we should be descending the Italian side of the mountain, and within sight of the lights of Susa, before midnight.

My hopes, however, were not to be realised.

Previous to our entering our vehicle the garrulous landlord of the Three Cranes informed us that, although we were travelling in haste, three other gentlemen, whose carriage had only turned the corner of the street as we entered the hotel, had shown themselves to be in a greater hurry still, for they had had six horses harnessed to their chariot, and before starting had despatched a courier on a blood mare, who was as fleet as the wind, to secure relays at Modane.

"What sort of men were they?" I asked.

"Oh, pleasant gentlemen enough. Germans, I imagine. They have been at my establishment a week—a whole week—and at least half a dozen times every day one or the other of them has been to the railway station, and there telegraphed to and received an answer back from Dijon. Half an hour ago the one who had been up to the terminus came rushing back, and ten minutes later they were on the road in the manner that I have described," answered the landlord.

"And do you know their ultimate destination?" I asked.

"Not the least in the world. Their luggage consisted of a small hand-bag each, unlabelled, and they merely called each other Herr Karl, Herr Fritz, and Herr Ripp. But one peculiarity about them was, that each carried a double-barrelled gun—with one barrel for shot and one for ball—and though they went out with them loaded every day, they seldom or never brought home any game," said the landlord.

"Oh! and have they got them loaded now?"

"Yes, and talk to each other as if their journey was for the object of wild boar shooting on the lower spurs of the mountain; but, lor bless me, if that was all, they needn't have been in such a hurry—the boars would have waited for 'em patiently enough," said Boniface.

I was of exactly the same opinion, but I made a careless reply, and the next minute our almost springless vehicle was rattling along the rough stony streets.

At a gallop we dashed across the beautiful bridge that spans the rapid Argau—an hour later crossed the more sluggish Aar, and a rivulet which has the wonderful power of changing into stone everything that is cast therein.

At six o'clock to the minute by my repeater we drew up before the only good inn at Modane, and here I tried to get a relay.

To my consternation I learnt that the three strangers had taken every horse that the landlord had in his stables, whilst those they had left behind were completely broken down.

They had evidently travelled with great speed, for they had gained nearly half an hour upon us in twenty-five miles. Ours had been tolerably tall travelling, but these German sportsmen had left St. Michelle five minutes, and had arrived at Modane twenty-five minutes before us.

What a hurry they must have been in to reach the boars!

To us they were terrible *bores* themselves.

Our postillions, however, declared that their horses were still fresh enough to reach Susa before midnight, if they only had a good feed of oats to work on; and so I engaged them for the further stage at a cost of five guineas.

The consequence was, that a couple of hours before midnight we had commenced the ascent of Mount Cenis, along the very road constructed by the first Napoleon, in 1810, for the marching of his legions into Italy.

CHAPTER XI.

AND IN THIS DON'T GET ACROSS IT.

IT was snowing hard, and blowing too, so that the horses, despite their feed of oats, had great difficulty in making head against it. As for the road itself, as it was invisible, it was somewhat hard to imagine that it had been constructed by three thousand men at a total cost of £810,000.

Louis Foucarte had been in pretty good spirits during the afternoon and evening. The inexpressible dreariness of the scene, however, now appeared to depress him again.

"Will you point out the place where you had the adventure with the people who murdered the Marseilles merchant?' he presently asked.

"Oh, we have passed it. I had forgotten to show it to you," I rejoined.

Not that we had done so, for the old stone cross and the tumble-down posting-house were still three miles ahead; but I thought I had best not allow his thoughts to settle on morbid subjects.

Presently I said—

"Come, you must not think of ghostly foes, for I much fear we shall have to encounter less shadowy ones. Unless I'm a very bad guesser, those three Germans, as the St. Michelle landlord calls them,

have betaken themselves to the mountain defiles to attack us at a disadvantage and rob me of my despatches."

"I'm sure I hope they may try," said Louis, calmly.

"What! with their three double-barrelled guns!" I rejoined, with a laugh. "On my word you are kind."

"Yes," answered Foucarte, looking me full in the face; "because I want to prove myself serviceable and useful to you, and that would give me an opportunity."

I forget what answer I made, but I know that we both of us carefully examined our revolvers, and placed them where they would be immediately handy to our grasp.

Then we both relapsed into silence for a considerable time, and at length I began to feel very drowsy.

"Are you sleepy?" I asked of Louis Foucarte.

"Not the least in the world," was the reply.

"Well I am, deucedly," I replied. "Will you keep watch whilst I have a nap, and then I will do so in turn?"

This my companion promptly agreed to do, and in less than five minutes after he had given me the promise I was as sound asleep as a tired traveller could be.

How long I slept I know not, but my companion aroused me by heartily shaking my shoulders.

"The postillions say that the snowdrifts are so deep that the horses can't move a step further," he said.

I looked out of both windows, and saw that even where we were the snow was above the hubs of the wheels.

As for the horses, spite of the intense cold they were dank with sweat and covered with foam, whilst their heaving flanks showed that their strength was almost spent.

"They say that there is a house yonder with stabling to it, and that we had better spend the remainder of the night there,' continued Foucarte, pointing over the snow as he spoke.

I looked, and at once recognised the ruins of the wayside auberge at which I had had so disagreeable an adventure a few years before.

It was not a time to be squeamish, however, for the snow was still falling heavily, and if we hesitated we might even be cut off from that haven, desolate though it looked.

Five minutes later, therefore, the horses, the carriage, and the two post-boys were under cover in the coach-house and stables, and I was busy tearing down and breaking up a door, in order to make a fire in the interior of the main building.

Foucarte had managed to get drenched to the skin by missing the pathway, and plunging into a pond that was concealed by the snow which had fallen on its half-frozen surface.

Fortunately, I had an old uniform in an accessible portmanteau—and this I insisted on his donning, as to attempt to open our baggage in such a situation was out of the question.

He retired into the carriage, and on his return I was amused to see that he had put on all the accoutrements as well as the necessary part of my discarded uniform; and a thorough soldier he looked every inch of him.

As he entered, Foucarte suddenly exclaimed—

"Hang it, we needn't have taken so much trouble, for there is a fire still burning in one of the upstairs rooms. I can see the ruddy glow on the white-washed wall of a passage."

"If 'tis as you say, our friends the three Germans have taken prior possession of the place," rejoined I.

Scarcely had the words escaped my lips when a gruff voice shouted through the casementless window—

" Surrender yourselves prisoners, or we blow your brains out."

I glanced round, and in the twinkling of an eye saw sufficient to instil terror into the stoutest heart.

Foucarte and I were both covered by the double muzzles of three guns, the barrels of which rested on the stone windowsill, thus insuring steadiness of aim.

The guns were at full cock, three forefingers touched three triggers, and three keen eyes glanced along death-dealing tubes as nonchalantly as though we were the wild boars that the precious sportsmen had come so far to shoot.

The worst marksmen in the world could not have failed to hit us at such a range, and that, too, ere we could stoop down and pick up our revolvers from the floor, where we had laid them whilst we broke up the door for firewood.

We were truly in a most unpleasant quandary.

"Kick those pistols over towards the window!" said the man who had before spoken. " Kick them over, I say, or you die on the instant. We are not fellows to be trifled with."

Though the attempt was almost certain death I stooped to pick up my revolver, hoping, at all events, to be able to send one rascal to his final account ere I perished.

But, before I could lay a finger on the weapon, "crash" went one of the guns, and my right arm fell powerless by my side; either a bullet or some small shot had penetrated it.

I dropped to the floor, feeling sure that my doom was sealed; but as no other shots followed I looked up, and saw Louis Foucarte holding something out at arm's length towards the three infernal marksmen, at the same time shouting, " Potorogna ! Brichka ! Potorogna !" as loud as he could bawl.

To my surprise the three Herrs at once recovered their weapons and came bounding into the room through the open window.

" A mistake, monsieur !" said he who was evidently their leader, approaching me. " A mistake, for which we beg most respectfully to apologise. We are three French police agents, acting upon instructions received from Paris, to capture, alive or dead, two Russian spies, now attempting to escape across the frontier into Italy. Have we your forgiveness ?"

"Yes," I muttered, for 'twas no good to be churlish. " And I wish to goodness I could give you back your wasted powder and shot. I fear I must keep the latter *nolens volens.*"

Louis Foucarte, however, bound up my arm, and we spent a not unpleasant evening, all things considered.

The three Herrs, now turned out to be three Monsieurs, were not at all bad sort of fellows, and when they had released our postillions, whom, previously to tackling us, they had surprised and lashed to the wheels of the chariot in the coach-house, they brought in quite a feast from their own travelling carriage, which they had concealed in a plantation of pine trees close by, and, making a tremendous fire, we ate fat capons and cold hams, with brown bread and fruit, washing all down with French cognac, until we felt remarkably friendly.

Then we all rolled ourselves in our cloaks, and with our feet to the cheering blaze soon sank into sound slumber.

CHAPTER XII.

THROUGH MYSTIFICATION WE ENTER SUSA.

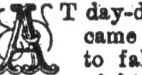T day-dawn the postillions of both carriages came in to say that the snow had ceased to fall, and what had fallen during the night had frozen so hard that there would be no difficulty in proceeding.

I gave instructions for the horses to be harnessed at once, and five minutes later we were *en route*, after having taken farewell of our acquaintances of the night before, who expressed their intention of haunting the mountain for another twenty-four hours in the hope of still entrapping the Russian spies whom they were in search of.

Louis Foucarte went out with them and smoked a pipe whilst our horses were being put to, whilst I remained by the fire, not seeing the fun of leaving it until the necessity obliged me.

Presently he hallooed out that all was ready, and picking up my precious despatch-bag, which had formed my pillow during the night, I hastened out of the house.

On the doorstep, however, I saw something gleaming, and stooping picked it up and looked at it.

'Twas a small square piece of wood, and on it was painted a black two-headed eagle, whilst underneath were the words " Potorogna ! Brichka ! Potorogna !"

Immediately I remembered that these were the very words Foucarte had shouted the preceding night to prevent the three men from firing at us again, and that this was the very piece of wood he had waved in so frantic a manner before their eyes.

I put it in my pocket, and an hour after, just as we had begun to descend the Italian side of the mountain, I returned it to its owner, saying—

"Here is your talisman. I picked it up on the threshold of the old house in which we passed the night. You should take more care of what seems to have a rare and most singular value."

My companion's face flushed redly, and his eyes flashed almost angrily, as he took the piece of wood from my hands.

"But for it you would not be alive now," he remarked.

"If so, then, do I owe you my life twice over," I made reply ; " and I assure you that I do not lack gratitude. Yet, tell me wherein lies the spell that gives that simple-looking little piece of wood such almost magic power ?"

" Don't ask me, my dear friend. I cannot answer you truly, and I don't wish to be forced to utter a falsehood. Enough that its influence has been for good. You will confess that, I suppose ?" rejoined Foucarte.

"Assuredly I will. Its presentation saved my life."

"Very well, then, let that be sufficient. And now to change the subject. Was not that tumbledown old building wherein we passed the night the auberge where dwelt the old man and old woman who murdered the Marseilles merchant ?" asked Foucarte, thus adroitly changing the subject of conversation.

" Yes, I confess it was," I answered. " I told you we had passed the place earlier in the evening, because I did not want you to brood over the ghastly and the horrible. I deemed that the object justified the deception."

" Thank you for the precaution," smiled Foucarte ; " but as it happened the postillions came to their final full stop exactly abreast of the old stone cross. It was all but buried in snow, but I saw it and recognised it from your description. However, that is past now and yonder is Susa, and away in the distance Turin with all its hundred spires."

We were dashing down the steep mountain road at a rattling trot, but not so fast as the broken, rushing, and roaring waters of the Dora Susina—a river formed by a hundred mountain streams—and the leakage of the deep and placid lake that crosses the summit of Mount Cenis at a height of 6,000 ft. above the level of the sea-swept valewards by our side.

Had our horses stumbled, shied, or fallen, we might have made a more intimate and more lasting acquaintance with this same Dora Susina by being precipitated a depth of some fifty feet into it ; for there was no protection of hedge, wall, fence, or rail to avert such a possible, and indeed probable, catastrophe.

We neither of us seemed to give the danger a thought, however, for Foncarte kept whistling a succession of opera and waltz tunes as he gazed out of one window ; and all my thoughts were centered on the block of wood with the two-headed eagle and the three words of mysterious import that were painted thereon, as I looked out of the other.

I could not make it out at all, but I felt certain of one thing—namely, that some mystery surrounded the person of my *compagnon de voyage* that he had not thought fit to explain to me, and would not explain even if pressed.

The horrible story he had told me the day before had carried all my credence with it for the time, but now I began to reflect it only after all explained two things—namely, why Wandering Jew-like he kept travelling over the face of the earth, and, secondly, who the old chasseur was who had awaited him at the Chemin-de-fer-du-Nord station.

It had not accounted for his leaving London-bridge Railway Terminus in the disguise of an elderly lady of title, nor the strange conduct of the three well-dressed men at the Paris railway station, who evidently knew him, and either wished to give to or receive from him instructions or information ; and now here was a greater riddle than all to solve, for had he not stopped three other men from committing, what upon calm reflection I could call by no other name than a cold blooded murder, by merely showing them a piece of wood with a black two-headed eagle painted thereon, and shouting the three cabalistic words "Potorogna ! Brichka ! Potorogna ?"

I had formed no solution to this charade of my first, my second, and my whole, when, after dashing at a gallop through some half dozen of Susa's dirties and most tortuous streets, we at last drew up suddenly in front of the Hotel di Tortoni.

CHAPTER XIII

THREE MEN HERE, THREE MEN THERE, THREE MEN, THREE MEN, EVERYWHERE.

T Susa we only stopped sufficiently long to partake of a hurried breakfast, then took train for Turin, which we reached an hour later.

There we found the express on the point of starting for Milan ; and at Milan, finding that we should otherwise have to remain for six hours, I engaged a special train to take us on to Trieste, thereby arriving at the latter port in time to catch the Austrian steamer for Constantinople, which we should otherwise assuredly have lost.

So far all had gone well, and I was able to congratulate myself that I had not lost a minute's time upon the road. I mean to say not a minute that I could by any possibility have saved.

Now all my anxiety for the time was gone, for over the vessel in which I was a passenger I had no control. She would take me alongside the British Admiral's flag-ship that lay off Pera, but she would take her own time to do it in, for the captain was a

stolid Austrian, and as doubtless his sympathies were with Russia he would not be likely to put on extra steam on my account.

During the previous two days' journey through Italy Louis Foncarte had, apparently in very great measure, recovered his spirits. He ate, drank, laughed, and conversed as cheerfully as any man could do who was travelling for his pleasure, and had left all his cares behind him.

I found him an excellent companion, and not unfrequently a useful one—for he was a magnificent linguist, and could make himself understood everywhere.

I had also begun to feel a kind of attachment towards him, for his manner was thoroughly genial and pleasant, and yet there was the indefinable something about the man which, even whilst it attracted, also repelled me.

Besides, three strange men still continued to start up when least expected, here, there, and well-nigh everywhere, always with fresh faces, and yet as I could not help thinking ever with the same design—namely to rob me either by force or fraud of my precious despatches.

And, strange to say, what disconcerted me still more was my firm conviction that on each, and every occasion of their so appearing, the sight of my travelling companion caused them to abandon their project, and, as sailors would express it, "sheer off."

As during the journey from London-bridge to Dover he had saved me from being murdered by three ruffians by force of arms, and as amid the snows of Mont Cenis he had saved me from being murdered by three other ruffians by shouting " Potorogna ! Brichka ! Potorogna !" and the exhibition of a piece of painted wood, so at Paris, and again at Turin, at Trompetta, and at Milan, a frown, a curling of the lip, a twist of the moustache, or an impatient and half-concealed gesture, had seemed to dispose at each place of three other men, who until they received the sign had dodged us, followed us, or stared at us pertinaciously.

True none of these interesting trios, since quitting Paris, had I seen pounced upon by the police ; but this fact did not comfort me in the least. They might not have aroused the suspicion of the authorities elsewhere, and besides what had that to do with their apparent knowledge of, and implicit obedience to, the slightest sign from my travelling companion?

These things I kept turning over in my mind as sitting on the quarter-deck of the good ship Cité de Vienne I smoked a cigarette, and watched the distant lights of Trieste sink gradually into the dark blue tideless waters of the Adriatic.

A quarter of an hour's calm reflection had almost convinced me that very many of my suspicions were the result of an over-wrought imagination, founded on a very strange yet accidental chain of coincidences, when, glancing suddenly around I saw another group of three men, standing just abaft the weather paddlebox, out of the wind and apparently earnestly conversing.

I confess that I started as though an adder had suddenly stung me, yet in another instant I smiled at what I considered my folly, for these three men were simply three Greek priests, who were doubtless on their way either to Corfu or Syra, islands that acknowledged that faith.

They were queer-looking fellows enough, clad in dark-green robes, trimmed with sables, that reached down to their very feet, and in their heads they wore rough fur caps, rather larger than the bearskins of our Grenadier Guards. Great gilt crosses hung from their waists, and their hair and beards were alike long and flowing.

They were conversing in an animated manner, and every few seconds the one or other of them seemed to glance round at me.

Chuckling at my own folly for thinking such a thing, I nevertheless dived down below, saw that my despatch bag was safe in the private state-room, that I had specially secured for myself, and ere returning to the deck carefully locked the door and transferred the key to my pocket.

On regaining the deck the first object that met my gaze was Louis Foucarte, in converse with the three priests.

I instantly darted half-way down the saloon staircase again, where I crouched under the deep shadow of the hatch, with only my eyes above it, determined to see and hear all I could.

I need not have been at such pains to conceal myself, for there was only the starlight to see things by, and I need not have taken such trouble to listen, for not one word of the conversation could I understand.

'Twas not modern Greek, and 'twas as assuredly neither French, Italian, nor Austrian. I did not know Russian, but I could not help fancying it had the guttural sound of that language.

Anyhow the conversation was carried on by gestures as much as by words, and by these I could see or thought I could see, that the three Greek priests were importuning Foucarte to let them do something, and that he was vehemently and scornfully denying them permission.

Once the tallest of the three priests threw back his robes and pointed significantly to a long knife that was sustained in a broad silk sash, but Louis Foucarte stamped his foot energetically on the deck, and seemed to intimate to the priest, by pantomimic gesture, that if he ventured to have recourse to it he should hang for it.

The conversation was continued for some time longer, but it grew gradually milder in its tone, and at last the three Greek priests—though I did not believe them to be such any longer—walked forward, and Louis Foucarte, turning on his heel, came right towards the saloon staircase.

I met him half-way up, and noticed that he started slightly as he remarked—

"I thought you had turned in half-an-hour ago."

"I went below with that intention, but altered my mind, and came on deck ten minutes since, when I found you so absorbed in conversation with those three interesting-looking members of the clergy, that I dived below a second time for a cigar. Will you take one?" and I offered him my case.

"Ah, they are three very interesting fellows—deeply read and well informed "—said he, as he accepted and lighted one.

"And wear knives," I rejoined, fixing him with a glance.

But he looked me calmly in the face, and said—

"So I perceived. Peculiar—isn't it?"

"Very," said I, "as is also the fact of their speaking Russian."

"Oh, that is not odd at all," rejoined Foucarte, with a laugh, "as very many of the Greek priesthood are educated in Russia."

"But you seem to speak Russian, too," I exclaimed.

"Very fluently. I have lived there. Many British officers speak Hindostanee, yet are they not niggers;" and Foucarte looked as though he would resent any further cross-questioning.

CHAPTER XIV

I DELIVER MY DESPATCHES TO THE ADMIRAL.

THE slight coldness that the conversation I have just recorded occasioned between Foucarte and myself did not pass away for a couple of days, by which time we were off Syra, where the three Greek priests were put ashore.

We lay under the lee of the island for more than an hour, for what reason I could never discover, and whilst doing so I had the mortification of seeing a little steamer of about five hundred tons' burthen dart out of the port over against which we lay, and glide away eastward under a tremendous head of steam.

She passed almost under our bows, and as she did so I recognised aboard of her the tallest of the three Greek priests—the possessor of the long broad-bladed knife.

He smiled grimly as his eyes met mine, and I felt for an instant that I would much have liked to have shot him, for that he was a Russian spy I had not the slightest doubt.

Turning away, I found myself face to face with Foucarte.

"There goes one of your precious acquaintances," I said.

Foucarte shrugged his shoulders, but said nothing.

"What do you take the man to be?" I persisted.

"Well, I should not wonder if he were a Russian, and perhaps a spy as well," he rejoined, with a smile.

"You give vent to your suppositions very calmly," I said. "I believe, nay know him to be the same thing, and last night he was very coolly suggesting to you my murder."

"Why do you think that? You are not murdered."

"Oh, that's because you would not allow him to do it."

"And is that why you are so offended with me?"

The question was asked so naively and dryly that I could not forbear from laughing. So I made answer—

"Of course I am infinitely obliged to you, but it isn't pleasant continually having one's life saved, and not to know how or wherefore it is done. It seems so confoundedly strange."

"So it is," answered Foucarte. "I own to having saved your life six times since leaving London. Well, what of that? In all human probability it will be threatened thrice more ere your mission is accomplished, and if you find my method of preserving it so very distasteful I will in the future refrain from interfering. Eh, what do you say?"

"I want to know how you succeed in doing it," I said.

"Ah, that's where you ask too much," returned my companion, smiling. "The physician who saves a patient from a dangerous fever will not always submit to be pestered by the convalescent as to what drugs he has used in the process. If the result satisfies you not, I can tell you no more."

"Then you refuse to be otherwise than a mystery?" I asked.

"Indeed, no; but inasmuch as I am only what your fervent imagination has made me, it is you who must disentangle your matted threads, and then you may be able to draw your own deductions," said Foucarte.

"That I decline to do," I answered, testily. "I have had ample reason for my suspicions, and you must either explain away the mysteries that surround you, or our friendship must end."

"Are you determined upon that course?"

"Yes, I am," I replied, firmly.

"Very well, then our friendship must cease for a time; but I foretell that it will be renewed when I save your life for a seventh time," answered Foucarte.

"Thank you, but I can henceforth guard my own," I said.

"I doubt it, but time will prove," and Foucarte bowed and turned away; but scarcely had he gone half a dozen paces when he returned and said with a quiet smile—

"I'll bet you an even tenpound note that I'll save your life again before the present week is over—save your life and your despatches as well. What do you say?"

"I accept the bet with pleasure," I responded.

"Very well, let us have a glass of wine on the strength of it."

To this proposal I agreed, and we went down into the steward's cabin, and had the wine forthwith.

After that Foucarte and I, though we conversed at table, and occasionally passed the time of day when we met on deck, were cool and distant to each other all through the voyage, which lasted some forty-eight hours longer.

At the end of that time, one bright sunny morning the Isle of Marmora hove in sight, then the Princes Islands, and a little later the gilded dome of St. Sophia, and the heights of Stamboul and Pera.

Whilst running through the English squadron that was lying in the very centre of the beautiful Straits, the steamer hove to, and lowered a special boat to take me aboard the admiral's ship.

Five minutes later I was in the cabin of the stately flag-ship, and Admiral Dundas was reading his despatches.

"Have you met with any particular adventures on the way?" he asked, suddenly looking up from his papers.

"A few, your excellency," I answered.

"I asked you," said the veteran, "because a rumour has reached us out here that Russian emissaries beset the four lines of route from England, and rob, and, where resistance is offered, murder every Royal Messenger from the Courts of Great Britain and France that they can lay hands on. Five messengers are at the present time missing, of whom we never expect to hear more—which is not remarkable since these Russian villains generally travel in companies of three, and are all well armed."

"I believe, sir, I have run the gauntlet of more than a score such fellows," I made reply, "but I had a very agreeable travelling companion, and we each of us carried revolvers."

"Ah, that accounts for it, perhaps," said Admiral Dundas, "I'm glad you escaped. Have you breakfasted?"

"Once, but I think I could do justice to another. The commissariat department of the Austrian Lloyds is not what it should be," I answered, for in all truth 'twas wretched.

"You shall join me then, for I expect mine to be served every minute," said the admiral.

I accepted the invitation gratefully, and a hearty meal I made.

During its discussion which lasted fully an hour, the admiral made me give him a full account of my adventures.

He seemed very much taken up with the peculiarities of Louis Foucarte, whose private history I of course did not tell.

I, however, at the admiral's request described his personal appearance as closely as I could, and when I had concluded Dundas exclaimed:—

"Why hang it all, that's a perfect word photograph of a fellow for whose apprehension five thousand pounds are offered."

"What is he then, your excellency?" I asked.

"A Russian noble called Kakalogg, and supposedly the head and motive power of all the spies that are spread over the continent of Europe. Can you put him in our hands?"

"No," I replied; "but I don't for one instant believe that, spite of the similarity, my late travelling companion can be the man whom you refer to. Besides, if he was," I added, "the thing would be equally impossible, for he saved my life, on at all events one occasion, at the imminent hazard of his own."

"Very well," replied the admiral, "I appreciate your feelings. Here are your despatches for the Sultan. Endeavour to deliver them before noon. If you will come aboard early to-morrow morning I shall have some ready for you to carry on to the allied generals before Sebastopol. If you will bring your friend with you, I shall be happy to see him."

And so we parted.

CHAPTER XV.

SHOWS HOW FOUCARTE WON HIS WAGER.

THE admiral's eight-oared gig was lowered away to take me ashore, and a quarter of an hour from the time of leaving the huge line-of-battle ship I was landed at Beicos Bay.

I had been instructed to take up my quarters at the Hotel Byzance, in the Grande Rue de Pera, and thither I accordingly journeyed in a caïque* drawn by two ponies, and driven by one of the fattest old Turks that I ever beheld, it being necessary that I should make some alterations in my toilet ere I presented myself before the "Light of the World," Abdul Medjid.

I found the streets of Constantinople narrow, tortuous, dark, dirty, and in every respect wretched. Here, there, and everywhere, however, I encountered European soldiers, and this gave me a most comfortable feeling in that far-distant land.

At the Hotel Byzance I learnt that I should not have much chance of obtaining an interview with the Sultan until his return from the Mosque of St. Sophia, where he spent the greater part of his morning.

I had, therefore, ample time to wash, change my apparel, and enjoy a general brush up; after which I strolled forth with my light despatch-bag in my hand, intending to walk to the palace slowly and leisurely, and thus see something of Pera and Stamboul on my way.

Pera is, so to speak, the European quarter of the city, and Stamboul the Oriental.

In the former division of Constantinople some of the hotels and shops would not do discredit to Paris or London; but in the latter such things scarcely exist, bare walls of houses, whose windows face inwards upon courts, forming the sides of the streets, and everything saleable or buyable being confined to the bazaars or huge market-places.

I found, however, numerous sights during my slow progress palace wards that both interested and amused me, more I own by their novelty than anything else, and at length I was fairly entranced by the eccentric conduct of some whirling Dervishes.

I had often read of these fellows—as who, indeed, has not?—but I never had the faintest idea of the wonderful manner in which they did revolve—apparently without the slightest exertion on their part—for all the world like tops, with arms outstretched, and white raiment fluttering in all directions.

The party that I gazed upon were five in number, all wearing very high conical fur caps, and the gravest of all possible faces beneath them. Their raiment was spotlessly white, and their short linen, ballet-girl-like-looking skirts, stood out all around them as they unceasingly whirled, now in this direction and now in that, affording a strong and ludicrous contrast to their great tawny, hairy legs, which, from the knee downwards, as well as their feet, were quite bare.

---

* The name is used indifferently for a boat and a carriage.

They seemed to attract little or no attention from the few passers-by, from which I argued that I was gazing upon no uncommon sight in the streets of Stamboul.

I was myself at length about to pass on, when, to my utter astonishment, the five Dervishes made a ring around me, so that I found myself hemmed in.

Then one of them, never ceasing his whirl the while, whizzed past me like a revolving Catharine wheel, and in doing so laid a hand on my despatch-bag, whilst another fellow, imitating his movement on my right, when he had come within a foot of me, drew a long, slender-bladed flissa from within the folds of his loose robes, and flourished it above my head.

I saw the full peril of my position at a glance, and that I only had myself to depend on, for the long, silent street seemed to be utterly deserted save by a mongrel dog or two.

Planting my left foot heavily on the stomach of the man who had hold of my despatch-bag, I doubled him up most effectually, and almost at the same instant brought the villain who menaced me with the flissa to the ground by a most energetic kick on the shins.

Then I essayed to tear open my overcoat and get at my revolver, which was in the breast pocket of my jacket.

Ere I could do so, however, all the fellows were upon me, howling and yelling like so many demons.

As they all brandished weapons of some sort or other, I gave myself up for lost, which no doubt I should have been had not a cavalry sabre split open the head of one, and lopped off the arms of two more, whereupon the rest took to their heels and ran away.

"I think you're a tenpound note to the bad," then exclaimed a merry, ringing voice, and looking round I perceived that my deliverer was Louis Foucarte, who handed me my despatch-bag, that he had just unfastened the fingers pertaining to a severed Dervish hand from the handle of.

I was completely staggered, as may well be supposed.

How I managed to thank my preserver I do not know.

I did it clumsily enough, you may be sure, and then I gazed with considerable surprise at his altered appearance, for he was clad in a rich and highly becoming huzzar uniform of blue and silver, with scarlet trousers and a light bearskin busby, surmounted by a blue and white plume.

He noticed my look of wondering surprise, and straightway proceeded to enlighten my curiosity with an explanation.

"I have bought a commission in the French Foreign Legion," he said, "with a clear understanding that I am to be attached to no regiment, but be allowed to fight who, when, and where I like. I have christened my uniform quicker than I reckoned upon."

"To the saving of my life and the losing of my wager," I rejoined. "Now, where may you have pitched your quarters?"

"Nowhere as yet, but I shall fix them at the Hotel Byzance."

"That is right, for there have I pitched mine. Shall bygones be bygones, or do you require of me an apology first?"

"I require nothing but a renewal of our friendship," was the reply.

"There is my hand upon that," I made answer; "I will never doubt you again. Doubtless you have often deemed me impertinent?"

"Oh, no! Travelling as you are, you are bound to be circumspect. Have you delivered your despatches?"

"To the admiral, yes. I am now on my way to deliver others to the Sultan. To-morrow I depart for the Crimea."

"Oh, so soon?" said Foucarte, with a shrug of the shoulders.

"Yes. I breakfast with the admiral, and depart directly after. By-the-bye, he invited you to breakfast also."

"Me?" said Foucarte, with a scarcely perceptible start.

"Yes, not by name, but as my friend and travelling companion. I think he is also anxious to see you because you so closely resemble a Russian noble and spy, for the apprehension of whom the united British and French Governments have offered a reward of five thousand pounds," I said.

Louis Foucarte laughed heartily, and then exclaimed—

"Egad, I'll accept your admiral's invitation. We will breakfast with him together, and then hey for the Crimea!"

"What! are you still intent on accompanying me thither?"

"Aye, and on to the Caucasus as well. That is to say unless you are really tired of my company," and he looked at me hard.

"That I am not," I rejoined; "and you keep giving me practical proofs of how very useful you are."

By this time we had reached the exterior of Abdul Medjid's palace, and as Louis Foucarte could not accompany me any further we parted, promising to meet at the *table d'hote* at the hotel at 6 p.m.

CHAPTER XVI.

THE BREAKFAST ABOARD THE FLAG-SHIP.

I FOUND his Serene Majesty the Sultan very approachable indeed. He received me with very great condescension and kindness, and after reading his despatches presented me with a very valuable diamond and emerald ring, which I still wear.

I was away from the palace before two o'clock, and having now naught but an empty despatch-bag, I felt as though freed from a heavy responsibility, and wandered all over the City of the Sultan, determined to see all that there was to be seen ere I returned to my hotel.

But this everything was only very little, for Constantinople is like a temple of Thespis at an English country fair—the best part is the outside, and what seems a perfect paradise from the blue waters of the Bosphorus, is naught but a large town of indescribably dirty streets, when you once land and proceed to give it a minute inspection.

I really was not sorry when the time came to bend my steps Pera-wards, in order to seek the Hotel Byzance and dinner.

Louis Foucarte had reserved me a chair next to his own, and after the repast was over (a very good one by-the-bye) I proposed that we should adjourn to a private sitting-room and crack a bottle of champagne.

This he heartily agreed to, and after we had duly discussed it, and I had paid my lost bet of ten sovereigns, we made up our minds to visit the French Opera House, where we witnessed a very indifferent performance of "Lucia di Lammermoor" and from sheer weariness took refuge ere the second act was over, in an adjoining café, where we were much amused by the drunken antics of a Highlander and a corporal of French Zouaves, whose extraordinary costumes rivetted universal attention.

We were not in bed a minute before midnight, yet nevertheless punctually at eight o'clock on the following morning we were at the waterside, bargaining with an extortionate lot of *caïgées*, for a caïque to take us aboard the admiral's flag-ship, and at length for at least three times the sum that a Thames waterman would have asked for treble the distance, we obtained one.

Our reception by Admiral Dundas was a very kind one, but the instant that his gaze rested on Foucarte's countenance, I saw him start and change colour.

Afterwards, during the progress of breakfast, he again looked at him fixedly, and whilst doing so observed, more by way of mental soliloquy than as addressing anyone—

"Truly I never saw so wonderful a resemblance!"

"To whom, sir?" asked Foucarte, with one of his quiet smiles.

"To that daguerrotype," answered the Admiral, opening a drawer on his side of the table as he spoke, taking thereout a likeness, and pushing it across to my friend.

Foucarte took it up, gazed at it steadily for a minute or two, and then passed it on to me, saying—

"It is indeed very like. Who may the original be?"

"A notorious Russian spy, sir—whom, could I lay my hands on, I would have swinging at my foreyardarm in considerably less than five minutes," answered the old admiral, testily.

"To judge from the expression of the fellow's countenance he is not such a fool as to thrust his head into the lion's mouth in any such absurd manner. May I trouble you, admiral, for another slice of that ham? I declare it's delicious. What may this Russian spy's name be?"

"Kakalogg" grumbled Dundas under his beard.

"Dear me! that sounds more Polish than Russian. Dunbar, let me have another glance at my double. I vow that this is highly interesting."

Foucarte stretched out his hand for the picture as he spoke, and I handed it back to him in silence—myself perplexed beyond measure at the wonderful resemblance, which was perfect as perfect could be.

He looked at it again and smiled.

"I detect one point of dissimilarity between us," he said, suddenly.

"Where? Where?" demanded the admiral and myself in a breath.

"Well, if you notice, his hair is brushed well off his right temple, showing a clear smooth forehead, whereas I let a curl or two cover mine to hide a birth-mark that I'm not altogether fond of showing to the world. See!"

He pushed up his glossy curls as he spoke with one hand, and revealed a clearly defined death's-head, as large as a shilling, a little above the centre of his right temple.

It was black as ink, and contrasted strangely with the whiteness of the surrounding skin. As I looked on it, I wondered how it was that I had never noticed it before.

"There," said Foucarte, "that must have come out in the likeness with the hair brushed right off the forehead—so please don't hang me by mistake for Monsieur Kakalogg, the Russian spy!"

He laughed, and the admiral laughed, and I laughed too, yet with a strange uneasiness I knew not why.

"Similarities in faces are sometimes very remarkable," said the admiral presently, "and though a death's-head is not always a pleasant imprint on a human face, I advise you to take care of your's, Monsieur Foucarte, for until Kakalogg is caught and hung, you don't know where or when it may save your life."

Foucart smiled, and said that he would value it as it deserved to be valued, and then the conversation turned on other topics, and did not revert to the disagreeable one.

After breakfast was over the admiral called me into his private cabin, and, whilst making up and sealing his despatches, told me to take care and deliver them into no hands but those of the Commander-in-Chief of the British forces before Sebastopol.

"And look ye, my lad," he said solemnly, as he seized me by the hand, and gave me a grip that almost brought the tears into my eyes. "The dangers you have left behind may be trifles to those that lie before. Russian cruisers are by no means rare in the Black Sea, no matter what newspaper correspondents may affirm to the contrary; but before those despatches shall fall into the hands of the foe you must, as a last resource, destroy them. Do you hear?—destroy them."

"I will do so. You may depend on me to the death," I said.

"That's right—that's right. And your companion—your companion. He seems a nice, genial, gentlemanly fellow, but don't trust him too implicitly. He's infernally like that Russian spy—and although of course he can't be he, yet don't trust him too implicitly. In fact, trust no one, my boy, out of old England."

I said that I would not, and then the admiral dismissed me with a warm shake of the hand, and a hearty God-speed, and, after he had wished Louis Foucarte a colder and more formal adieu, we took our departure.

Three hours later we were both of us aboard a large French steamer bound straight to Balaclava Bay, with stores and winter clothing for the troops—articles which, poor fellows, they stood sadly in need of.

A fierce strong east wind was blowing straight in our teeth, and there was every probability that we should have rough weather of it in the Black Sea.

CHAPTER XVII.

A GALE IN THE BLACK SEA.

AS it turned out, the prognostications of the weather were amply verified, for no sooner had we left astern of us the two giant headlands that guard as it were the entrance to the Dardanelles, than the storm burst upon us with all its fury, and never had I witnessed such a storm before.

The waves rose in fierce and vast inky billows that threatened every instant to engulph us, whilst the wind absolutely shrieked through the rigging and cordage like the wailing of a million of tortured fiends.

The sky was as gloomy-tinted as the ocean, and a low strip of coast line far away to the leeward looked a dusky green by comparison.

The steamer seemed to make little or no advance in the teeth of the gale, and her great paddle-wheels appeared to beat the waters almost despairingly.

The captain came up to us wrapped in his warm furs, yet with icicles hanging from his thick beard, and declared that if the gale grew worse he must put back.

"Put back! Don't do that whilst there remains a single chance of the vessel's holding together," I said. "I am the bearer of despatches of vital importance to the allied generals before Sebastopol, and a delay in their transmission may cause the loss of thousands of lives."

"And if I do not put back you will in all probability bear your dispatches to Davy Jones," replied the captain, with a grim laugh. "We haven't made a quarter of a knot in the last hour."

"But," I said, earnestly, "a quarter of a knot is something. We at least hold our own, and the storm may abate as suddenly as it arose."

The captain shook his head until quite a shower of icicles were scattered on the deck around him.

"Well," he said, "as I have a passenger of such importance on board, I will do my best," and away he went forward, staggering, strong as he was, in the teeth of the fearful blast.

"If," said Foucarte, calmly to me, "the captain had refused to go on, do you know what I should have done?

"Shot him, and taken the steamer to Balaclava myself."

"The deuce you would!" said I, a little startled at the calm, assured tones in which he spoke. For Foucarte had a peculiar knack of making his words carry conviction with them.

"I would, and so should you, if you value your duty as I think you do. Put back! Pshaw, it's ridiculous! This powerful steamer could face twice such a gale. Look yonder, too, there is something that should make our captain ashamed of what he said."

I followed the direction indicated by Foucarte's finger, and saw a beautiful schooner yacht, trying hard to beat up to windward.

She was undoubtedly English in build and rig, and bad as the weather was, we could see aft quite a large party of ladies and gentlemen.

"What do you think of that?" asked Foucarte, as he re-adjusted the slides of his telescope.

"Why, that they must be remarkably tired of their lives, to attempt to cross the Black Sea in such a cockle-shell, and in such weather," said I.

"You English are famed for what, you will pardon me, if I term it foolhardiness," said Foucarte, with a smile.

"That foolhardiness, as you call it," I replied, a little nettled at my friend's sarcastic tone, "has won for us the admiration of the world—a prize worth a little risk."

"All that it will win for those yonder," said Foucarte, with a laugh, "is probably a bed of Black Sea mud. 'Tis a pity though, for I can swear that some of those ladies on board are young and pretty."

"You must have both good eyes and a good glass to make that out, but perhaps it is instinct that tells you."

"There is one thing that I cannot make out," said Foucarte, who was still intently watching the yacht.

"And that is?" said I.

"This—that yacht is holding nearly the same course as ourselves; she has hardly canvas enough set to make a pocket-handkerchief, while we are under a full head of steam, and yet she is going faster than we are."

"Impossible!" said I.

"Look for yourself," replied Foucarte. "Watch her steadily for a few minutes, and if you do not then acknowledge the truth of what I say I give you leave to pitch me overboard."

I watched, as Foucarte asked me, and in five minutes I had to own that he was right.

Just then the captain came hurrying towards us, with such an expression of alarm upon his face as I never remember seeing upon any other human creature's before.

"What is it?" we both said in a breath.

"Grand Dieu!" he exclaimed, passionately clasping his hands together. "We are lost. We have drifted into one of the currents which feed the whirlpool. Only a miracle can save us!"

"God help them on board that yacht then," I said. "If this powerful steamer is in danger, what must be her fate?"

"In ten minutes you will see," said the captain; "we can make a harder fight of it, and in an hour we shall know our own fate. Meanwhile, messieurs, watch that yacht, it may be interesting, since perhaps we are doomed to the same death."

The Avegnon's course was slightly altered, so as to take her across the powerful current which was striving its best to hurl her to destruction, and Foucarte and I, crossing to leeward, watched the doomed yacht, as faster and faster it flew, in the very teeth of the wind, towards the fearful whirlpool.

We could see now quite clearly the point where the opposing currents met, lashing themselves into a white fury, and seeming to heap themselves one upon the other until they rose high—even above the mighty billows that rode on every side.

The captain's prediction was fulfilled to the letter; in less than the ten minutes he had mentioned the yacht reached the fatal spot. One mad rush into the very centre, then she was whirled round twice or thrice and disappeared for ever!

My pulse throbbed, and I could feel my heart beating wildly, but pity was soon swallowed up in apprehension for our own fate. In an hour we should know whether we also were doomed to perish in that awful vortex.

CHAPTER XVIII

WE HEAR THE CANNON'S ROAR AT LAST.

HAPPILY the captain was wrong in his surmises, though for very nearly an hour from the disappearance of the yacht, the most dreadful apprehensions oppressed all on board.

At the end of that awful period of suspense, however, it became clearly apparent not only that we were out of all reach of the whirlpool-feeding currents, but that we were rounding the gigantic cape as well.

With the joyful feelings produced by a state of comparative safety, I now indulged in a nip of raw brandy, and asked Foucarte to tell me the Legend of the Kaidoum.

"It is not a legend but a positive truth," replied he. "The incidents have occured within the present century, and there are people still living who remember them distinctly."

"That will make the narrative all the more interesting," said I.

"Well, if quite the other way, 'tis not a very long one, and the telling will scarcely take five minutes," rejoined Foncarte.

And he forthwith commenced his yarn as follows—

"As you are doubtless well aware, the Crimea was wrested from its old possessors, the Krim Tartars, in the year 1801.

"Kaidoum Ali, its previous ruler, was a Tributary of Turkey, as is the Khedive of Egypt at the present moment.

"He was a great warrior, and a Pasha of five tails, and for years before Russia took upon herself the task of humbling him to the dust, he waged predatory warfare against Wallachia, Bulgaria, aye, and sometimes even against Poland.

"During one of his marauding incursions into the latter kingdom, he captured a young and beautiful princess, and took her back to form the chief ornament of his harem.

"The grey ruins that you behold on the very summit of that awful precipice are the ruins of his then castle.

"The Polish princess, however, won the fierce Krim Tartar's heart, and in such a manner that instead of making her one of his hundred mistresses, he absolutely married her, and built a Christian chapel for her to worship in.

"But three months later the beautiful Pole sickened and died.

"Old Ali Kaidoum either with or without

reason, just as likely as not without. suspected that the young ladies of his harem in jealousy poisoned her.

"After the funeral he therefore made a terrible example, selecting exactly half of their number to suffer death.

"Five he burnt alive at the stake; five he threw into cauldrons of boiling water. Ten he had torn to pieces by wild horses, and another ten thrown naked into a pit and suffocated by quicklime thrown in on the top of them. The remaining twenty had to jump one by one from the summit of that cliff into the sea, urged thereto by poisoned arrows discharged at them by Ali Kaidoum from one of his palace windows. Happily the rapidity of falling through the air must have given these latter almost a painless death."

"What a horrible fate!" I exclaimed, shuddering. "And what became of this infernal rascal?"

"He was slain in the defence of his stronghold, of which, as you perceive, the Russian soldiery left scarcely one stone upon another. His body, with those of the other slain, was thrown into the cauldron of the whirlpool."

"And the surviving ladies of his harem?" I asked.

"Oh, they were allowed to depart whithersoever they would. Russian officers took two or three of them to wife, for not a few of them were incomparably lovely, and all were young."

"Gentlemen," said the captain, interrupting us at this moment, "I have the pleasure to inform you that immediate danger is over. The gale is at last moderating."

This was capital news indeed, and we both went down with him into the cabin to drink a safe conclusion to our voyage in some excellent champagne brandy.

Then we made what breakfast we could on cold meats, bread, and bitter ale, after which, perfectly tired out, both of us sought our berths, and slept soundly until darkness had once more set in.

A very different darkness from that of the preceeding night, however, for the stars glittered in the dark blue vault of heaven like a million diamonds sparkling from out a velvet pall, whilst the sea was calm as calm could be.

The good ship Avegnon was making rapid progress, too, the more so as the fresh northerly wind enabled her to use sail as well as steam.

Nothing happened very remarkable for the ensuing twelve hours, but about sunrise a cry from the mast head of "A sail on the larboard quarter!" brought telescopes into speedy requisition, and by their aid we could perceive a free-rigged-ship standing towards us with every stitch of canvas set, even to moonrakers and skyscrapers.

The captain gave it as his firm conviction that she was a Russian frigate, and hauling down the tricolour, which erstwhile had been gaily fluttering at our mizen peak, he promptly ran up the two-headed eagle in its place, thereafter clapping on more steam.

Never perhaps had the old Avegnon done such tall walking over the great highway of ocean as she did on this memorable occasion, whilst her captain swore and growled by turns, the former manner of giving expression to his pent up feelings preponderating as soon as he found out that the stranger was running fifteen knots to his twelve.

At last a puff of white smoke came from the pursuer's bows, as a polite intimation to heave to.

Then, as our captain paid not the slightest attention to the summons, a round shot speedily followed, and away went the upper half of the Avegnon's funnel.

''Twas all up with us now. The lambent tongues of flame burst forth from the shattered chimney, threatening a conflagration. To save the ship the fires in the furnace had to be banked down and the steam let off.

"What steamer's that?" roared a voice from the stranger's quarter-deck, directly she forged up alongside—a voice that set me quite at ease as regards my despatches.

"The Russian prize Czarina—late the French transport Avegnon—name not yet painted out," answered our captain.

"Yield yourself then to her Britannic Majesty's frigate—Corunna," replied the voice from the stranger's quarter-deck, and up went the Union Jack in place of the Russian eagle.

"Oh, it is all von grang meestake—von gr. ng meestake," answered our delighted captain. "I imagined you Roosian and ran away—you Engslish stead. Hooraw!"

"You've given us a pretty chase," said the epauletted and cocked-hatted English post-captain, as he looked over his towering bulwarks down upon our decks, "and I suppose we shall have to return good for evil by towing you into Balaclava Harbour."

"I can't reach there any other way," answered our skipper, dolefully, "and I think there's another gale rising."

The long and short of it was that the British frigate took us in tow, and about six hours later we sighted the headlands of Balaclava Bay.

But long before that we heard the thunder of heavy ordnance in the distance, away to the right.

"The allies have commenced the bombardment," I said, addressing Foucarte, who was standing by my side.

Receiving no reply, I glanced round, and saw that he was very pale. A stream of blood was flowing from his under lip.

"What is the matter?" I asked. "Are you ill?"

"Ill!—no. Why do you ask such silly questions?" and Foucarte dived below, apparently in a tiff.

Three hours later we dropped anchor in Balaclava Bay—at length the seat of war was safely reached.

CHAPTER XIX.
A DASHING CAVALRY SKIRMISH.

IT was evening when we reached the bay, and evening had changed into night before I could effect a landing.

At last, however, after having paid the captain the promised hundred pounds, I managed to secure a boat, though not without great difficulty, and dived below to get my dispatch bag and portmanteau, and tell Foucarte that we could be put ashore there and then.

But to my surprise no Foucarte could be found.

In vain I called his name all over the ship. He was clearly not aboard. He had succeeded in landing first.

I did not feel the slightest doubt about the matter, though how he could have succeeded in getting ashore puzzled me greatly.

A tremendous wind was blowing, and a heavy sea was rolling even in the most sheltered part of the bay, added to which a driving storm of snow and sleet blew from the shore, rendering even the bow of the steamer invisible from the stern.

We could hear other leviathans of the deep plunging and rolling at their anchorage all around us, some of the steamers blowing their fog-whistles lustily, to prevent a possible collision, but all sounds seemed to be roared down by the thunder of the distant cannon.

I had had to promise my boatmen a guinea for landing me—and I felt very thankful when I sprang on terra firma that I was alive to pay it them, for thrice during the short pull ashore we had been within an ace of capsizing, and nearly the whole way I had been baling out water with my hat as hard as ever I could work, and had I ceased my exertions but for an instant I verily believe we should have been swamped, so many seas did we ship en route.

AN INSTANT LATER THIS OBJECT ASSUMED A PERPENDICULAR ATTITUDE, AND REVEALED ITSELF TO BE AN ARMED COSSACK.

No. 3.

Ashore at Balaclava, however, I found that my difficulties and perils had but commenced.

I had thought that I should have had no difficulty in reaching the Commander-in-Chief's tent from the port, that friendly lines of red-coated soldiers would have stretched the whole way, that I should be as protected from all extraneous danger as in the streets of London.

Instead of this I found that I had before me a nine mile ride, part of which ride was swept by the cannon balls from the Malakoff and the Redan, whilst at other portions of the route there would be great danger of being buried alive in a snow drift, or of being set upon by marauding bands of Cossacks and robbed and murdered.

This was by no means delightful intelligence, but my duties brooked not of delay, and so I lost no time in procuring a horse and a guide, in company with whom—after a stiff glass of grog, and a crust of bread and cheese at a suttler's shanty, rejoicing in the name of "The Czar's Head"—I set forth.

Oh, what a truly horrid night it was. It had ceased snowing, and a full moon shone out now and then between great masses of riven grey clouds—shone out upon a vast treeless and shrubless expanse of hill and plain, covered with white snow as with a pall.

Here and there gleamed red watch-fires, few and distant at first, but seeming to increase in number towards the brow of the distant hills, behind which lurid glows, as of the northern lights, continually flashed and faded, accompanied by a roar that was really deafening.

The horse I was mounted on was a sorry beast, a mere anatomy of loose bones, and with the snow up to his knees, 'twas impossible to get more than three miles an hour out of him; whilst my guide—a trooper of the Army Service Corps—rode an animal not one whit superior.

"Your cattle don't seem up to much," I ventured to remark.

"They are like ourselves, sir, overworked and underfed," replied the trooper, with a laugh. "If this state of things continues much longer, the Russians, who fight like very devils, will have little difficulty in driving us into the sea."

Having given him permission, as it were, to unloosen his tongue, my companion let it wag to its utmost tension. He told me how that sickness, hunger, and semi-nakedness were destroying the army far more effectually and speedily than Russian shot and shell. How that regiments which had come out a month or two previously a thousand strong, were now reduced to a quarter of that number, through exposure to the wintry weather without sufficient food and clothing, and without ever having been under fire.

He was still chattering away on these dismal subjects, when his attention was suddenly attracted by something far away in the front.

He spurred to my side, clasped my arm, and pointed to where, at a distance of about two miles away, a dark cloud seemed to be crossing the white snow.

"They are Cossacks!" he said, almost breathlessly. "The murderous thieves are going to make a raid on one of our sleeping cantonments."

"I can scarcely distinguish them to be men at all at this distance," I remarked. "Are you sure that they are foes?"

"Oh, yes; my sight is very keen, and sharpened, may be, by continually looking out for danger. I wish we could give the alarm. A pistol shot will scarcely be heard so far away, yet 'tis all that we can do," and as he spoke the trooper plucked forth a pistol from his holster and fired it in the air.

At once drawing my revolver I imitated his example, and fired three shots in rapid succession.

Almost before the sound of the last had died away we heard a bugle ring out, followed by the blare of a trumpet.

"Hurrah!" shouted my companion. "They heard us. We have saved them from having their throats cut in their sleep. Let us spur on, I may be able to show you a pretty sight."

'Twas easy to spur, but very difficult to make our horses quicken their pace thereby. We did succeed in getting another half a mile an hour out of them however, so that in a very few minutes I, too, could see the Cossacks quite distinctly.

They were nearly a thousand strong, all mounted on shaggy ponies, and armed with long spears. They were crossing the snow-clad plain as silently as an army of spectres, and in a confused mob, without any military order or regularity.

The pistol shots and the answering alarm of bugle and trumpet peals had disconcerted them for an instant, and brought them to a full halt, but they were now proceeding in their original course, doubtless thinking that they would still have time to strike a severe blow and escape before any active retaliation could be offered.

If such was their thought, they counted without their host, for suddenly we heard a ringing cheer, and a body of cavalry appeared above a distant hill-top, and the next instant came swooping down upon the Cossacks, with all their sword-blades and brass helmets gleaming in the moonlight.

"By George! the Second Dragoon Guards are on them! Now we shall see sport!" exclaimed my companion, rapturously.

As I had never seen an encounter between cavalry, I drew rein and gazed with intense interest at what was about to take place, and, in truth, it was a splendid sight.

The wild screaming yells of the Cossacks as they saw the British cavalry o'ertopping the hill and bearing down upon them were awful to listen to—so much did the cry sound like that of wild beasts—but they showed no token of craven fear. The Dragoon Guards consisted only of a couple of troops—a mere handful of men compared to the closely-swarming hosts of Russians below.

But in spite of the dissimilarity in numbers, the brave English dragoons rode straight at them, regarding the thousand bristling spears no more than if they had been a thousand nodding bulrushes.

Little chance had the Cossack ponies of withstanding successfully the charge of the dragoons' dark bay blood horses, albeit that they and their riders were half-starved with hunger. With a cheer and a shout they rushed down on the wall of bristling lance-heads, and broke it asunder like a paper barrier with the shock.

Over rolled the Tartar ponies and Tartar riders by scores. The dragoons rode through and through them, trampling them underfoot like a field of nettles.

Five minutes from the first shock of the charge the Russian Irregular Cavalry were in full retreat, and the dragoons, after following them for about a quarter of a mile, sabring them like sheep, drew off, in answer to the shrill summons of the recall trumpet, and rode along backwards up the hill, whose snow-clad slope was now thickly dotted with dead and dying Cossacks, a red-coated brass-helmeted dragoon scattered amongst them every here and there.

CHAPTER XX.

A PRISONER OF THE COSSACKS.

NOT until I saw the dragoons ride up the hill, and perceived that the crowd of runaway Cossacks were coming straight in our direction, did I feel any uneasiness about my own and my companion's safety.

Then it at once occurred to me that we were in imminent danger of being slain or captured, and the same idea seemed to strike my guide at the same time.

"Good God, sir!" he said. "Let us get out of the way quickly, or we shall be ridden down and killed."

Get out of the way! Yes. but how? The Cossacks were galloping down upon us in an extended and irregular crescent of a quarter of a mile in breadth, with each horn well advanced.

Nothing would accelerate the speed of our horses, nd even if we escaped beyond the horns of either escent, the Cossacks could not help perceiving us that plateau of white snow, and they would be to give us chase.

ll of these thoughts I unlocked my bag, took my precious dispatches, and concealed them een my flannel vest and my skin.

did this as we rode swiftly on, that is to say as ftly as our horses would go.

What I dreaded came to pass.

We could not evade the left o'erlapping wing of the Cossack force.

They saw us and bore down on us with guttural ries of delight.

An instant later a hundred spears and swords seemed to be flashing around our heads.

I saw my companion, after shooting one Cossack, and severing the head of a second with his sabre, felled to the ground and transfixed by at least a score of long reedy lances.

Then I was myself knocked from my horse with a blow that deprived me of consciousness.

*   *   *   *   *

When I regained my reason, I found myself inside a hut which seemed to be constructed of mud or turf.

It had but the dimensions of a moderate-sized potatoe burrow, and the floor whereon I lay was wet and slimy. It possessed a small aperture by way of door, just big enough for a man to crawl in at, and another in the centre of the roof which served the purpose of escape hole for the smoke that rose from a fire lighted beneath it.

This delightful residence, if residence it was, with floor, walls and roof of earth, and totally devoid of furniture, was, despite the fire, which gave much smoke and little warmth, about as cold as cold could be, and my teeth were immediately playing the most lively tune, whilst my body shivered and shook in time to the music.

An intense pain in my head made me endeavour to raise my hand to it, but I found that this was impossible owing to my arms being tightly pinioned to my side.

Then I tried to stagger to my feet, but, lo and behold, my legs were bound in like manner.

This dual discovery brought back to my dazed remembrance the encounter with the Cossacks, and the way I had been knocked, stunned and senseless, out of my saddle.

I was without doubt a prisoner of these savage warriors of the plains, and within one of their huts.

Scarcely had I come to this conclusion, when the entrance to my prison house, through which the bright moonlight had hitherto streamed, was darkened by an object that was evidently creeping in on all fours.

An instant later this object assumed a perpendicular attitude, and revealed itself to be an armed Cossack.

"Armed to the teeth" was an expression that I had often come across in penny romances, but I never realised fully what it could mean until now.

My visitor might however be described as being thus armed without any exaggeration. In his right hand he carried a spear, and in his left a dagger; whilst on one side of his belt hung a sword, in company with a long knife, both scabbardless, and on the opposite side no less than three pistols; a short carbine being in addition strapped to his back.

He wore a cap of steel, spiked, and with a red and white turban twisted around it; a cuirass, rusty as it well could be; a blue jacket; a pair of voluminous red breeches; and naked legs from the knee downwards.

The strange-looking individual, whose yellow skin and oblique eyes betrayed his Tartar origin, even more than his incongruous dress, stared at me fixedly for a minute or two, and then kneeling down carefully examined my bonds.

He seemed satisfied with his survey, and was about to retire when I intimated to him by signs that I was thirsty and wanted something to drink.

Directly he understood me he shook his head jocularly, and went through the pantomine of tying a rope around his neck and then drawing it tight and choking.

Having thus signified by dumb show that as I should be hung on the morrow I couldn't by any possibility need water overnight, he chuckled and withdrew.

––––––

CHAPTER XXI.
I BID THE COSSACKS GOOD-NIGHT.

DIRECTLY he had gone I set to work puzzling my brains how best to effect an escape.

I didn't at all relish the idea of remaining there until the Cossacks thought fit to hang me, especially as they had determined that the wants of nature should not be supplied *ad interim*.

I was fearfully thirsty, and was beginning to feel hungry as well, added to which the tightness of my bonds gave me intense pain.

My precious despatch, too—there it was inside my flannel vest, and perhaps the safety of the whole army depended upon its safe delivery.

My despatch-bag had been stolen, but the all-important papers were safe.

This fact, even more than my own peril, made me resolve to strain every nerve to make an escape before morning.

It was very well to resolve to escape, but the how was a much more difficult question to solve.

I had nothing wherewith to cut my bonds, and I couldn't get at them with my teeth—as to bursting them asunder, that was a matter of sheer impossibility.

All at once a brilliant idea struck me, however. There was the fire still burning brightly—my thongs were made of raw cow-hide. If I could roll into the flame, these might burn and burst.

I at once acted upon the idea suggested. My clothes were all of wool, and I did not fear being burnt to death. I rolled over the floor and into the fire, contriving to get my hands between my thighs, and to keep my head well out of the flame.

Thus I lay, rolling round and round, for nearly a minute, my agony being intense the while. Then I rolled out of the fire and smoke, and made a desperate and sudden effort to snap asunder my arm and leg bonds.

I succeeded—the fire had done its work. I was free.

"Free!" the word seemed a mockery as I involuntarily gave it utterance. Free in the hut of the Tartar, with doubtless vigilant sentinels on the outside, and an army of foes camped around me. Bah! the word was out of place.

I had dared so much, however, that I should have been worse than a fool had I hesitated to dare more.

The agony of my burns, too, made me desperate. My clothes were in some places almost burnt off me, and the backs of my hands charred and half roasted.

I carefully searched the hut for a weapon of some kind, but found none; the place was perfectly bare.

Dismayed, but undeterred by this discovery, I dropped down on all fours and crept out of the hut.

Directly I got outside I looked cautiously round, and saw a number of similar huts scattered in every direction, most of them half buried beneath the snow.

Here and there red fires gleamed brightly, and

around them strangely clad forms were grouped, apparently chatting and conversing.

Just behind the hut in which I had been confined stood a small grove of trees, and from their inmost recesses I could hear the constant neighing and whinnying of horses.

For a few minutes I did not dare to move, for fear that some concealed sentinel or other might sight me and shoot me down.

But neither by the exercise of ears nor eyes could I detect the proximity of such an individual.

I therefore commenced to crawl towards the grove of dark pine trees, from whose recesses I had heard the neigh of horses.

The cold snow felt refreshing to my burnt and blistered hands, and the bleak east wind seemed to restore much of my vigour and spirit. In snake-like wriggles I progressed slowly, sometimes burrowing under the snow so as to pass the dangerous neighbourhood of a watchfire.

At last I reached the confines of the pine grove.

Emboldened by my immunity from detection hitherto, I was about to rise to my feet in order the quicker to reach the piquetted horses, whose forms I could dimly see between the tree trunks, when I suddenly perceived a prostrate figure lying right in my path, either dead or asleep.

Asleep I soon detected by the loud breathing, and that he was a Cossack by his gaudy and incongruous dress.

Besides, none but a Cossack could sleep with impunity in a snow hollow as this man was doing.

Noticing that he was well armed, and in anything but a light slumber, I determined to appropriate his sword and a brace of pistols to my own use.

I experienced not the slightest difficulty in doing this, and in less time than it takes to record the fact, the pistols were transferred to my belt, and his long straight sword was firmly grasped in my right hand—the scabbard I had not ventured to deprive him of.

Feeling much more confidence in myself now, I proceeded on my way until I got amongst the horses, who were piquetted in groups of a dozen to a tree.

I was not long in choosing a steed, in drawing his girths tight, and in clapping his bridle on.

I was in the act of lengthening the stirrups when I heard the report of a gun, and the whiz of a bullet past my ear.

Looking round, I saw a Cossack running towards me, with a pistol in either hand.

In a twinkling, however, I was in the saddle, and had cut the rope that bound the horse to the tree.

Striking him sharply with my knees and heels, I urged him to full speed, guiding him south and by west, the direction in which I thought the English camp must lie.

I had not gallopped more than a hundred yards or so, when another Cossack rose right up in my path.

It was the man I had deprived of sword and pistols.

He discovered his loss just as I recognised him, and, with what I presume was an oath, hurled a knife at my head, following it up with his sword scabbard.

Both happily missed me, but the latter taking effect on the flank of my galloping steed, drove it on still faster.

I whirled round the back of my late prison house, darted past a score or two huts more, on the very wings of the wind, and then for miles and miles before me a snow-covered plain seemed to stretch away until it met the horizon.

I felt now that a chance of escape really did exist.

CHAPTER XXII.

SHOWS THAT I BRAGGED BEFORE CLEAR OF THE WOOD.

I HAD had many a carbine and pistol discharged at me whilst running the gauntlet of the Cossack huts, but not a bullet had found its billet save in the white snow-wreaths, so that, although I heard the Cossack trumpets blowing, and knew that in a minute or two at the most I should be hotly pursued, I began to think that I bore a kind of charmed life, and was not going to be caught.

Inspired by these thoughts I turned round in my saddle directly I was out of range, and brandished my sword, wishing my Cossack hosts a contemptuous "Good night."

The old proverb, "Never brag before you are out of the wood," is a very wise one. I had violated it, and so was to be taught not not to do so in the future.

Scarcely had I bidden the Cossacks a contemptuous good night when I found myself pursued by at least three score of them.

My own nag was evidently fresh, however, and so I at first felt very little uneasiness.

I tucked my bare sword under my left arm. therefore, and steered in a bead line for where, far away, I could still hear the thundering roar of heavy ordnance.

I rode as lightly as I could, but for all that, many minutes had not elapsed before, on looking around, I felt convinced that the Cossacks were gaining on me.

'Twas plain that they thought so too, for by the bright moonlight they saw my backward glance, and shook their tasselled spears in derision.

Then all at once, a long, peculiar, and sustained whistle came across the snowy plain.

The instant he heard it, my pony pricked up his ears, and began to rear and plunge.

In vain I tried to urge him on, but when the whistle was repeated, the shaggy little brute wheeled round, and, despite all my efforts to restrain him, tore back towards the approaching Cossacks.

The animal had been accustomed to obey its master's whistle, and its master, mounted on some other pony, was evidently amongst my pursuers.

I had not the slightest control over the little brute, whose mouth was as hard as a granite rock, and who had, moreover, got the bit between his teeth.

I heard the loud laughter of the Cossacks now scarcely more than a quarter of a mile away.

In another five minutes I should be borne into their very midst, and be again their prisoner.

The thought was horrible.

But an idea suddenly struck me.

If I couldn't make my steed go my way, I needn't allow him to take me his, *nolens volens*.

Directly I found him struggling through a snowdrift, therefore, I flung myself off, and allowed myself to sink under the icy pall.

I went down a yard or two at the least, and let the snow fall over me.

In this position I lay as still as I could for the chattering of my teeth in my head. hoping that the Cossacks would not succeed in finding me.

Presently the trampling of hoofs surrounded me on all sides, and my spirit died within me at the dread that they had noticed the spot where I had fallen.

To and fro, backwards and forwards, hither and thither, rode the Cossacks, uttering guttural cries and exclamations as they passed and repassed.

They had clearly not noticed whereabouts I fell.

My heart felt elated for an instant, then sank again.

Even if they had not seen me drop yet how could they help finding me if they only took sufficient pains?

And they evidently were doing so.

I could hear them thrusting their long lances again and again into the snow-covered earth.

Presently one transfixed my sleeve, and I had hardly congratulated myself on my lucky escape, when another passed through the fleshy part of my left arm.

The pain was agonising, and I could hardly repress a shriek. I did, however, for I felt that my life depended on my silence, at the cost of a nearly bitten through lip.

I now expected no other than that the next lance-thrust would pierce my heart or chest, but I was doomed to be pleasurably disappointed, for though the devilish spears kept dig-dig-digging around my head and body for some time longer, not another wound did I receive, and after the lapse of another quarter-of-an-hour or so—which seemed to me about a century—I heard the Cossacks ride away.

Allowing about ten minutes for them to get out of sight, I struggled out of the snow wreath, and looked around.

Not a Cossack was anywhere to be seen.

I examined my arm and found that the snow had stopped the bleeding. Then I listened for the roar of the cannonade, but lo! it had ceased. A dead silence reigned around. I had only the moon and stars to guide me.

I knew that if they did not guide me somewhere I should be a dead man before day-dawn, for I already began to feel that terrible drowsiness which is the inevitable forerunner of death from cold and exposure.

Horror of horrors! When, having marked out my direction, I tried to advance, my legs refused to perform their office, and I fell forward with my face in the snow.

Again I struggled to my feet, but only again to fall.

My legs I thought must be already frost-bitten, and, rolling myself round into a sitting posture, I began to rub them with my right hand as hard as I could.

Happily I succeeded in restoring the circulation of the blood, when, once more assuming the perpendicular, I rushed on, determined that at all events I wouldn't allow myself to freeze any more.

It was heavy walking in all conscience, the snow often being above my knees. What would I not have given for a deep drain at a rum or a brandy bottle? But the wish was an idle one, a very idle one indeed.

After I had walked at least seven miles I stumbled and fell over something. On rising, an irresistible curiosity seized me to discover the nature of the obstacle.

I scraped away the snow that covered it, and the pale moonlight shone on the still paler face of the hapless Army Service Corps trooper who had accompanied me as my guide from Balaclava to the front.

He was stone dead, and the blood that had flowed from a score of wounds was frozen in thick clots over his chest, which one broken spear still penetrated.

I could do nothing for the poor fellow, so I covered him over again with his snowy winding sheet, as much to baffle the sinister designs of two dull black heavy-winged looking vultures that hovered in the air above as for any other reason.

Then I staggered on again, knowing that I was at all events in the right direction, a fact that was presently confirmed by passing several slight snow mounds, from which arms, legs, and helmeted and turbaned heads every here and there emerged, pointing it out as the spot where the English dragoons and the Cossacks had fought and fallen a few hours previously.

Presently I began to see what looked like the outlines of long rows of tents in the distance; and, inspired by this token that I was approaching the camp of the Allies, I stepped blithely out, nor halted until I was brought suddenly up by a gruff "Qui va là?"

I started. Before me stood a tall French grenadier in the uniform of the Imperial Guard, with his bayonet at the charge.

I explained to him that I had just escaped from the Cossacks, and was looking for the British camp.

'Twas clear that he did not believe me. What soldier would have taken the word of a miserable looking scarecrow such as I was?

"Avancez et je feu!" he cried, threateningly. "Où est la consigne, Monsieur!"

I told him how that under the circumstances I knew neither watchword nor countersign. That I had only that evening landed at Balaclava, and an hour later had been captured by the Cossacks.

"C'est drôle!" exclaimed the huge grenadier, with a shrug of the shoulders. "Rendez vous un prisonnier, monsieur."

There was no help for it, and so rather than have a bullet or a bayonet through me I threw my sword and pistols to the ground, and surrendered myself.

Then two of the grenadiers came up from a neighbouring camp-fire, and marched me off between them to the tent of the *chef de bataillon* which stood at some little distance.

This officer, a veteran whose once tawny moustache and imperial had grown grey 'neath the suns of Africa, heard my tale very patiently, and, what was better, believed it.

He made me drink nearly a quarter of a bottle of brandy, eat the leg of a fowl and some capital biscuits, and then, hauling out a portmanteau from underneath his camp-bedstead, he forced me to don a suit of mufti, and then proceeded to call a guard to conduct me to the tent of the English general.

How I thanked him I know not. Luckily he was a blunt soldier who disliked a superabundance of gratitude, and, presently, after bidding him a warm and hearty farewell, I mounted a beautiful grey charger, and, surrounded by half-a-dozen French Lancers, rode gaily away.

For miles and miles, as it seemed to me, we trotted down streets of tents, silent as though they were pitched on an unpeopled solitude. But one of my companions told me that each one contained seven sleeping soldiers.

Every now and then we would pass a watchfire, with half-a-dozen men grouped around it, and a sentry with shouldered rifle marching up and down in front, and at last we turned a sharp corner in this interminable city of canvas, and I involuntarily drew rein awestruck, yet delighted, at the magnificent spectacle that my gaze rested on.

CHAPTER XXIII.

THE SORTIE FROM SEBASTOPOL.

BEFORE me lay a vast camp, covering, as it seemed, five hills and the slopes between. I had passed through the French camp, and that which I now looked upon was the British—a barren track of land, about a mile in width, cut up into ridges and deep gullies, dividing the two.

Beyond the British lines rose Sebastopol, with the grim Malakoff and the green slopes of the Mamelon and the Redan distinctly visible, and more dimly so, because further away, the dark grey forts that frowned o'er the ocean, and the tall raking masts and the black hulls of the Russian fleet that lay locked up inside the harbour.

The sullen boom of the ocean, though a good three miles away, was distinctly audible, and, save the long wailing moan of the wind, it was the only sound that broke the stillness, for Russians, English, and French alike seemed to be buried in profound repose.

It was not so, however, for, before we were a quarter of the way across the neutral ground that divided the English from the French camps, we observed that we were cut off from the former by an immense column of green-coated infantry, which, like a huge glittering-scaled python, was ascending one of the gullies, the sides of which were sufficiently steep to conceal them from sight until we were almost upon them.

"*Mille bayonettes!* 'tis a Russian sortie. We must gallop back and give the alarm. *Allons, monsieur,*" and the French *sous officier*, who had charge of my escort, wheeled his horse round as he spoke.

I had no resource but to do the same, for the Russian columns interposed between me and the British camp, and cut off all communication with it.

Back we rode on the spur, therefore, the troopers shouting as they rode, at the very top of their lungs.

At the first watch-fire the sentry discharged his rifle; the signal was repeated from post to post.

Then bugles warbled and trumpets blared, the brattle of drums sounded far and near, mingled with the shouts of command, yet we still rode on.

"We mustn't drop you on the way, or, being in mufti, you might be mistaken for a Russian spy, and then it would be a case of the bullet or the cord before you could attempt, far less give, any explanation," said the sergeant.

I felt that he was right, and yet 'twas hard to be riding away from my own countrymen just when they were in imminent peril of a surprise.

I knew that the alarm had been given, and I could tell by the distant firing that the action had commenced, and was being hotly maintained.

"Would you like to see a little of what war's like, monsieur?" asked the sergeant, as we rode on at a gallop.

"I confess that I should," I made reply.

"Then, if you don my undress uniform, which is in my tent hard by, you may ride in our ranks, and, if we are in luck's way, charge with us. What do you say to that?"

"Well, my life is scarcely my own to risk," I said; "but if by donning a uniform I may succeed in getting to the tent of the British General any the quicker, I'll soon clap it on."

"Very probably you might," answered the obliging *sous officier*. "Even the Russians would forbear from hanging as a spy a captive wearing a uniform. Besides, we might charge right up to the British lines, and so carry you within gunshot of your General's tent."

"Good," I said; "I will borrow your uniform."

The result of my determination was that, some twenty minutes later, I was trotting to the front in the disguise of a French lancer, a solitary unit of as gallant a looking regiment as it had ever been my lot to gaze upon.

I knew as much about the management of a lance as any plough-boy, but I knew that it was used for sticking enemies with; and, being as good a horseman as Leicestershire foxes and bullfinches could make me, I felt that at all events I should not disgrace my French friends by my riding.

I found it pleasantly exciting—the clatter of arms and accoutrements, the neighing of horses, and all the pomp and circumstance of war.

We passed fast-forming infantry regiments and chains of artillery.

My friend the sergeant, who rode on my left, chattered unceasingly, and pointed out to me all that was worth noticing *en route*. But before very long we were to the front, and the battle-field lay before us.

The moonlight had given place to the cold grey of early dawn, and so everything was clearly visible.

Two Russian infantry columns had attacked the right and left of the British force almost simultaneously, and these were still hotly engaged, now gaining ground and now losing it, fighting with the dogged resolution for which Russian and English soldiers are alike remarkable.

But a third column, stronger and mightier than either of those that had attacked the flanks, was now rolling up the slopes to assail the British centre.

It looked like a vast green ocean billow, slowly rolling forward, but its crest was composed of glittering steel.

The famine-stricken, disease-decimated British, had few men indeed to spare to oppose this new danger.

The centre had been already weakened to strengthen the wings, which, in spite of these reinforcements, could scarcely hold their own against the ever-increasing volume of Russian soldiery that were being hurled against them.

The English staff, a mass of many-coloured men and horses, were distinctly visible, so little were they hemmed in by their own red-coated soldiery. The tide of battle was rapidly rolling thitherward, threatening to cut the army in two with a wedge of bayonets.

At this moment, however, to the intense surprise of the French regiments of horse and foot that were rapidly forming in battle array along the entire opposite length of what I have called the neutral ground, a regiment of kilted Highlanders came up from the rear of the British centre at the double, deployed and formed in line two deep, with a front of a good quarter of a mile, and about five hundred yards in advance of the staff.

"What soldiers are these?" asked my friend the *sous officier*.

"Highlanders—the forty-second, I think," I rejoined.

"Fools!" growled the *sous officier* under his glossy moustache; "as if they could check those onrolling columns for a single instant with an extended line only two deep."

"I'll bet you a bottle of champagne against a cigarette that they hold the Russians in check until reinforcements come up," I cried, entering into the full excitement of the thing.

"Done!" responded the sergeant; and we shook hands preparatory to watching with breathless interest a *combat à outrance* that was evidently near at hand.

I will reserve its description for another chapter.

CHAPTER XXIV.

SCOTCH HIGHLANDERS AND FRENCH LANCERS.

NO sooner had the thin red line of kilted warriors thrown themselves into battle array than the heavy batteries in the Redan, the Mamelon, and the Malakoff commenced to open fire. Shot and shell came looming through the air, making great gaps in the British ranks; and under cover of this terrible cannonade the heavy Russian columns that threatened the British centre surged onwards against the Scottish line that so silently awaited their attack.

There were five thousand men at the least, all packed in close column, the hinder ranks pressing hard on the heels of the front, and all bellowing forth the name of the Czar.

They thought to sweep away the line of petticoated soldiers who ventured to oppose them, in so extraordinary and apparently weak a formation, as a bounding horse would sweep away a gossamer spider-web stretched from bush to bush across his path.

They were soon undeceived, and in a terrible manner.

A stream of fire appeared suddenly to flash adown the whole Scottish line—a tempest of leaden balls to bring their leading columns to a dead halt. The instant they began to advance again another burst of smoke and flame, with its accompanying torrent of death-dealing *pilules*, caused their advanced files not only to halt, but to waver, and, ere their officers could reform them, the Highlanders, with a cheer which we could distinctly hear, even above the roar of the cannonade, charged down upon them with the bayonet.

At the same instant a squadron of English Hussars were launched suddenly upon the flank of the Russian columns, rendering their confusion irretrievable. They reeled, broke, and fled, pursued by the avenging British steel.

"Glorious! glorious!" exclaimed the French *sous officier*, "those petticoated warriors of yours are heroes, every man of them. Our grenadiers of the Guard could not have done better, hanged if they could. Your cigarette, monsieur."

I took the cigarette, and lighted it. Such trifles were allowed in the somewhat loose service of France. Then we turned to watch how the fight went in other parts of the field.

And now a superb regiment of French Zouaves went past at the double. They were going to relieve the hardly pressed British right.

At the same time a Russian cavalry regiment was descried coming up the slopes with the evident intention of heading the Zouaves back.

"Now it will, perhaps, be our turn, monsieur," said my friend, the *sous officier*, loosening his sword in its scabbard. "Are you open to wager another bottle of champagne on it?"

"Against another cigarette—yes," I rejoined; "but this time I hope that I may lose—cordially hope it."

"Ah, I perceive that you are a regular *croc mitain*, monsieur, laughed the *sous officier*, shrugging his silver-epauletted shoulders. "Well, all the better, for we shall soon be in the thick of it."

His words were prophetic, for, scarcely had he spoken them when an *aide-de-camp*, whose horse was covered with a lather of foam, rode up to the colonel, and, pointing with his sword towards the advancing Russian cavalry, said—

"Those fellows are coming on at a trot. It is your task, *mon cher colonel*, to send them back at a gallop."

"A task that I will accomplish," answered the colonel, stroking his iron-grey moustache.

Then, turning to his men, he shouted—

"*Mes enfants*, it is our turn at last. *Chargez! Vive l'Empereur!*"

The trumpets rang out, the eagle-surmounted tri-colour bent to the breeze, a thousand red and white pennons fluttered, and a thousand lance-heads gleamed, as at this instant the sun showed half its blood-red disk above the ocean waves; and with every lip set, every cheek flushed, every eye sparkling, the gallant regiment, in open order, swept down the hillside.

But the trot quickly changed to a gallop, and, in obedience to another trumpet blast, the ranks closed up nearer and nearer, until we were riding holster to holster and boot to boot, with our steel sword-scabbards, long bits and chain bridles jingling, and our brassed-bossed schapshas and bright accoutrements glittering in the sunshine, whilst the broad rustling silk of the Imperial and regimental colours waved defiantly above our streaming plumes of blood-red horsehair, as we poured down like a mountain breeze on the white and gold cavalry of the Czar.

A dull red flash, followed by a hoarse booming sound, made me instinctively stoop forward almost to my saddle bow; and it was well I did so, for a Russian cannon ball whizzed just above my head, and tore to pieces a poor lancer in my rear.

Then I saw the flash of sabres along the Russian line, and the next moment, with a shock such as might have been caused by the collision of two heavily-charged thunder-clouds, we pierced the opposing squadrons of Russian horse like a wedge of steel.

The murky cloud of dust stirred up by so many hoofs seemed to my bewildered vision to be full of helmeted and schapshad heads, of gauntleted hands, the bright points of levelled spears, of brandished swords and waving standards, whilst the air was laden with cries, tumultuous sounds, shrieks, groans, cheers, commands, and imprecations.

Rearing horses and dying men went down on all sides, but with the dash and élan peculiar to French cavalry we burst right through the Russian dragoons, breaking through their close array of horses heads and cuirassed breasts, cutting, slashing, and thrusting right and left, and trampling them down like a field of ripe corn.

My grey charger bore me bravely, but bewildered by the fury of the charge I knew not for a moment whether I was on earth or in Pandemonium, until a heavy blow from a sabre on my schapsha recalled my energies with the instinct of self-preservation, and then I found myself thrust rather out of the press, and opposed to a Russian officer in a brilliant uniform, and mounted on a powerful black Smolensko charger, in whom I at once recognised Louis Foucarte.

For a moment I was so astonished that my antagonist would not have had the slightest difficulty in slaying me had he felt so inclined.

Previous to this encounter I had run a Russian through with my lance, and then dropped the weapon, not knowing how to withdraw it with my horse dashing on at full speed. I now held my drawn sabre in my hand, and having been an adept at both foils and single-stick when at college, I felt, the instant that I recovered my astonishment, not at all inclined to shirk the encounter.

"Foucarte, you are a liar and a traitor!" I shouted.

My adversary grunted something by way of reply, shrugged his epauletted shoulders, and then slashed at me savagely.

Our swords clashed, and for a moment were engaged up to the very hilt. Then we watched each other warily, with blade pressed against blade.

"Yield yourself a prisoner!" I cried. "I don't want to take the life of a man who has thrice saved mine!"

But Foucarte merely grinned in reply, and made a sudden feint at my right side, changing it into a rapidly delivered lunge at my heart, by which he got just inside of my guard, and ripped up an inch or two of my gold lace.

This stirred up my usually sluggish blood to fever heat, and I retorted with slash and thrust, thrust and slash, in such rapid succession that my antagonist was reduced to the necessity of acting solely on the defensive.

At last his long straight but slender sword snapped short off at the hilt in parrying a blow from my heavier weapon, and, ere he could draw a pistol from his holster or I had realised the fact of his being defenceless, I had passed my weapon through his body.

The instant I had done so my battle fever and blood-lust passed away from me, and I would have dismounted to discover whether he yet lived, and if so, render him any assistance that lay in my power, but ere I could do so I was swept away by a rush of men and horses to quite a hundred yards distance, and suddenly a hand was laid on my shoulder, and a voice shouted in my ear:

"There's a gap now, *mon camarade*. Dash through it. The British general and his staff are looking on within rifle range of us."

CHAPTER XXV.

I DELIVER MY DESPATCH AT LAST.

THE voice and hand pertained to my friend the *sous officier*.

A glance shewed me that he was right, and that now was my chance.

I put spurs to my horse and made a dash for it, for the momentary gap might soon close up again.

I shot it, however, and the next instant I was

clear of the press, and sweeping up the opposite hill-side like a hunted fox.

Once only I looked back. It was to see the Russian dragoons galloping in panic-stricken confusion towards Sebastopol, with the French lancers riding their rearward squadrons down like a field of white poppies. Oh, it was a terrible yet a glorious sight.

But as I rode on, with cannon-balls hurtling by and rifle-bullets whistling past my ears, I saw with joy how the battle was going in other parts of the field.

On the left, the side nearest to me, the British Queen's Own and the Thirty Second, helped by the French Zouaves of the Guard, were rolling the Russian columns, still manfully contesting every inch of ground, back towards Sebastopol, with repeated bayonet charges.

The Russian central column, pressed hard by the cavalry of the Light Division, had already entered the beleaguered city, and the gallant horsemen were riding back in triumph, pursued now and then by an iron ball from the Mamelon or the Redan; and away to the right our flying artillery were pounding away hard at the rear of the third column of retreating Russians, and pounding with considerable effect, too.

The sortie had failed; the allies were masters of the field.

It took me but five minutes to gallop from the frightful mêlée of struggling men and horses to the summit of the little knoll on which the British staff was grouped.

"Whom have we here?" exclaimed Lord Raglan, as I rode up. "A French lancer? What do you want my good fellow?"

"Not a French lancer, but a Queen's Messenger, my lord," I replied. "This uniform was donned to enable me to get to you the sooner. It has been successful."

"Why, when did you arrive in the Crimea, then?"

"Last night I landed at Balaclava, and set out for camp, but was captured by the Cossacks *en route.*"

"And they let you go again?" asked Lord Raglan.

"Not a bit of it, my lord. I saved them the trouble of hanging me by running away. I reached the French lines, and, not daring to cross in front of the advancing Russian columns in mufti, for fear of being shot, or, if captured, hung as a spy, I borrowed a French sergeant's spare uniform and charged with his regiment," I answered.

"By heaven you have acted promptly and acted well. Come with me to my tent. General Simpson, I leave you in charge of the field. There is little more to be done—nothing, in fact. The Russians will go quietly home to their breakfasts—that is to say, if we haven't already given them a sufficient stomachful," said Raglan.

Then, turning to me, he added—

"Come along, I am anxious to see my despatches."

We rode side by side, and presently we reached the general's tent.

Throwing the reins of our horses to two soldiers, we entered it together, when, to my utmost surprise and consternation, whom should my eyes rest on, reclining negligently in a camp chair, and apparently reading a novel, but Louis Foucarte.

I know that I must have staggered and turned pale, for Lord Raglan looked at me curiously and said—

"You've over exerted yourself—you feel faint—a little wine will soon revive you. Count Pollaki, will you let this gentleman have your chair? he has come a long journey and undergone some severe vicissitudes. Mr. Harry Dunbar, a Queen's Messenger, the Count Eugene Pollaki, an illustrious Pole, who has left the service of Russia for that of England."

"Very happy, I'm sure," remarked the individual I had been introduced to as a Polish count, springing to his feet and bowing profoundly. Pray sit down, my dear sir. None but the brave serve the chair, as your Mr. Pope has it. On chair—chair—no, I think it's *fair* in the original, but it's all the same, I suppose. Now, do sit down."

I did as I was invited, for I was sorely in need of rest, and believe I should have on the ground if there had not been a chair to fall into.

I made no reply to Count Eugene Pollaki's politeness, however, save by a bow, for he was Louis Foucarte I had hardly a doubt, and yet, if so, who then was the officer whom I had run through the body only half an hour previously?

I was fairly puzzled, and, an instant later, I was more puzzled still, for the Polish count running his fingers lightly through his hair, pushed it back off his forehead, and I saw that the distinguishing feature of Foucarte, the birth mark of the death's-head, was not there.

Lord Raglan forced me to drink three or four glasses of wine, and then sat down to read his despatches.

Scarcely had he perused a quarter of their contents, however, when he brought his fist down with a crash on his camp desk, exclaiming—

"This news has been forestalled—the instructions are worthless. Some treachery has been at work, Mr. Dunbar."

CHAPTER XXVI.

MADE PRISONERS BY THE RUSSIANS.

"COUNT EUGENE POLLAKI," said I, when, on leaving the General's tent, we found ourselves alone together. "Fate seems to cast us in each other's way."

"And very kind of Fate it is," was his smiling reply. "I like a pleasant companion above all things, and I have been unable to find one among the foes and oppressors of my country, whom the allies have locked up in yonder city."

He pointed towards Sebastopol, and smiled as he returned my supercilious gaze.

"Come, come," I said. "This is all very well, you know, to strangers, but you can't impose on me, Monsieur Louis Foucarte. I am ready to accept the situation because I can't help it, and in the presence of others you are Count Pollaki, but when alone pray let us drop the farce."

"Farce?" I don't understand you, sir," replied my companion, drawing himself proudly up.

"Do you mean to deny," I said, looking him sternly in the face, "that we have travelled in each other's society all the way from London to the Crimea, and that you have always represented yourself to me as Monsieur Louis Foucarte, by birth a Frenchman, travelling the world over in order to drown a great grief."

"Assuredly, I do," was the haughty retort. "I am a Pole, was born at Warsaw, and for the last six years have served, compulsorily, not from choice, in the Russian army. From that hated service I escaped last night, after having been shut up for long months in Sebastopol."

"Thank you for the explanation," I said, not believing a word of it, however. "All that I can say in reply is, that there is another individual in the world so like you that did you see the reflection of his face in a mirror you would swear it was your own."

"Oh, if *I* could so swear, of course I cannot feel surprised at another's being prepared to do the same," retorted my companion, with a smile. "I've no objection to being called Monsieur Louis Foucarte, until you are perfectly convinced that I am not he. It is a pretty name, and my greatest ambition would be to be a Frenchman by birth."

Of course after this I could say nothing further.

I accepted his outstretched hand, and apologised for my apparent rudeness.

The General had advised me to travel in uniform, so as to escape all risk of being hung as a spy if captured by the Russians.

Count Pollaki had already attired himself in the blue and silver uniform of a French hussar, and speaking the language, was able to sustain the character to perfection.

I chose the uniform of a British lancer, the most gorgeous and resplendent in the service, well knowing that with a martial yet semi-barbarous people, like the Circassaians, an abundance of scarlet and gold would carry no little weight.

A couple of splendid chargers were placed at our disposal, mine being a beautiful black Smolensko stallion, and Count Pollaki's a superb grey, with a good share of Arabian blood in his veins, as was evidenced by his thin expanded nostrils and soft gazelle-like eyes.

After a substantial, though coarse, breakfast—for even British field officers had to rough it pretty severely at that period, and the rank and file had to put up for weeks at a time with dry bread, mouldy cheese, and coffee made with green berries—we set out, with our pockets filled with English gold, and our stomachs with salt beef, Bass's pale ale, and hard biscuits, upon a journey of a thousand and some odd miles in length.

We were by no means destined to perform it, however—at all events, not at that time, for obstacles and difficulties that we counted not of lay in the way.

We had not left the British camp a couple of miles in our rear when, crossing a narrow valley, we found ourselves suddenly surrounded by a host of Cossacks.

They seemed to rise out of the very earth, and to sweep down upon us from every point of the compass.

Escape was impracticable.

Count Pollaki and I looked at each other.

"If these fellows take us prisoners instead of killing us, remember that I am Louis Foucarte, a Frenchman," he said, solemnly. "Count Eugene Pollaki, a court-martial of Russian officers would award a short shrift and a remarkably long cord too."

"I understand," I rejoined. "I will testify in your favour. But they haven't got us yet."

"Nor shall they," answered my companion, "until a score of them have bitten the dust. They have felt the weight of my sword before, have these cursed spawn of the Don and Volga, and I have a long score still to settle with them."

I made no reply, for the time had come for actions, not for words.

From north, south, east, and west the Cossacks, on their little rough, shaggy ponies, were sweeping down upon us, their tasselled spearheads flashing in the sunshine.

Our only course, if we meant to fight at all, was to dash at the force that came sweeping along to bar our path, and cut a way through them before those to right, to left, and in rear of us could come up.

We knew it to be next to an impossible feat, but yet we never hesitated.

We set spurs to the splendid battle-steeds and rode right at them.

Rode with a yell and a shout that rang loud above the guttural cries of our foes, which sounded more like the yelpings of hungry dogs than any other earthly noise.

We expected no other fate but to be riddled with spear thrusts; but we both resolved, I think, to have our innings out before we were clean bowled over.

I know I gripped my lance as though I had meant to drive it through a wall of stone, instead of through quivering flesh and muscle; but through the latter I drove it pretty hard, for when we crashed down on the Cossacks I sent it through a front and a rear rank man with the force of the shock, which very nearly hurled me out of my saddle in turn—a catastrophe which would have been fatal.

Of course I had to relinquish the weapon, but, drawing my sword, I laid about me right and left, and was surprised to find what a number of Cossacks I could kill without receiving a scratch in return.

Not but what I think my great powerful charger did most of the work, for before his broad buffeting shoulders the small Cossack ponies seemed to go down like skittles before a well-played ball, leaving me to strike whilst their riders were in the act of falling with them.

Eugene Pollaki, or Louis Foucarte, whichever he might be, kept nearly abreast of me, and proved himself an accomplished sabreur, slicing Cossack heads open as though they had been ripe melons.

Had the Cossacks restricted their attack to us I really think that, despite their long spears, the points of which we shred off as though they had been poppy-heads, we should have cut our way through them.

Discovering us to be invulnerable, however, and beginning to entertain a wholesome horror of our flashing and death-dealing sword-blades, the dastards began to direct their attack at our horses, spearing them in chest and flank, whilst they kept beyond the reach of our sabres.

The consequence was that ere we could cleave our way wedge-like through their compact array, the noble animals fell, faint from loss of blood, to the ground.

Ere we could disentangle ourselves from the stirrups we were pounced down upon, stunned with the flats of sword-blades and the butt-ends of lances, and then tightly bound with lashings of raw cows'-hide.

Whilst undergoing the latter humiliating indignity a Russian officer (doubtless the colonel of the Cossack regiment), dressed in a rich green and gold uniform, came up, and regarded us intently from underneath his shaggy brows.

Suddenly his lips expanded into a malicious grin as, apparently recognising for the first time my companion, he said—

"Ha, ha! Count Pollaki; so you have come amongst us again. You will be accorded a warm reception, believe me, when you re-enter Sebastopol."

My companion replied to this remark in French, telling the officer "that he did not know what he said, not understanding Russian."

The officer shrugged his epauletted shoulders and smiled.

Evidently the assertion did not go down.

He walked away, however, and remounted his horse. Then he gave the signal to march.

Closing up around us the Cossacks drove us on with lance pricks and the blows of sword scabbards, making us keep pace with their ponies.

'Twas hard work to do so, but we valued our skins too much to hang back.

How we both prayed, I have no doubt, that a French or English cavalry patrol party might turn up and rescue us, but our prayers were unanswered.

We were driven on in the manner that I have described for at least a dozen miles, and then we found ourselves at the mouth of a cave, the entrance to which was almost concealed by a luxuriant undergrowth of scrub.

Half-a-dozen Cossacks then dismounted, as did the officer, and we were pushed into the cavern with oaths and laughter.

———

CHAPTER XXVII.

INSIDE SEBASTOPOL.

THE underground passages that we threaded seemed to extend for two or three miles, and at quarter of mile intervals or so we passed sentries leaning upon their muskets, in queer little niches, that caused them to look more like statues than living men.

At last, above the trampling of our feet along the vaults and subterraneans, I thought I could hear very loud and very beautiful singing in the distance.

Every instant I became more assured that I was not deceived, and before long I could make out that it was some grand anthem, sung by at least a thousand voices.

I glanced inquiringly at my companion, but he walked with his eyes on the ground, with the general air of a man whose interest in the world and all earthly things was for ever gone.

But the thundered chaunt grew every instant louder and louder; and when, having arrived at the end of a passage longer than any that had preceded it, we began to ascend, the noise was deafening.

The next instant a trap-door, or something of the kind, was thrown open, at the top of a steep flight of steps, by a Cossack, who had dashed in front for the purpose, and on ascending these steps and passing through the aforesaid trap-door, we found ourselves within an immense church crowded with Russian soldiers.

High mass was being performed, and at least a thousand candles blazed on the high altar, before which a score of priests in vestments stiff with gold and glittering with precious stones were officiating.

The vast church was literally packed with soldiers. All down the long nave stood the cavalry of the Imperial Guard, the Chevalier Guardsmen of the Empress, in uniforms of white and gold, standing nearest to the altar steps.

The aisles were closely packed with the green-coated, black-helmeted infantry of the line, and the galleries were full of the brown-coated and brass-helmeted artillery.

Altogether there were at least ten thousand men of all arms present, who at certain points of the grand and imposing ceremony joined in the choral service with one heart and one voice.

Then, after the waving of silver censers, and the ringing of bells, came the elevation of the Host, and, as the sacred receptacle was raised aloft, three thousand swords leapt from their scabbards and flashed in salutation, whilst twice three thousand muskets were presented, the butts the next instant descending on the marble pavement with a crash that sounded awful as the knell of doom.

Our wild and half barbarous custodians, the Cossacks, had involuntarily halted to gaze awhile upon the grand and imposing spectacle, but as the congregation sat down, and a grey-bearded priest ascended the pulpit to deliver a sermon, they drove us on again; and a minute later we had issued forth from the church-porch into one of the streets of the city.

It was a broad and stately thoroughfare, with what, in days of prosperity, must have been handsome shops.

Most of these now had their shutters up, and the walls of many of the houses were ventilated by the passage therethrough of French and English cannon-balls, whilst some had fallen down altogether, and blocked up the pavement.

Even as we passed along, in reply to a heavy and ominous boom from the Malakoff, a shell came hurtling through the air, and, striking the high gilt spire of a neighbouring church, exploded and blew it to fragments.

One heavy stone and a sheet of crumpled-up copper fell amongst us, killing one of the Cossacks, and so maiming another that he had to be left behind.

Our escort hurried on after this at the double, nor paused until they had brought us to a building whose architectural features were a villainous cross between a barracks and a town hall.

Into this we were hustled and driven with most unnecessary cruelty, and presently found ourselves before a tribunal of Russian officers, who were all seated around a green-baize covered table.

"A hundred strokes with the knout, and then to be shot," I heard one of these officers exclaim, as we entered the hall, and then there was led past us by two brown-coated gendarmes a pale, horror-stricken looking wretch, clad in a ragged French uniform, but whose broad, flat-featured face showed him plainly enough to be a Russian deserter.

When he had been removed we were led forward in turn; but during our momentary detention in the background the Cossacks had relieved us of our lashings, and taking advantage of having my hands at liberty I had drawn my dispatches from the inside breast pocket of my uniform, and tearing them unperceived into the minutest fragments, had scattered them over the floor of the court.

"Your names, nationality, and rank?" exclaimed the officer who sat at the head of the table. "You first, sir," nodding to me.

"Cornet Harry Dunbar, of her Britannic Majesty's 18th or Royal Lancers," I replied.

"Now, sir, you?" said the Russian, turning sharply upon my companion.

"Louis Foucarte, Lieutenant of Hussars in the army of France," was the reply.

"I can prove him, General, to be a deserter from Sebastopol—a renegade Pole, by name Count Eugene Pollaki," exclaimed an officer sitting on the president's right.

"I recognise him as the same," said another.

"What answer do you make to this double charge?" asked the president, sternly.

"I will leave my comrade to answer for me," said the Pole, with a huge French shrug of the shoulders. "He will testify that we have only just come out from Europe together, by way of Paris, Mâcon, Dijon, Mont Cenis, Milan, Trieste, the Adriatic, and the city of the Sultan."

"Can you do this?" asked the president of the tribunal, appealing to me.

"I can," I made answer, again inclining to the conviction than my companion was Louis Foucarte, owing to his accurate knowledge of the route by which I had come out: "I can indeed; and we only landed in the Crimea a matter of twenty-four hours ago."

"Ugh, take that down. We will accept it for what it is worth," said the president, addressing a clerk who, habited in plain black, was taking minutes of the evidence in a large book.

I was very much nettled by this observation, which, like all the rest, had been uttered in French—the higher classes in Russia always using that language.

"General," I made answer in the same language, "could I face you for one instant on neutral ground I would force you to apologise for that gratuitous insult."

I was vouchsafed no reply, unless a cold imperturbable stare might be regarded as one.

Then our examination continued.

"What were you doing so far away from your lines when captured?"

As the General continued to stare hard at me whilst he was speaking, I naturally concluded that the question was asked of me, and so replied—

"We were bound on a diplomatic mission to the Caucasus."

"What, to the outlaw, Schamyl?"

"No, to Prince Schamyl. Call people and things by their proper names, General, or I shan't be able to understand you."

I saw the President bite his under lip this time with rage.

Then he continued—

"Answer my questions without making any remark on them, sir. But, first of all, surrender up your dispatches."

"I have already done so, to your remarkably dusty floor," I made answer. "If you've anyone in Sebastopol clever enough to put the pieces together into anything like intelligible shape, you are lucky."

The General swore roundly at this.

"Let him be searched!" he roared.

I was searched, but of course nothing of any importance was found on me.

"Now the other one," cried the General.

Then my companion had to undergo the same indignity, and with the same result.

The General was furious. The fragments of the torn despatches were searched for and picked up off the floor, but many dirty boots had trodden on them, and I had ground and hacked a good many with my spurred heels out of all decipherability.

Nothing could be made of them, even after a great soiling of fingers, and almost of nose tips.

"I don't believe a word that either of you has stated," suddenly exclaimed the General, "and if you cannot tell me the precise errand on which you say you were journeying to Schamyl's camp, I will have you both shot as spies."

"The usages of European warfare will prevent your doing that," I replied. "We were captured in the uniforms of our respective regiments, so that you *dare* not treat us as spies."

"Russians dare everything and anything that they choose. Usages of European warfare? Bah! Russia is large and strong enough to make her own usages. Come, tell me your mission to the Caucasus, or dread the worst?"

"You know well enough, General, that, as an officer and a gentleman, I dare not betray my trust. Shoot or hang me by all means, but don't waste your time in trying to extract from me secrets that I would rather die a hundred deaths than not carry to the grave with me," I said.

"Are you equally punctilious?" asked the General, with a sneer, addressing my comrade.

"Try me, General," was the retort.

"Well, then, what was your mission?"

"To offer Prince Schamyl a wager that, as one Circassian is a match for three Russians, so either an Englishman or a Frenchman is a match for six," was the reply.

This answer was a daring but a rash one, for it turned not only the General but every officer present into bitter foes at once.

To make matters worse, several witnesses were now brought forward to prove that my mysterious comrade was Count Eugene Pollaki, amongst others three officers of his own regiment, so that I was again perforce driven to the conclusion that he was in all verity not the man he had all along pretended to be.

This settled the case. I was declared to be a perjurer and a liar, and my companion to be a renegade and a deserter.

When a show of hands was called for, not one was raised in our favour, and we were sentenced to be shot at midnight.

Then we were at once led away and marched ough the streets to a place that, until we entered we supposed to be a prison.

CHAPTER XXVIII.
MIDST THE DYING AND THE DEAD.

AND it evidently had been a prison once. Now it was worse—worse than a hospital; worse than a lunatic asylum; bad as a pest house.

We were led inside the outer gates, which crashed home and were locked in our rear.

Then across a paved court and into the body of the building.

Sentries with loaded rifles and fixed bayonets appeared to be plentiful enough.

Nor did locks, bolts, and massive clattering chains seem to be wanted.

Yet, when we were ushered into the presence of the stern, grim-looking governor, and he was told that he would be responsible for our custody until midnight, when we were to be led out to be shot, he said, turning to us—

"Go through that low archway, gentlemen; and choose any cell that you may prefer. They are all open for you to look in."

Wondering very much what he could mean, we walked on without our guards, but no sooner had we passed through the archway indicated, than a sort of portcullis dropped down in our rear, effectually, as it was composed of stout iron bars, cutting off our retreat.

Before us lay five passages, branching off from where we stood, like the spokes of a wheel from its hub, and cells evidently opened on either side from each.

What kept us a minute or two from advancing further was the awful stench that seemed to come down the long low passages, accompanied by a horrid babel of shrieks, laughter, cries, sobs, and groans.

I glanced in my companion's face for an explanation.

He looked very grave and very pale.

"What place is this?" I asked.

"It was the great military prison," he made reply. "I fear that it is now the fever and cholera hospital. I think I've heard so."

"Gracious Heaven!" I rejoined; "and those poor wretches who are screaming and yelling so must be mad with delirium."

"Very probably," rejoined my companion.

We walked on, and entered one of the cells.

It seemed to be empty, but, before we had taken three steps across the floor, I fell over something.

I felt it was a human body.

I got up, and rushed out of the cell.

Count Eugene Pollaki followed me.

We passed one or two others, in which men were yelling and shrieking, and then ventured to enter another, in which a light was burning.

But, oh! what a horrid spectacle met our gaze. Never shall I forget the sight.

Two unhappy wretches, nearly naked, lay at the point of death.

Ghastly was the expression of each of their faces. One was of the hue of lead, but seemingly sprinkled over with flour—poor wretch, he was suffering from floury typhus, the most terrible of all fevers.

The other was cramped two-double with the excruciating agony of cholera—'twas evident that he was too far gone to utter groan or cry. His pale blue lips were parted, showing his white teeth gleaming horribly, as they half bit through a black and withered tongue. His eyes gleamed with a stony glare, and seemed to be bursting from their sockets.

But the most sickening sight of all was the massive naked shoulder of this man, which had been split by a sword stroke to the bone.

Sick unto death almost, I fled from the awful scene, and my companion fled with me, not one whit less affected.

We did not dare to enter another cell after that, but we crouched down at the end of one of the long corridors, and there tried to shut out the dreadful sounds that surrounded us on every side.

This was difficult to do. We essayed to converse, but we had nothing lively to talk about, and soon relapsed into silence.

Thus hour after hour passed by, each one seeming a leaden age, until we took to counting the heavy ticks of a clock that faced us at the opposite end of the corridor, and in this employment must, I think, have fallen into a state of semi-idiotcy.

"YIELD YOURSELF A PRISONER," CRIED HARRY DUNBAR. "I DON'T WANT TO TAKE THE LIFE OF A MAN WHO HAS THRICE SAVED MINE."

No. 4.

I know that, as far as I was concerned, the ticks, at first scarcely audible, seemed to grow louder and louder, until at last I fancied I could feel them like heavy blows on my brain, as well as hear them like the clashing of iron hammers on steel anvils.

Then I must have fainted, for when I awoke it was quite dark.

I was awakened by a hand laid on my arm.

I looked up, and saw Count Eugene Pollaki bending over me.

He held a torch in his left hand, and a single glance showed me that he wore a sword.

Behind him stood a gaoler, with an immense bunch of keys dangling at his belt, and half a dozen Russian soldiers.

"Come," he said to me, with a smile, "it is time we were on the move."

"To our place of execution?" I gasped.

"No, on our tour to the Caucasus."

He spoke in English, a language the Russian gaoler and soldiers could not be supposed to understand.

"What can you mean, Count?" I asked, wildly.

"The tribunal have relented, or, rather, seen through their error. A substitute has been found. I will explain fully anon. Come!"

I needed no second bidding, but, springing to my feet, declared myself ready.

"This way, then."

I was led hastily through a couple of passages, and then out into a paved court.

As we entered it a volley of musketry rang out.

"Let us go some other way," said the Count.

"Impossible, your Excellency," replied the gaoler, "'twould be as much as my place is worth."

We walked on, therefore, a shadowy file of helmeted soldiers with shouldered arms seeming to flit before us in the distance.

Suddenly the light of the torch, carried now by the gaoler, flashed on the body of a man lying prone on his back.

The Count uttered an oath, and tried to interpose his figure between the light and the corpse.

But before he could do so I had recognised the face that pertained to the bullet-riddled body.

It was identical with his own.

His reflection in a mirror could not have been more like him.

Was the dead man Louis Foucarte, and the living one Count Eugene Pollaki; or the dead man the Count, and the living one Louis Foucarte?

I was unable even to guess which was which.

CHAPTER XXIX.

SHOWS HOW WE GOT OUT OF SEBASTOPOL.

HOW can I describe my sensations as my gaze wandered from the dead to the living and from the living back to the dead again, both the exact semblance and counterpart of the other, save that one face was white as monumental marble, and the other, I thought, flushed and confused.

"Good God! What is the meaning of this?" I gasped.

"Ample time to explain that on the road," was the half-angry retort. "We are still within the lion's den, remember."

The Count, as he spoke, linked his arm within mine and led me away, whispering in my ear, as we crossed the paved yard, with the Russian soldiers tramping on in front and in rear—

"Do you forget the important service you are engaged in that you would suffer an idle curiosity, awakened by a mere casual likeness between two men, to spoil all?"

"No," I said, "a thousand times no; but that poor devil whom they have shot is as much like you, Count, as your own reflection in a mirror could be. Who the deuce is he?"

"Your travelling acquaintance, Monsieur Louis

Foucarte," answered Count Eugene, with a shrug of the shoulders; "very probably it is he. You have said we are much alike."

"Ha!" I ejaculated, "so it may be, but I sincerely hope not."

"Do you feel such a very warm friendship for him, then?"

"Well, considering that he has been the constant preserver of my life, and that I am the sole confidant of his melancholy and romantic history, I *should* entertain such a feeling."

"But do you?"

The question was sharply asked.

"Yes, if it comes to that, I assuredly do, notwithstanding that there was much that was mysterious and unlovable about the man. He deserted me in the most strange manner at the end of our journey, and I've never seen him since."

"He might not have been able to help himself, poor fellow," replied the Count, in the same low whisper that we had all the way conversed in. "Well, you have, in all human probability, seen the last of him, now; and your time is too precious to honour his memory by a single thought. The present demands all our attention and care."

"Crash!" went the brass musket-butts of our infantry guard on the stone pavement at this juncture.

I looked up and saw that we had reached a kind of guard-house, and presently out from a room which contained a large and cheerful fire came a richly uniformed officer, with a chest scarcely broad enough to contain the number of medals and orders that sparkled thereon.

He spoke a few words with the young sub who had charge of our guard, glanced carelessly at me, but more scrutinisingly at my companion, to whom after a keen inspection he raised his hat, and invited into the guard-room.

The Count remained there some little time, much to my annoyance and disgust, for I could not see why he should be treated with greater courtesy and consideration than myself, he being in French and I in British uniform of officers equal in rank to each other.

I had to pocket the slight, however, and exercise the slender stock of patience I possessed.

Through the open door I saw him take wine with the Russian officer, and shake him by the hand.

"Strange cordiality," thought I, "towards a deserter, wearing openly the uniform of a foe. Well, wonders will never cease."

Really it did not seem as though they would, for presently Count Eugene Pollaki came forth, accompanied to the very door by the *decorée* Russian officer, at a wave of whose hand the gates of the fortalice were opened, and we were suffered to walk forth into the streets without any guard soever.

"Our Russian enemies are d— corteous," I observed.

"The most polite people in the world," was the reply.

"Do you know I wish it was not so?" I asked.

"Do you? And why so pray?" and he looked at me keenly.

"Because I should have more faith in their sincerity."

"Oh, if you look for sincerity in a Russian, you'll never find it," laughed Pollaki. "But come," he added, "we are on *parole d'honneur* to make our way, without once halting to look around us, to the south-eastern gate of the city, where we shall find horses awaiting us."

"Horses, what horses?" I asked.

"Oh, I don't know what horses," answered Count Eugene, with a laugh, again linking his arm within mine, "but good ones I've no doubt, since they are supplied through the chivalrous generosity of the Grand Duke Constantine.

"What, is the Grand Duke in Sebastopol?"

"Yes, he arrived here two hours ago."

"And entered the city, despite its close investment?"

"Yes, despite its close investment!" and Count Eugene nodded.

"Hang it, our fellows should have captured him."

"Had they we two should by this time have been past discussing the subject. To the Grand Duke we owe our lives and our liberty. I was taken before him whilst you lay in a deep faint on the dungeon floor. He told me that he had heard of the brilliant way in which we had fought in defence of our dispatches, that he could not with honour avail himself of an advantage that had been obtained by a hundred combating and overcoming two, and, so saying, he bestowed upon us two horses, and gave us a safe conduct through the city and through any roving bands of Cossacks that we might encounter outside."

"In that case he is a noble specimen of a prince and soldier," I rejoined. "Dispatches, happily, we can do without. I was instructed to proceed onwards to Circassia, even if, by any misadventure, I lost or was deprived of them on the road. I bear my instructions clearly enough in my head."

"That is well; for, believing such to be the case, I gave the Prince my word of honour that we would not return to the camp of the Allies, who, by-the-bye, and to change the subject, are keeping up a tolerably good pounding to-night."

"They are indeed," I rejoined, for the roar of the cannon and the hollow boom of the mortars was in truth incessant, and, in more than one place, heavy wreaths of black smoke showed that some building had been set afire. The British parallels are close up to the Redan now. I shouldn't wonder if it were captured within the week."

CHAPTER XXX.

ON FOR THE LAND OF SCHAMYL.

"WE had best not talk of that here," said Count Eugene, turning far redder, I thought, than the occasion demanded. "Many Russians understand English as well as they do their own native tongue; nay, better, for some high-class Russians cannot speak Russ at all fluently, French being the only language admitted into fashionable circles. A still tongue makes a wise head, therefore; and, by-the-bye, you had better keep your cloak drawn well around you, for your scarlet coat underneath is deucedly bright in hue."

I followed Count Eugene's advice, and halted to do so.

The momentary pause saved my life, for a cannon ball crossed the street we were traversing only a half-dozen yards in front of us, passing through the walls of a house on the opposite side.

A piercing scream, and a woman rushed out of the door, almost naked, with a bleeding shoulder, and in her arms a headless babe.

The passing ball had decapitated it.

"Come on," said Count Eugene, gripping me by the arm again. "Never mind the woman; we can do her no good, and it may be our turn next, if we linger in this infernal place. Ha! thank Heaven, here is the south-eastern gate."

He showed the Grand Duke's pass to the officer who had command of the gate guard, and two magnificent horses were led forth, of pure Smolensko breed.

We were not sorry to throw ourselves on their backs, and, even as we did so, the gates were rolled open by grey great-coated Russian soldiers, and the officer, with a bow and a smile, wished us a *bon voyage*.

Well, here we were outside Sebastopol, it is true; but with a ride of at least two hundred miles before us, through a hostile country most of it, and with mountains and deserts to cross; and, lastly,

an arm of the sea, where one might watch for months for a means of transit and find none.

I knew absolutely nothing of the country or the language of the people that inhabited it; but I knew that, until our arrival in Circassia, I should have to rely entirely on Count Eugene Pollaki, and the knowledge did not console me, for I had managed to conceive for him, though I could not exactly tell why, a most insufferable dislike.

All Louis Foucarte's bad qualities seemed to be intensified in him, and all his good ones entirely wanting.

I felt that every obligation he placed me under I should hate him the more for it, and yet I could not have adduced one solid reason for my antipathy.

The night was dark as pitch, save when a passing rocket occasionally illumined it with a brief and ruddy light.

The thunder of the cannon still sounded in our ears, and away to the left the camp fires of the allies looked like gas-illumined London as seen from Hampstead Heath.

Before us, however, was gloom and shadow.

It looked like the Valley of the Shadow of Death, and I felt my flesh creep with a nameless horror, which was all the worse because I could not tell precisely what occasioned it.

Does an inner and momentary glimpse of the future, forgotten as soon as seen, sometimes occasion this strange and unaccountable feeling?

I shall ever firmly believe that that was what overcame me then.

Ah! had not the vision been as instantly forgotten as it was seen, I would have passed my sword through Count Eugene Pollaki's body then and there, and have left the Crimean vultures and wild dogs an uninterrupted supper.

"You feel cold?" said he, noticing my involuntary shiver, as he noticed everything, down to the veriest trifle.

"Rather," I made answer. "The night is bleak, and now I really think we are in for another fall of snow."

"I hope you may be mistaken, for, if fresh snow should fall and lie deep in the mountain passes, 'tis very likely to serve us for a pall and shroud in one. Crossing the Tchatyudag in early February is no joke, I can tell you; particularly when St. Krun and Otouz come after, by way of dessert."

"Well, you are guide and pioneer," I said. "It is a game of follow my leader, and wherever you go I go too. But, how about crossing from the Crimea into Circassia? The Strait of Kertch is in no part less than ten miles wide, I am informed."

"Where we shall cross, from Choungelsk to Tinsitarskan, it is a dozen," was the calm reply.

"Then, how are we to accomplish the feat? No ship or boat floats on the Sea of Azov or sails up the Cimmerian Bosphorus, as the Strait of Kertch is poetically called."

"You are well informed, so far," answered Count Eugene, "but we shall not need a boat to cross the strait from the Crimea to the Caucasus. We shall ride over."

"What, ride over twelve miles of open sea?" I laughed.

"It sounds strange—don't it?" retorted Pollaki laughing too, "but the feat is possible, for all that, for the strait is fordable in no less than three different places."

"A strait connecting two seas! it sounds incredible," I said.

"Until you know the why and the wherefore," said Count Eugene. "The Azovskago Moré, or Sea of Azov, though many thousands of square miles in extent, is nowhere deeper than twelve or fourteen yards, and the boggy marshes of the Putrid Sea drain much of its waters, whilst still more is sucked up by the Kosa Arabatskaia, a porous sandbank, a hundred miles in length. But, besides this, a far greater volume of water escapes subterraneously (only twice seeking the light in the lakes of Temsouk and Kouban), from the Sea of Azov to the Black Sea than ever flows through the Strait of Kertch, which in parts is almost dry in the summer."

"You are wondrously well informed upon the subject, and I thank you for the information," I said. "You must both have travelled and read a good deal."

"I have travelled far more than I have read," was the reply. "It would puzzle you to name a place in the habitable world that I have not been in."

"I'll bet you ten to one I'll name one place, in three guesses, that you've not been in," I said.

"I accept the wager in guineas," replied Count Eugene.

"Done," said I. "You've never been in Greenland."

"On the contrary I was sojourning at Cape Desolation only last year," answered my companion.

"Never mind, I'll have you this time. You were never at the Isle of La Terre Adele, within the Antarctic Circle," and I laughed with the certainty of triumph.

"Bah! I was wrecked on the north coast of that very island three years ago on board the whaling ship Gulliver."

"The devil you were!" I ejaculated, for I was astonished out of all my proprieties. "Well, then, now for a last chance. You were never down in the diving bell at the Polytechnic Institution in London."

"Oh, that's not fair," said Count Eugene. "When you come to in the water, in a diving machine, in a particular building, that's in a certain street, of a capital, of a certain country, you increase the chances against my having been there a hundred-fold, and I've a right to remonstrate."

"Do you then remonstrate?" I asked.

"Well, I won't in the present instance, because it happens that I paid a penny to go down in that particular diving bell only last summer twelve-months on my return to Russia through London. I only said I had a right to remonstrate."

I could see him grin by the light of the cigar that he was smoking.

For a moment or two I was too astounded to reply.

Then I burst forth with—

"Hang it, you are even a more extraordinary man than Monsieur Foucarte, and I fancied him the greatest traveller that I had ever come across. The ten guineas are yours. I will pay you to-morrow when I can see to count the money. I don't believe any other fellow in the world could have won such a wager."

"Probably not," answered Count Eugene; "but I have been a traveller from my early youth, partly because a Pole has no home and no country, partly to try to forget and drown a great grief, or rather dreadful memory which I shall nevertheless carry with me to the tomb."

"Gracious heaven!" I exclaimed. "Why, that was poor, unhappy, murdered Foucarte's very excuse."

Count Eugene made no reply, unless an energetic pull at his cigar might be interpreted as such, and I felt an icy chill traversing the top of my head, and from thence running down my spine, as for an instant I realised the possibility that I might be travelling in company with the ghost of my late travelling companion.

I was awoke from this dismal strain of thought by something white and wet flying in my face.

"We must keep close together or we shall be parted. Egad, how it snows!" exclaimed my companion impatiently.

I then saw that it was snowing heavily.

Immediate and actual danger banished imaginary fears from my mind.

"If this continues for an hour it will be our grave," I said. "The drifts are frequent and deep now."

"Yes, but there is a shelter a mile further on."

"I'm precious glad to hear it. But what kind of a shelter?"

"Patience, friend, patience. The snow will fill my mouth if I answer too many questions. Wait till we gain the haven, and you won't object to it, I'll dare swear," and not another word could I extract from him on the way.

CHAPTER XXXI.

A PASHA OF MANY TAILS.

AT this dreary juncture of affairs the wind began to blow, and each moment rose higher and shriller.

Had it been in our backs it might have helped us on somewhat, but being directly in our faces it blew the frozen particles of snow with such force and fury before it, that we were almost blinded by the storm.

Even our horses, Russ by birth though they were, could scarcely make head against it, and several times essayed to turn round, so that an iron grasp had to be maintained on the reins, with fingers that seemed to be changing into ice.

In the lulls of the storm I could hear Count Eugene growling maledictions on everything sub-lunary beneath his snow-laden, and icicle-drooping moustachios, and even I was fain to find relief in sundry "*mille tonnerres!*" for French swearing is more innocent than our own, and yet quite equal relief to the surcharged temper. Surely there can be no more harm in exclaiming, "A thousand thunders!" than in ejaculating "A thousand mutton chops."

Well, anyhow it didn't help us on much, and more than once I thought we had come to the end of our journey and our lives at one and the same time.

Happily 'twas not so, for a Russian horse has as many lives as an English cat, and apparently possesses continual relays of strength and pluck; for frequently, when seemingly on the point of lying down and resigning themselves and ourselves to a mightily disagreeable fate, they would revive magically, as it were, and push on for awhile with renewed activity and vigour.

"Do you know which way you're going?" I asked Count Eugene, at length, for I could not see my horse's head before me, and so, of course, no landmark of any kind was visible.

"Yes," was the reply. "You will see red lights gleam through the white snow wreaths in an instant."

Even whilst he was speaking I thought I saw them.

Yes, there could be no doubt about it.

There they were—ten, twelve of them.

Was he a prophet, a conjuror, a magician, or merely a lucky guesser?

Whilst I was wondering, our horses came to a dead stop again.

Great iron gates barred our further progress.

"How the deuce shall we make the people hear?" I said. "The house seems situated a long way within the grounds."

"We will admit ourselves," answered Count Eugene, and, dismounting, he drew a key from his pocket, and with it opened the great gates.

"You make yourself very much at home," I remarked.

"I do—everywhere," he made curt reply.

After I had ridden through, he closed and relocked the heavy gates in our rear, and then walked on beside his horse.

Presently we found ourselves in front of what looked like a fine mansion, in the Turkish style of architecture.

Count Eugene told me to dismount, and scarcely

had I done so when four men, in rich but strange uniform, came out of the house and took our horses, whilst two more stood on the steps to be our conductors into the interior.

We were greeted by a perfect blaze of light directly we had entered, through gates of polished brass and doors of glass, into a vast hall, which was hung round with trophies of the chase, and a glittering assortment of antique weapons.

The floor was of marble, and, in the centre, an exquisite fountain threw a volume of perfumed water almost up into the star-domed roof.

We traversed this superb hall in silence, and were ushered into a room at the opposite side, where carpets, ceiling, and tapestried walls were of blue and silver.

Upon a large divan, in the very centre of the room, sat a venerable Moslem, looking very much like the Nabob on the pickle-bottles, for he was attired in Asiatic garb, and not in that ugly, non-descript, Mahomedo-Franco-Zouave costume, which during the last half century the Turk has so much affected.

He was smoking a hubble-bubble pipe with an air of tranquil enjoyment, while a beautiful girl, with a bare bust that not one of Titian's Venuses could have excelled in voluptuous contour, and pear blossom could not have exceeded in beauty and purity of tint, was sitting at his feet, playing on a harp.

She sprang up, and dropped her veil around her, as we entered the room, and her Turkish master opened his eyes and gazed at us with an air of blank surprise, not altogether unmixed with displeasure.

"Can't help it, your excellency," said Count Eugene, in a jaunty, flippant manner that I had never before noticed in him. "The snow storm without was a deuced deal less inviting than your well-lighted rooms, well-served dinner, and sparkling hock within, so we have dropped in to regale on all three. Egad! for the nonce, it is fortunate that during the winter months you sleep through the short days, and live, move, and have your being during the long nights, when, with warm fires and a myriad lights, you can forget that it is winter."

"Bismillah! The summer and its increase were given us for our good, the winter and its snow for our bane; but, luckily, the bane can be shut out, and an artificial summer can be produced. Why has Allah given to man brains if he is not to use them for his own comfort?" and the old Turk laughed until his fat sides fairly shook.

"Then you rise with the moon, and with the moon seek your couch, which being the case, I should think it was close upon dinner-time," said Count Eugene, drawing forth and consulting a costly gold repeater.

"By the blessed Well of Kishon you are right! There goes the gong. Can it really be three o'clock in the morning?"

"To the very second, as surely as you are Rimnik Bouzes Tirgskoulis Formoz Bakou Gasilkoi, Khedive of Salghur and Pasha of Three Tails. Likewise, as surely as this is my friend and travelling companion, Mr. Harry Dunbar, whom I have great pleasure in introducing to you as one of the many thousand gallant Englishmen who have come to fight your battles for you," said Count Eugene with a profound, but as it seemed to me, mocking bow.

"I'm glad to make his acquaintance," said the Pasha, whose name is so short that I shall depend upon my readers bearing it in mind. "His presence in my poor abode covers it with honour," and his little beady black eyes glittered and scintillated like those of an amiable snake as he held out his fat paunchy hand.

I wasn't sure whether he intended me to kiss or to grasp it, but the latter courtesy being more in accordance with my feelings, I seized it and wrung it fervently

But the Pasha was evidently a stranger to many of our customs, this one in especial, for my hearty pressure of his digits elicited a yell, and, when I let them go, he muttered something under his beard about "a son of burnt fathers," gazing at his released fingers the while most ruefully.

Had not the gong sounded a second time, louder and more sonorously than on the first occasion, goodness knows what might not have come of it; but that sound, helped perhaps by an appetising smell that crept into the room either under the door or through the keyhole, seemed to appease him, and rolling off, rather than rising from his divan, he told us to follow him, and with slow and pompous steps led the way to the dining hall.

CHAPTER XXXII.

IN WHICH I HALF MURDER MY HOST.

"A QUEER card, isn't he?" said Count Eugene, as we followed the Pasha across the marble hall at about a dozen paces in his rear. "We shall have some fun with him by-and-bye when the wine unthaws his dignity."

"I thought good Moslems didn't drink wine," I observed.

"Nor do they, but bad and indifferent ones do. Old Rimnik Bouzes Tirgskoulis and the rest of it worships Bacchus and Venus, and throws all other divinities and prophets overboard," answered Count Eugene, who spoke English fluently, and without the slightest foreign accent.

No end of gorgeously-clad domestics were hurrying hither and thither, conspicuous among them being negroes with hideous faces and thick blubber lips, whose black skin was made to look blacker still by their attire of blue and white, the white predominating.

"These," my companion informed me, were the eunuch custodians of the Pasha's harem, and with their enormous scimitars and inlaid pistols they looked terrible fellows enough in all conscience.

The dining-hall was a splendid room, and the tables were most sumptuously laid.

From the number of plates I concluded that the Pasha and his ladies were in the habit of dining together, but that on our arrival their presence had been forbidden, no Moslem caring for Ghiaour eyes to gaze upon the belles of his harem, save and except the slave dancers and posturers.

That Pasha of ever so many tails was certainly a judge of good living.

I believe he kept a French cook, for I'll vow the names of the dishes were the only Turkish part about them.

As for the wines, they were simply superb.

Hock, moselle, champagne, and even Hungarian Tokay were passed round with no niggard hand, so that tongues were soon loosed; or, at all events, mine and the Pasha's were, for I don't believe Count Eugene's was capable of such a process, and I also believe that his head was wineproof.

At a signal from the Pasha his dancing slaves at last came in; young girls clad in diaphanous muslin, through which their exquisite shapes and snow-white skins were as clearly visible as though their clothing had been transparent clouds.

They danced, and their tiny feet scarcely touched the floor; they sang, and their voices were as the music of the spheres.

The flashing eyes, the waving perfumed hair (black and gold often mingling in the mazy whirls of the dance), the witching smiles, the exquisite complexions (never exposed to cutting winds or burning sun), the bare, rounded arms, flashing with many circlets of gold and gems, the tiny ankles and plump little white feet, the slender, swaying, zone-girt waists, from which sprang busts as full and Hebe-like as enraptured painter ever dreamed of and despaired of reproducing on canvas with a tithe of their actual beauty, the white, heaving shoulders, and still whiter bosoms, panting with the prolonged exertion. the swelling hips, whose velvet softness and marble whiteness were preserved by the most costly unguents, and by their never reposing on aught harder than couches of down; all combined made one wonder how Moslem could ever hope to find aught more lovely and adorable, even in the dark-eyed houris of Paradise, of whom liberal Mahomet apportions to each true believer five hundred.

I gazed, and gazed, and gazed, in a happy and delicious dream, from which I would fain have had no awakening, until an incident occurred that aroused me painfully therefrom, and stirred up within me the fury of a demon.

How she aroused his anger I do not know—perhaps by bending her soft lustrous eyes more frequently on us than on him, perhaps by some error in her dancing that I could not detect—possibly for some prior offence that he had just recalled to his memory; but the Pasha suddenly sprang from his seat, drew a heavily-thonged and ivory-handled dog whip from his belt, and commenced to lash one of the youngest and most lovely of the dancing girls in a brutal manner across the back and shoulders with it.

I saw three livid lines scored on a skin of snow. I saw the soft dimpled flesh quiver beneath the strokes, and I arose in turn, Count Eugene sitting stoically still the while.

Whether she saw any sympathy in my face I know not, but no sooner was I on my feet, than the beauteous dancing girl bounded forward with a cry, and threw herself into my arms, her lustrous tear-swimming eyes raised to mine in an agony of supplication for protection.

I threw my left arm around her and drew her to me.

I felt her bosoms of snow throb against my chest, whilst one milk-white but whip-stained shoulder almost touched my lips.

How could I help but kiss it? I should have done so had it cost me my life.

Her perfumed breath was on my cheek, the glory of her hair almost dazzled my vision, and even in that position the brutal old Pasha was bad and mad enough again to slash at her savagely.

Methought that I myself could feel the blow that smote the beautiful flesh as certainly as I felt the quiver of her divine form, and saw the upheaving of the expansive chest, with the faint blue veins just showing through the clear and transparent skin.

The next instant I had seized a heavy decanter from the table and shied it at the old Pasha's head.

The aim was a true one, and the old Turk went down as though from the blow of a battering ram, his forehead covered with blood.

I scarcely know what followed.

The Pasha had lots of armed dependents close by.

I called upon Count Eugene to aid me, but Count Eugene never stirred.

The other dancing girls fled, and the one whom I had tried to befriend was torn from my grasp, and, half-naked and bleeding, dragged by the hair of the head along the floor and out of the room.

A dozen knives and scimitars glanced before my eyes, before, in my confusion, I thought of drawing my sword.

I was beaten to the ground, dragged out of the dining-room, and through many passages, until we got to a cold, grand hall, from the centre of which a trap-door was raised, and I was pushed down through the aperture into darkness.

I fell a considerable distance, and then, utterly helpless, saw, with sensations of horror that I cannot describe, the trap-door replaced, and heard the receding steps of the Pasha's retainers as they strode away.

There I was—perhaps in a prison, perhaps in a wine cellar, but just as probably in a tomb.

And the dancing girl! Perhaps, instead of be friending her, I had sealed her doom.

She had been clasped to the breast of a Frank—doubtless she would atone for it as a kitten atones for being born.

CHAPTER XXXIII.
AND IN THIS AM BURIED ALIVE.

THE cellar or vault in which I was imprisoned was as dark as pitch, or at least so it seemed when I was first cast down into it, but as my eyes became acustomed to the gloom, first one object and then another became dimly visible, until I could pretty well make out my surroundings, which were not altogether agreeable.

The floor of my dungeon, for I mentally dubbed it the most disagreeable thing I could think of directly I discovered that it was not a wine-cellar, was of beaten earth, and its walls and roof were of stone, dripping with foul moisture, and adorned with rank fringe.

These walls seemed to be a favourite promenade and *pleasaunce* garden for a few colonies of spiders and blackbeetles, enormous and ugly wretches, any one of which would have been sure of first prize in a Spider and Beetle Show at the Crystal Palace.

Of less lofty aspirations, little green lizards and huge brown, venerable-looking toads wriggled and hopped along the mud floor, sometimes stopping to stare at me, with brilliant but blinking eyes.

Their companionship was neither soothing nor pleasant, for I could not banish the impression that both toads and spiders might owe their bloated and aldermanic proportions to frequent civic feasts upon the bodies of defunct prisoners.

Directly this idea occurred to me I looked round in search of something that would dissipate it, but naught could I see except huge boxes of strange shape, covered with hieroglyphics, lying in tiers on stone shelves, or standing upright in odd corners.

"Hang it, I wonder if, after all, they are the Pasha's wine bins," I muttered, to myself, and as I did so I congratulated myself on the fact that I had a knife in my pocket, containing a corkscrew.

Deciding mentally that, if so, those standing perpendicularly must be the empty ones, and those lying horizontally the full, I approached the shelves and daintily lifted the lid of one of them.

Heavens! A hideous whitey-brown face with dropped jaws and open eyes glared stonily at me.

I uttered a cry of horror, for I gazed upon a corpse.

The body was richly habited in blue silk, white satin, and gold, all faded now with age and damp; but another tint pervaded the chest—the dark purple hue of coagulated and dried blood.

You may be pretty sure that I replaced the lid as quickly as I could, but yet my foolish curiosity tempted me to raise another.

This time I gazed upon a beautiful young girl, whose face looked as calm and placid as though she was asleep.

She was dressed in white, and veiled like a bride, but round her throat was a livid ring, telling the sad tale that she had been strangled.

I had seen enough—more than enough—and it needed not the sight of a heap of mouldering skulls in the corner of the vault to instil into my mind the very acmé of horror.

I replaced the second coffin-lid even as I had done the first, feeling faint with the sweet yet pungent smell of the herbs that preserved the body from decay.

I went and sat down in the middle of the floor, as far away from the embalmed bodies as I could.

I regarded the bloated toads and the great obese spiders with a greater horror than ever now, and actually shuddered when the former stopped to wink and blink at me with their jewelled eyes, and when the latter ran over me, or fell with a dull "flop" on my head or face.

Doubtless they had worked their way through the rotting wood of the lower tiers of coffins, and found in them larders exactly suited to their tastes.

I was morbidly calculating how they would like me, and how long I should be able to keep them waiting for a repast, which I fancied, from their sly glances. they were looking forward to with some curiosity, when I saw a thin white streak of light above my head, each moment growing wider and wider.

I perceived at a glance that it was caused by the trap-door being raised slowly with a lever.

A minute later it was thrown entirely back, and a long and broad step ladder thrust through the orifice, down which came tripping half-a-dozen gaudily clad negroes, each with a drawn scimitar in his hand.

These hideous and repulsive specimens of humanity drove me back into a corner, and kept me there with many jabbered threats, which I should not have understood but for the accompanying brandishing and whishing of their scimitars all round my head, whilst a dozen more bore down upon their shoulders a coffin, which they placed upon an empty shelf, and precipitately retired.

Then, the half-dozen who had menaced me spat in my face, devoutly wishing that "jackasses might defile my grave" (which I thought would very probably happen, if they frequently visited the vault after I had perished therein), and cut after their companions.

The trap-door was replaced, the light died out and I was again in darkness.

Some five minutes elapsed before my eyes got accustomed to the gloom a second time, but, directly I could again see my surroundings pretty clearly, I staggered across the floor towards the coffin that had just been laid on the empty shelf—a terrible foreboding in my heart that I should know the face and form that was lying still in death within.

Tremblingly I raised and threw back the lid.

My worst fears were confirmed—I gazed upon the lovely countenance of the poor dancing girl, whom, intending to befriend, I had instead doomed to death.

There she lay, looking more beautiful, if possible, than in life, but those rounded limbs would never again shine snow-white in the dance, and that still warm bosom would never more throb with exertion, excitement, or pleasure. The ivory throat was encircled by a livid ring. She also had been strangled.

I bent forward and pressed my lips to her icy brow; I kissed her hands and beautiful feet, and then essayed to replace the coffin lid, but in doing so a kind of faintness came over me; the dungeon and its coffin-filled shelves seemed to swim round—I tottered—tried to recover myself—failed, and sank to the ground in a deep swoon.

CHAPTER XXXIV.

THE ESCAPE FROM THE VAULTS.

HOW long I lay in that unconscious state I really do not know, but I was aroused by some one pouring brandy down my throat out of a pocket flask.

Presently he spoke, and I recognised the voice as pertaining to Count Eugene Pollaki.

A minute or two later I could see his face.

"How did you get here?" I asked directly I could speak.

"By the same way that directly you are strong enough I shall lead you out by; so take another pull at the brandy bottle, for it is broad daylight, and high time for us to be *en route*." he made reply.

"I wish, instead of troubling yourself about me you had used your influence to save that poor girl who is strangled there," I said, nodding my head towards the coffin, whose lid I had not been able to replace.

"Well, I tried my best," said the Count, but in a jovial careless way that made me hate him. "'Pon honour I used no end of eloquence over the matter; but old Bluebeard was as stubborn as a mule. He was for having her torn in pieces by wild horses, each wrist and ankle being bound to a leg of a different charger, which would then be spurred in an opposite direction until she was dismembered. After nearly an hour's palaver, however, I got her sentence commuted to strangling, which was done in an instant with a silk scarf."

"And did she seem to suffer much pain?" I asked.

"Oh, no, very little, if any," was the reply. "She was made kneel down, her wrists being first bound to her ankles. A black eunuch then approached her from behind, threw a green silk gold-fringed scarf over her head, looped it behind, and then digging his knees into her back, drew the ends tight. A heave of the chest, a shudder, and 'twas over."

"You do not seem to have been much horrified by the spectacle, Count."

"Well, no. I have seen a similar scene enacted before. Pooh! she was only a slave, and slaves should be careful not to offend their master. Nevertheless, 'twas you, my friend, who signed her death-warrant. I believe the Pasha only whipped her for our entertainment, and you must needs shie one of his own wine bottles at his head."

"The old brute, I wish I had passed my sword through his heart! Is he injured seriously?" I asked.

"Not a bit of it," replied Count Eugene. "I left him half an hour ago walking about with his head bandaged up. and calling loudly for his breakfast, after which he intends to subject you to some ingenious torture or other previous to having you decapitated—a feat he means to perform with his own hands and his own scimitar. He thinks that I have departed, leaving you to your fate."

"You may do so," I said; "for I've no wish to survive her."

"What! not to survive the dancing girl—the mere toy of a fat Turk's leisure, and as devoid of mind and soul as a waxen doll!" exclaimed Count Eugene, impetuously.

"She was beautiful enough to be able to afford to dispense with all other attractions," I answered.

"Bah! the same remark applies to the waxen doll; but if her death has made your own life valueless to you, do not forget that it may still be valuable to others, and that, therefore, it is your duty to preserve it. You are a Queen's Messenger, engaged upon an important duty. Fulfil that duty first, and then, if you like, return to the Pasha and tell him he will oblige you by cutting your head off," answered Count Eugene, with a sneer.

"I thank you for reminding me of my duty," I said. "To tell the truth, I had forgotten it. I will be ready to accompany you in a moment."

I sprang to my feet and crossed the floor to the open coffin.

For an instant I gazed at the vision of loveliness within, then picked up and replaced the lid.

As I did so, the clattering of sabres and the ring of spurs echoed on the stone floor above.

"Be quick!" said Count Eugene, in a hoarse whisper; "we have already wasted valuable time. The Pasha and his eunuchs will be with us in another moment."

"Push on," I said; "I am myself again now!"

Scarcely had the words escaped my lips when the trap-door began to rise, revealing the white leather boots and blue baggy trousers of the eunuchs who were grouped around.

Count Eugene seized my wrist, and whispered in my ear—

"Run with your head down, the ceiling is low in places."

On we dashed like a couple of hounds in leash.

A flood of daylight seemed to pursue us for an instant, and then was blotted out again.

But we heard the great stone trap-door fall back well enough, and the rattling of sword scabbards as the Pasha and his armed servitors came down the ladder.

We never stopped to look round, however, but dashed on through the darkness as no men would have had the nerve to have dashed, except such as were running for their lives.

Once I nearly came to grief over a heap of skulls or some other human relics, and once I nearly slipped up through placing a foot on the slimy back of a toad or lizard; but in each instance I recovered myself before Count Eugene's grasp on my arm grew taut.

We were evidently rushing down a series of long narrow passages, our foes in hot pursuit; but they did not seem to gain on us, and before very long, to my unspeakable joy, I saw daylight shining in through the mouth of a cavern a little way ahead.

'Twas a pleasant spectacle, and gave us fresh hope.

Another minute and we had actually gained the cavern's mouth, where grew an old tempest-torn pine tree, to one of whose lower branches two saddled and bridled steeds were tied.

I at once recognised them as those which we had ridden the preceding evening.

"Throw yourself into the saddle quickly," said Count Eugene; "I see our pursuers in the distance, and we afford too good a mark to be easily missed."

Even as he spoke a couple of Tunisian muskets rang shrilly out, and a couple of balls whizzed by unpleasantly near to our ears.

We mounted in hot haste, a bullet passing through my left epaulette as I kicked my feet into the stirrups.

As we wheeled round and dashed off another volley was sent after us, but the leaden missiles this time flew wide, and we had no more to fear.

We looked back once to see Rimnik Bouzes Tirgskoulis Formoz Bakou Gasilkoi, Khedive of Salghur and Pasha of three tails—but still (the vile old murderer) closely resembling the Nabob on the pickle bottles—foaming, dancing, and gesticulating at the cavern's mouth, and no doubt hurling every possible invective after us, which, happily, were as harmless as the bullets of his eunuchs, who now stood grouped in his rear.

I had half a mind to ride back and shoot him down, and assuredly should have done so had I been my own master; but the importance of the service on which I was engaged restrained me, and so I turned my head away, and rode doggedly on.

"We have escaped a great peril," said Count Eugene; "but a still greater one, though of a very different nature, lies before us."

"What is it?" I asked, indifferently.

"Well, as we are precluded from trying back, and so gaining the main road, which will soon be swarming with the Pasha's retainers, who are good chaps at an ambush, though contemptible enough ones in the open field, we shall have to ride along the Devil's Pass," answered Count Eugene, impressively.

"And what kind of a place may that be?"

"Oh! a deucedly rum place at the best of times, far less when the road is rendered slippery with frozen snow. The Devil's Pass is a narrow path traversing a mountain side, about four feet wide, with a sheer cliff rising on the left and an unfathomable abyss on the right."

"Why, it would be certain death to traverse such a path in weather like this," I said.

"By no means You over-rate the danger. There are at least two chances in a hundred that we get safely across," answered the Count, with a cold, icy smile. "Anyway," he continued, "it is the only practicable route the pig-headed Pasha has left us."

"And how far on is this mountain?" I asked him.

"You may even now see it in your front," was the reply, and following the direction of his pointing finger I saw, rising above the clouds, about twelve miles away, two snow-covered peaks, resembling a mountain that had been split in twain by some fell enchanter's sword.

CHAPTER XXXV.
SHOWS HOW WE CROSSED THE DEVIL'S PASS.

BY this time we had ascended some three hundred feet of the mountain's height, and from that elevation beheld a prospect of valley, plain, and ocean, indescribably grand, embracing a bold semicircular sweep of at least a hundred miles.

Almost beneath our feet was a roaring cataract, to look down upon and listen to the hoarse brawl of which was nerve trying in itself, when mounted upon a spirited and restive horse.

Still up and up we went, however, the pathway having a zig-zag tendency, that made the ascent anything but laborious.

As we attained a higher and yet higher altitude, the cold became so severe that it was difficult and painful to draw one's breath.

Count Eugene and I spoke little during the ascent.

He appeared to be meditative, whilst I, for I am not ashamed to confess it, felt very nervous, an indescribable presentiment having taken possession of me, to the effect that something terrible would happen to one, or both of us, before we descended to the plains again.

The very elements seemed to be impressed with my ill-omened forebodings, for the sky, which had been so blue and sunny when we commenced the ascent, was now flecked with heavy, reefy clouds, that appeared to be hurrying towards a common centre.

Then a furious hailstorm, each frozen particle as large as a marble, set in, and blew with such force that our faces were soon cut and bleeding, and we could scarcely prevail upon our horses to face it.

"This isn't exactly agreeable, is it *mon ami?*" said Count Eugene Pollaki, turning in his saddle, and regarding my discomfiture with a reckless laugh. "Peste, it reminds one of a *fantasia à la clarinette* in Algeria, where I have had the honour of serving under Bugeaud and Canrobert. Russian soldiers are not, such clever marksmen, are they?"

"Hardly, or the allied armies would be swept from off the face of the earth," I rejoined. "Thank goodness, however, the storm is passing away."

"Yes, and at a happy moment, for our upward course is at an end, and we are at last fairly opposite the pass. In five minutes we shall be traversing the Devil's Ridge," replied Count Eugene.

"And if our horse's shoes are at all worn, very probably at the bottom of it," I growled, for I heartily wished the Devil's Ridge, where its name implied it should have been, in the centre of a region where it would have been geographically and climatically impossible for it to have become snow-clad or ice-coated.

"That's almost a matter of heads and tails," laughed my companion in reply to my last observation. "We'll keep at the top if we can."

As he spoke the sky momentarily brightened, the clouds parted, and the cold wintry sun shone down on the snow covered mountain, whose double peak, with the vast crevass between that looked as though it had been cleft by a Titan's sword, still rose to a height of at least a thousand feet above our head.

This crevass, midway between the mountain's peak and base, we had to traverse, very much like cats walking along a narrow window ledge.

'Twas a feat as hazardous and daring as for two

men to ride around the Whispering Gallery in the dome of St. Paul's Cathedral with the gilded railing first torn away.

Count Eugene Pollaki was right. In less than five minutes we were on the Devil's Ridge, and I immediately voted it to be well deserving of its name, for it was as devilish a place to attempt to cross as the most daring lunatic ever conceived.

We rode of necessity in Indian file, Count Eugene about two score paces in advance.

To do him justice, he never shrunk from being the first to encounter every danger, and, in fact, often insisted on doing so as a right.

The pathway was about five feet wide, certainly ne ver more, and was frequently somewhat less.

On our left rose the precipitous mountain side, a sheer cliff, to a height here and there of at least a thousand feet.

On our right yawned an awful chasm, apparently bottomless, and to a depth, as I afterwards learned, of eleven hundred feet.

From the bottom of this always arose the roar of waters, as though seething and boiling from a subterranean Niagara.

I do not hesitate to affirm that at any part of the pass had I raised my arms, in the shape of the letter T, the middle finger of my left hand would have touched the black cliff, and a pebble dropped perpendicularly from between the forefinger and thumb of my right would have fallen into the roaring torrent below.

I must admit that, despite the icy coldness of the air, I was bathed in perspiration directly we were fairly on the ridge.

I had never felt such a sickly fear even in the charge of battle.

Terrible and dangerous as the pass was, enhanced now to an immense degree by the slipperiness of the frozen snow that covered it, its perils seemed to instil no alarm into the breast of my companion, who rode on, whistling airs from the newest operas, and in the very narrowest parts frequently turning in his saddle, with a light-hearted laugh and word of encouragement, to see how I was faring.

His beautiful and glossy-coated steed stepped out as proudly and as steadily as though pacing Rotten Row or the Champs de Mars, but mine, on the other hand, frequently snorted and trembled, as its great eager eyes sought the bottom of the gulf, and found it not.

I could see that the poor animal was almost as terrified as myself, and this terror sometimes caused it to trip, slip, or stumble, on which occasion, it is needless to say, my heart was almost in my mouth.

Then, suddenly, Count Eugene reined up, and allowed me almost to come up with him ere he again urged his horse on.

I noticed that his light-heartedness was gone and his face deadly pale.

"Is there any unexpected danger ahead of us?" I asked.

"No—that is to say, I can hardly tell," was the reply. "Perhaps your ears are rather quicker than mine. Do you hear any horses' hoof-strokes in addition to our own? Don't be alarmed—only tell me."

I listened and decidedly thought that I could.

But a distant neigh rendered my belief a certainty.

"Good Heavens!" exclaimed Count Eugene. "It is even as I feared."

"What is as you feared?" I gasped, dreading I scarce knew what.

"Why, other horsemen are traversing the pass, and towards us. We cannot see each other because the crescencular sweep of the mountain stops the view, but in less than five minutes we shall meet face to face, and then the weaker party must go to the wall, or rather, in the present instance, go from the wall and drop into the abyss."

"I scarcely understand you," I gasped, though I

knew that I did thoroughly, I only hoped against hope that his next reply would destroy the horrible conviction that had impressed itself on my mind.

Instead of doing so, it stamped it indelibly there.

"Don't you see?" said Count Eugene, "that it will be equally impossible to turn or to pass each other, and that consequently we must either pitch them over into the abyss, or allow them to pitch us."

"Heavens, I do see it!" I exclaimed. "What a frightful alternative."

"Frightful or not, it is the only course left open to us."

"And to think that these men never harmed us."

"They will have the same comforting reflection that we have never harmed them," replied my companion. "Ah, here they are."

I looked over his shoulder and saw two Cossacks mounted on shaggy ponies, and armed with long lances, carbines, swords, and pistols, riding leisurely and nonchalantly along the ridge.

But they saw us almost as quickly as we perceived them, and then their conduct and manner suddenly changed.

They brandished their spears, and intimated to us by signs, that we should wheel round and retrace our steps.

They knew as well as we did though that to attempt to do so would be certain and immediate death.

Count Eugene asked them in Russ "if they took us for greenhorns, and to try how they could manage wheeling round themselves."

CHAPTER XXXVI.
WE GIVE THE COSSACKS TO THE ABYSS.

IN reply to this very natural question, the foremost Cossack pointed his lance in a threatening manner towards us."

At the same instant Count Eugene whipped a revolver from his holster and levelled it at the Cossack's head.

"You have still a chance for your lives," he, at the same time, shouted. "Slip down over your ponies' tails to the ground, push them into the abyss, and then creep under our horses' bellies to safety."

But the Cossacks, whose ponies' lives are as precious to them as their own, rejected this counsel with the scorn they thought it merited.

Affection for their dumb favourites set apart, a Cossack would sooner be killed in the saddle than doomed to a life of pedestrianism. Walking is their aversion, and no doubt the majority of the Cossacks die without having walked a dozen miles collectively during their lives.

Count Eugene evidently saw by the way in which the foremost Cossack still continued to handle his lance that he meant mischief.

Perhaps the fool took him to be a bad shot.

If so, he quickly undeceived him on that all important point.

Dropping his muzzle he fired at the horse instead of the rider, and the pony, maddened by the agony of its death wound, gave a hideous shriek, reared nearly bolt upright, and backed into space.

In an instant—in the twinkling of an eye—horse and horseman had vanished from sight for ever, but I could hear their bodies rebound from crag to crag in their descent.

The second Cossack was evidently appalled by the tragic fate that had overtaken his companion, yet knew not how to escape a similar one, for Count Eugene's pistol was now levelled at him.

He endeavoured, after a moment's hesitation, to slip to the ground over his horse's tail; but the pony resented such a method of dismounting by a kick that sent its master after his companion.

Methinks that even now I can see the ghastly, horror-stricken face of that poor wretch, as with it upturned, he fell into the yawning gulf which was to be his grave.

The yell of unutterable agony and fear that escaped his lips no pen can describe—no other noise resemble.

With my steed reined in until his haunches pressed the dark mountain side, whilst his fore hoofs were planted on the hard, slippery snow within a couple of inches of the edge of the precipice, I gazed with feelings which I cannot even now analyse, down into the dread gulf that had entombed the two ill-fated Cossacks.

My very blood seemed to freeze and suspend its functions; whilst my brain reeled with a strange pain and lightness.

It was a mercy I did not lose my seat in the saddle and fall over the precipice myself.

I was aroused from this horror-stricken and almost imbecile stupor by another pistol shot and another crash.

Another white, wounded, yet still living object swooped down into the vale of utter blackness.

It was the Cossack's pony.

My own steed snorted at the sight, and half-reared.

His hoofs struck a handful of stones and pebbles from the edge of the precipice into the abyss.

It was a miracle of miracles that we did not accompany them.

Had he not quickly swerved round broadside on to the wall of rock on our left we must have done so.

"Hullo, that was a close shave. Keep a steady hand on the reins, my friend. The road is clear now, and heaven grant that it may keep so," exclaimed Count Eugene, noticing my narrow escape.

"I hope it will," I said. "But at what a price our safety has been purchased."

"How so?" The value of the powder and bullets could not have exceeded twopence, English currency," laughed my companion.

"I alluded to the sacrifice of human life," I rejoined.

"Oh," laughed Count Eugene, "I never thought of that. *C'est drôle.* I daresay in your little island a man has his money value. I perceive it by the smallness of your armies. Out here it is very different, and as for Cossacks, pshaw! they are a mere drug in the market at all times and seasons."

"But for all that they have souls and hearts and feelings like the rest of us," I rejoined, feeling rebellious at this cold-blooded sophistry.

"Have they? Well now if so you have made a discovery that no Russian Czar, prince, or noble has made before. Regarded as a fighting machine the Cossack in his way is admirable, looked at in any other light I fear he is a mistake, and has no place in Nature. As for killing one, either in hot blood or cold, of a necessity or for mere pastime, I should think no more of it than in bagging a hare," rejoined my companion, with a suggestive shrug of the shoulders.

"You speak like a Russian instead of a Pole," I answered. "Like one who from his childhood upwards has been accustomed to look upon the lower classes as mere beasts of burden, going with land on its sale, as part of the live stock, along with the cattle, horses and sheep."*

"I certainly may have imbibed some of those ideas," said Count Eugene, hurriedly. "But look, we are at the end of the pass."

We had been slowly and warily riding on during the whole of this little discussion, and glancing up I really was delighted to find that our long continued and awful peril was so nearly over.

Hope accordingly reanimated my heart, and I do believe my poor horse, who was black with sweat and quivering in every limb, felt it too.

As to Count Eugene, he rode on as unconcernedly as ever, whistling his invariable opera tunes.

* Serfdom was not at that time suppressed in Russia.

I ought to have been deeply thankful to him for having, by his promptness and unflinching nerve, saved both our lives.

But I wasn't. I hated him. I couldn't conceal from myself the feeling; and try to master and overcome it, though I frequently did, I ever made a miserable failure of the attempt.

Five minutes later we were on the sloping mountain side, and the terrible Devil's Pass was in our rear.

CHAPTER XXXVII.
WE STAY THE NIGHT AT A TARTAR HUT.

ALL that day we rode on and on and on, for it was too cold to halt anywhere, and not even a peasant's cot was to be seen.

I was afraid that the night would perforce be a repetition of the day, but Count Eugene declared that before dusk we should sight a Tartar hut and in it find rude accommodation.

I was delighted to receive this oft repeated assurance, for our horses were evidently much in need of rest, and as for myself, unaccustomed to such a severe climate, I felt that if exposed to it through a long Russian winter's night, I should utterly break down.

Count Eugene was right, however—he always was—and just as a deep violet twilight was veiling the scene, we came in sight of the mud-walled, flat-roofed Tartar hut he had spoken of.

In less than ten minutes we were at its door; upon knocking at which we were welcomed by a venerable old man, with the longest hair and beard I had ever seen, save in the case of Mynheer Rip van Winkle, after his sleep of forty years, as represented on the boards of Old Drury.

We were bidden bring our horses inside with us, and our host secured them to two rings that were attached to the thick wooden post which supported the centre of the roof.

Against this post stood the small Russian charcoal stove, and on the top of this stove lay the bright brass samovar, upon which, at all hours of the day and night in Russian and Tartar houses and huts, stands a large teapot full of simmering tea.

We were bidden to make ourselves at home, and did so as well as we could on two hard wooden settles, which, in conjunction with a rude table, seemed to be the sole furniture of the place.

The old Tartar placed before us, by way of supper, milk and eggs, black bread, lemons, sugar, and tea.

The repast was more sumptuous than I had expected; but I shall never forget the Tartar's surprise on seeing me pour milk into my tea ere I drank it.

He expressed it by raising his hands, rolling his eyes, and twice declaring that "The ways of Allah are wonderful!"

Perceiving his consternation, I looked round to see whether Count Eugene was guilty of the same solecism.

Not a bit of it.

I believe that that wonderful man was intimately acquainted with the habits and customs of every people under the sun, and in China would have eaten puppy dog pie, or in Tauraunga have partaken of baked missionary, intuitively knowing the very tid bits, too, just as he would have appreciated a whitebait dinner at Greenwich, or a Fricandeau-au-papillot at Les Trois Freres.

To see him cut a thin slice off a lemon, drop it into a glass tumbler, pour the tea over it, place a large lump of sugar between his teeth, and then, raising his glass to his lips, suffer its contents to slowly percolate through it until it was drained and with it the sugar melted, was a sight worth witnessing.

I made not the slightest doubt that had he been in a Highland shanty, and a jug of water and bottle of whiskey been placed before him, he would have tossed off a wineglassful of the raw spirits first, and a tumbler of the water atop of it, as naturally *a l'Ecosse* as he would drink his tea *a la Russe.*

When the frugal meal was over, and no meal in my life did I ever more enjoy, our host put a bottle of vadschoi before us—a very strong and potent native brandy made from corn.

Then he produced three pipes and a bag of Georgian tobacco, and curling ourselves up on our wooden settles, with our horses munching a feed of beans and hay as they lay on their beds of fern, and the charcoal fire giving out a genial heat, we began to feel comfortable.

After puffing away in silence for about a quarter of an hour, for our Tartar host, when he condescended to converse, which was only on very rare occasions, did so by signs and pantomimic contortions that were not particulary entertaining, I began to think seriously of going to sleep.

I counselled Count Eugene to follow my example, and he yawned, stretched himself, and said that he would.

Our bedsteads were not conducive to slumber, being of hard wood, and perfectly destitute of bed, mattrass or palliass.

Russian travellers always carry a bed and pillow with them.

Fatigue, however, is a capital soporific, and with my saddle for my pillow I was sound asleep before Count Eugene had finished his last pipe.

It seemed to me that I was awakened after only a very few minutes' slumber by the sound of singing.

I unbuttoned my eyelids preliminary to emitting a growl, for no man, especially one dog-tired, likes to be aroused suddenly from his first sleep.

But I gazed upon a scene that completely tongue-d me.

Count Eugene was sitting at the table smoking d sipping corn brandy with an officer, who was bited in a green and gold uniform that I knew to Russian.

They were evidently on amicable terms, and I could make out, though my knowledge of Russian was so very limited, that the officer in green was urging my travelling companion to sing a song.

From this I concluded that it was his singing that had awakened me, and that now Count Eugene would in turn effectually prevent my going to sleep again.

I was far too somnolent still to puzzle my head as to how the Russian came there; how it was that Count Eugene was so friendly with one of the race of oppressors, as he delighted to call all Muscovites, whether or no we were his prisoners or he ours, et cetera.

Yet directly Count Eugene began his song, the words thereof raised strange and unaccountable feelings and remembrances in my breast.

" In the halls of day there is silence and gloom,
  The old lord lies dead in the great Blue room ;
  The casement is open, the wind roars loud,
  And ruffles the plaits of the dead man's shroud."

A feeling of horror crept through my veins, and I somehow felt that I was going to hear something that I had heard before.

" A bird of prey, all black and grim,
  Flies up to the window and looks in at him !
  Then flaps its wings with a goblin croak,
  So low it would seem that the dead man spoke ;
  And next, by its horrible instinct led,
  It perches itself on the coffin-head."

Already a too keen, a too terrible remembrance told me what was coming—but I listened on—

" Ah ! the yellow beak has plunged full deep
  In the sockets where, later, the worms will creep ;
  Eyes and nose and cheeks are bare,
  And the carrion-crow is still feasting there—
  Gorging and feasting, fast and full,
  Till its wings droop down and its eyes grow dull."

I shuddered as I lay, but still listened—

" Yes, the long sharp bill is steeped in red,
  And smeared with the spine of the fleshy dead ;
  Instead of those features grim is seen
  A deep red patch where the face has been !
  And heavy and dull, in the tainted air,
  The foul black devil is sleeping there."

" Good God ! He will appear upon the scene now !" I muttered inaudibly to myself

The song continued—

" Hark—hark ! 'tis the rattle of hoofs beneath,
  And voices resound in the chamber of death ;
  Torches are gleaming about the hall,
  And steps are heard on the stairs to fall."

" Yes—yes," I again murmured, " I know he is coming now."

" With the fumes of the liquor still in his head,
  The young lord enters the room of the dead ;
  What horror arose at the fearful sight—
  Some fainted, some fled, and some prayed from fright !
  And some did shriek and wail full loud
  For the mangled corpse in its bloody shroud."

I could scarce contain myself now to hear the awful song to its end, and yet by a great effort I did succeed.

" But the young lord looked with tipsy eye,
  Then scared them all with a sudden cry—
  'A crow—a crow !' by this liquorish bird,
  My fine old father has kept his word ;
  To his word, ye can see, he did true remain,
  For he swore I should ne'er see his face again !"

The song was ended, and I sprung from off my wooden bedstead, and advanced upon the singer.

"'I will stand this mystery no longer. Who are you, and how do you dare put into verse, and sing for a stranger's diversion, a dreadful secret of which I and the chief actors therein are the sole recipients."

" Well, come, that's good," said Count Eugene, throwing himself back in his chair, with a boisterous laugh. " You ask me who I am after a formal introduction, and being my travelling companion for a month, and next accuse me of making and singing a song out of some incidents or other that you and sundry third parties alone know anything about. Pardon me, my friend, but that sounds very like an Irish bull."

" I cannot help it," I rejoined. " My surprise and utter astonishment must excuse me. The incidents of your song were told me in strict confidence as events that had really happened, as the history of great griefs. You can fancy my feelings, therefore, at hearing them incorporated in a song."

" And who told you this dreadful tale pray ?"

" Oh, that I am not at liberty to inform you."

" Well, as it happens, I am not so bound down. What I have just sung I read as a poem, in an old number of either 'Chambers' Journal,' or 'Household Words,' whilst on a visit to England, a year ago. It chimed in with my own morbid ideas, and so I set it to music, and it's the only song I sing."

"'Chambers' Journal,' or 'Household Words ?' Impossible !" I gasped, more in mental soliloquy than as addressing Count Eugene. " Surely it cannot be."

" Thanks for your scepticism, which I take as a personal compliment to myself. I tell you a fact though for all that. It was quite a long poem for I only got off by heart the most telling verses. Hang it, I ought to remember the author's name. It began with R. R. I know. 'Twas either Richard Reed, or Robert Reece, I think the latter. It struck me at the time that for awful weirdness and for arousing emotions of horror, it beat Hood's 'Dream of Eugene Aram,' Poe's 'Raven,' and many another celebrated piece of the kind, into a cocked hat."

I was too astonished and stupefied to make reply. His words carried conviction along with them.

" I beg your pardon, and I firmly believe you," I stammered forth at length, " yet it is very strange."

THEY TREATED THE RAJAH WITH NONCHALANT LEVITY, MUCH TO THAT DIGNITARY'S DISGUST.

"So strange that I fear, my friend, that you have been duped by an adroit story-teller," laughed the Count.

"Perhaps so," I rejoined, "but yet as you yourself declared this evening, there are more things in earth and in hell than are dreamed of in our philosophy. Anyhow, I owe an apology to yourself and friend for having disturbed your *tête-a-tête.* I freely render it, and with your joint permission will e'en get back into bed again."

I looked round as I spoke.

Heavens! Count Eugene was alone.

The Russian officer had disappeared.

"Your friend has left the hut," I said.

"My friend!" exclaimed Count Eugene, looking round. "Why what the deuce do you mean? Our worthy host has been curled up in yon corner and sound asleep for a good half an hour. I certainly don't admit our horses on terms of companionship."

"I mean the Russian officer who was sipping brandy and smoking with you. He to whom you were singing the weird song," I answered.

"By Jove, you can scarcely be awake yet. I was singing to myself, *mon ami,* as I often do. No Russian or any other officer has been here, I give you my word on it," and Count Eugene laughed uproariously.

"But I say there has," I answered, hotly, for I was not going to disbelieve the evidence of my own eyes. "Why he wore a green uniform and large bullion epaulettes, his chest was covered with stars and orders, and—I'll wager you ten to one that there he goes at the head of a troop of Cossacks or some other infernal light horsemen."

I moved towards the door, outside and past which I felt convinced that I heard the rapid passage of a small body of cavalry across the frozen snow, but, ere I could gain it and throw it open, Count Eugene barred my path, with his sword bare in his hand.

"Excuse me," he said, with an ironical bow, "but you have given me the lie direct, and by opening the door to look out you would repeat it by implication. I must resent the insult. Draw and defend yourself."

CHAPTER XXXVIII.

FORDING A SEA OF FIRE.

UNWILLING to be thought a coward I rushed to my bed, seized my sword, and, unsheathing it, advanced upon him.

I was by no means a skilled swordsman, though, on the other hand, a very tolerable one.

At the third pass, therefore, I felt convinced that the Count was merely playing with me; for that he was a perfect master of fencing I could not entertain a doubt.

He proved this to be the case before long by sending my sword spinning from my grasp, after which he deliberately sheathed his own weapon.

"Why don't you ask me to retract my words?" I asked.

"Because I know you English are so stubborn," was the reply.

"Why, then, don't you take my life?" I demanded

"For the simple reason that it is not your own to give or mine to take. You have secret instructions for the chiefs of the Caucasus, and were I to pass my sword through you, with you they would die, and mine would almost be a useless mission. No, no, my good friend, my honour is sufficiently avenged, and you are at perfect liberty either to open the door or to retire to bed."

"It would be of no earthly service opening the door now, anyhow," I rejoined; "so thanking you for your lesson in sword-play, I will even wish you good-night for a second time, and try to get my sleep out," and picking up my weapon I sheathed it, and again sought the hard boards, but for a long time lay awake wondering whether Louis Foucarte's tale was all a sham, and if so whether Count Eugene's might not be the same.

Sleep, however, did at last come, and then endured for far too short a time, for when Count Eugene woke me up, and I opened my eyes to discover that it was broad daylight, I felt as though I had not been asleep an hour, and every whit as tired as though I had had no rest at all.

The Count was as genial and affable as could be, and made no mention of the events of the preceding night, events which I was quite ready to ignore, even whilst I retained my own convictions intact, for the remembrance of being worsted in a sword bout is by no means agreeable.

Our Tartar host had slept through the whole affair—or else pretended to sleep, which came to pretty much the same thing.

He now got us a breakfast in the shape of black bread, eggs, and dried fish, which we washed down with brick-tea and copious draughts of mare's milk.

Giving the Tartar the largest silver coin that we each of us possessed in return for his hospitality, with which remuneration he seemed to be extremely well content, we led out our horses, tightened up our girths, and, mounting, rode away.

The day was one of bright sunshine but intense cold, so that I was very glad to pull on my great fur gloves and draw the sealskin-lined collar of my military cloak up around my ears.

Whilst doing so I noticed at least a hundred hoofprints of small unshod horses or ponies in the surrounding snow.

"Our friends of last night," I said, nodding towards them meaningly; but Count Eugene would not understand me, and abruptly launched forth into conversation.

* * * * *

Nothing of any importance occurred during the two ensuing days, but on the morning of the third we were riding along cliffs that overhung the sea, and Count Eugene, pointing to a dimly-visible violet-hued mountain that rose high into the air far across the dark-blue ocean, said, with a nod of the head—

"Behold yonder the junction of Europe with Asia in Mount Kouban. One half is in one continent and one in the other, yet, nevertheless, both are in the Caucasus, and close under its northern shadow lies the town of Anapa."

"I have heard of that place," I said.

"As who has not?" was the response; "for that port trades in more lovely merchandise than any other in the world."

"What kind of merchandise is that, pray?" I asked.

"The beautiful girls of the Caucasus," was the reply, "are shipped there for the Stamboul market, sometimes in scores and hundreds at a time."

"Oh, indeed," I rejoined, calling to mind a few white-haired pink-eyed specimens of the genus Circassian that I had seen exhibited in shows at fairs, and thus failing to feel inspired. "And what is that picturesque village down in a hollow almost at our feet?"

"Oh, that is Choungelok, from whence we cross over into Circassia. You can see the oposite coast very clearly, if you look right over Choungelok's roofs."

"And is that wide arm of the sea opposite, the Strait that we have to cross on horseback?" I asked.

"It is," was the nonchalant reply.

"Hang it, it looks a deuced long twelve miles."

"Ah, you see the morning is hazy."

"And it has the appearance of being deep enough for 'The Twelve Apostles' to sail up or down.

"Appearances are very deceptive then, for nowhere along the ford that I shall conduct you across is the water more than four feet deep. I will show you a very strange phenomenon in passing if wind and currents serve."

"And what may the phenomenon be?" I asked.

"A sea literally on fire," was the response.

"On fire. By George, you must be chaffing," I laughed.

"'Pon honour, I am not. I will set it on fire myself, with that very unromantic conjuror's wand a wax vesta."

"Well, I sincerely trust that winds and currents may serve. But how comes it to depend on them?"

"In this manner. I could set the sea aflame in any case but if the wind did not blow in a contrary direction, we should suffer by the experiment, for the flames would devour us," said Count Eugene.

"I would run a very strong chance of their doing so in order to witness so wondrous a phenomenon," I rejoined. "I have never read or heard of such a thing."

We had now entered the Town of Choungelok, and loking down the narrow ravine between the two hills on which it is built, could see the leaden-coloured waters of the Putrid Lake, stretching away for miles to the north, its banks covered with a yellow, dark, and decaying vegetation.

"No fish swim in it, and no bird can fly across without dropping dead upon its waters," said Count Eugene. "Men turn faint and fall whilst yet a hundred yards away from its bank. It is deemed to be accursed."

"But cannot its poisonous qualities be explained by natural causes?" I asked.

"Well, some attempt to do so by saying that when General Jelisavetgradski, the Russian Commander, conquered the Krim Tartars under Akmetchet Ali on the bloody field of Soultamoko, two hundred thousand of he dead, wounded and prisoners, were cast into this lake, raising the height of its waters by a couple of feet and poisoning it for evermore.'

"It may be so," I rejoined. "But here we are at the water's edge, and the sea itself is calm as any lake."

Such was indeed the case, for not a ripple disturbed the placid waters of the Cimmerian Bosphorus, more commonly known as the Strait of Kertch.

The opposite shore looked dim and hazy in the distance.

I would certainly have fought shy of pulling it in a boat.

To ride across anyone would have deemed a matter of sheer impossibility.

Count Eugene seemed to read my doubting glances, and an almost imperceptible smile curled his thin lips as he spurred his horse into the water.

I followed his example, and we rode straight out to sea for more than half a mile, the water not rising higher than our horses' knees.

"This is awfully jolly," I exclaimed.

"Yes, quite a new sensation—isn't it?" laughed the Count. "Makes one feel half Centaur and half Neptune. Here we are in mid ocean, as it were."

I looked round—the Crimean shore looked a long way off already, and away to the right the dark waters of the Black Sea flashed here and there white with foam.

Another hour's steady riding and we were in the very centre of the strait.

Here, for a short quarter of a mile or so, our horses had some difficulty in maintaining their footing, and at one time, I believe, were actually off their legs; but the water soon got shallow again, and as it did so, the vast and grand headland of Taman seemed suddenly to show out distinct and clear in our front.

"Have you forgotten what you said about setting the sea on fire?" I asked, presently, of the Count.

"Oh no," was the reply; "but we have not yet reached the spot where the feat is practicable."

We spoke no more until, some five minutes later, Count Eugene, who had been riding a little in advance reined in his horse to a halt.

"Here is the spot," he said. "And fortunately there is nothing to hinder the success of the experiment."

I drew up in turn, deeply interested.

"Keep a firm hand on your reins," said the Count, "or your horse may shy and throw you. Mine knows better than to act so foolishly."

He let his bridle fall on his horse's neck, drew a fusce box from his pocket, struck a wax vesta thereon, which burned brightly, for there was not a breath of air stirring, and leaning over in his saddle touched with the blazing tip the surface of the water.

There ensued a strange kind of report, more like an explosion of pent up gas than that of gunpowder.

A lambent tongue of flame leapt up out of the sea, like that which springs from the mouth of a huge siege mortar, quivered and flickered for a brief moment, and then settled into a steady and roaring blaze, each instant covering a larger tract of sea.

"Spur on! Spur on!" cried Count Eugene. "You can turn for another look when you are a little further off. The heat will be intense directly."

I did as he advised, and he imitated my example.

When we next paused to look around the fire covered a space of sea as large as a small field.

It burnt in a clear yellow flame without smoke, but accompanied by a peculiar roaring sound.

It seemed to flicker almost on the surface of the water, but was sufficiently in it to cause the sea all around its margin to bubble and hiss as water in a pail does when red hot iron is plunged into it.

It had now apparently attained its utmost dimensions, and after surveying it for some time with intense interest and astonishment I, seeing that my companion was becoming impatient, wheeled round, and rode on by his side.

"How the deuce is the phenomenon to be accounted for?" I presently asked, unable to conquer my curiosity. Of course I'm not going to believe that there's any magic or dire sorcery in the affair, but at the same time it's deucedly odd to see a sea set on fire with a match."

"And yet the explanation is after all very simple," answered Count Eugene with a laugh. "Firstly, though, the sea has not been on fire at all."

"No?" I exclaimed, more astonished than ever.

"Why, of course not. Nothing will make water burn. But underneath this Strait of Kertch are numerous springs of naphtha. Now, naphtha being lighter than water rises to the surface, but being at the same time a volatile spirit, it does not mix with or become impregnated with the water up through which it rises. Wherever it is seen like a scum upon the surface of the waves, it may be set fire to with impunity, and will burn for days until a high wind or a rough sea put it out," said Count Eugene.

Thus was the mystery explained, and a quarter of an hour later we were on Caucasian soil.

CHAPTER XXXIX.
A CIRCASSIAN CHARGE.

WE seemed to have entered another world, for though the scenery of the Crimea is bold, that of the Caucasus is grand and stupendous in the extreme.

Hills rise o'er hills, and mountains overtop mountains, until the topmost peaks are lost amongst the clouds.

Far up the slopes of many we could see cold and glittering glaciers, like tempest-tossed seas of ice, and sometimes a roar, louder than that of the loudest thunder, would announce an avalanche of millions of tons of snow, from some mountain top to valley.

The sky became leaden and overcast, and then no description in Dante's "Inferno," no picture of Gustave Doré could have exaggerated the majestic gloominess of the scene.

I could almost imagine that we were on the threshold of some awful and unknown world.

But suddenly we heard a fearful yelling and shouting, whooping and howling, as though legions of fiends were battling for the mastery in some narrow gorge.

"That is the Circassian war-cry," said Count Eugene. "There is hot work going on at the top of the pass we are ascending. We must take care not to put a foot in it."

"Do you think they are fighting each other?" I asked.

"Oh no," was the reply. "I can hear the shrill Russian cheer, but it is uttered in accents of despair. Let us get out of the way, or in a minute or two we shall be overwhelmed."

"Will the tide of battle roll this way, then?"

"Indisputably, since Russia lies at our backs, and the mountaineers are the victors. It takes ages to subdue mountaineers. England found it so with the Highlands of Scotland and Wales, did she not?" and Count Eugene fixed me with a keen and penetrating glance.

"She certainly did," I made answer. "But hark to the shout of victory. How it echoes from mountain to mountain. I hear shrieks, groans, and the thunder of horses' hoofs."

"Let us ride up into this canon," said Count Eugene. "In the dark and narrow defile we shall be unperceived, and shall be able to witness the mingled flight and chase sweep by at our leisure."

Even as he was speaking a couple of riderless horses came dashing down the pass at a mad gallop.

"Now," said Count Eugene, "not a moment is to be lost."

I was quite aware of the fact, and required no further pressing.

I spurred after him up the black canon, and in an instant the darkness of Erebus concealed us from the view of the curious, for to right to left and in rear of us rose wall-like precipices of black rock to the height of, at least, two thousand feet, effectually shutting out the light.

We commanded a clear view of the pass we had just quitted, however, for we looked out as from a darkened church into a lighted street.

Nearer and nearer came the sound of resounding hoofstrokes, and now I could hear in addition to the shouts, cheers, and battle-cries, what I knew from the tones in which they were uttered to be supplications for mercy, all mingled with occasional pistol shots, the clash of swords, the jingle of chain bridles, and the rattle of accoutrements.

Then more horses flew by riderless, and two or three with them dragging along their dead masters, whose feet had become entangled in the stirrups.

Then with a rush, and a burst, and a roar, came the main body of the defeated cavalry, riding helter skelter, and each striving to be foremost.

Many a green uniform was splashed here and there with scarlet, many a helmet was bent and battered, many a sword was broken, and many an eagle shred away.

They had evidently fought well, but they were just as assuredly in wild panic now, as well they might be, for the wild horsemen of the mountains were close upon their heels.

Another moment and they also hove into view, coming sweeping down the pass like a mountain torrent.

Above their towering sheep-skin caps waved an embroidered shirt by way of banner, the bodies of many were clad in chain-mail, and crimson horsetails fluttered around their galloping chargers. Their appearance was wild and barbarous, but at the same time superb.

But Heavens, what kind of missiles were they hurling after the retreating foe, every one of whom that they overtook they scimitared or poignarded without mercy.

I could not imagine at first for what reason they kept continually bending over in their saddles.

But when they arrived opposite to us, I could see that these wild horsemen were picking up stones off the ground without checking their headlong pace for a single instant, and continually hurling them with most accurate aim and crushing force at the retreating Russian dragoons.

Had I been told of such a feat, I should have considered it an impossible one, and the apparent ease with which it was accomplished confounded and astonished me almost beyond measure.

The retreating and the pursuing waves of horsemen had all swept by in the short space of a quarter of an hour, and we rode out of the canon again.

Not a horseman was visible, but dead chargers and their riders lay pretty thickly around, together with here and there a wounded Circassian.

Suddenly, in turning an abrupt corner of the pass we found ourselves face to face with a tall, stately white-bearded warrior, mounted on a cream-coloured Arab charger, of rare beauty and symmetry.

He was followed by about a score of other horsemen, one of whom held an enormous sheathed sword aloft.

"We have found him of whom we are in quest, a hundred miles further to the westward than we had any right to expect," said Count Eugene, in a low tone. "You look upon Schamyl, the Prophet Chief of the Caucasus."

CHAPTER XL.

SCHAMYL, PROPHET AND CHIEF.

ON hearing these words I gazed with considerably more of interest on the advancing cortege.

Schamyl I knew to be the tall, stately, white-bearded chieftain on the cream-coloured Arab steed, for he had a look that indisputably declared him to be a leader of men.

He was of middle-height, and apparently of about sixty years of age. His keen, eagle-eyes, flashed brilliantly from beneath black, well-defined brows, but his hair was of a bright blonde colour, and his beard white as snow.

He wore a papash, or high cap of sheepskin, so high and large in fact that his whole wardrobe might have been contained therein.

His dress was of a dark green material, and heavily trimmed with the fur of the black fox.

On each side of his chest were sewn round brass cases in rows, and filled, according to Circassian custom, with rifle and pistol cartridges.

A long sword hung from his left shoulder, a rifle in a green-baize case was slung at his back, in company with a single-barrelled pistol, whilst depending from his richly wrought girdle was a formidable dagger, cased in a velvet sheath, and possessing an enjewelled hilt.

His followers were very similarly dressed and armed, and I noticed with some surprise that their stirrup irons were tied together under their horses bellies.

By the time I had made all these observations we were so close to the advancing cortege that some explanation of our presence was absolutely necessary.

Some of Schamyl's followers had drawn their swords or levelled their pistols at us, very probably taking us for Russians.

If we did not quickly disabuse them of the idea they would make very short work of us.

I did not understand a word of their language, but I unfastened my cloak, and throwing it back revealed my bright scarlet uniform beneath, at the same time drawing forth a pocket-handkerchief in the semblance of a most gorgeous Union Jack.

"Ah, you are British," said Schamyl, in as fluent English as I spoke myself. "You are British, and as such are welcome."

Of course I returned a suitable answer, whilst Count Eugene explained in the same language that he was a Pole in the French service, and that we l ad been sent from the camp of the Allies on a diplomatic mission.

"We will listen to it later in the day," said Schamyl. "When the sword is red in our hands we give our thoughts to no subject but victory. We have just hurled back a marauding body of Russian horse into the plains, that are as flat as those who dwell therein. Now, however, we shall return to our camp, and after you have rested and partaken of our hospitality, then we will hear you to the end."

And the warrior prophet extended a hand to each of us.

Having thus welcomed us, Schamyl and his murids wheeled round to escort us to the camp, which we were informed was at no great distance up the mountain.

Far it certainly was not, but the way was so steep and rugged that our unaccustomed horses sometimes slid back as much as they advanced, and frequently required a smart application of the spur to urge them on at all.

In fact it was like clambering up a constant succession of house-roofs, with, now and then, the edge of a precipice to skirt, just perilous enough to bring back to my recollection the horrors of the Devil's Ridge.

When, however, we had reached an altitude of some thousand feet or so above the pass or gorge in which the cavalry combat had taken place, the ascent grew less steep, and the ridable ground so wide that we could progress in clumps or mobs again, instead of in Indian file.

Suddenly, as I was riding somewhat carelessly on, talking to Schamyl, I felt that something was giving way under my horse's feet, and only by a very prompt action of the rein and spur did I succeed in preventing him from falling into what looked like a rather deep pit, covered with brushwood.

Directly we were secure on *terra firma* I looked down into this seeming booby trap, and thought I saw human heads moving about therein, whilst at the same minute cries and supplications ascended from below in some unknown tongue, which I supposed to be Circassian.

I could tell, however, that the voices pertained to women and children, and I exclaimed, addressing Schamyl—

"Some unfortunates or other have fallen into that pit, and are praying to be rescued."

"It is nothing," answered the Prophet Prince.

"Pardon me," I rejoined; "but I am sure that I see heads and can hear voices. Ride a little nearer, O, Schamyl, and you will see and hear the same."

"I am aware of it, but it matters naught," said Schamyl, in the same cold unmoved tones as before. "It is but the wife and children of Abar Boolan. She slew her husband's murderer, Baroon Fassam, and so, with her family lies buried for three months, at the expiration of which time she will be re-wedded to whoever will marry her. Sekar, I have said it."

"But the poor wretch will surely die ere three nights, far less three months, have expired," I replied. "The snow must lie deep around her and her hapless children. It must be icy cold down there."

"The daughters of Circassia, praise be to Allah, are hardy, or they would not bring forth warriors. This woman and her children are fed daily, and their health will not suffer," was the retort, uttered in such a tone as was evidently meant to check any further questioning on the subject.

Horrified, however, at what I considered such inhuman treatment, I was not to be thus easily silenced, and continued with—

"She supplicates in tones of great agony, O Schamyl, and the children's cries are touching. If she is thus imprisoned according to your laws, cannot you for once, in commemoration, we will say, of this morning's victory over the Russians, temper justice with mercy, and set her free."

The Prophet Prince drew rein, stroked his beard, and for a minute or two seemed to be turning the matter over diligently in his mind.

Then looking up, he said with a smile—

"Be it as you say. I will show mercy—not in commemoration of our victory over the Russians, for Bismillah, that is a thing of every day occurrence, but in order to mark, as with a white stone, the day of your coming amongst us. Looloo Boolan and her children have already been in the pit two months. After she has been liberated and had a bath, you shall see how little the incarceration has injured her. You shall witness her nuptials also with the Murid Ali. They shall come off immediately after presentation."

Of course I tendered no end of thanks for the mercy accorded to the poor prisoners, and the compliment paid to ourselves in the character of ambassadors.

Then, with no little curiosity, for the affair fairly puzzled me, I asked—

"How comes it that this woman, who, knowing the fearful punishment that would be her doom, nevertheless so heroically avenged the murder of her husband, is ready so soon to wed another?"

"Because it is another of our laws that no woman may remain a widow for more than three months, unless she be old and past child-bearing. Bismillah, the Russian hordes kill so many of us that we cannot have too many sons to keep our weapons from rusting when we in turn lie useless in the grave," answered Schamyl, lifting his hands and eyes heavenwards.

Then he added, with a deprecating gesture—

"You may think our punishment for such an act as this woman has committed unjust, or, at all events, excessive. Know, then, that in times of peace we should have applauded the act, but now we are at war with the Russ; her knife robbed our army of a good sword, for Baroon Fanam's heart was tough, and his arm was strong, and we punish her for the robbery—not for the taking of life."

Whilst thus conversing, we had been riding on and on, and presently we all drew rein before the grand, but gloomy, mouth of an immense cavern that opened right into the mountain's side, apparently to a great depth.

Dismounting, we entered it, leading our horses.

They were taken from us inside, however, by a number of rudely armed warriors, and then Schamyl led the way to a part of the cave (a long way off, it seemed) where the softest of Persian carpets and pillows strewed the ground, and arms and accoutrements of the richest description hung from the walls of natural rock.

Here Schamyl welcomed us for a second time, and, in obedience to his command, a bevy of young girls, between twelve and fourteen, but already possessed of woman's contour, bare-armed and, from the knees downwards, bare-legged also, with that exquisite rounding and plumpness of limbs, and delicate softness and purity of flesh that constitute the chief charms of Circassia's fair daughters, washed our feet, gave us slippers, and a little later brought in and handed to us cups of fragrant coffee, black, bread caviare (prepared sturgeon-roes), and plates of delicious fruit.

Scarcely had we satisfied the wants of the inner man (for precious hungry we were) and feasted our eyes for a little better than half an hour upon the delicious and somewhat intoxicating beauty of the dark-eyed nymphs who surrounded us, when an exclamation from Schamyl caused us to look up and we saw slowly, and with rare symmetry of motion, advancing down the cave a beautiful being who in both face and form surpassed in perfection all others present, as the fair white moon at its full supasses in beauty each and all the stars and planets that surround her.

She was certainly not more than twenty years of age, and yet was accompanied by three children, the youngest just able to toddle unsupported, each one of whom gave promise of growing up beautiful enough to do credit to their mother.

"Behold the woman on whose behalf you interested yourself, and who owes her present liberty to your intercessions," said Schamyl, and then he addressed her in turn, hastily I thought, though I knew not what he said.

She came up to me, knelt, seized my hand and kissed it, whereupon, not liking such servile homage, I sprang to my feet and lifted her up, noticing as I did so the richness of her dress, the dazzling whiteness of her expanded chest, the dimpled beauty of her shoulders, and the perfumed silkiness of her wealth of golden hair, that almost swept the ground.

I almost envied the Murid Ali, who doubtless thinking that I had gazed quite long enough at the charms of his intended, presently came forward to relieve me of her near presence.

He was a tall, gaunt, eagle-eyed man of about forty, and I involuntarily pitied those pretty shoulders that his young bride possessed, if she ever succeeded in rousing his anger, and a stick or sword-scabbard happened to be handy.

Schamyl and the other murids now rose, and invited Count Eugene and myself to accompany them and witness the wedding.

We proceeded down many a subterranean passage in the dark mountain side, all of them dimly lighted with oil lamps, until we at last reached a smaller cavern than that in which we had partaken of food, and which was fitted up somewhat in the manner of a Mohammedan Mosque.

'Twas soon evident that Schamyl himself was to be the priest who would unite the apparently ill-assorted pair.

It was a very simple yet somewhat impressive ceremony, and when it was over we all returned to the cavern we had first occupied, and coffee and pipes were handed round, and much smoking and sipping was done in silence, Mahommedans not being a talkative race, and all intoxicating drinks forbidden by the Koran.

At last, however, at a sign from the Prophet Prince, the company began to disperse.

The bride and bridegroom went in one direction, and the dark-eyed, cherry-lipped, white-armed waiting-maids made a swoop upon the three children and vanished in turn in another.

Then the murids and warriors departed in a more staid and stately manner, and at last Schamyl, Count Eugene, and myself were alone in the cavern.

"What do the Allied Chiefs of England and France require of me?" Schamyl then asked.

"Know then," I said, "that on the 26th of the present month, Zarif Mustapha Pasha, with forty thousand infantry and cavalry, and a hundred and twenty pieces of artillery, whose contemplated movements are most carefully masked, will attack, take, and destroy, Tiflis, the capital of Georgia, which is garrisoned by only twenty thousand Russians, whom they will cut to pieces; and thereafter, falling on the army of Prince Babutoff at Gumri, will drive it, and the smaller contingents of General Kemti at Dowchet, and of General Novotroff at Passanasur, back into the Southern Caucasus, where we depend upon your cutting them off from the great military road leading from Georgia to Vladikankus, and, if possible, exterminating them."

"It shall be done," said Schamyl, half drawing his sword in his excitement. "It shall be done, and I shall be more your debtor than you mine by the information that shall enable me to strike so deadly a blow at my accursed foes. For twenty years have I been a thorn in the side of Russia, but now I will be a hornet's sting. How many men think you the gallant Turks will drive back for us to destroy?"

"Out of thirty-five thousand they will have to conquer and overcome, nine or ten thousand may

very likely succeed in gaining the mountains," I replied.

"To lay their whitened bones there!" replied the Prophet Prince, with a wild and reckless laugh. We will give their bodies to the wolves, and their hearts to the eagles. Bismillah! I have said it!"

CHAPTER XLI.

THE IMAUM TELLS THE HISTORY OF THE HOLY SHIRT.

COUNT EUGENE and I sat with Schamyl, the Imaum, for more than an hour, discussing and arranging the minor details of the movement that was to prevent the Russian army of Georgia from ever again treading European soil.

The Count left me to do most of the talking, to such an extent, indeed, that I began to wonder for what earthly reason he had accompanied me to the Caucasus.

I had all along fancied that in this expedition I was the subordinate and he was the leader, yet save a few passionate utterances concerning the grievous wrong that Poland had suffered at the hands of Russia, with assurances that if Schamyl backed us well up in this matter the Allied Powers would see that the integrity of his dominions was preserved from all incursions of the Russians on the north, he said nothing of any consequence whatever.

When we had pretty well discussed matters threadbare, Schamyl again called in his murids, who seemed to be staff officers, council, and priesthood all in one, and we had to go over the whole matter again.

They, however, took it up just as enthusiastically as Schamyl had done, and likewise declared that not a single Russian of the army of Asia should cross the Caucasus to the great military road alive.

Scarcely had the excitement of these holy murids cooled down a little when it was again aroused by the blare of trumpets, the crash of timbrels, and the hoarse boom of unbraced drums from outside the cave.

"Our gallant horsemen have returned," said Schamyl. "Let the captains enter and deliver their report."

One of the murids rose, and quitted the cave, but presently returned, followed by three young men, dressed in the universal papash and long flowing robes of green, who carried their long straight swords unsheathed in their hands.

They knelt before the Prophet Prince, who solemnly blessed them, and then asked quietly, and with a smile—

"What have you to tell me, my children?"

"Oh, holy Schamyl, it is the same tale as usual," answered the youngest of the three youths; "we chased the foe almost up to the walls of Himri, when the cannon suddenly opened upon us, and we had to retire, leaving many dead upon the field."

"And how many of the foe, think you, have escaped?"

"But a handful—a score at the most; and they were mounted on Arab horses, stolen from us," said another youth.

"It is well. They rode to the encounter a thousand strong. Now tell me of our own losses."

"Twenty killed and forty-five wounded—many of them not seriously."

Schamyl's countenance at once lighted up with pleasure.

"It is well," he said. "See the latter be seen to, and a feast be at once spread for my gallant warriors."

The three youths bowed and retired, and Schamyl then told me that the younger was his son.

Of course I congratulated him upon being the father of so fine a youth, and upon the victory his horsemen had obtained over the Russians.

Then, overcome by a curiosity that I could not repress, I asked the origin and the meaning of the strange shirt-standard that I had seen borne by his troops.

"It is the holy shirt of the founder of our religion. Aboo Moslim, who was slain by my side at the taking of this very Himri by the Russians, a score of years ago," said Schamyl. "He was the first Moslem, since the death of the more holy people, privileged to hold direct communication with the Almighty, a privilege which, through him, I, in common with the entire priesthood, now enjoy upon taking the oaths, and devoting ourselves to death, if necessary, in the defence of the faith."

I had heard something of this new religion of Safism before, but, regarding it as a mere spurious outgrowth of Mahommedanism, born of fanaticism, I felt little interest in it, though I doubted not that it had in a great measure enabled the Circassians to maintain their independence for so many years against the overwhelming forces of the Russians.

I still experienced curiosity in the matter of the sacred shirt, and the defence of Himri, however, and pressed the Imaum to favour us with the tale.

He appeared to be nothing loath to do so, and straightway launched forth into the following narrative:—

"Aboo Moslim was, from his earliest youth, a reader of the Koran, and the possessor of a lofty pride, a strong love of independence, and great earnestness of character.

"Disdaining the sports and amusements of his youthful companions—except such as partook of a military nature, and in them he soon taught himself to excel all rivals—he withdrew from their society whenever the opportunity offered, to meditate upon the sayings of the Prophet, and to read his book in the most solitary recesses of the mountains.

"On the summit of Mount Ebbrouz, which rises to the height of eighteen hundred feet above the level of the plains below, the great Allah one day alighted, and told his servant that, as long as a hundred faithful sons of Mahomet remained banded together in the double capacity of priests and warriors, devoting themselves to death in the defence of their faith and of their country, the unbeliever would never triumph over us.

"These priestly warriors were to be called murids, and Aboo Moslim was to be their head and chief.

"In token of his authority he was to repair to a cave that pierced the very depths of the mountain, and in the very farthest recess, marked by a green stone, he would find a consecrated shirt and sword.

"The former was made of one piece of soft chamois leather without seam, and over it were scattered texts from the Koran in stamped gold.

"The sword too, hilt, guard, and blade, was made from one piece of iron, and the weapon was so heavy that Aboo could scarcely carry it out of the cave and down the mountain side to the village wherein he lived.

"He told the Elders what had happened, and the will of Allah was immediately carried into execution.

"Aboo, then only in the eighteenth year of his age, was the next day placed in command of an army, he having in only a few hours formed his band of a hundred murids from the bravest and most godfearing of the youths of his acquaintance, qualities that are generally found together in the Caucasus.

"Wearing the sacred shirt and sword, though the latter was too heavy to use as a weapon, Aboo Moslim, the first of our Imaums, waged successful war against the Russ, for more than ten years never experiencing a defeat, and during all this time he and his murids held frequent personal communication with Allah on the summit of Mount Ebbrouz,

a mountain to whose icy and snow-clad summit none but a murid can now climb, and often in the darkness of night they who watched at the mouth of the cave, which none but a murid dare approach, saw with their inspired vision the glorious form of the archangel Isragel, whose heart-strings are a lute, and who has the sweetest voice of all God's creatures, hovering between the moon and the earth, and pointing with a spear tipped with flame, in the direction in which the Russ was about to make an attack, or in which we were to deal him a deadly blow.

"At last, however, whether it was that we failed to make an attack during the first quarter of the moon (a period most propitious for all offensive operations) or neglected to turn back upon some occasion when a hare darted across our line of march (a sure warning sent by Allah that to proceed would be disastrous), I know not; but, be that as it may, we in three days suffered three defeats at the hands of General Garbatoff, and only escaped annihilation by throwing ourselves into the walled town of Himri.

"The Russians, having got us into a trap, resolved to keep us there. Garbatoff sent off for reinforcements, and in less than twelve hours as many thousand infidels had surrounded the walls and laid siege to the place.

"I was Aboo Moslim's favourite murid and his right-hand swordsman in the field.

"Many a consultation we had upon the best means of getting out of the place and cutting our way back to the mountains through the beleaguering hosts of Russians, but the project seemed too insane a one to be carried into execution, and neither Allah, nor Mahomet, nor Isragel appeared to comfort us.

"Every hour the Russian hordes seemed to grow more immense. Heavy cannons were brought up and placed in position. Then the bombardment commenced and was continued for four days and nights, the Russians not even daring to rush in through the breaches they had made, though they outnumbered us by at least twenty to one.

"Aboo Moslim, foremost amongst us murids, was ever in the hottest fire, encouraging his men, for again and again, when the walls lay in heaps of ruins, the Russians rushed over them to the attack, though only to be again and again repulsed with terrible slaughter.

"But at last, out of the force of twelve hundred and fifty Circassians who had ridden into Himri, only twenty-four murids remained alive, while the numbers of the Russians seemed inexhaustable as ever.

"Another assault was made and met as boldly as ever. Aboo Moslim, covered with wounds, and dripping with his own and his foeman's blood, urged the remainder of his small force to fight to the last gasp; and, directly his own sword fell from his grasp through weakness, dropped on his knees and briefly committed his soul to the God of Armies.

"Then beckoning me to his side, he bade me take off and don in his stead the holy shirt, and, repairing to the stables, saddle his horse and cut my way through the Russian lines.

"'You will succeed; for even with glazing eyes I see as in a vision the Circassian hosts rushing to battle with this shirt as an all-conquering flag, and you as their annointed leader. Go then; it is the will of Allah;' and so speaking he died.

"Of a necessity I obeyed, and, as I rode out through a breach in the old wall, I saw the last of the twenty-four murids cut down.

"Out of the original hundred I alone survived, but Aboo Moslim prophesied true, for I rode through the whole Russian army protected by the holy shield, and a sword that I knew well how to wield, at the trifling cost of two bullet wounds and a bayonet stab. And now I am Imaum, in Aboo Moslim's place."

CHAPTER XLII.

A BABOON FOR A ROOM-MATE.

THE Prophet Prince's story, and his simple manner of telling it, made a great impression upon me.

It seemed as though, in the course of a few hours, the scene had been changed by some fell enchantment from the middle of the nineteenth century to the mediæval age.

And nothing was there in our surroundings to dispel this illusion, for many of Schamyl's followers wore shirts of chain mail and caps of spiked iron.

The kindness of one and all was, however, great, and the day passed so rapidly, that darkness veiled the scene at least a couple of hours before I had expected it.

Then great lamps were lighted, and, to divert us, wild, barbarous music was played, and a strange but not ungraceful dance was indulged in by a troop of young Circassian maidens, who possessed great beauty of face and form.

I saw amongst them none of those white-haired, pink-eyed, eyebrow-less, doll-nonentities, that generally pass for representatives of the Circassian race at European shows and exhibitions.

On the contrary, many of the girls had golden, others rich glossy brown, and some few jet black hair, but in every instance it was of great length and luxuriance, and allied with arch and well defined brows, long drooping lashes, the brightest of eyes, and the most dazzling of complexions, with features delicately cut as those of a Greek statue.

Their limbs, too, were most exquisitely rounded, with waists of the tiniest dimensions, swelling grandly upwards into the fullest and most voluptuous of busts.

This perfection of figure is produced by the adoption of a broad and tight girdle, placed around the waist at the age of twelve, and never removed until the bridegroom cuts it asunder with his dagger on the nuptial night.

Directly the Prophet Prince imagined that the music had been continued long enough to weary us, supper was ordered to be brought in, the meat whereof consisted of salted boar and bear, the bread of rye, whilst for drink we had some finely flavoured coffee and mare's milk, sugar being an unknown luxury in the Caucasus.

When we had done discussing this frugal repast, we were led away by two of the murids and shown our respective beds, which consisted of two heaps of dried ferns, with a bear skin for a coverlet, and another rolled up for a pillow.

They were not far apart, but situated, as it seemed to me, in one of the very further recesses of the vast labyrinth of subterraneans that formed Schamyl's underground palace.

True, the passage seemed to extend a considerable way further, but shrank to such small dimensions that it would have been a matter of impossibility to traverse it in an upright position, or, in fact, in any but a creeping attitude.

The murids blessed us before they went away, and solemnly committed us to the keeping of Allah.

A minute later their footsteps had ceased to be audible in the distance, and Count Eugene and I were alone.

We were too dog-tired to be very communicative, however, and, with a few common-place remarks, we took off the tightest articles of our attire, and turned into bed.

"To bed, perchance to sleep." Ah! "there was the rub," indeed.

First of all I found it so icy cold that I had to get up and put on all my clothes again, even though a fire of tissels, or dried cows'-dung, had been lighted a little way adown the passage for our especial behoof.

Next I was fain to wrap my bearskin coverlet around me until I was fairly coiled like an Egyptian mummy; but even then I could not get comfortably warm.

The bats kept me awake, or sometimes they fluttered by so close to me as almost to brush it with their leathery wings.

At last, however, in spite of bats, cold, and everything else, the wants of nature asserted their sway, and I fell into a sleep of profound and deep.

How long it lasted I know not, but it was abominably dream-haunted, and I was at length aroused therefrom by a reality so disagreeable that my nightmare-ridden slumbers were insignificant when compared to it.

Strong, bony, and deathly-cold fingers clutched my throat—a heavy form was crouched in strange attitude on my chest. Two fiery stars, or rather glowing cigar-tips, which I knew must be eyes, glared into mine out of the darkness, and a foetid breath fanned my face.

The fire had died away into a few red embers, so that the form of my foe was absolutely viewless, but that he was of large size his weight proved, while his strength was more than sufficiently evinced by the muscular power with which he clutched my throat.

Gracious heavens! he was assuredly throttling me.

With the instinct of self-preservation I threw out my hands.

One clutched a hairy wrist, the other a hairy body.

The latter I withdrew with a cry, for a snap, accompanied by an angry snarl, was made at one of the fingers, which was bitten through to the very bone.

Horror-striken, I wondered what kind of a foe I was pitted against; but even whilst wondering I actively resisted, for I felt that to relax my efforts for an instant might mean death by strangulation.

I had got him by both wrists now, but I saw by the rapid approach of his eyes that he was lowering his head to bite me again, so I clenched him tighter than ever, threw my own head up for his chin to come in contact with, and the same moment by a most vigorous effort dislodged his superincumbent form, and gave him a violent kick in the region of what I guessed to be his stomach.

I heard his teeth clash together like castanets. I heard him puff and grunt as though the wind had been knocked out of him. His clutch on my wrist relaxed as he rolled off me. Another instant and I had sprung to my feet.

I had not given my foe his quietus however, for he was up as soon as I, and instantly grappled with me.

By the position of his blazing eyes I could see that he was not nearly so tall as myself—probably not more, indeed, than five feet in height; but directly he clutched me and I clutched him in turn, I found that he was of herculean build, and by no means a foe to be despised.

Was he a man? It seemed so, for he fought upon two legs. And yet was there ever a human being so covered with hair? Wherever I touched him 'twas as thick as a dog's coat, only coarser and more matted.

Gripped together and reeling to and fro, I tried to taunt him into speech, for I felt that could I hear him utter a single articulate word, no matter in what language, the spell that hung over him would be broken, and much of dread and horror being dissipated, I should fight him on more equal terms, and with more confidence of victory.

But nought would he utter but a strange kind of jabbering and hissing that was unearthly in the extreme, whilst I could hear his great teeth constantly grinding and clashing together, though he no longer made any attempt to bite.

That he understood the principles of wrestling was very plain, for he frequently threw a clumsy, and, as I could feel, very handy leg around mine, in an attempt to trip me up, and dug his hard bony knuckles into my back to throw me over.

I soon began to be conscious that I should go to the wall the first.

Though a very giant in stature compared to my antagonist, his strength far exceeded mine.

He had suffered me to exhaust myself, playing with me meantime; but when he saw that I could no longer resist him successfully, he put out his whole strength, and down I went to the ground again. Then, by a prodigious effort of strength, I managed to push him through the aperture into the open air. No sooner had I got him there than my overtaxed strength gave way.

Once more, then, he leapt on my body, clutched my throat with his deadly talons, and bit with a savage snarl at my fingers whenever I attempted to clutch his wrists with them.

Then, and not till then, I screamed for help.

As I did so the fiery eyes enlarged, and an angry snarling growl escaped my antagonist's lips.

I screamed again, but the words seemed to gurgle inaudibly up through my throat, whilst at the same time my eyes felt as though starting from their sockets. There was a strange rush of blood to my head, a sensation of departing consciousness, a painful and horrible feeling of suffocation.

At this critical juncture, however, when Death was so near that his arrival could only have been calculated by seconds, there was a flash as of torches, the reverberation of a shot, and, with a howl of mingled rage and agony, my murderer relaxed his grasp on my throat, sprang to an upright position, howled again, and then fell back across me dead.

I struggled to my own feet then, and, though my rescuer—Schamyl himself—was hurrying towards me with his rifle still smoking in his hand, my first glance was towards the foe he had rid me of.

I own that I was not much surprised at discovering him to be an enormous ape, with almost as great a girth of chest as an African gorilla.

I recollected having read that such a breed of apes inhabited the mountainous defiles of the Caucasus. Doubtless this one had made his home in some snug little hollow at the end of the subterranean in which our beds had been laid.

Schamyl asked me if I was hurt, and, on my stating that my injuries were but slight, declared his satisfaction thereat in no stinted terms.

In fact, in all save a very sore and tender throat, and a most painful finger, where the ape had bitten it, I felt nearly myself again—so much so, that it only needed a drain of brandy and some sticking-plaster to set me all right.

I knew, however, that no brandy was to be obtained from such devout Mussulmen as the Caucasians; so I thanked Schamyl first of all for his rescue, and then complimented him on his good aim, which, in sober verity, had been a wonderful one, taking into account the flickering and uncertain torchlight and the way in which the ape and myself were huddled up together.

We then made our way back to the cavern, and I began asking questions about the habitat of the beast.

Presently he interrupted me by asking with some surprise and concern what had become of my companion.

I looked round. Count Eugene's bed was empty!

CHAPTER XLIII.

SCHAMYL DREAMS AND I SUSPECT.

"CAN craven fear have made your friend desert you in the moment of danger?" asked Schamyl.

"He is as bold as a lion," I rejoined; "I never saw his courage shaken, even by the most deadly peril."

"Then what can have become of him?" exclaimed the Prophet Prince. "We must make a search."

A search was made throughout the cave in every direction, but no Count Eugene was to be found.

"This is very strange," said Schamyl. "'Tis plain that he has quitted the cave, and quitted it surreptitiously, for some special purpose; for no man would walk abroad for pleasure—or, at all events, no man of western origin—on such a night as this. I half suspect your friend to be a traitor."

"To be a traitor?" I gasped.

"Yes, a traitor. A wolf in sheep's clothing. I have had my suspicions from the first. Have you entertained none?"

"None—that is to say——"

I paused, remembering that I had from time to time entertained frequent and many.

"Ah! I see I am right," said Schamyl, with a quiet smile; "this is not the first time that Count Eugene has acted unaccountably. His name is Polish, but his features are peculiarly Russian. He declares that he represents France, even as you represent England; yet at our conference you gave a brief statement of facts, and he spoke only empty wind. I watched his face closely and keenly whilst you were speaking, and, though he masked his features admirably, yet did he seem to be more astounded at your disclosures than ever I was, who did not in the least expect them."

"I know that he was really and veritably despatched by the allied generals, even as I was," I made answer. "I was introduced to him by and in the tent of British commander-in-chief, who seemed to be well acquainted with and to put great confidence in him.

"It is very strange," said Schamyl; "for your cries awoke me from a dream wherein both of you figured prominently, and my dreams are ever prophetical of the future or true pictures of the past."

"What might have been your dream?" I asked.

"I will tell you," answered Schamyl, gravely. "I dreamt that the right men set out from the allied camp, but that they were taken prisoners by the Russians, who shot the patriot Pole, and substituted in his place a wily Muscovite, who bore a most wonderful likeness to him, in order that he might accompany you hither, gather the reasons of your journey to the Caucasus, and send the information to his own people. You were just leaving your prison in his company, and crossing a grim walled yard by the light of a lantern, when your cries awoke me, and I rushed to your rescue."

I was so astounded by the relation of the Prophet Prince's dream, that for more than a minute I could not reply with a single word.

The sight of that Russian lazar-house, mis-called a prison, and the courtyard wherein lay the corpse of him whom I had come to the sad conclusion must have been Louis Foucarte, recurred to my memory so forcibly, as to be absolutely painful.

Then came the rapid and sudden thoughts: Was it Louis Foucarte who was still with me?—had he been a Russian agent and spy all along?—had he deserted me at Balaclava to go straight to Sebastopol, thinking that I could be of no farther use to him, and that, when I and the Pole were taken prisoners thither, had he procured the execution of the latter in order that in his dress and name, he might accompany me to the Caucasus, and there gain still more information that might be useful to his Government? Pooh! the idea was too romantic and improbable; so I dismissed it from my mind at once.

I could not but confess that Schamyl's dream bore a most startling resemblance to what had really occurred within the walls of Sebastopol however, and the Prophet Prince declared that an immediate search should be made for Count Eugene.

CHAPTER XLIV.

TWO TRAITORS DETECTED.

IT must have been about an hour past midnight when we set forth from the cave.

Schamyl would not permit anyone to accompany us.

It was icy cold, and I was astonished to see some hundreds of Circassian warriors sleeping on the exposed mountain side, in the deep snow, as comfortably and cosily to all appearance as though reposing on couches of down in the bedroom of a well-appointed hotel.

I expressed my surprise to my companion, but Schamyl was equally astonished at other people not doing the same in other climes.

"In our country to do so would be death," I said.

"Then it must be much colder in your country?"

"No," I answered; "it is cooler in summer, but far less cold in winter. We never have such an icy wind or such deep snows as yon seem to have here, and yet the strongest of us could not sleep out of doors a single night in a snow drift without paying the penalty of his hardihood with his life."

"Oh, then your people cannot be so strong and robust as ours," said Schamyl. "Let us now look for footprints."

"If we find them, we shall scarcely be able to follow them up without torches," I replied.

"Oh, yes, we shall; the night is dark, but the snow is white. You will see clearly enough presently. Had we brought torches, those whom we wish to surprise would see us from afar off and easily evade us."

"Those!" I ejaculated; "are we in search of more than one?"

"Yes, oh, friend of my soul! we are in search of two—a traitor unto me and a traitor unto thee, but not united in the same person. Listen, and, whilst looking for the tracks, I will tell you of him whom you know not.

"A week or ten days ago a deserter came to us from the Russian ranks. He was a Circassian born and bred, but a dozen years ago, in a sortie from Temir-haw Toura, he was captured by the Russians, and forced to serve in their armies—a usual fate with our unfortunates. Well, we gave him a hearty welcome, a horse and arms, but, ere he had been with us two days, I could see that he was no longer a true son of the Caucasus, and ere four had elapsed I half suspected that he had come back amongst us as a Russian spy.

"I have waited for some proof of his guilt, and believe that we shall find it to-night. When I awoke I missed him from my side, where, for special reasons, I had allowed him to sleep. My idea is that we shall find him and Count Eugene, as he calls himself, together—that, in fact, the one was sent hither to await the arrival of the other. Ha! this looks as though I were right indeed. Here is a double track leading towards the summit of the mountain."

I bent down.

I could see it plainly too.

"Draw your cloak closely around you," said Schamyl. "Let no gleam of pistol-barrel or sword-scabbard betray our approach in the semi-darkness. We can still converse, for the direction from which the wind blows will carry away the sound of our voices."

I muttered an assent, though I had nothing to talk about.

"I had a better opinion of this man at first," said Schamyl, still harping on the same theme, "for when he deserted he brought with him two pet pigeons, which he declared that he loved as his own life; and I have generally found that people who can warmly attach themselves to dumb animals or to flowers are to be depended on. There are, I suppose, exceptions to the rule."

I should think that there were indeed. Directly I heard of the pet pigeons, I became every whit as suspicious as Schamyl himself—nay, even more so.

No longer did I feel the cutting wind in my face, or heed the deadly numbness that beset my nose, toes, and finger tips.

I felt that my travelling companion, Count Eugene, Louis Foucarte, or whoever else he might be, was at all events a traitor and a spy, and that Schamyl's deserter was an accomplice, with *carrier* pigeons sent purposely to meet him here, and promptly despatch, by means of his sagacious birds, to the Russian armies of Europe and Asia, intelligence of whatever understanding I came to with the Prophet Prince.

The track was not difficult to follow, and the snow was, happily, soft and deep, instead of frozen and slippery.

Taking advantage of every bit of shadow that offered itself, and at other times frequently creeping on all-fours, so as to resemble wild animals more than men, we ascended higher and higher, until suddenly the flutter of wings caught my ear, and, looking up, I saw a grey-and-white bird rise from behind a rugged rock.

I at once plucked my revolver from my belt and fired.

The first shot took no effect, but, undismayed at this, I discharged barrel after barrel until at last the bird dropped to the ground mortally hurt.

I sprang forward and picked it up.

'Twas even as I suspected—a small scrap of paper was attached to its left leg.

"How foolish! you have spoilt all," said Schamyl.

"On the contrary, I have saved all," was my rejoinder.

I untied the scrap of paper from the pigeon's leg, unfolded it, and read aloud the following:—

"*Forty thousand Turks, with* 120 *guns, attack Tiflis on the* 26*th. Concentrate armies of Prince Bebuloff and General Kemti thereat by forced marches. Mount every gun on the walls. Relief will soon come.*"—J. R.

Schamyl stood as one thunderstruck; he had evidently never heard of a carrier pigeon before.

"Would that bird have flown all the way to Tiflis?"

"Yes," I replied, "for doubtless he was brought from there for the especial purpose of being sent back thus loaded."

Before Schamyl could make reply we were both seized from behind with no gentle grasp.

So strong was my own assailant that he had hurled me to the ground in a twinkling.

Schamyl, after an ineffectual struggle, shared the same fate.

Our cowardly assailants then bound us, and ordered us to march quietly before them, on pain of being shot.

CHAPTER XLV.

COUNT EUGENE UNMASKS.

WE had no course left open to us but to obey.

Count Eugene was doubly as strong as myself, and the Russian spy who had overcome Schamyl was a perfect giant, being little, if anything, less than seven feet in height, and possessed of proportionate girth.

Threatening us with instant death should we utter a cry for succour, or make any unnecessary noise, they drove us before them for some distance up the mountain, and then in through a small hole, scarcely large enough to admit the passage of our bodies, into a small cave that would have held about a dozen men closely packed.

A fire of dried cow's dung burned at one end, and in a kind of rough cage beside it I saw, to my joy, the second pigeon.

"What means this conduct?" I demanded angrily of Count Eugene, directly I found myself at liberty to speak without having my brains blown out.

"Am I, then, to believe the worst of you?"

"You are at liberty to believe what you like, since you will die within the hour," was the reply.

"What! do you intend to murder us?"

"You have forced upon me the necessity, *mon ami*. I am not naturally a bloodthirsty man, but when I am driven to choose between the sacrifice of other lives and my own, why on such occasions even my nearest and dearest friends go to the wall, as a matter of course."

He spoke lightly, mockingly almost, and his eyes seemed to blaze with a savage glee that was more devilish than human.

"But if you can clear yourself from the suspicious circumstances that surround you, your life will be in no danger soever," I rejoined.

"That cannot be done; you know it well enough, *bon garçon*. The mask can be worn no longer, so I will throw it aside as useless. I confess that I am a Russian—that I have danced in attendance upon you from the hour of your leaving the Foreign Office in London until now, with the exception of a brief holiday that I took upon our first landing at Balaclava, and that during that period I have sent frequent and important intelligence to my Emperor and his generals, founded on the contents of your despatch bags, and what not."

"Then you *are* Louis Foucarte?" I stammered.

"Amongst other fictitious characters, yes."

"And not Count Eugene Pollaki?"

"Yes, him also if you like," was the retort.

"But who are you really? A doomed man may surely have his curiosity gratified in such trifles."

"I am one for whom your British Admiral off Pera was ready to give an immense reward for the capture of, either alive or dead. The fool! to gratify his wish I breakfasted with him, and yet he let me go scot free. Of all the dullards on the face of the earth, you Englishmen are the worst."

"But you disarmed the Admiral's suspicions by the birth-mark of the skull and cross-bones," I rejoined.

"Which were specially drawn and painted for the purpose. Do you see anything of them now?"

He pushed the hair up off his temples.

The mark of skull and bones was utterly gone.

"You are a clever villain," I said; "but I had my suspicions of you in the tent of the commander-in-chief."

"Scarcely, for I never was there."

"Never there?" I stammered.

"Assuredly not. You were therein introduced to the real Count Eugene Pollaki, a Polish deserter from Sebastopol. When you two were captured by the Cossacks, and brought into Sebastopol, the Count was shot, as any other deserter would have been, and I again had the honour of becoming your travelling companion," said the accomplished spy, with a deprecating shrug of the shoulders.

"Then the story of a great grief told by Louis Foucarte, and the tale of Ghost Glen narrated by Count Eugene, were merely ingenious pieces of fiction got up to deceive me?" I asked.

"Exactly so" was the retort. "The first was founded upon the poem which you heard me singing to General Mouraviffe, and narrated to dissipate your rapidly gathering suspicions; and the latter was wholly imaginary, and told, as well as I can recollect, for very much the same reasons. Should I not make a good novelist?"

"Excellent," I rejoined; "and I am glad that you confess at last that there was a Russian officer with you in the Tartar hut the night that I swore to you that I saw him there. Now tell me, if you will be so good, what made you save my life so often from other Russian spies (for I know them to have been such), whom we met in threes so frequently on the road?"

"Because they were ignorant fellows, who could not distinguish between a rook and a crow. They would have slain the goose for the sake of the one golden egg that is carried in its despatch bag. I, however, received special instructions that this goose was of so rare a breed that it would continue to lay egg after egg, each one of larger proportions than the preceding, and so I was to pay it close attention, and carefully abstract each egg as it was laid. The egg that was dropped at Pera any of our common hands might have taken, by killing the goose in the Dover train, on the Paris platform, in the Mont Cenis pass, on board the Austrian Lloyd's steamer, or even in the streets of Stamboul, but these bunglers could have done no more; they could not have broken and devoured the contents of the egg laid for the breakfast table of the British Commander-in-chief before Sebastopol, nor the far finer one that was to form a *bon bouche* for Schamyl, Prophet and Prince of the Caucasus, and now our prisoner along with the goose in question;" and the wily Russ bowed and smiled ironically.

I felt so enraged, that, had I not been bound, I would assuredly have sprung upon and strangled the grinning spy where he stood.

Our conversation being carried on in French, Schamyl did not understand it.

My curiosity to know more mastered, however, my rage, and I again eagerly questioned him.

"How did you know the nature of my despatches to the Admiral, the Sultan, and the Commander-in-Chief? I kept the closest watch and ward over them."

"Except when you slept. Upon four occasions I drugged your wine ere you retired to your cabin, or your hotel bedroom. I then came in, for I had duplicate keys of every door, and opened your despatch-bag with a quill-pen. Yes, it may seem strange; but I know the way for all that, and read and studied your papers, whilst you comfortably snoozed."

"But my despatch-bag possessed two Bramah locks."

"My little bits of quill-pen were too strong for them though. Properly handled, they will open any lock."

"But you left one ere I delivered those addressed to the British Commander-in-Chief?"

"Not before I had perused them though. I landed in such hot haste at Balaclava, in order to place the information in the hands of our generals before it could reach yours, which a band of Cossacks were to endeavour to prevent its ever doing, by making you prisoner whilst on your way to the camp. They seem to have done so; but you escaped them. Your information, however, reached your Commander-in-Chief too late to be of any service, for ere then we had taken measures to guard against the measures that he was instructed to adopt."

"Curses upon you!" I exclaimed, no longer able to control my passion. "Unbind my arms; give me back my sword, and I will quickly punish you for all this despicable spying and surveillance!"

"And you actually expect me to assist you in doing so? Come, that is rather cool!" laughed the Russian. "But you should have the modesty to remember that, when I have given you the chance of punishing me with the sword, you have proved yourself to be scarcely competent to do so."

I bit my lips in silence, for this was a home thrust.

"Ah!" said the Russian, with a sneer. "I see that you remember. Be content, then, with the fate that is in store for you—for you and for this barbarian who calls himself a prophet, and whom you would stir up to wage war against holy Russia as well. Just outside this cave there is a round deep hole in the ground, that is reported to be bottomless. A stone thrown into it rebounds against the sides with ever fainter and fainter reverberation until it at last ceases to be audible, and yet finds no resting place. You two shall explore its depths, and then come back if you can and tell us all about them. Ha! ha! ha! What

AS THE SHOT TOOK EFFECT, THE HORSE REARED, AND BOTH RIDER AND HORSE DISAPPEARED DOWN THE YAWNING ABYSS.

fun, to send a Queen's Messenger with despatches to the centre of the earth. A new route, my friend——eh?"

I did not reply—the thought was too horrible.

The Russian turned to Schamyl, and in English gave him the same explanation as to his fate.

The Prophet Prince thereupon replied in the same language—

"You may try, but you will not succeed. Heaven decrees for its servant a very different death from that to which you would doom him. Perhaps the very gulph in which you have determined to hurl us will instead swallow you up," said Schamyl, solemnly.

"That we will soon see," retorted the Russian, with a fierce oath. "Ivan, help me drive our prisoners forth and to cast them into the pit that has no bottom. We can then return and despatch the other pigeon with later and still more important intelligence than the first could have taken, even had these fools let it live."

He glared at us in turn as he spoke, pointing meanwhile to the other bird.

Then Ivan and he drove us out of the cave through the narrow opening, even as they had driven us in, by a liberal application of their sword-scabbards to our persons.

CHAPTER XLVI.
THE TURNING OF THE TABLES.

FORTH from the cave we were half led, half dragged, hastily pushed round a sharp escarpment of rock, and there at our very feet yawned a horrible crevasse in the mountain's side, which seemed to split it asunder to its very base, a thousand fathoms of pitchy darkness.

"You remember the Devil's Ridge," said Louis Foucarte with a sneer; "I saved you then, did I not? You were still useful, you know. Now I have squeezed you dry, like a sponge."

I made no reply.

In my hideous position I could not give taunt for taunt.

The winner has ever the right end of the joke, and I was the loser.

How I envied Schamyl his imperturbable calmness, for his features might have been hewn from marble, for any emotion they betrayed.

He was telling his beads, like a devout Mussulman. They engrossed all his thoughts.

Louis Foucarte and his accomplice conversed for a moment in Russian, each grasping us tightly the while, and then they bade us leap into the abyss.

"That would be self-murder, a crime which admits of no repentance," said Schamyl, calmly. "We will relieve you of no portion of your sin, so consummate yourselves what you have commenced, for the deed will be in every way worthy of you."

"'Twill lie very lightly on our consciences, old gentleman, I can assure you," answered Foucarte, with a reckless laugh. "Ivansvitch, I will pitch the Englishman over, and do you serve the Prophet in the like manner. His pretended sorcery and hocus-pocus won't serve his turn now, I imagine."

I felt his grasp on my collar tighten. I knew that his fingers were contracting for a sudden and strong push.

With my arms bound to my side, and my legs also loosely secured, I was perfectly powerless to resist.

I believe my hair stood erect, and my blood turned to ice during the awful moment of suspense that followed.

I say moment, instead of moments, advisably, for it could have been but one, when I saw Schamyl, as I supposed, launched headlong into space, and scarcely had my eyes fixed upon his descending figure, when I myself fell, not forward into the gulf, but backwards on the frozen snow.

I believe that I fainted, but if so my swoon

must have been of very short duration, for when recovered therefrom Schamyl was at my side, a group of armed murids were around us, and Louis Foucarte was standing on the brink of the precipice above, and bound, even as I had been.

"I thought I saw you falling down the crevasse," I said to Schamyl.

"It was the villain Ivansvitch," was the reply. "Just as he was in the act of pushing me over, the holy murid Mereddin pulled me back from the brink of the abyss with one hand, whilst with a buffet from the other he sent the traitor to explore its depth. Truly God is great, and the camel-driver is his Prophet.

"Some one must have saved me in a like manner," I said.

"The murid Empoli preserved you even as the murid Mereddin rescued me," was the reply; "had they not advanced with the swift yet velvet tread of the panther, so that their approach was not heard until their clutch was felt, we should now have been where we are about to despatch the arch spy and traitor who accompanied you hither."

I now noticed for the first time that Foucarte stood with his back to the abyss, and that at a distance of about twelve paces from him, about half-a-dozen Circassians were ramming home charges in their rifles.

He saw my glance first at him and then at his executioners, and shrugging his shoulders, said, with a laugh—

"*C'est le malheur de guerre*, Monsieur Dunbar. Quite a little melodrama of the Port St. Martin or the Victoria kind, is it not?" I wonder if those gentlemen are such slow loaders and bad marksmen as to give me time to do a cigarette before they send me *en voyage*."

His glossy black moustaches curled in a smile that showed all his white teeth, and he proceeded to roll up a cigarette as calmly as though he was seated at a café, and merely waiting for a cup of *café au lait* or a *demi lasse* of brandy.

I could not but admire his consummate coolness, not one particle of which I had myself possessed when occupying the same unenviable position five minutes previously.

The Circassians, I think, experienced the same feeling.

Heroic themselves, they could not but admire heroism in another, even though it was of so distinct and different a type. Their admiration did not incline them to mercy, however.

The ramrods were refixed, the death-dealing tubes were levelled, and, simultaneously with the shrill command to fire, Foucarte dropped his cigarette, smilingly bowed to his executioners, and, with a meaning glance at me, awaited his doom.

It was not an instant in coming.

The dozen rifles rang out as one, and Foucarte clapped his left hand on his chest, turned deadly white, and then toppled over backwards into the terrible abyss, in a moment passing out of sight.

"So perish all spies and traitors," said Schamyl calmly. "The villain has done more harm than three thousand open foes would have been capable of effecting, but yet we should be deeply grateful that Allah did not permit him to do more—that we do not at this instant lie as he does, at the bottom of that abyss of perpetual night."

And, rising, Schamyl led the way back to the cave.

CHAPTER XLVII.
I AM INTRODUCED TO ILLUSTRIOUS PRISONERS.

AFTER we had partaken of a substantial breakfast, for day had by this time dawned, and the Circassians breakfast at sunrise and sup at sunset, taking no more between, a cabinet council was held in the Hall of the Murids.

A stormy and puzzling debate ensued—a debate to which I could give very little assistance, for none of us knew with any certainty whether a previous pigeon might not have been despatched to the Commander-in-Chief of the Russian army of Asia, with a full account of our deliberations and plans.

Schamyl determined to act, however, as if such was not the case, and, with his army of mountain warriors, to seize and hold the great military road as soon as possible.

Then the question arose, would it not be wise for me to push on through Georgia to Kars, and from thence on to the army of Omar Pasha, warning Sir William Williams, the gallant Englishman who held the former place against such overwhelming odds, and the equally gallant Hungarian who had embraced Islamism, and was now the boldest and most skilful general in the Ottoman army, that our carefully matured plans might all be frustrated, and so to attempt to carry them out with greater circumspection and caution.

"But how am I, an English officer, unacquainted with the Russian tongue, to traverse the whole of Georgia, which swarms with their troops, without being taken prisoner?" I asked.

"That part of the business is easily managed," replied the Prophet Chief. "We have here as prisoners, the Russian Princess Chafchevadsey and her daughter Katinka. I have set them up to ransom at twenty thousand roubles, and their relatives and friends have already paid eighteen thousand on account. Now, under the circumstances, I will let them off what remains due, and you shall escort the princess and her daughter back to Prince Chafchevadsey, the husband and father, who happens to be the very Russian General who is investing Kars. They will be the very best of safe-conducts through Georgia, and ensure your arriving in perfect safety at all events as far as Kars."

"The idea is a superb one," I replied; "and though I have no instructions, either from my Government or from the allied generals, to proceed farther, yet under the circumstances I will take upon myself the responsibility of doing so, for my official duties are all carried out, and I am to a certain extent my own master."

Schamyl was evidently pleased at my decision; he signed to the other murids to withdraw, and to one of them he gave some whispered instructions, the result being that this particular murid presently returned, leading with each hand a prisoner, evidently the two Russian princesses.

One, the elder, was a tall and majestic looking woman of forty; the other a beautiful maiden of nineteen.

That they were mother and daughter was evident at a glance, for they were, to use the language of the poet, "alike, yet oh, how different!"

As may readily be imagined, the younger lady attracted my attention the most, for hers was a peculiar type of loveliness, with her immense masses of jet-black shining hair. Her well-arched brows and long drooping lashes, equally ebon, but veiled soft gentle eyes of the deepest violet. As to her features, they were classically Grecian, her complexion creamily delicate, her figure petite but exquisite in its proportions, and her smile the sweetest, I think, that I had ever witnessed.

I was introduced by Schamyl as a Christian officer who had offered to be their escort through Georgia, and he informed them that though he had not received their full ransom, yet he could not allow so favourable an opportunity to pass of returning them in honour to their own people as a present.

The ladies thanked him, and regarded me, as I thought, with some favour.

The eldest princess addressed me in French, and was evidently delighted that I could converse with her so fluently in that language.

The result was that my escort was most graciously accepted, and Schamyl thanked, with much volubility, for setting them at freedom before the full indemnity was paid over.

"It shall be honourably forwarded, nevertheless," said the elder princess; "together with the full value of any horses that you may lend us to perform the journey."

* * * *

Half-an-hour later we were in the saddle.

The elder princess riding the horse that had belonged to Louis Foucarte, alias Count Eugene Pollaki, and the younger, a beautiful Circassian pony that had been presented to her as a free gift by Schamyl. I, of course, was mounted on my own tried steed.

The princesses bade the Warrior Prophet adieu, more as if he had been their father, than their captor and gaoler.

It was very plain that they had received naught but kindness and consideration from his hands.

I own that I was rather sorry to bid so fine a modern representative of our own middle ages farewell myself, but "necessitas non habet legem," so I wrung his hand, lamenting that the laws of the Prophet permitted no stirrup-cup of sparkling wine, threw myself into the saddle, and galloped after my fair charges, who, in company with the mounted guide lent us by our host, had got some way in advance, while Schamyl was giving me parting assurances that if a single soldier of the Russian army of Asia succeeded in crossing the Caucasus alive it should not be his fault.

Once fairly on our journey, I found the ladies most agreeable, which was more than might have been expected with so long and fatiguing a journey before them.

As the guide, a wild, extraordinary looking warrior in chain mail and armed to the teeth, understood no language but his own, we were able to converse unrestrainedly.

I asked the elder princess how they came to fall into the Warrior Prophet's hands, and she answered me as follows—

"Were I to confess that we had been captured in such a manner by any foe but Schamyl and his mountain warriors, it would be imputing a disgrace to our own brave soldiers. The Circassians, however, are such an extraordinary race of people—so patriotic, so brave, and so unconquerable—that I feel no reluctance to make you acquainted with the full facts of the case exactly as they occurred.

"A very few words will suffice to tell the tale.

"Three thousand of our best troops were encamped under the fortress of Vedago, within full shelter of its guns.

"Sentinels were posted, and every precaution taken, for my husband, Prince Paul Chafchevadsey, had the supreme command.

"I and my daughter had a tent in the very centre of the camp, where we naturally deemed ourselves to be as safe as within the walls of our palace at St. Petersburg.

"At midnight, however, we were awakened by some one in our tent, and, before we could give the alarm, we were seized, gagged and bound, carried out in strong arms, and placed on horseback. Our captors sprang up behind us, and we were borne with lightning speed towards the mountains.

"Many of our soldiers woke up and offered resistance, but were cut down like autumn wheat.

"Once, I believe at least a hundred mounted dragoons threw themselves across the path of our captors, but they withstood not the Circassian charge for more than a brief second, when they were all stretched dead or dying on the plain. A whole squadron of cavalry sent in pursuit failed to overtake and deliver us, and an hour later we had ascended the forest defiles and were captives in Schamyl's care."

"Rather a dashing exploit," I remarked.

"You will say so when I tell you how many warriors accompanied him on the expedition," said the princess.

"I should not wonder if he only had as many hundreds as your army had thousands," I hazarded at a guess.

"Your conjecture does you credit, but you are far out, notwithstanding," answered the princess, with a smile, "for Schamyl had with him only twenty men, and of that small number he took back with him fifteen alive."

"And what were your own losses ? "

"Ah, that we have never been able to learn," sighed the princess, "for we have been captives ever since ; but at least a score must have been slain, and thrice as many wounded."

"And has Schamyl treated you kindly in captivity ? " I asked, scarcely knowing what to say.

"Had we been his daughters he could not have been kinder or more considerate," answered the princess. "We leave him with a deep respect for his chivalrous and noble character, with a keen appreciation of his many excellent qualities, and with a great regret that the policy of Russia should aim at wresting from him the dominions that he is so worthy to reign over."

She fell into a reverie, and I was not sorry, for it gave me more time to study the charming countenance of Katinka, my taste ever having been to prefer daughters to mothers, when the latter are the shady side of forty, and the former the sunny side of fifteen.

When Katinka began to talk in turn, her voice was like the sound of silver bells, a voice which it would have been pleasanter to listen to had it talked nothing but nonsense, than that of the greatest philosopher emitting wisdom at every monosyllable.

Suddenly the badinage and merry ringing laughter changed into an exclamation of terror.

Following the direction of her terrified gaze, I saw an enormous tiger standing in the middle of the road and lashing its sides with its tail.

The terrible-looking brute was between us and our Circassian guide, who was riding leisurely on, about a couple of hundred yards in advance.

I knew that some writers had asserted the existence of tigers in the Caucasus, whilst others had laughed them to scorn, declaring the formidable animal was totally unfitted to inhabit such a climate.

The brute who barred our path was most unmistakably a tiger, and a large one too.

Not so immense, certainly, as those of Bengal, and considerably darker in colour, its fur being more an umber than an ochre, but it had the true tiger stripes and great massive head, and was no more like a panther, a puma, or a leopard than it was like a seagull or an old woman.

It was crouching for the spring as I drew forth a pistol and aimed it at its head.

Happily, it was a revolver, so I had six chances of settling him.

My horse trembled so that I knew it would be a case of chance entirely.

As for the Princess Katinka's steed, it was rearing violently, and the Princess Chafchevadsey's had wheeled round with her, and was fleeing madly down the pass.

"Crack ! " went three barrels of my revolver, and then I paused to see the effect of my fire.

Glorious ! the tiger was crippled in two of its legs.

It had fallen in the middle of a spring—a spring that, had it not been arrested in mid-course by my bullets, would have enabled the brute to fasten its talons in the swelling breast or rounded limbs of the beauteous Katinka.

Though crippled, it was not yet placed hors de combat, however, and the way it gnashed its great yellow fangs as it now crept, instead of bounding, towards me, emitting meanwhile the most terrible roars, was awful to behold.

I was about to discharge the remaining barrels of my revolver at it, when I saw our Circassian guide coming down the pass at a headlong gallop.

He made a sign to me not to fire, and so I recovered my weapon, wondering the while what his intention could be, and set myself to curb and control the prancings, rearings, and kickings of the Princess Katinka's horse.

In this I presently succeeded, and I had just complimented her in French on her splendid seat in the saddle, when she uttered a cry of surprise, and, again following the direction of her gaze, I saw that the Circassian was dismounted and on foot, attacking the tiger sword in hand.

It was a daring deed, for, though crippled, the immense and savage brute was not one whit disabled in any other way, and its fangs were as hungry for human flesh as ever.

We both expected to see the man get the worst of it, and we peered anxiously through the cloud of dust that encircled the light, to see how he fared.

I determined to restore the balance of power with a bullet or two directly. I clearly saw that he was getting the worst of it, for I knew that in that case alone would he excuse my interference.

I had no opportunity of offering my aid, however, for after about five minutes' hot and close engagement, we saw the Circassian standing with one foot on the dead body of the tiger, whilst leisurely wiping the blood from off his sword-blade with a wisp of grass.

With one strong and well-directed lunge he had reached his antagonist's heart.

He returned his trusty weapon to its scabbard, remounted, and rode backward down the park in search of the Princess Chafchevadsey, as calmly and composedly as though he had just performed the most common-place achievement.

She was discovered calmly riding back to rejoin us, for she had at last succeeded in bringing her runaway under control.

We then resumed our march southwards.

CHAPTER XLVIII.
WITH THE WANDERING KALMUCKS.

AFTER following the course of the Karakcouban river for many days, sleeping on beds of dry fern in caves of a night, and living for the most part on dried caviare (sturgeon roes) and chamois flesh, with sometimes a jerked hare, trapped overnight, for a dainty, we at last reached the grim Marsukh Dag mountain, and crossed it into Mingrelia, bidding an eternal farewell to the Caucasus.

At Patzow, the first frontier town, our guide bade us adieu, solemnly calling down the blessing of Allah on our heads.

We were sorry to lose him, for in his rough way he was a noble fellow, but his safety would have been compromised by his proceeding further, and so there was no help for it.

He refused to accept of any reward for his services, being evidently as proud as he was poor—a common attribute of the inhabitants of mountainous regions.

After he had gone, we travelled on and on, generally sleeping in wretched inns now, though they scarcely deserved the names of huts, until we reached Nagameri.

Here we came to more mountains, and in crossing them I had a most strange and ludicrous adventure, which, however, might have ended very seriously.

Evening was just changing into night, and we were all three wondering whether we should be able to find a cave to sleep in, or have to camp out wrapped in our furs, on the bleak mountain side, when I noticed a fire burning brightly a little way down a deep and narrow gorge.

We drew rein, and for a minute or two pondered upon what was best to be done under the circumstances.

The clearly-blazing fire was a pleasant prospect to half frozen travellers, but then those who lighted it might be very objectionable, in fact, most unsafe characters to enter amongst at any time, leave alone at night.

It was proposed then that I should go forward and reconnoitre, leaving the ladies some way up the pass; so, resigning to them the custody of my horse, go forward I did, and from behind a great fragment of rock, I obtained a very good and comprehensive view of the encampment.

It was somewhat a large one, and there were women and children, which gave me some confidence in my travelling companions being awarded a kind reception.

They looked by no means fierce either, even though they were dressed in the most gorgeous of oriental garbs, and were armed with ivory-handled, velvet-sheathed scimitars, long pistols, with jewel-inlaid stocks, and knives and daggers, *ad infinitum*, hung, strung, and stuck here, there, and everywhere.

But their features, though half concealed by the voluminous folds of their great yellow and crimson turbans, looked grave and benign, and in every way trustworthy, and so I concluded that they were merely armed for self-defence, and determined upon trusting to them.

Quitting my place of concealment, I advanced boldly into their midst, salaaming right and left, and then popping a finger in my mouth, and patting my stomach with my disengaged hand, to show that it was in urgent need of being revictualled.

The orientals nodded and grinned, and pointed towards a second fire, where I perceived that their women were engaged in rather extensive culinary operations.

I pointed towards those women, and then towards the defile, where I had left the two princesses; patted my stomach, and popped my finger in my mouth once more, thereafter holding up my thumbs to signify that I had two female companions in as bad a state as I was.

My pantomime was perfectly understood, and in return dumb show they bade me return and fetch my companions, which I proceeded to do, fully persuaded now that we had fallen amongst most hospitable folk.

I told my princesses what had happened, and my opinion of those who had offered us hospitality.

The elder made me describe their dress and general appearance as closely as I could, and then expressed her opinion that they were a wandering tribe of Gouriel Kalmucks, who were oft-times very rich, being, in fact, travelling merchants, who worshipped the sun and revered the ashes of their fathers, which they carried about with them from place to place; but that they were by no means either treacherous or bloodthirsty, though strongly addicted to horse-stealing whenever they came across animals worth the taking.

On this account, we determined to walk into the oriental encampment, and the princesses rode down to the spot where I had left my horse, and discovering a small cave, we led them all into it, and I tore down, and flung in a lot of green ferns and long tussochy grass that grew around its mouth, for we had long ago left the land of glaciers and snow behind us, and reached a region where the nights were not much colder than they are in England, during the month of April or early May.

When we had done this I gave to each of the princesses a hand, and in this melodramatic fashion we descended the hill, and walked up to the fire, around which my turbanned acquaintances sat, cross-legged.

Three cushions had been already placed for us, and down on them we plumped, crossing our legs, acknowledging the jabbering of our hosts with nods and wreathed smiles, and looking longingly and very continuously at the second fire, from which the most savoury smell now began to assail our nostrils.

We had not, in truth, very long to wait, though to us it seemed an age and a half.

Yellow earthenware basins, containing wooden spoons, were placed in each of our laps, and then a woman came round bearing an enormous pitcher, that she nearly staggered under the weight of, and out of which she poured about a pint of what closely resembled pea soup into each of our basins.

I was so hungry that my wooden spoon, laden with the hot thick yellow syrup, was in my mouth in a twinkling; but no sooner was it in than out again, and I was on my feet executing the most wonderful can-can possible, with the Princess Chafchevadsey for a vis-à-vis, whose steps were scarcely less remarkable than my own, whilst we both kept panting and puffing and blowing and popping out our tongues at each other as though we had been a brace of heathen Chinese.

The Princess Katinka, who had not yet tasted the yellow mess of liquid fire, stared and laughed at our antics, whilst the turbaned orientals uttered hoarse grunts of applause, fancying that we had got up the entertainment especially for their delectation, I suppose.

"Boo! ha! pu-r-r-r!" spattered the Princess Chafchevadsey, kicking up behind and before the while.

"Boo! ha! pu-r-r-r! bah!" echoed I, doing the same, and then whirling round in my agony.

"Boo! ha! pu-r-r-r!" echoed a hoarse voice, and there was the chief of the Kalmucks trying to imitate us, bounding up and down like a gutta-percha ball, his turban all awry, his legs flying hither and thither, and his rubicund face very nearly black-red.

We both of us came to a full stop at this truly remarkable sight, and dropping many tears, as much with laughter now as from the inward burning of the "hell broth," for I can call the fiery soup by no more appropriate title, watched our dancing host—his followers every whit as open-mouthed with astonishment as ourselves.

But, good heavens, what did his unearthly dance merge into, when he had no longer the princess and myself as a copy? Why, into a genuine Irish jig, as I'm a sinner.

He twirled an imaginary shelalagh, whooped, and "covered his buckles" at each step as neatly as Kathleen Mavourneen's most favoured swain, whoever he might have been, could have done.

When he had stopped from sheer fatigue, as everything from a railway engine to a blow fly must do in the end, he seemed to recollect himself, and sat down, evidently much mortified, and as he readjusted his turban, he muttered, "Allah il Allah! Allah pesal Allah!" underneath his bushy beard.

By this time all the rest of the Kalmucks had empty basins, and were clamouring vociferously for the next course, which we were just as impatient for the arrival of, hoping that it would be some fish, flesh, or fowl, that would satisfy the cravings of hunger and take away the diabolical burning that we still experienced in our throats as well.

By we, I mean, the Princess Chafchevadsey and myself; for the Princess Katinka, taking advantage of our experience, had forborne to touch the savoury mess.

Presently a lot of women came up, each bearing on a long wooden skewer a little animal trussed and roasted, of about the size of a large rat.

Whether they were rats or baby rabbits I'm sure I don't know, but as they were offered to us on nice green leaves, and we were awfully hungry, we pitched into them without the slightest scruple, and found them to be delicious.

Saucers of boiled rice succeeded to these succulent little creatures, and then hot coffee, in little tiny cups, without milk or sugar, was handed round, serving as an appropriate conclusion to the repast.

Directly the meal was over two women came up to my companions, and invited them to accompany them, pointing to a tent that stood at a little distance, and intimating by signs that they were to sleep therein.

They were perfectly understood, and the princesses having bade me good night, requesting that we might start on our journey early the next morning, bowed to our entertainers and withdrew, my eyes following the beauteous form of Katinka—on whom I could not disguise from myself that I was pretty considerably spoony—until she was out of sight.

Then I was about to intimate a desire that I should like to retire too, when the Kalmuck chief tipped me a wink that was puzzling in the extreme.

CHAPTER XLIX.

AN UNFORTUNATE PINCH OF SNUFF.

NOT content with blinking his venerable eyes, the Kalmuck chief came round and squatted on one of the vacant piles of cushions at my side.

Then he gave me a dig in the ribs with something that he had concealed under his left arm, winking away with forty-horse power the while.

I was alarmed at first, but, looking down, I perceived that, instead of the muzzle of a pistol feeling for a handy place between the ribs, it was the corked top of a strangely shaped bottle, that he he was prodding me with.

"Goot, goot, oh, Allah, how goot!" he said, winking again.

By Jove, the old boy could speak a little English!

I drew the cork and tasted it. 'Twas indeed good.

'Twas the very best old Irish whisky !

I took a good taste, and smacked my lips ardently.

The old chief was evidently much pleased at my pantomimic commendation.

He took a good pull at the bottle in turn, gasped, smacked his lips, patted his stomach and corporation, and then passed it on to his next door neighbour, who went through precisely the same ceremony, and again the bottle travelled on its course.

I was now completely mystified, for the Kalmucks, in common with the Mohammedan and all other Asiatic creeds, abjure wines and ardent spirits as liquids thrice accursed.

I had certainly got amongst rather an extraordinary set of believers and philosophers.

Now, as I said before, the bottle, which as well as I could make out was of leather, was a prodigiously large one, and so quickly did it travel round and round in a circle, there being no table for it to come to a halt on, that the Kalmucks soon gave evidence of the potency of the spirit contained therein, by their loud and unconstrained laughter, and their frequent hiccoughy declarations that Allah was great, and the camel-driver his sole prophet !"

At length, however, the chief, who had drank more whisky than any other two of us, and had been humming something sotto voce between his frequent pulls for some time past, broke out suddenly with—

"'Gramachree makruskeen, slanta gae, mavourneen :

Gramachree makruskeen lawn.'

And ain't that foine Turkish, anyhow ? "

"And be jabers, is it an Irishman after all that ye are ? " exclaimed I, falling into the humour of the thing, and delighted to find a Paddy amongst the Kalmucks.

"An Oirishman ! De the blessed Saint Pathrick —Saint Mahomet, I mane—indade ye're intirely mistaken. It's a true Turk I am—a second cousin to the Great Mogul his blessed self, an' I was never nearer the Cove o' Cork than—than—than— than——"

"Than Passage West," I responded, with a laugh. "Come, it's no good to deny it—you may be a very good Turk to everyone else, but it won't go down with me, my friend."

"Ye can't make me out to be an Oirishman at all, at all—nohow," was the petulant retort.

"I'm glad of it," said I ; "for they're a nation of dirty bog-trotters ; and as for Saint Pathrick, why he was the greatest old fool and vagabond that ever ate potatoes."

"What is it that ye're a daring to remark agin Saint Pathrick, ye spalpeen ? I'd have ye to know he was a rale Oirish gintleman o' credit and renown," exclaimed the Kalmuck chief, angrily, as he sprang to his feet, with his turban all awry again, and flung himself into a particularly good boxing attitude.

I could hardly speak for laughing, as I exclaimed—

"What can a jolly old Turk like you know about Saint Patrick, the patron of old Ireland ? "

Dull of comprehension as the whisky had made him, he saw well enough that I had abused Saint Patrick and the Irish people to make him put his foot in it beyond recall, and so he flopped down again on his cushions, and held out to me his hand.

"I was a ribil, and so now I'm an outcast," he said, with a genuine touch of feeling. "But still God bless auld Ireland. I've presarved the sacret of distilling her whisky, and that is all that I have presarved ; so woe betide the hour that I was timpted to take up with them Peep o' Day Boys, for they was the ruin ov me at all, at all."

He subsided into a deep, and apparently an unpleasant reverie, seeing him in which state, I suppose, my left hand neighbour thought that a little attention would be polite on his part.

Anyhow, he pulled from out a pocket what I took to be an immense antique snuff-box, evidently of pure gold, unscrewed the lid, and handed it to me.

"A funny looking snuff, in all conscience," I muttered to myself ; and so it was, for the mixture was of a pale ashen grey ; but, fancying that it would be very impolite on my part to decline the proffered courtesy, I dipped my finger and thumb into the box and took a pinch.

Pshaw, what a diabolical flavour it had to be sure ! 'Twas frightfully pungent, however, and made me sneeze at once, so I concluded that it must be some wondrous compound or other peculiar to Kalmuck tastes.

But what was my surprise to behold the offerer of the snuff hastily and angrily screw on the lid of his box, replace it in his pocket, and draw his curved scimitar ?

What had I done to offend him, for with me it was that he was wrath. I could see that at a glance.

I sprang to my feet, and had just time to interpose my sabre-blade to ward off a most malignant slash.

Before I could return the compliment, my jovial Irishman had thrown himself between us.

"What the devil's the matter now ? " he asked of me.

"Dashed if I know, for the life of me," I replied.

He then talked some kind of gibberish to my companion.

I suppose he was putting the same question to him.

He was answered this time, and, turning to me, he said, with eyes brimfull of fun, though he spoke very gravely—

"Faith, me friend, ye've been sniffing up yer audacious nostrils the ashes of this gentleman's grandfather !"

"The devil take his grandfather's ashes! What will he attempt to pass them off for snuff for then?" I ejaculated, feeling very indignant and fearfully sick at the same time.

"But he didn't, me friend," explained my acquaintance from Cork. "Sure and he was only exhibiting them to ye as a great treat, because his grand-dad was a famous man in his way—never thinking you'd go and gobble them up."

"I didn't gobble them up, thank heaven; but I snuffed them up, which is nearly as bad. Oh! give me another taste of whisky, do!" said I, faintly.

"How can I pass the bottle and hauld this fellow's hands at one and the same time? Help yerself, me buoy, and may it teach ye the art o' discrimination in heathen countries," said the chief; and sure enough I saw that he had hold of the beggar's wrists, and was gripping them as in a vice.

I saw the whisky bottle on the grass, and at first I thought that it was empty, but I put it to my lips, tipped it upside down, and so managed to squeeze out at least a wine-glassful of its contents.

I felt better after that, and with much equanimity saw the chief bundle his subordinate out of the way.

The other Kalmucks treated me with anything but friendly looks the while, and I was not sorry when the Cove of Cork returned to my side.

He took me away at once to his own tent and told me he would bring my friends to me there, after I had had two or three hours' sleep, as after what had occurred it would be better for us to steal quietly away before day dawn.

CHAPTER L.

A FRIEND IN THE HOUR OF NEED.

I LAY down on a bed of heather and was soon fast asleep, for I was really well-nigh worn out with fatigue.

How long my slumber lasted I really do not know, but I was awakened by a sudden puff of cold air, and a flapping sound as of the canvas of a tent being raised and then let drop.

I was very drowsy, and had shut my eyes to go to sleep again, when I thought I heard stealthy footsteps.

I raised myself on an elbow and listened.

No; all was as still as the grave.

No living object met my view as my eyes glanced round.

True, the lamp of perfumed oil that swung from the ridge pole gave a very flickering and uncertain light, and left many dark corners, but yet the tent was surely untenanted.

Assured of this I was about to resign myself to slumber once more, when this time a clatter behind my head assured me that I was not alone; a fact that an instant later was impressed still more unpleasantly on my drowsy faculties by seeing a gliding, glittering object give a sudden and cat-like spring, and poise itself before and above me in the shape of a turbaned warrior with a long and gleaming dagger raised to strike.

Diable! here was a romantic-looking midnight assassin with a vengeance.

I peered up into his coffee-coloured, turban-shaded face, and recognised the Kalmuck who honoured his grandfather's ashes.

"Go back to bed, and don't be a fool," said I.

"Gobble boo flobbetce crashabrick can!" answered he, or something very much like it.

"Git out wid ye, mavourneen," said I, thinking he might have had a lesson or two in Irish from the Cove of Cork. "Git out wid ye, acushla!"

Not a syllable of my choice Milesian did he understand, however, that was very clear.

He muttered something in reply that sounded very like a Dutch oath, just for the sake of having the last word, I suppose, and then out shot his long, skinny, sinewy, eagle-beaked looking left hand, with the amiable intention, I fancy, of clutching me by the throat, so that he might make sure of striking true with his dagger-armed right, the scoundrel!

Instead of clutching my throat, however, the old fool ran his four fingers into my mouth. Not to give him too much credit, I certainly helped him to perform the feat, taking some pains with the instruction.

No sooner had he got them in than he found that he couldn't get them out. He also made the discovery that I was in no immediate need of a dentist, and that my jaws were remarkably strong, and my molars very tenacious.

He howled and I bit. I bit and he shrieked. Still, I had only one hand in limbo, and the other was capable of an immense amount of mischief.

I tried to clutch it with my left, but as its brother had caught a Tartar, it was too wily to be trapped in turn.

Down it came in a semicircular sweep, and an instant later the long curved crease or dagger that it so firmly grasped would have found a redder sheath than its habitual one of crimson velvet; had not a friend indeed, and heaven knows a friend in sore need, put in an appearance at the right moment.

The sharp crack of a pistol was followed by the dropping of the crease on to the ground, so close to my left eye that it nailed my left ear to the soil, and by the dropping of my intended assassin backwards, so suddenly, that my teeth not having time to unlock, my head was pulled up off the ground, my novel and single earring coming with it, and then suddenly changing its mind, giving a wriggle and falling to the grass, whereon I gave a shriek of agony and disgorged my dead foeman's brown, skinny fingers.

It was all over in an instant.

The next, I recognised in my preserver my Irish Kalmuck, a bullet from whose pistol had sent the reverer of his grandfather's ashes to rejoin that grandfather in another world.

With him were the two princesses.

Of course I thanked him as eloquently as I could for having saved my life—and very thankful I felt, I can assure the reader, for no one exactly knows the value of his own life till he finds some one else awfully intent upon taking it away from him.

"Me friend," said the Cove of Cork, "I'm sorry I had to shoot one of me own followers to preserve yer life, for in case of attack by Arabs, or Turks, or Cossacks, we are none too many of us; and Baboo Azimoolah Kinginfako Ali Moozibar was a tough warrior in his way. But it couldn't be helped nohow; and fair and aisy goes far in a day, as well here as in auld Oirland. Now, however, you must all three don the cloaks that I carry on me arm, and let me conduct you to where yer animals are concealed, for ye are sure to git settled off by ain or the ither, directly the camp is astir, if ye remain in it."

Of course I could not argue the point with him, as he knew, no doubt, the habits and characteristics of the set of blackguards he ruled over better than I did.

We all three disguised ourselves in his cloaks, therefore, and he led us out of his tent and through the slumbering camp until we reached the cave.

There he produced another bottle of whisky, a small one this time, and insisted upon our pledging him, which I, after the fright I had just gone through—for I was frightened, I can tell you—felt not a bit disinclined for, and the princesses, imagining it to be some rare and costly liqueur, followed suit, and declared it to be very good.

We then shook hands with our host and deliverer, and he having given us an idea of the route that we were to pursue, we mounted, and set out by the light of a very clear and nearly full moon, and ere day-dawn were descending the mountains on the other side.

CHAPTER LI.

ARRIVAL AT ALEIK KONI—MY RECEPTION.

WERE I to dwell upon every event of interest that attended our march, or rather journey, from Mingrelia through Gonniel and Akhaltsik, to Kars, I should swell the limits of my tale to the dimensions of a three-volume novel.

I have no desire to trespass so far upon my readers' patience, however, and so will content myself with telling them that about three weeks from the time when I incautiously mistook a condensed Kalmuck gentleman for something near akin to "Irish blackguard," we arrived within sight of the domed and flat-roofed city of Kars, and an hour later were within the lines of the Russian army, which for months past had closely invested it.

I must admit that I was somewhat sorry that the journey was over, for it had been a most pleasant one—more pleasant, perhaps, owing to the many strange perils and adventures that had beset its every stage, but most pleasant on account of the presence and constant society of the Princess Katinka, who seemed to me more lovely every day.

It was all over now, however, for in another half hour or so I should have to bid adieu to her for ever.

I was in no very amiable mood as we rode adown the long streets of Russian tents, ever and anon passing a formidable battery of heavy siege guns—some silent but watchful, others belching forth smoke and flame with a roar that seemed to shake the very world.

The sturdily-built, impassive looking soldiers of the Czar crowded the great camp, as ants crowd an ant hill. Here the fur-capped, balloon-breeched, blue-coated Cossack—there the green-uniformed, brass-helmetted dragoon; in one place the chain-mailed Russianised Circassian—in another the high conical bearskin-capped grenadiers of the regiment of Paul; while artillerymen and brown coated linesmen were everywhere.

Passed on from general of division to general of division, we at last reached the tent of Prince and Marshal Paul Chafchevadsey, and were passed in by two gigantic grenadiers who were on duty outside.

Prince Chafchevadsey's surprise and joy upon beholding his wife and daughter, found vent in first of all sweeping all the breakfast things off the table with his left arm, and springing to his feet and frantically embracing them.

At least ten minutes elapsed before the ladies found any opportunity of introducing me—a ten minutes rather awkward for a bystander; but at last the introduction was effected, and then the Prince commenced hand-shaking at such a rate that I began to dread the possibility of my arm being dislocated in the operation.

At last he ceased, however, and ordered a breakfast for four, a command that I was very glad to hear given, being as hungry as a hunter.

The prince and I became very sociable during the meal, and the ladies took the opportunity of telling him of how many perils and dangers I had shielded them from during the journey, and of my wish to enter Kars.

"There cannot be any serious objection to your doing so—that is, unless you are the bearer of despatches," said the prince.

"I shall be most happy to submit to being searched," I rejoined, "if you consider such a step to be requisite."

"Certainly not," replied the prince, with some hauteur, "your word of honour will amply satisfy me."

"Then I unhesitatingly give it," said I, for, as the reader is aware, I had nothing even in the nature of a despatch about me.

"I will then allow you to enter the city," said the prince; "but, remember, I cannot allow you to leave it again. Once there you must stop, or else, returning here, remain as a prisoner on parole until Kars has fallen."

"I only request permission to enter the city, your highness. If I grow tired of the confinement, the diet, or aught else, and seek to leave it, 'twill be my own fault if a Russian bullet makes my journey a short one," I remarked, pointedly.

"Ah, I quite catch your meaning," laughed the prince. "Well, I have promised to pass you in, but I really can't do more. To get out you must rely on your own bravery and ingenuity. Remember, the place is most closely invested."

The conversation then flowed into other channels, and the breakfast having at length been duly discussed (and to do it justice, neither before or since have I partaken of so good an one in camp), champagne and bottled porter were introduced as drinks of kindred excellence.

It is really surprising the love that the Russians have for English bottled porter, which, even in the palace of the Czar, is brought in with the dessert and supplied out of wine glasses. Though a great porter drinker myself, such a way of imbibing it is to me particularly nauseous.

Prince Chafchevadsey seemed rather surprised that I preferred the champagne—which was really very tolerable—to our own national drink, as he was pleased to term it; but I explained to him that it was made national by being drunk out of immense pewter pots, which seemed to surprise him, and naturally so, for I daresay his porter, which would have been sold at three-pence the quart in London, cost him about half a guinea a bottle.

After breakfast came the unpleasant ordeal of leave taking, and then I was placed under the charge of a young cornet of dragoons and a troop of horse, and away we dashed at a gallop, Kars-ward.

CHAPTER LII.

THE LOSS OF A HEAD—MY WELCOME TO KARS.

NOW, as the young cornet in question could not speak a word of any language, save his own—a most rare thing amongst Russian officers, who are, as a rule, the best linguists in the world—he did not prove a very entertaining companion.

We dashed along at a merry, spanking pace, however, to the musical accompaniment of rattling sword scabbards and jingling chain bridles, the neighing of our horses, and the pad-pad-pad of their iron-shod hoofs.

An army under canvas, on the march, or in actual engagement, ever presents a grand and a spirit-thrilling sight—a sight which has somewhat the effect of champagne upon the system; and I must admit that a Russian army, notwithstanding the sombre colours of its uniforms, looks almost as well as any other—its soldiers are so tall, so burly, so well set up, bearded, and determined looking.

They do not fight for the love of it, like the French, or for glory (for none but the officers ever get any), but they fight because they are paid to be food for powder, and it would be greater trouble to run away than to fight and fall.

I had plenty to interest me during our ride, therefore; for though, strictly speaking, a civilian, I yet knew a good deal about war and its armaments, and, what is more, felt a great interest in all things military.

When we got to the extremity of the Russian lines, the cornet sent a dragoon to right and to left to bid the cannon in the advanced trenches and parallels cease firing upon the town; and, directly they had done so, he drew his sword, and, fastening his white pocket handkerchief to the blade, we cantered on towards one of the gates.

As we neared it, however, a turbanned and

villanous-looking Turk levelled a rifle over the wall and fired.

The bullet hit the cornet's helmet, but glanced off the tempered steel, half-stunning him, and causing him to reel for an instant in his saddle.

Fearing that this solitary bullet might be the avant courier of a volley, I reined up; but as I did so, I saw the turbanned head flying over the wall, minus its body, and a stern-looking, smoked-begrimed English officer, in a purple-black and ragged uniform, and a blood-dripping sword in his right hand, standing on the parapet, from behind which the treacherous Oriental had taken aim.

I saw the Russian cornet's eyes light up with pleasure, and his lips murmur something, which I have no doubt was equivalent to either "Well done!" or else "Served him right!" He waved his impromptu flag of truce afresh, and once more we cantered forward as we saw that the gate was on the point of being opened, and the drawbridge lowered.

Signs, however, were made that the Russians would be permitted to come no farther, and when once understanding them, they made no efforts to do so.

They saluted the officer on the ramparts with their swords, and then the cornet having shaken hands with me, English fashion—an absurd and idle ceremony possibly, but one which I very much preferred to either French kissing or Muscovite nose-rubbing—he galloped rearwards with his troop of dragoons, and I rode slowly over the drawbridge, and under a very deep and thick archway lined by British light infantry, into Kars.

Scarcely was I well inside the gates, hardly had the ponderous drawbridge rattled and clattered up in my rear, than I felt my hand clasped in just such a friendly grip as a grizzly bear might have given, whilst a hearty, genial voice exclaimed—

"I don't know who the deuce you are, but as someone from the outer world, and more especially as an Englishman, I bid you welcome to Kars."

I looked down, and perceived that my hand-shaker was the seedy-looking, purple-coated officer, who had cut off the Turk's head for treacherously firing upon a flag of truce.

"Thank you," I said; "I'm very glad to greet an Englishman, too, after seeing none but Circassians, Mongolians, Kalmucks, and Muscovites for so long. But pardon me, I want an immediate interview with General Williams, the Commandant."

"General Williams, the Commandant, addresses you in person," was the laughing retort; "if you are in a hurry to confer with him in private, dismount, throw your reins to any of these fellows who stand around, enjoin them not to eat it, and then come along with me."

"Not to eat my horse?" I exclaimed, rather aghast.

"Yes, not to eat your horse; but perhaps I had better tell them, for the beggars mind me," and, whilst I was dismounting, the Governor of Kars roared out some order in Turkish, I presume, to the crowd of Bashi-Bazouks and Bono Johnnies who surrounded us, whose import I could not at all make out.

I followed him through two or three dark and narrow streets, villanously filthy, and full of the most abominable stenches, until we reached a kind of open space resembling a square of three sides, into one of the houses forming which he made his way, preceding me up a narrow and steep flight of black, ricketty, and almost tumble-down stairs.

Then he entered a room almost bare of furniture save a deal, knife-chipped table, and two chairs, into one of which he flung himself, bidding me take the other.

Scarcely had I done so when he exclaimed—

"Now tell me the worst, without beating about the bush. I can bear it better than this terrible uncertainty. The allies, have they been beaten out of the Crimea, and have the Russians sent you to tell me this, rightly conjecturing that I should accept it as the truth from the lips of no one but a British officer?"

"Far from such being the case," said I, "there is every reason to believe that Sebastopol is tottering to its fall, nay, very probably it has already fallen; for when I quitted the Crimea, now more than a month ago, our trenches were close up to the Mamelon and the Redan, and it was thought that the Russians were falling short of ammunition."

"What on earth brings you here, then?" he asked.

I told him as concisely as I could, and also how pressing a necessity there was of my hurrying on to the army of Omar Pasha at Erzeroum.

"Yes," replied General Williams; "I see the necessity, but am at a loss to devise the means. You say that you ought to be gone at once, and I agree with you on that point."

"There can be no two opinions on it," I urged; "or Omar Pasha may commence military operations against, as he imagines, a weak and scattered enemy, and instead, find himself confronted by an army powerful enough to crush, or even to annihilate him."

"And if his army were so annihilated, the war in Asia would be virtually over, and my long and stubborn defence of Kars a feat barren of all useful results. Yes, you must assuredly leave the town as speedily as ever you can. The means alone baffles me, for we are closely invested by a force five times as large as we can muster, and we have eaten nearly all our horses for food," said General Williams.

I shrugged my shoulders, for I could say nothing.

"All that I can do for you," said the general, after nearly five minutes' deep thought, "is to mount every horseman who has a horse left him, and at their head you must issue forth under cover of night, and endeavour to force your way through the sleeping Muscovite army. There exist ten chances to one that you will be cut to pieces to a man, and one chance in about a hundred that you yourself will be cut to pieces. Do you feel inclined to attempt the running of so terrible a gauntlet?"

"The thing must be done," I replied, "for duty and necessity command it. That is, unless we can improve on the scheme."

"I fear not," replied the general; "yet stay. I am having constructed a small balloon, which I meant to send up the night after to-morrow, with a solitary inmate and letters and despatches for England and the Crimea, in the faint hope that the aërial postman may escape Russian bomb-shells, rockets and bullets, pursuing cavalry, and every other contingency, and descend somewhere or other from whence he will be able to forward his despatches and tell our friends at home and elsewhere, who are alive and who are dead, and how we fare within the walls of Kars."

"Yes; and you would suggest——" I began.

"That if, by a miracle, the cavalry sortie fails, and you are driven back into Kars, that you play the rôle of the aëriel postman," answered the general, very calmly.

"Agreed," said I; "though I tell you plainly that I don't understand the management of a balloon, in the least."

"Nor does a single soul in the place," was the reply.

"Does anyone really understand the construction of one?" I asked.

"In a bungling and unworkmanlike fashion, yes."

"But where do you get your silk?" I asked.

"We have none, and so will substitute paper."

"But your gas—there you will experience a difficulty."

"An insurmountable one, and so we have recourse to warm air."

"Why that was Mongolfier's old and exploded system, and his balloon very naturally became a prey to the flames, so that Mongolfier fell and was killed," I rejoined.

"Just so; I recollect the occurrence perfectly, but then Mongolfier made two previous ascents in safety."

"Yes," I rejoined, "and five years later one Olivari deemed that he had perfected Mongolfier's invention; his balloon also became a prey to the flames, and he, too, was killed," said I.

"He was," answered the general; "but not until his second ascent. Billorf, an Australian, started the next paper hot-air charged balloon, and I allow that he was killed the very first time that he ascended, but desperate straits require oft-times desperate devices to get out of them, and as we have neither silk nor gas, why, what are we to do?"

"What you are going to do, most certainly," I rejoined. "And if I cannot get to Omar Pasha by means of horse, sword and pistols, why I will endeavour to do so by means of paper and hot-air. We must wait for a north-east wind, however, for Erzeroum lies to the south-west, and that would facilitate travelling in the right direction amazingly; otherwise I might get blown back to the Caucasus."

"That is very true; we must so wait," said the general.

"And Kars—how long can you still hold out?" I asked.

"Oh! we have still black bread and water, but that has been our sole food for weeks, and we are getting accustomed to it. I hope you have breakfasted, for that's the only fare I can offer you."

"Thank you; I will try it for dinner, then," I rejoined. "I think, as we have fully arranged everything, I should enjoy a stroll round the town. I want to see if besieged Kars resembles besieged Sebastopol."

"I can't offer to accompany you, for I've had no sleep for three nights. After an hour's nap I'll gather up some horsemen," said the general; and so I set forth alone.

CHAPTER LIII.

A HORRIBLE ADVENTURE IN KARS.

BEFORE I had walked a distance of a quarter of a mile I could see that I was in a town where famine was making fearful ravages with the inhabitants.

Skeleton-like forms, with hollow, haggard faces and greedy eyes, encountered me everywhere. Seated on one doorstep, I saw a Bashi-Bazouk eating a live rat. The shops and bazaars were all closed. No meat, no bread met the view.

But the low wail of famine-stricken women and children was drowned by the brattle of the drums, the shrill blare of the Turkish trumpets, the popping of musketry, and the roar of the cannon.

The Russians were bombarding the place with vigour, for the crash of falling masonry was sometimes loud as the boom of the great siege guns, and now and then the falling of a shell would be followed by a great explosion.

Groups of soldiers were hurrying hither and thither, all ferocity and excitement—Bashi-Bazouks, Kurds, Turks proper, Armenians, and English infantry, the latter in the proportion of one to ten of the rest.

Often I would meet a convoy of killed and wounded, journeying hospital-ward from the walls —often would I see the bodies of the dead of both sexes cumbering the streets, often half buried, and oft-times crushed out of all human semblance by fallen buildings, of which, in all probability, they had been the occupants.

I was nearly growing tired of this gloomy and terrible wandering, and had almost begun to wish that I had never set out on it, when my attention was attracted by a graceful female figure, wrapped in the most costly of cashmere shawls, who, as she passed me by, bestowed on me the most arch and piquant of glances through the eyelet holes of her yashmak.

The eyes that had for a moment beamed upon me were as large and liquid-looking as those of the gazelle—eyes that, though so soft and gentle, sent a current of fire, as it were, through one's veins. I had noticed, besides, as she passed, the smallest of jewelled hands, and the tiniest and whitest of feet clad in sandals.

Of course I concluded that she was young and beautiful. She could not be otherwise with such feet, and hands, and eyes, and so, very naturally, I turned round to gaze after her.

She had stopped also to look back at me.

Not only stopped, but she was beckoning me to follow her.

I hesitated—I know not why—for certainly never before nor since have I hesitated to obey the behest of beauty, no matter at what hazard or at what risk.

And yet on this occasion something seemed to hold me back.

But the Turkish girl stamped her little foot with impatience, and, raising her yashmak, revealed, though for a moment only, a face of such exquisite loveliness that it cast the charms of Katinka into the deepest shade.

Dropping her veil, she beckoned again, and now even an anchorite could not have avoided the temptation of following her.

And I was very far from being an anchorite.

Wondering what on earth she could require of me, I slightly inclined my head in acceptance of her invitation, and thereafter followed her through street after street until at last she darted into a narrow alley, and from thence in at an open doorway, or rather a doorless way.

Here she paused at the foot of a black oaken staircase, and put her finger on her lips to imply caution.

Having signed to me thus, she glided rather than ran up the stairs, the twinkling of her snowy feet being quite sufficient to reveal in the deep gloom the path I had to follow.

At the head of a third flight of stairs she again came to a halt, and waited until I was beside her.

"Beautiful being—fair as the fairest rose in the Sultan's garden," I began; but the maiden shook her head.

It was plain that she did not understand what I said.

I essayed the same compliment in French.

Still only a shake of the head.

I tried German—without a hope of success, however.

And I was right; there was no success. I might have known that such beautiful lips could not have given utterance to so guttural a tongue.

She gave me her hand, however—oh, so petite and deliciously soft! The object was to lead me through, it might have been, half-a-dozen passages, all as dark as night, but I took the opportunity of raising it to my lips and kissing it fervently.

At last we emerged out of the darkness into light.

Into a richly-furnished room, in which a number of fair women were congregated together, dressed in the most sumptuous of apparel, be-diamonded and perfumed.

Some of them were reclining idly on piles of soft cushions, some were grouped together in converse; one beautiful young creature was playing the mandolin, and two others, equally charming, were singing most sweetly to the accompaniment of the music.

What struck me at once as peculiar was that they were all unveiled, and, instead of striving on my entrance to conceal those charms which nature had so abundantly lavished upon them, as Turkish, and, in fact, all Mohammedan women generally do, they seemed to display them with as much generosity and prodigality as possible.

I must own that when my fair guide dropped off her yashmak and many shawls, she was the most lovely of them all, a moss rose amidst a bed of other flowers, all lovely, yet in that respect far inferior to their queen.

I could not help wondering where, and among whom I was. How were all these girls so plump, glossy-skinned and rounded in proportion, in a city that was a prey to famine, wherein even the commandant could only get dry bread, and not too much of that.

I came to the rapid conclusion and conviction that they were the ladies of some harem, whose lord, together with all his guards and male followers, had been slain in the defence of the city, and that, finding themselves at freedom, the ladies had determined, for a while at all events, to enjoy themselves as they listed.

And yet this explanation was not altogether satisfactory, for it did not in any way explain how every one of the party was so sleek and comely in appearance.

Another moment's reflection convinced me, however, that I was a fool under such circumstances to reflect at all. I was in paradise. Why draw thoughts of earth within its magic influence? Why not yield myself unreservedly to all the delights of the hour?

Ah, why not indeed? Such an hour might never occur again, and yet I could not overcome the feeling that some terrible peril threatened me.

The other women had begun to group together, and cast sidelong glances at me whilst they conversed.

I was evidently the subject of that conversation, and I could not help fancying that dozens of a minute or two ago soft lustrous eyes, now glared at me wolfishly.

I had noticed one of them shut the door, and, as I thought, lock it, thereafter abstracting the key and dropping it into her bosom. Ruby lips, too, seemed to contract, and flushed cheeks to pale as though a sudden awe or terror had fallen upon the assembly.

Suddenly, however, a burst of song broke forth, the mandolins struck up, and two of the youngest and most lovely of the maidens began to dance.

What pen can describe the grace and pure poetry of their motions?

I gazed, enchanted, at the sight, but in the midst of it came the sudden and abrupt clash of a cymbal, and simultaneously therewith I felt a sharp stab in the back.

I seized the plump white arm of my companion at once, and buried my thumb and fingers so deep in the soft and yielding flesh, that she uttered a cry of pain. and dropped to the ground a small and jewel-hilted poignard.

"Did you invite me hither only to assassinate me?" I asked. forgetting that she spoke not a word of English.

"Annette Scasci!" she screamed—"Annette Scasci!"

Thereupon another of the beautiful creatures came up, a flush on her cheeks and a smile on her lips.

"Monsieur conjectures rightly," she said, with a shrug of her alabaster shoulders, and in the purest French. "Monsieur is brought hither to enjoy a happy death, and to preserve unimpaired the health and the charms of the most beautiful women in Asiatic Turkey."

"Kindly explain yourself, mademoiselle," I said.

"Very well, monsieur; that is easy. We are the inmates of a besieged city, whose inmates are dying by hundreds of famine, whilst those who do not so die, yet become, through insufficient food, the most miserable looking of objects. Such should we become did we not adopt some ruse whereby to replenish our larder. A woman in Turkey, monsieur,

without she be young and plump and satin-skinned, either becomes one of the most degraded and hard-worked of slaves, or she is sewn up in a sack, thrown into a river, and permitted to drown like a dog. We have no wish for either fate—we have resolved to maintain our health, strength, and beauty at any and all risks; in short, monsieur, you were enticed hither to be killed and *eaten*."

"Eaten!" I exclaimed, a thrill of the most intense horror causing my very hair to bristle on my head.

"Yes, eaten, monsieur. Would you not sacrifice yourself for our sakes? Fie, fie, where is your chivalry as a soldier? Is it not a more agreeable thought than that of dying in the battle-field or in the hospital?"

She laughed merrily, but I could see that the gaiety was forced, and worn with a great effort.

"I must say I've a very strong objection to be killed at all. Can I not buy my freedom. I have a very well-filled purse, and its contents are entirely at your service."

"What is the good of gold, when there is no food for gold to buy? No, monsieur, a cart-load of diamonds would not purchase your exemption. You are our ninth victim. The first, second, and third, we slew like dogs in the dark corridors without. Since then, we have sought to alleviate the pangs of death, if not annihilate them. I will open a vein with the point of my dagger, and you shall expire slowly and painlessly, beguiled by the sounds of singing and music."

Every member of the beautiful troupe had gathered around me now, each one with a drawn dagger in her hand.

"Mademoiselle, such a death would be very sweet had not life still a strong hold upon me, and dying thinking of naught else but earthly delights—a strange terror—— As a French girl and a Christian you must know what I mean."

"But I am not French, and I am not Christian. I am a Circassian and a Mahommedan. I learnt French from a Russian prisoner who could speak all languages, ere I was sold by my parents to the Turks, and, therefore, I do not know what you mean."

"Then you and your followers are resolved to slay me?"

"Yes, if you insist on calling it by so harsh a name."

"But what if I resist. I wear a sword, woman."

I drew it as I spoke and menaced her with the point.

She rushed right on with her beautiful chest bare.

Hastily I lowered the blade lest it should hurt her.

"Ha!" she exclaimed, with a laugh; "I knew that my beauty would disarm you. Nay, point your sword again, run me through the heart if you can. I will allow you to do so. If you can do so, I will consent to be a meal for my syrens, and you shall go away free and unharmed."

She tore down her dress.

"There!" she said, mockingly; "thrust, and so preserve your life."

"Yes, run her through the body—'tis easily done," said the girl who had brought me to the house, in a low whisper.

"I cannot," I said; "I could not if it was to save myself from being burnt alive."

"Then will you yield graciously to your fate?"

Ere I could reply there was a great crash, and something like a globe of fire rushed by me, the wind thereof causing me to reel and fall.

I was on my feet in an instant, and looked around.

A horrible, heart-rending, and sickening sight met my gaze.

The beautiful woman who had braved me to kill her lay on the floor cut in two by the red-hot cannon-ball which had passed right through the house.

No. 7.

HE SENT MY SWORD SPINNING FROM MY GRASP, AFTER WHICH HE DELIBERATELY SHEATHED HIS OWN WEAPON.

She was dead, as were two of her companions, two or three more being seriously injured by the flying missile.

The shrieks and screaches of the injured were piteous to listen to—the aspect of the dead, revolting and fearful. An instant had sufficed to change beings the very acmé and perfection of earthly beauty into severed, crushed, charred, and hideous-looking heaps of flesh, and bones, and rags.

I hope I may not be accused of cowardice or destitute of feeling when I declare that after one glance round, I dashed at the door, burst it open with my weight, rushed through the dark passages and down the three flights of stairs thereafter, never pausing until somehow—by instinct I believe, for I never stopped to inquire the way—I reached the tall house in the square, in which General Williams had fixed his head-quarters.

There I sank into a chair, and absolutely fainted away.

CHAPTER LIV.

THE UNSUCCESSFUL SORTIE.

AFTER the horrible adventure I had encountered in the morning, I actually longed for the approach of night, that I might forget it in the incidents of the sortie.

And night at last came, and with it some three hundred horsemen, in every variety of uniform, and mounted on every variety of steed.

They were all that General Williams could gather together, and in truth they were a motley group. My hopes of being able to cut my way through the Russian cordon at the head of such men as these, seemed very problematical indeed.

The attempt had to be made, however, and I knew that I had the best men that could be procured, and as many as ever the commandant could muster.

We left the city by its south-western gate. The night was luckily a dark one.

I had given orders that not a word should be spoken in the ranks, and for extra precaution's sake the horses had been unshod and muzzled.

Of the courage of my motley troop I had little fear. The Turk, though a miserable infantry soldier, is always a bold and daring horseman.

We had got to a distance of about a quarter of a mile from the city walls, when a Russian sentry challenged, but so near were we to him before he perceived us, that ere he could repeat his question or discharge his musket, he was cut down.

A second, five minutes later, was served in the same manner, but with the third we were not so fortunate. He challenged and fired the same instant, and one of our troopers tumbled out of his saddle.

The Russian trumpets seemed to ring out simultaneously. "We must ride for it now," said a young officer, in French; "speed alone will save us."

We set spurs to our horses and did ride with a speed that, considering how dimly indistinct everything was in the gloom, was terrible in itself.

And presently we could see that our path was barred—an opposing wave of man and horse was rushing through the gloom to meet us.

I could plainly see the commanding officer leading them on, owing to his horse and uniform being alike white. He waved his sword on high, encouraging his men.

"Close in!—close in!—charge!" shouts our leader, waving his sword in turn; and on we went with the speed now of the whirlwind, our wild horsemen calling upon Allah and the Prophet, and brandishing their lances aloft.

Everything seemed easy now, whilst the blood was up, whilst the brain boiled, and the heart beat as though it would burst, with that ecstatic rapture that every man must feel when charging with a crowd, with a good horse under him, and a tried sword in his hand.

The Russian cavalry note our desperate resolution, and waver. They thus lose the heavy momentum which is everything in a charge, and as we crash against them, we roll them over, man and horse, with the very impetus of our charge.

Lance-thrust and sword-cut, lunge, slash, and ringing pistol shot succeed. Our men call on their Prophet more frequently, and many of them are fast departing for that luxurious paradise of dark-eyed houris which he promised to all who fell in battle.

And in the midst of it all I find a foe in every way worthy of my steel, an officer evidently of high rank, who introduces himself by dealing me a furious head cut with his long sabre, which I am only just quick enough to guard.

I catch a quick and hurried glance at his face, and the sight of it almost causes me to drop my weapon.

Heavens! it was the face of Louis Foucarte, of Count Eugene Pollaki, of the Russian spy whom I had seen shot, and fall headlong backwards into that horrible crevasse in the Caucasian mountains.

So astounded was I, that I might for a minute or two just as well have been unarmed.

Indeed, had not another brace of combatants pushed their horses between us and so given me time to recover my presence of mind somewhat, I should assuredly have fallen beneath his sword.

As it was, however, I came up to time, calm and cool as the blade of my sword, convinced that I only had to deal with a wonderful resemblance after all.

Cuts and thrusts were interchanged with lightning rapidity, and sparks of fire frequently flew from our clashing weapons. We neither of us spoke, the work was too real and earnest to permit of idle badinage, but we certainly did our very best to cut each other's throats in a skilful and workmanlike manner, with the least possible loss of time.

Which would have eventually succeeded in slaying the other, I really do not know, for, just when the excitement was at its height, the Russian cavalry broke and fled in the wildest confusion, bearing my foeman with them.

The heavens fairly resounded with the battle cries of our men. The disorganised foe, in a panic-stricken mob, rode pell-mell into a regiment of infantry that was forming to support them, and thereby rendered the aforesaid infantry innocuous for harm, whilst we dashed on afresh, wondering how many more obstacles there yet were to encounter and overcome.

More than sufficient, as it turned out. A battery of field artillery presently begins to gall our left flank, a regiment of infantry opens fire on our right, and a regiment of Navodski hussars shows up in our front.

Our horses are tired and blown, those of the foe are fresh—our men are weary and dispirited, those of the enemy proud, fiery and exultant, feeling that they have got us well under their thumb—our men are few, the majority of them wounded, the foe outnumbering them by at least three to one. No wonder that they are confident.

We rush furiously on them, however, despite a withering fire poured in by the infantry upon our flank, which empties many saddles.

I set my teeth, and nerved my muscles for the encounter. But it was destined to be one of very short duration this time. We were ridden down and crushed into the dust and dirt, apparently with as much ease as if we had been a company of field poppies.

Then crash—my sword was broken off to a jag against a brass helmet, and I turned to fly in turn.

'Twas high time to do so, if I wanted to escape with my life, which very few seemed to be doing, judging from the number of turbans, fez caps and shaven heads that strewed the ground around.

To go forward was impossible, for a sea of onrolling men and horses blocked the path. To fall back on Kars seemed equally, or nearly, a feat of impossibility, but something had to be attempted, and so I turned rein and gave my horse the spur.

Away, fleeter than the wind, we flew, with half-a-dozen Russian troopers hard at our heels, and ever so many more darting like meteors in all directions.

Kars was a good mile distant, but I had no hope of reaching it. The feat seemed impossible, and yet I tore on, determined to give it at least a chance.

How many foemen I cut down, or how many succeeded in wounding me, I know not. Many a wound was not felt at the time. All that I was aware of was that every instant the lights of Kars seemed to be nearer and nearer, until at last they gleamed so near that hope returned, and I believed that I might yet be able to gain one of the gates with life.

Scarcely had this new hope been born, when my horse bounded into the air, fell upon his knees, recovered himself, and went down again, this time to rise no more.

I disengaged myself from the stirrups and sprang to my feet. A riderless charger instantly knocked me down again. Once more I rose, and it was to see a mounted Cossack charging down at me with his long, ready lance in the rest.

I had no sword, and my pistols were discharged. I was completely at his mercy, when, happily, a bullet from the ramparts stretched him low.

I rushed towards the gates now, but another Russian intercepted me. I launched both my pistols at his head, and had the satisfaction of seeing the last knock him out of his saddle.

As he fell the gate was thrown open. I was caught as I was in the act of falling to the ground through sheer weakness, and dragged within the gate. I was safe!

CHAPTER LV.

"HE WHO WOULD SOAR SHOULD FEAR NO FALL."

THE sortie had failed, utterly failed, and there now remained for me only one way of getting out of Kars.

By balloon!

It was a desperate expedient, or at all events I thought so.

I knew very little about balloons or ballooning, and I made up my mind that a rifle or a cannon-ball would pierce the silk envelope that confined the gas, and bring me to earth in no time.

I had undertaken to go, however, and Sir William Williams had promised to provide me with a balloon and an aëronaut.

At the time of which I write the science of aërostation had not reached the perfection to which it has since attained, and many a gallant fellow who ballooned it out of Paris and Metz, during the late Franco-Prussian war, dropping calling-cards derisively into German camps as he passed over them, might feel inclined to laugh at my trepidation, in committing myself to what was then a newer, or at all events a less understood, element.

Besides, everyone has his bête noir, and I own that mine was ballooning.

Just before leaving England I had read a treatise on the subject, and had been struck by the fact that nine out of every ten aëronauts broke their necks at the second or third venture.

No, aërostation was not my fort.

I had been down in a diving bell, down the deepest copper mine in Cornwall, and down in the omnibus at the new Paddington Hotel, but up amongst the clouds—ah! that was another affair altogether.

I thought of red-haired Queen Bessy's advice to Raleigh, "He who would soar should fear no fall;" but I could not apply it to my present case.

Besides, Raleigh soared and did fall, his head and trunk parting company in the process.

However, the thing had to be done, and, though inwardly craven, I was not going to stick the white feather in my cap for daws to peck at.

The sortie had failed, the turn of the balloon had come.

Whilst breakfasting with Sir William Williams, he informed me that there was enough gas in the city to inflate a score of balloons, and, what was better still, that there was a balloon, and an aëronaut who was ready to place himself at my service that very afternoon.

"So you see," said Sir William Williams, "things could not have turned out better than they have."

"Indeed, they could not," I replied, making a mental reservation or two.

Then I added cheerfully, "Of course I am ready to go up at any hour."

"Just what I anticipated your saying," was Sir William's retort; "but the balloon will take three hours to inflate, so that the earliest moment at which you can start will be twelve at noon."

"Very well; that hour will do nicely," I said. "I'll trouble you for another cup of coffee."

"Why, you take the affair very coolly," said my host. "Nothing appears to have any effect upon your nerves."

"Doesn't it?" thought I to myself. "Oh, dear, doesn't it?"

But I said aloud, "I rather like the idea of the thing."

"You must be sure to make the aëronaut ascend high enough to escape any possible rockets that may be aimed at you by the Russians. A rocket shoots to a great height. If such a missile were to pierce the silk gutta-percha-coated balloon, you would fall to earth like a stone—that is to say if you were not blown to atoms by the explosion of the gas."

"Yes, yes, just so—if I wasn't blown to pieces by the explosion of the gas," I repeated, half dreamily, but with a smile on my lips.

"Then they may throw shells at you from their mortars. You will have to trust to Providence to keep clear of them—for I don't think you will be able to rise high enough to be safe from such missiles. They have mortars that will throw a shell or a red-hot shot in a parabola with a maximum altitude of five thousand two hundred and eighty-six yards, or a little above three miles, and you can't ascend to such a height with safety."

"And why not?" I asked, taking a glass of brandy.

"Because, although we have any amount of gas wherewith to inflate, we none of us know its exact expansive power, and so there might be great danger in testing it, by ascending to too great a height. The proper gas to use for the purpose is hydrogen evolved by the contact of water with iron and sulphuric acid, but we can only give you common coal gas, which is very inflammable."

"Oh, very inflammable is it?" I ventured to remark, filling up another glass of brandy as I did so.

"And by-the-by, you must be careful which way you drift when you get amongst the upper currents of air. Balloons sometimes travel with inconceivable rapidity, and a descent into the Black Sea or the Caspian would be certain death."

"Yes—yes—yes, that's understood," I replied. "But suppose we change the subject to one more cheerful, my dear Sir William. How much longer do you think you can hold this place?"

"I don't know," was the somewhat gloomy retort. "When fathers and mothers take to devouring their own offsprings—when a filthy kite or vulture cannot be bought under five guineas, and a rat brings literally its weight in gold, the end must be at hand. You have been eating mice stew for breakfast; and that delicious rabbit, as you have called it, caught them in its then form of a fine tabby. We shall have to try traps in future. Poor Tommy would have lived another week possibly, had I not been resolved to honour her Majesty's representative by a feed above the common."

"I'm sure I don't know how to express my gratitude for your kindness," said I, quaffing yet a third glass of brandy, lest pussy should persist in returning to express hers, a *catastrophe* which a certain heaving of the stomach indicated as likely to ensue.

"Oh! don't mention it," retorted Sir William. "Duty is duty, and when we can combine pleasure with it, why all the better. Tell Omar Pasha, if you are lucky enough to reach his lines, to advance with all haste, you know, or he will find our skeletons, instead of our bodies. Now, have a bit more curried Tommy. Here is a fine leg!"

"No, thank you," I answered. "I have already fared sumptuously," and I felt strangely reconciled to the balloon from that instant.

* * * *

Well, the morning wore slowly away, for I didn't go out, having seen quite sufficient of the horrors of Kars already.

Dinner time came, but I resolutely stuck to some boiled rice and a couple of mouldy ship's biscuits.

Sir William had evidently an accomplished cook, but I distrusted his entremets and his made dishes in toto.

And at last the hour arrived, and a baggy-breeched Turco came to tell us that the balloon was ready.

"Come old fellow, another glass of wine," said Sir William, heartily, as he sprang to his feet. "We may never meet again, you know."

I felt that very strong myself, and a sort of something in my throat rose up and met the sherry half way, nearly choking me.

"Come," said Sir William, giving me a heavy slap on the back, that effectually put me to rights. "In the old days of bigotry and superstition that would have been taken for an evil omen, wouldn't it?"

"Yes, I think it would," I stammered, with the tears still in my eyes. "But come along, for who cares for signs and omens now?"

I was in full uniform, and my pockets were bulging out with the letters that the besieged British and other officers had entrusted to me to post or deliver, should I ever succeed in safely passing over, and dropping somewhere or other out of reach of the investing foe.

The governor and his aide-de-camp walked down with me to the great square in the centre of the town, where my aërial conveyance was in waiting, held firmly to the ground by grappling irons.

'Ah," said Sir William, glancing at the empty car. "Where is the aëronaut? He should be aboard, awaiting us."

A pale-faced, excited-looking woman pushed her way through the crowd, and grasped Sir William's arm with her long skinny fingers.

"He's dead!" she said in a hollow voice. "Some starving Turks set upon him and killed him, half-an-hour ago. Oh! God, I saw them tear his clothes off, disjoint him with their long knives, and eat him in great mouthfuls. I am come to you for justice."

"You shall have it, my good woman—you shall have it. Go straight to Government House, and await my return. If I find the rascals, I will hang them. But what on earth are we to do for another aëronaut?"

That was indeed the question.

Aëronants are rare personages in a beleaguered city, especially an Asiatic one, and without an aëronaut how could I ascend or steer myself when aloft?

"Do you know anything about the management of a balloon?" asked Sir William, turning hopelessly to me.

"About as much as a Methodist preacher would know about the handling of a three-decker in a hurricane," I answered.

"Then you refuse to trust yourself alone in a machine that you do not understand how to manage?" said the perplexed governor.

"Rather," said I. "If I did, I know that I should never come down again. There are quite risks enough to be run with an aëronant."

We all stared at each other, looking as foolish as we could well look, whilst the great balloon tugged, and tugged, and tugged to get free—the aërostal bobbing about in the strangest manner imaginable.

Then all at once a voice cried from out the crowd—

"I understand the management of a balloon well enough. If the gentleman will entrust himself to my care, I'll guarantee to drop him a good score of miles the other side the Russian lines."

The speaker came forward—a tall, thin man, in civilian dress, with a broad-brimmed felt hat, slouched down well over his eyes, and the lower part of his face muffled up in a comforter, so that very little of it could be seen.

A cloak draped his form from head to foot; but there was nothing strange in cloak or comforter, for the air was bitterly cold and a keen cutting wind blowing.

No sooner did this strange, muffled-up individual step so boldly forward, than I felt a confidence in him, and, grasping his hand, I exclaimed—

"I will go with you, whoever you are."

CHAPTER LVI.
THE AERONAUT IS NOT ALTOGETHER TO MY LIKING.

HE made no reply except a mute pressure of the digits, and then, dropping my hand, he scrambled into the car.

"By George, you're right lucky!" said Sir William, turning to me. "I congratulate you, my boy—I congratulate you."

He patted me on the back towards the balloon, and pushed me towards it.

At last I reached it, and scrambled into the car in turn.

"You'll find a hamper of good things down amongst the ballast bags," said Sir William, standing on tiptoe to look over the edge of the car. "'Pon my word, you look quite comfortable in here," he added.

Now, as the car was perfectly round, being five feet in diameter and the same in height, and its circular seat fitted with soft cushions, whilst bags of sand (the ballast) formed its floor, it no doubt did look very comfortable whilst resting within twelve or fifteen inches of terra firmâ.

But then how would it look and feel when a couple or three miles above it, and still moving through space?

The governor never thought of that—but I did, as I glanced around at the equatorial circle, the compass, the barometer, and the great black swaying, groaning globe above, that to me seemed to have swollen to dimensions vast as those of the dome of St. Paul's.

But I shook hands with the gallant defender of Kars, and thanked him for the hamper, which I devoutly hoped contained liquids alone, and no fricasseed cats, mice, or rats.

"Bon voyage!" said he,

shouted a lot of young officers who had gathered together to witness our departure.

Then the amateur aëronaut sprang on the edge of the car, and, holding on to a rope, shouted in a deep stentorian voice—

"Cast off, lads—cast off. Now, then, all at once."

Then the grappling irons were promptly let go, and an instant later the twelve cords that passing down from the aërostal through the equatorial circle had bound the balloon to mother earth were cut adrift from the grappling irons and held in the hands of a dozen strong, lusty men.

"Let go—let go! Now then, all the same instant," roared the aëronaut, in a voice of thunder.

They did as they were bidden. The crowd cheered. I looked over the edge of the car—we were rising —a mounted soldier might have gallopped beneath us.

I looked up, and in that short interval we were on a level with the house-tops.

We were ascending with a vengeance.

I glanced over the side of the car again, waving my handkerchief in reply to thousands of hats and handkerchiefs that were waved below, until the wavers seemed to grow as small as bees and flies, and the houses no bigger than those that compose a toy village.

We drifted over the dome of the great Mohammedan mosque.

It looked like a small umbrella, and yet we were still going up—up.

I started upon seeing two objects diving downwards, rebound from one of the slender minarets, and from thence fall into a street.

I turned round and saw my compagnon de voyage in the act of throwing over a third bag of ballast without untying it.

"Have a care," I said; "sand weighs heavy when packed in a sack. It is very easy to rip up the bag and let it fall in a shower—then it can hurt no one. But in solid form it may kill people in a crowded city like Kars."

"What do I care?" grunted the aëronaut, pitching a third, and then a fourth sack over; "Kars and its defenders may go to old Clootie for me."

"You are no true Englishman to speak like that," I said.

"Englishman! I would not accept the title. Nor Frenchman, Russian, or Turk either. I'm a citizen of the world, and a poet."

"A citizen of the world, and a poet!" I ejaculated. "How so?"

"Well, the world is my home, the tender muse is my delight."

"I hope I aren't going aloft with a madman," I muttered to myself.

Then I said aloud—

"The barometer has fallen to 24 inches. Kars is a mere dot on the plain below—we are drifting south-easterly over the Russian hosts that environ the city on that side. How high are we above ground, think you?"

The aëronaut seemed to be making a mental calculation for a minute or two, and then he said, quite unconcernedly—

"About sixteen hundred mètres, or a little more than a mile."

"We must go higher," I replied; "a Russian shell may reach us at this degree of altitude. Ha! here comes a missile."

A fiery snake, or what seemed like one, was dashing up at a rattling pace directly towards us.

But suddenly it broke, and fell in a million of crackling stars earthward.

It was a rocket, and it had happily fallen short— far short.

"We are out of range of those ugly customers, at any rate," laughed my companion, grimly. "Shall I take the opportunity of reciting an ode— an ode over which I have taken great pains?"

"Ode(e)ar no," I replied, making a vile attempt at a pun. "Some other time if you please—I want to soar a little higher than Parnassus now, to avoid the possible consequences of a Russian shell."

"We should have to shell out if it did reach us," replied my travelling companion, with a chuckle. "You see I can pun as well as yourself. I hope we shall not be punished for being such punsters. We might be, in a very pungent manner."

"Hang it, here comes a shell!" I ejaculated.

Before the words were well out of my mouth a ball of seeming fire had risen from the earth below, passed over the aërostal, and fallen on the other side into space.

"That was an ugly customer!" I exclaimed, with a shudder.

"A rough and reddy one in the shape of a red-hot shot," said my compagnon de voyage; "but hear my ode."

"For heaven's sake drop poetry, and stick to prose," I said.

"I thought it was sufficient for one of us to be prosy," retorted my eccentric aëronant. "But how can you expect a human being named Homer-Virgil-Anacreon-Moore-Byron to remember any other language than that of the gods?"

I was now more than ever convinced of my companion's insanity.

"Is your name really Byron?" I asked.

"Homer-Virgil-Anacreon-Moore-Byron," he replied.

"But your surname is Byron—I may call you Mr. Byron?"

"Well, I suppose you may. I am certainly more Byron than the other names. A pun again! But you didn't seem to catch it."

"I am so fearful lest we should catch something else," I rejoined. "Here comes another red-hot shot. Ha!"

The glittering parabola was described, and the messenger of fire and death passed over the top of the aërostal again, this time so closely that the vast globe of pent-up gas quivered, undulated, and roared with the concussion of air that was caused by its rapid passage.

"Mr. Byron, this will never do," I said. "We must ascend higher. We are well within range of those infernal guns, and are sure to be stricken sooner or later. Throw over more ballast, in heaven's name!"

"With pleasure," was the reply, and the poet whipped out his knife and cut open the bags, bearing my former remonstrance in mind.

"Hold!" I roared; "pitch them over as they are. We are amongst foes now, who are trying all they can to kill us. Why, then, should we be over merciful unto them? While we were hovering over Kars 'twas a different matter."

"As you will," retorted the aëronaut, with a sigh and a shrug of the shoulders. "But the poet, you know, has no foes save vice and prejudice."

Bang! flash! and up came another fiery messenger.

It was something horrifying to watch its dazzling parabola, not knowing but what it might describe in its course the aërostal or the car of the balloon.

But the agony, though terrible, was, at all events, short.

It passed so close, below the aërostal now, that the stout, taut ropes that held the car thereto hummed as telegraph wires hum in a still breeze.

But Byron now, as though awaking for the first time to our danger, threw over three bags of our sand ballast.

The balloon rose at once, as rises an eagle.

The rapidity of its upward flight almost made me giddy.

The air grew icy cold.

Flash! bang! another shot was discharged at us.

The report sounded fainter now.

I looked over the side of the car, and saw the red-hot ball of iron rise, describe its arc, and then fall.

At its greatest altitude it must have been at least a thousand yards beneath the car of the balloon.

"We are out of range now—we need ascend no higher," I remarked to my aëronaut; for I felt my blood was turning to ice in my veins, and my nose and ears were beginning to bleed.

"We have no choice but to rise until we reach a current of air of the same specific gravity as the peculiar conveyance in which we float," was the reply. "Ah, we have reached it!—we are now voyaging horizontally."

"At what pace?" I asked with some interest, for I longed to descend into warmer latitudes.

We were enduring the cold of the Arctic regions. His answer did not console me in the least.

"The breeze is very light," he said, meditatively. "We are certainly not sailing faster than a mile an hour, if that, and in a south-westerly direction."

The very direction in which I least wanted to go; and then the pace, oh, it was killing!

I looked down, and men of the size of bees and wasps had changed into men of the size of ants.

The colours of the Russian uniforms were obliterated by distance.

Their army was an army of mites, their tents were snowy hillocks, their flags were withered autumn leaves.

Still apparently almost under us, though I knew that we must have left it miles to the north-west, Kars looked like a small water-coloured drawing of a town; in short, man and his works had sunk into insignificance, though those of nature look grander and more immense than ever.

From that terrible altitude the eye took in a circle of at least a thousand miles. Mountain and plain, hill and vale, land and water, river and sea—ay, sea—for the Pontus Euxinus was visible like a cold grey fog, ever so many score of leagues away—with the lofty Caucassian ranges rising dim and cloud-like into the heavens on the right.

"We are out of range of all missiles," said the aëronaut; "and as we shall be floating at this altitude for some hours, you will have time to hear my ode; in fact, there is no other way of agreeably passing it."

I queried if this would be an agreeable way to me, but I saw that poetry was the aëronaut's hobby, and being clearly mad on that point, I feared to make him madder by a refusal.

"Go ahead," I said, therefore, "and I will listen as well as the intense cold will let me. If my teeth insist in playing a musical accompaniment, you must excuse me."

And he politely promised that he would.

CHAPTER LVII.

VIRGIL-HOMER-ANACREON-MOORE-BYRON'S EPIC.

"MY epic is a very short one, but for all that I expect it, when published, to take the shine out of the 'Illiad,' 'Paradise Lost,' and everything else of the kind," began the aëronaut by way of prelude. "It is strongly dramatic and narrative. I go in for narrative and dramatic poetry. Listen:—

'There once was a school in the kingdom of Russia,
Sore haunted by the ghost of a very dead usher.
Two naughty boys poisoned him—'tisn't a cram—
With isosceles triangles in raspberry jam.

But when the wind blew and when the snow snew,
These wicked lads thought of the usher they slew;
In compunction they swallowed twelve balls of red
        worsted,
And ten conic sections embedded in custard.'

Here he came to a full stop, and ejaculated with a wave of the hand and an expression of triumph—

"There, what do you think of that? There ends

Book I. you know. Won't Milton, Dryden, and the rest of them, have to look to their laurel honours upon Mount Parnassus, eh?"

"I should like to hear Book II. before I venture to express a positive opinion on the matter," I said, modestly.

"So you shall, my boy—so you shall," rejoined the poet, gushingly. "Now then, after a brief rest, we fire away again:—

'Then the reverend principal, kind-hearted soul,
Cut his throat with hot coffee and powdered French
        roll;
And a junior teacher, an unamiable fellow,
Asphyxiated himself with a cake of chrome yellow.

The cyphering master, so affected was he,
That he scraped six slate pencils up in his tea,
Then oxygenating three bottles of ink,
He mixed them together and quickly did drink.

And monsieur from France fell into a trance,
Lying so awfully still that he had to dance;
And thereafter being seized with a fit of despair,
He gobbled down his moustache and chewed up all
        his hair.'

"There, that's the end of the second book, and an epilogue will complete the poem. What do you think of it now?"

"I—I—I like it very much," I stammered. "But I should still like to hear the end, if you please, before I criticise it."

"Then you shall," said the aëronaut, solemnly. "The end is the climax, and the climax is the end. In a word, the end is everything. In it we reach the dénouement of the awful drama. Here it is:—

'Now that once-haunted school cannot be seen
Half so clearly as if it never had been;
But in each hush of the gale appears the usher,
Gliding past on his head betwixt Russia and Prussia.'

"There, what do you think of that?"

"I—I think it's very talented," I said, unwilling in my then perilous position to say aught that could by any possibility annoy my companion. "I think it so clever that if it were offered to 'Punch' or 'Fun' I make no doubt that——"

"Perish 'Fun' and 'Punch,'" roared the aëronaut. "You insult me, sir; you bitterly, you ruthlessly insult me; or, rather, you have a heart that has never known the ring and the fire of true poesy. Well, that can be amended. Epic poetry has its birthplace in the moon, and to the moon can we ascend. Oh, chaste! oh, beauteous Luna! we come! we come!"

He set to work throwing out the bags of sand as he concluded.

"Madman!" I exclaimed, "what in heaven's name are you about?"

"Higher, higher!" he shouted. "My muse cannot soar too high, and you, stranger, must lose all the earth-worn littlenesses of the globe you have so long dwelt on before you can appreciate poetry such as mine."

I thought that very probable, but yet I had no wish to gain a good opinion of the aëronaut's epic at such a cost.

"Stop!" I said. "We will go to the moon at some other time. I begin now to see the grandeur of your verses, to appreciate the tragic and dramatic vein that runs throughout. It would be a pity for the world to lose such a genius, and the moon will possess no appreciative audience."

"Fool!" exclaimed the aëronaut. "How little you have followed the wondrous and marvellous discoveries of late years. The moon uninhabited? Ha! ha! ha! One would think you were a seventeenth centuryite, when, I believe, people seriously thought that the orb of night was made of green cheese. Know then, dotard, that the moon is inhabited by—*an old man and his dog.*"

"I know that," I gasped, wildly; "but he is a woodman, and how can a cutter of sticks appreciate poetry such as yours?"

"He cannot be such a stick as you are," was the retort. "Prate not to me of sticks, or cutters thereof, or I will force you to cut your stick, and rid myself of a miserable encumbrance by severing the ropes that attach the car to the aërostat. Do you hear, slave?"

Hear? how could I but hear when he bellowed so loudly.

The deuce a doubt of his madness now.

His muffler had dropped from his face, and his cloak from his shoulders.

A brush of his right hand sent his hat flying into space.

His face, his features, his wildly-glaring eyes stood revealed.

To my horror and dismay I recognised Louis Foucarte!

Or, at all events, the man, whatever his name might be, who I had hitherto had every sound reason for believing had found his grave at the bottom of that deep, dark crevasse in the Circassian mountains.

CHAPTER LVIII.
AN OLD FRIEND IN YET ANOTHER DRESS.

THE discovery was electrical.

At first, I thought that it must be his ghost, but a moment's reflection convinced me that ghosts can't lift up and heave over heavy bags of sand as he kept on doing.

He turned round and seemed to read my very thoughts.

"Ha! ha!" he laughed; "that fall didn't dash my brains out, it only cracked them. But I know what I'm about. I'm all right enough when nothing excites me. At these altitudes it's excusable for a fellow with a piece of broken skull working into his brain to be a little eccentric. Ha! ha! ha! the moon will set all that to rights."

I noticed that he was foaming at the mouth.

His eyes were really terrible to look at.

I could see them through the blood that began to trickle from my own.

I glanced earthwards over the side of the car, and uttered an ejaculation of agonised horror, for the world was apparently gone.

There was naught but clouds above, around, and *below*.

"Louis Foucarte, Count Eugene, or whatever your name may be, let us descend," I said. "I don't care where we land, in the midst of the Russian camp even, so that it be somewhere."

I could hardly get the words out of my mouth so cold was I.

My very breath had turned into icicles on my moustache.

Every syllable dropped from my lips as though in frozen atoms.

I shook as one palsy-stricken.

The encircling clouds seemed to turn blood red and to rain showers of gore.

I could hear the aëronaut's laughing retort, however.

He knew no cold nor fear—madmen never do.

"Return to earth," he shouted, "at the commencement of our voyage? That would be folly, indeed. We have the old world, with its sins and follies, its temptations, and soul-fettering ties, beneath us. We are as the birds—we soar heavenwards."

I saw that reasoning with such a man was absurd, but a brilliant idea struck me, and I said—

"Have you not some duty to perform before you quit the earth for the moon? Are you not pledged to steal my despatches, and give them over to your Russian employers? I know you would not willingly soar even heavenwards with such a matter unfulfilled."

"True, true, I thank you for reminding me," said the aëronaut, as one in a dream. "I remember something—yes. I clearly remember something. Ah! your despatches. That was it. Give them me."

"They are no good to you whilst we are in the clouds," I said. "They will be of no service to the old man in the moon. You have to give them, or report their contents, to the Russians. Let us descend, then. After you have obeyed duty's call we can go up again."

I thought to deceive the madman, but lunatics are wary enough at times, and the aëronaut gave me an answer that I was perfectly unprepared for.

"I have a quicker way of keeping my word," he said, whilst his eyes glowed with devilish glee. "I will drop you overboard, despatches and all. If you are spoilt by the fall the writings will be intact, that is one thing—the sabretash will protect them."

"But I may fall into wrong hands, or where none can see me," I said, my very hair standing upright on my head with horror. "We must be far to the south-east of the Russian army of investment now. If you would see where you can drop me to the best advantage, you must not, at all events, descend until you can tell what is beneath us. Don't you perceive that there's sound reason in what I say?"

"Yes, there seems to be," he sullenly acquiesced. "I will do as you advise," and he pulled open the valve for some of the gas to escape.

The rushing sound that followed was like that of a distant waterfall.

We descended rapidly, and in strange, eddying gyrations.

We pierced the lower strata of clouds again, and saw the beautiful green earth, about three miles beneath us.

No army, no besieged city were to be seen, but a vast panorama of mountain and plain—the latter intersected with roads that looked like threads, and rivers that, at that giddy height, looked no wider than narrow white ribands.

"You see I am right," I said, turning with a shudder from my brief downward gaze. "The Russian army is not in sight. Drop me here and I should never be discovered. In performing your duty properly you will have to descend, and take me a prisoner to the Russian lines. I have information in my possession that will save the Russian army of Asia from annihilation.

If ever a deliberate falsehood was excusable, surely 'twas then, in order to effect an escape from the most horrible of deaths.

I spoke so earnestly that I evidently deceived the lunatic.

"I suppose it must be so," he growled, still suffering the gas to escape.

Down—down—down we still went.

At length we saw some Lancers galloping beneath us.

Their gaudy uniforms and brass helmets declared them to be Russians.

We were not half-a-mile above the surface of the earth then, and the aëronaut caught their attention by means of our signal flags.

They drew rein, and gazed up at us wonderingly.

"Now," thought I, "directly the car is within fifty feet or so of the ground, I will drop over the anchor, glide down the cord, and throw myself on the protection of those troopers."

So full was I of this thought, that for nearly a minute I did not look round, and what made me finally do so was the discovery that the balloon was no longer descending, but floating stationary in mid-air.

No sooner had I made this alarming discovery, than I felt a grasp on my arm.

I glanced up with a creeping, chilly feeling of horror, and saw the form of the mad aëronaut towering above me.

He had a long, dagger-bladed knife between his teeth.

In his eyes was the glare of murder.

Another instant, and the weapon was at my throat.

I was powerless to resist.

My nerve and strength alike were utterly gone.

But suddenly the maniac seemed to alter his intention.

He threw me down in the bottom of the car, and placed a foot heavily upon my chest.

Then he commenced, coolly and deliberately, to cut the cords that attached the car to the aërostal, muttering the while—

"The balloon will rise higher without the impedimenta. A double turn of the rope around the wrist will serve my purpose well."

His words gave me an idea.

A rope might save me too.

And as he cut and slashed, I tried to wriggle myself away from beneath his superincumbent foot, and to grasp at anything, no matter how slender, that would give me but a few seconds longer tenure of life.

But vain my efforts.

I was as weak as any child, and the madman's restraining foot seemed heavy as a nether millstone.

One—two—three cords were cut through.

The car lurched over at an angle of ninety-five degrees, for it was now only sustained on one side.

But the madman crawled up, upon what I shall now call the weather rail, and again slashed away with his knife.

Two ropes yet attached the car to the aërostal.

He made a leap and clutched one of these high up.

Then, slash—slash—and I felt myself falling through space.

But I was brought to with a sudden jerk, that seemed almost to cut me asunder, and then I was aware that I was rising again with inconceivable rapidity towards the clouds.

My head hung downwards, and thus I could clearly see how rapidly the earth was receding from me.

I saw the car of the balloon fall thereon and rebound, frightening the horses of the mounted soldiers until, one of them rearing bolt upright, fell back upon its rider.

But then all these objects grew dim and blurred. Up—up—up, higher—higher—higher, my nose, eyes, and ears began to bleed again, and, almost ere I remarked it, I was amongst the clouds once more.

I knew now how I had not fallen to earth along with the car.

I had been caught in the gyrations of the long rope to whose end was attached the anchor.

In falling out it had formed a noose and knot around me.

The aërostal, released from the weight of the car and all its ballast, was now rising with me at a pace of at least a hundred miles an hour into the sky again.

How awful, how terrible was my position!

Higher—higher—and higher yet.

The hundred miles an hour became a hundred leagues.

I had got into a strong upper current of air.

As a consequence, the balloon had changed its perpendicular course for a horizontal one.

Yet naught but burning fiery clouds were to be seen, from which lambent tongues of lightning seemed to me to be for ever darting, whilst the vast aërostal boomed, and roared, and quivered with the rage of the pent-up gas that threatened at any instant to burst its fragile envelope of silk and gutta-percha.

And if it did, what then?

Ah! what then, indeed?

CHAPTER LIX.

I DESCEND FROM THE CLOUDS—WHERE?

YES, I was being whirled along in the midst of fiery clouds.

Driven by the wind, I was travelling at the rate of a hundred leagues an hour in a horizontal direction.

Thunder clouds were crashing together and bursting beneath me, with forked lightning darting and quivering therefrom.

What a horrible position to be placed in.

Dragged through space by the heels.

The beautiful world shut from my view.

As a tail is to a kite, so was I to that big, roaring globe of gas that was tearing with me, perhaps, to the moon—perhaps, *nowhere*.

For space is vacuity, and vacuity is nothing.

Blood fell dripping, dripping, dripping into the clouds below, from my eyes, nostrils, and ears.

My head seemed to be swelling to as vast dimensions as the booming aërostal.

And yet I kept my reason, though I prayed, oh, ever so agonisingly, to lose it.

Every moment I expected to see the balloon burst asunder like a shattered world.

The rarity of the air had caused it to swell to almost twice its original size.

A few hundred yards higher and the gas must explode.

I knew quite enough of balloons to be sure of that.

I knew, too, that directly it happened, the great globe of gas would collapse like one of those painted air balls that are sold to children in the street, when pierced by a pin.

Then I should fall to earth like a stone.

But I should be suffocated long before reaching it with the rapidity of passing through the air.

These were horrible thoughts—horrible!

I was aroused from them by a singing.

The singing of a weird and awful song.

I could not make out the words, nor for a second could I imagine who was the singer.

Then I recollected the madman, my companion.

I remembered that he had sprang up and caught a severed rope just ere he had cut in twain the last one that bound the car to the aërostal.

With an effort, I then glanced upwards, and saw that he was still there holding on to the rope now with both hands, supporting the whole weight of his body in mid air thereby.

His position was even more terrible than mine.

But he seemed to be utterly unconscious of it.

He was singing away quite unconcerned.

But his wrists and hands were like marble.

And the veins stood out on them full of black blood.

I saw that he could not hold on much longer.

Had he been sane, he must have let go long ago; but madmen are impervious to pain.

At least, they are to a very great extent.

That is to say, when their mania is upon them.

I could not take my eyes off the man.

I found myself betting with an imaginary shadow how soon he would relax his grasp and fall.

Surely I was going mad, too.

It must have been so, for my terrors began to evaporate, and I began to feel a wild glee as I swung like a pendulum on the anchor rope.

I did not guess then that this ecstatic feeling must have been caused by the rarity of the atmosphere, which had somewhat the effect of laughing gas upon me.

And I still betted away with my imaginary shadow upon how long the madman would hold on.

And when I won I would laugh wildly, and when I lost, I believe that I swore most profanely, too.

At last my fellow victim perceived me.

"Ha! mon ami, you are there. It is well."

That's what I think he roared out to me.

I believe that I made some reply that provoked his anger, for he removed his right hand from the rope to shake his fist at me.

Then I heard his left wrist snap with its long tension, as snaps a bow when drawn too far.

A terrible yell followed, and I saw the madman fall—fall—fall into the leaden clouds that drifted and rolled far down beneath.

One glance I caught at his dead-white face and his glaring eyes, and then the masses of dim vapour seemed to enfold him in their embrace and hide him from my view.

I was absolutely alone in space now.

And yet my wonderful elation of spirits continued.

I still held communion with my imaginary shadow, and now fancying that the clouds rolling so far beneath had assumed the shapes of bears, and lions, and elephants, and bet with him on their racing powers, and was the witness of an imaginary Derby in the sky.

I was diverted from this train of ideas by a sharp blow on the face and a shrill croak.

I looked and saw that a monstrous eagle was hovering just over me, and apparently on the point of swooping down upon me.

My madness disappeared at that sight.

It must have returned, or I should not have so quickly known that my grim visitant was an eagle.

But I felt at once, that no other bird could have soared so high, and I also felt at once that the cruel bird had determined to hook my eyes out, for a special tid bit appetiser, before he consumed the rest of my face.

The idea was an agonising one. What nightmare could have been half so horrible?

I yelled and screamed, in order to frighten the eagle away. I threw out my arms, and kicked out my legs, unmindful of the fact that I might somehow or other wriggle myself free of the anchor rope, and fall downwards through the clouds.

But the eagle was at last frightened away, though not before my hands were severely lacerated by its beak and claws.

But it only left me to find another foe in the soaring booming aërostal, which seemed at last fully to have aroused its rage.

Perhaps it deemed it to be a rival monarch of the sky; anyhow, it attacked it again and again, pecking angrily at the vast glass globe.

I knew what must surely happen, as the eagle returned again and again to the charge.

I knew that his long, crooked, cruel bill, was sharp, and that the gutta-percha and silk coating of the aërostal was thin.

Nor was I wrong, for at last a heavy wheezing sound smote my ears, and a warm, stinking vapour fell upon my face.

I knew that it was the gas escaping from the aërostal, which the eagle had punctured with its beak. Surely it was all over with me now.

But as yet it escaped slowly, and the descent of the balloon was slow and gentle.

Yet the eagle might make a score more escape-holes for the gas to ooze out, and each would accelerate our downward progress.

Then, directly the gas was all gone, I should fall like a stone and be dashed to pieces.

But happily the stinking coal-gas frightened or disgusted the eagle, so that he flew away.

Then a slight ray of hope returned to me.

I was descending slowly and gently.

There could be no mistake about that.

Presently I was in the midst of the clouds.

Then I was beneath them, the sun and the blue sky were blotted out, and a cold rain was pouring downwards on my face.

I could see the world below me again, now see it like a panorama; about four miles off towns, fields, ruins and woods, like an old picture map of the seventeenth century.

But the aërostal was fast collapsing.

And every instant I fell faster.

Yes, clearly, at last, it would be like a stone.

But hope returned to my breast, as suddenly I beheld a mountain—a mountain to which Mont Cenis, or Mont Blanc, would have been as tiny babes, rising for tens of thousands of feet into the air, as though on purpose to receive me in its snowy embrace.

Down—down—still inexorably down.

Yes, surely I should descend upon the mountain.

But the descent was now so quick that I could scarcely draw my breath.

"After all, it is death," I thought.

And then my brains seemed suddenly to burst asunder, and consciousness forsook me.

*   *   *   *

When I recovered my reason, I was lying half buried in a snow wreath, as cold as death.

I opened my eyes. A rope was round my body, which seemed to hold me down to the ground.

But was it ground? I dropped myself a few yards over the snow, and came to the edge of a cliff, over which I peered.

I looked down a sheer precipice of at least two thousand feet in perpendicular height.

Then there was a ledge and a steep slope of another three thousand feet, while the heads and crowns of lesser hills rose up in wild confusion around their ice-clad monarch.

I drew my head back from the giddy abyss in shuddering horror, and crawled back to where I had first lain.

Then I pondered how I should rid myself of the rope, that was nearly cutting me in two.

I recollected that I had a knife in one of my pockets, and with great difficulty a half-frozen hand managed to drag it forth.

More difficult still was it to open it and cut through the cord: but at last I managed to do it, and then to rise to my feet, and stamp some life into them.

I looked around me. There was the anchor in one direction, hitched tightly in a crevice of the rocks, and in another, the utterly collapsed aërostal, still hissing through its many wounds, but not louder than a dozen or two of copper tea kettles.

"I can never remain here," I muttered to myself. "It is colder than the Arctic regions—I should be dead long before the morning."

I shuffled along as best I could, for to remain still was death; but it was very difficult to move.

And dangerous, too, for I might at any instant step into a thinly iced-over crevasse.

In which case I might also be buried alive.

The snow was slippery as slippery could be, and I had very little strength left in me.

But still I staggered around and between the frozen hillocks that formed the summit of the mountain, in search of the opposite side.

Suddenly, however, I came across an object built by hands—an object that caused me a thrill of astonishment and awe.

My hair rose erect on my head, and I uttered a cry, for I was looking upon Noah's Ark!

CHAPTER LX.

ON THE TOP OF MOUNT ARARAT.

THERE could be no doubt about it. There was the wreck of the first ship that had ever floated upon the great waters, preserved, almost miraculously, amidst the eternal ice and snow for scores of centuries.

What three-year-old child, who has ever possessed toys, or looked upon them through a shop-window, is there that would not, in an instant, have recognised that strange structure, with its sloping roof—half house, half ship.

Upon that sloping roof lay snow—icicles drooped from its edges—the great doors in the sides, through which the animals had trooped out, two and two, were wide open, doubtless just as they had been left by Noah and his sons.

It was a weird and an awful sight to look upon —weird and awful more on account of its associations than aught else.

I was alone with the mighty past—with that great house-ship that alone floated when the whole world was drowned. But I was more lonely even could have been Noah, for I had no companionship whatever.

I could not have entered through those open doors, into the interior of the ark, for worlds. Doubtless it would be warmer there—doubtless I could live there through the night that was rapidly coming down in gloom and storm; but I would rather have died out in the snow, the sleet, and the icy wind, than have gone in there to seek refuge.

Here it suddenly struck me that, as the inmates of the ark, and all the four-footed denizens thereof, must once have descended from the summit to the base of the mountain, the road, after all, could not be a very difficult one to traverse.

Ah! but how was I to find it?

That was indeed the question.

Besides, in those thousands of years, avalanches, mountain slips, falling rocks, &c., might have totally obliterated the old pathway, or, at all events, have made it impassable to the feet either of man or beast.

Anyhow, I would try and find it.

And there was clearly not an instant to lose.

It struck me that I would give much to take away a relic of the Ark.

My knife was in my hand, why should I not?

I crept up, tremblingly, to the antique ship.

I touched its hull with my hand.

I even dug my knife into its hard, frozen timbers, and then a great fear seized upon me, as the thunder crashed, and the forked lightning quivered and flashed above, below, and around me, and I fled.

Fled I knew not whither, and with a terror I had never known before.

It was a miracle that I did not go right over the awful precipice, of so many thousands of feet of perpendicular height, that I had peered over half-an-hour before.

Providentially, I must have taken an opposite direction, for, presently, I found myself rolling down a frozen incline a great deal faster than was agreeable.

Down, down, down—blinded with snow and cut with the sharp projections of the rocks—I rolled, until I again fainted.

When I recovered therefrom it was moonlight instead of twilight, and a moonlight so bright that I could see every object distinctly.

I could see naught below but mountains, peaks, a ruined city or two, a river, and far away in the distance the waters of a lake.

I glanced backwards up Mount Ararat, and saw between its summit and the sky the form of the Ark still resting.

The moon was shining immediately over its roof, and its entire and gigantic outline was as distinct as well could be.

I shuddered and turned away, again turning now my whole attention upon the best way of getting down to the base of the mountain.

I found, after a great many slips and slides and falls, that it was almost as well to trust to chance as to care; but I still stumbled on, for 'twas death to attempt to sleep in such altitudes; and after escaping destruction a hundred times, by next to a miracle, I came to the top of a precipice that shelved almost perpendicularly down to an immense depth.

I knew that a slip down this would mean to be dashed to pieces at its base; but, on the other hand, I found it impossible on so slippery and already inclined a surface to turn myself round to re-ascend.

What was to be done, then?

Nothing clearly could be done, except creep round the brink of the crevasse in search of some easier place either of ascent or descent at another point.

But this was a dangerous feat on an incline steep as a house roof, slippery as ice could make it, and with a precipice of profound depth, that the slightest slip would be sure to launch me into.

Truly, if I escaped this danger, also, I should have good reason for thinking that I was born to be hanged.

I crept on, and on, and on; but the slippery hill side was just as steep on my left and the precipice as perpendicular on my right as when I had first attempted its circumnavigation.

And looking up I saw that heavy clouds were about to obscure the moon.

Did they do so whilst I was in such a position I must assuredly be lost.

That thought made me crawl quicker.

But I grew so giddy as I looked at the abyss on my right, that I resolved, if possible, to do as Blondin does, cast not a glance at the depths below, but keep my eyes fixed on the path I was following, and that path only.

'Twas not quite as narrow as Blondin's rope, but then it was far more slippery, and not so true and level for the feet, either.

I was, in fact, soon obliged to take my boots off, or I must have lost my balance.

In my stockinged feet I no longer slipped, that was one comfort.

But then my feet presently became so benumbed that I could not feel them beneath me or be sure where I placed them.

And whilst I was thus situated, the clouds swept over the moon, enveloping the whole scene in the impenetrable gloom and darkness of night.

I could not see my hands before me, and my feet were so frozen that I could not tell whether they touched the ground or not. I had no resource but to cast myself on my back, therefore, and thus wait until the moon once more shone out.

I lay for several minutes at full length, with my arms outstretched in the shape of a cross. But in spite of this I presently felt that I was slipping, and that do what I would I could not check my downward course.

I went very slowly at first, but the pace soon increased; I tried to grasp at something, but only seized upon snow, that either balled or melted in my grasp.

Then I shot and slid downwards so rapidly that I lost my breath again, though not my consciousness, and I kept thinking to myself, "at all events this is no precipice."

It was no precipice. In copying Blondin, I had unwittingly left the precipice behind me, but I was descending a preciously steep hill for all that.

At last it struck me that I saw the gleam of a fire, far, far below, and heard the hum of human voices; but I was travelling so quickly, with sometimes head uppermost, and sometimes that I could not be sure of anything, until at last my headlong course was suddenly brought to an end by alighting upon something comparatively soft, and seeing rising on one side me a stone structure that looked very like a chimney.

Then I looked over the side of the thing, whatever it was, that had broken my fall, and saw two rough-looking men sitting before a fire.

———

CHAPTER LXI.

I ASTONISH THE CHARCOAL BURNERS.

THE fire was a bright and lurid one, and shed its rays far and wide over the landscape.

They showed me that I was lying on the roof of their hut, a miserable edifice of mud, with a reed-thatched roof, whose softness had, doubtless, saved me from a broken limb in falling down the mountain slope thereon.

I was much obliged to it, at any rate, but I did not like the look of its owners at all.

They were bearded, savage-looking fellows, with black faces and blacker dresses.

I could see by the felled pines that lay around, and by two or three other fires that dotted the hill still lower down, that they were charcoal burners.

A respectable trade, doubtless, but one which, from past experience, I had no great penchant for choosing my hosts from.

The reader will guess why.

Needs must when the devil drives, however, and these men, at all events, were not Russians, that was one comfort.

I called out to them, therefore, and after awhile they heard me, and looked up.

But when they at last saw me, their surprise knew no bounds, and, instead of helping me to descend, they ran away.

I had, therefore, to reach the ground as best I could; but this difficulty was but a trifle to those that I had encountered before.

The hut was not very high, and as on one side of it the snow seemed to be soft and tolerably deep, I rolled myself off the roof into it.

The fall did not hurt me much; but I was so bruised and battered with my previous rolls and falls, that I could not rise to my feet, and so had to crawl towards the fire.

I did this in order to get thawed, for I felt that I was frost-bitten in almost as many places as I was bruised.

I soon reached the fire, and at first its genial heat was most pleasant; but presently I began to feel the most frightful pricking pains all over, which quickly grew into positive agony.

I crawled away from the fire then, and into the hut, where I slunk into a corner, and for awhile writhed in my pain like a scotched snake.

I soon felt, however, that it was giving me the use of my limbs back, and so I grew reconciled to it—at all events bore it with more equanimity.

Then, at last, as my pains grew less, I remembered that I had tasted no food for many hours, and I began to feed ravenously.

So ravenous, that I really could have eaten with appetite the cat râgout of the Governor of Kars.

I looked around the hut, and nothing could I see but two or three rough wooden stools and a heap of dirty sheepskins.

The floor was formed of hard-beaten earth, and the walls apparently of the same.

There was no grate indoors, but an open hearth, formed of a single cracked flagstone, and the icy wind roared down the chimney as down a funnel, and then whistled around the interior.

A more wretched apology for an abode I had never been the denizen of.

But, then, beggars could not be choosers, and certainly I was an uninvited guest.

And, if I didn't like my quarters, there was the mountain side to which I could rebetake myself.

This last thought made me very reconciled.

Anything was better than being frozen to death.

But still I was as hungry as well could be.

And there seemed to be only the sheepskins and the three-legged stools there to devour.

And they required considerable powers of mastication.

I scrambled to my feet, and proceeded to make a more careful investigation, however.

Few things can be found without looking for them.

There might be a loaf of black bread, or a few eatable roots, in some corner or other.

And if so they would be worth the search.

But I searched, and searched, but found them not.

After I had done I went back to my corner again, and crouched down as before.

But I had hardly done so, when I heard voices and footsteps, and glancing towards the open doorway, I saw it completely blocked up with grimy forms, and fiery, wondering faces.

There were not two, but a dozen charcoal burners now, and they looked anything but amiable.

They wore long bare-bladed knives in their girdles too, and they looked like fellows who were accustomed to use them on any or no provocation.

I began to wonder if it wouldn't have been just as well if I had voyaged earthwards in the car of the balloon. Death seemed just as near now.

The charcoal burners began to bellow and bawl at me, but their language sounded to me as much like double Chinese backwards as anything else, I could not make out a word of it.

They seemed to see this, for presently they beckoned me forth, and I had no help but to go.

When they had got me outside the hut they felt me over, and seemed to be greatly astonished at the cut of my clothes, my gold lace and epaulets, and above all my bootless feet.

Then the two men whom I had first seen sitting before the fire pointed up to the roof and made signs as though to tell the others that that was where they had seen me first.

Then they all uttered grunts, and two seizing me by the arms, asked me by pantomimic actions where I had come from.

In reply, I pointed to the mountain top, now rising in the clear moonlight, many thousand feet above us, in the blue starlit sky.

They knew what I meant well enough, but they shook their heads incredulously.

They evidently could not believe that I had come down, and they regarded me suspiciously.

But I signified to them that they might see for themselves if some of them would scramble into the roof and see the traces of my descent.

I could not make them understand me for a long while, but at last I seemed to succeed, and they did as I had hinted, and some went up the steep mountain side, in the rear as well, presently returning with cries and exclamations of "Allah il Allah," and so forth.

They drew away from me now, as I thought in terror more than in anger.

I thought this, because they did not handle their knives or glance at me menacingly.

And presently, having conquered their fears in some measure, they came up to me again and examined me more carefully than before.

'Twas evident that they looked upon my dress as heathenish, outlandish, unintelligible.

But presently an idea seemed to strike one of them, and he ejaculated gutterally, a word that sounded to me like "Japhets."

Then another grunted a word like "Shem."

And another one that sounded more like "Ham."

Then they all nodded and grunted and shuddered; and putting this and that together, I could see that they took me for one of the sons of Noah, who had in some unaccountable manner or other revisited in the flesh the scenes of the mighty past.

I hardly know whether I felt flattered or otherwise. I certainly felt gratitude in one way, namely, at the thought that I had now no longer any fear of personal violence from these poor Mohammedans, who have as devout a belief in the Old Testament as ourselves.

But then, what would they do with me?

I tried to lead their thoughts in another direction

"STRONG BONY FINGERS CLUTCHED MY THROAT, TWO FIERY EYES GLARED INTO MINE, AND A FŒTID BREATH FANNED MY FACE."

by several times shouting, "Omar Pasha," as loud as I could bawl.

At last they seemed to understand me; and no sooner had they done so than they stared at each other, and then simultaneously commenced to slap their hands and exhibit the most extravagant expressions of delight.

I could not understand a word of what they then commenced to jabber about, but it struck me that they imagined that one of Noah's three sons had returned to earth in the flesh on purpose to bear to the army of Omar Pasha some intelligence or unearthly aid that should give it a victory, terrible and decisive, over the Russian hosts that had overrun and desolated Georgia, Mongolia and Circassia.

I was taken within the hut and given food and drink. I was given a bed of pine leaves to sleep on, and a huge fire was lighted on the cracked hearthstone to give me warmth.

I could also just make out from the explanations of my hosts, that on the morrow I was to be forwarded somewhere, though for the life of me I couldn't make out where.

CHAPTER LXII.
THE TENT OF OMAR PASHA.

WELL, not to make my tale too long, for doubtless the reader is somewhat impatient to get back to the siege of Sebastopol, which, all this while, the gallant Allies—English, French, and Sardinians—are pounding away at night and day, with more cannon and mortars then had ever been brought to bear against a fortified place before, I will cut short as possible my progress from Ararat to the Turkish head-quarters at Erzeroum.

Suffice it is to say then, that early the following morning, after a breakfast of black bread and onions, washed down with spring water, my hosts sent me forth on a mule, and with a sure guide as far as the Bayazid, in Armenia, a distance of about forty English miles.

The man, poor as he undoubtedly was, would not take a single coin for this arduous duty, which occupied from daybreak until nightfall.

But, as persuasions were of no avail, I was forced, nolens volens, to let his services go unpaid, and sleeping at a miserably dirty inn, I the next morning set forth with a troop of Bashi-Bazouks for Topra Kaleh, a distance of something like a hundred miles.

I was on this occasion seated on the charger of a Bashi-Bazouk who had died of black fever the previous day, at Bayazid; but it was the only animal to be obtained, for my friend the charcoal burner had taken his mule back with him.

He was a savage, evilly-disposed brute, who could kick, rear and bite, and perform other disagreeable antics to perfection.

But he had go in him for all that, and in the deep demi-pique Turkish saddle, with its broad shovel stirrups, and with a severe Turkish bit in his mouth, with which I could have broken his jaws had he been too mischievously disposed, I felt thoroughly the master of the spirited animal that I bestrode, and certainly much preferred it to the mule of the preceding day.

And it was a beautiful creature to look at, in all faith—mettle, courage and endurance were all apparent in the mottled satin-skin, the flat sinewy legs, the full muscular neck, broad forehead, shapely muzzle, wide red nostrils, quivering ears, and wild, yet gazelle-like eyes.

He could gallop on, mile after mile, hour after hour, with a stride unwarying, and apparently as untiring, too, as clockwork.

My companions, however, were such magnificent horsemen that I was thoroughly ashamed of my own powers.

Like the Circassians, they could fling their lances ahead of them and pick them up off the ground as they rushed past them at a headlong gallop.

Of course I could not understand a word of what they said; but they were very kind and polite in their way, and chatted to me incessantly, apparently quite contented with my nodded answers.

From Topra Kaleh I travelled in their company to Erzeroum, within a few miles of which city Omar Pasha's army of Asia was encamped in cantonments.

It took us five days' journeying from Bayazid to Erzeroum, and that was good travelling, too, for the distance was at least two hundred and fifty miles, over the most infamous of roads that it is possible to conceive.

But at last the journey was accomplished, and one bright, sunny day we reached the Turkish camp.

It was noon, and not a sound pervaded the Turkish cantonments, save the occasional snort of an impulsive steed.

Picketed in rows, the gallant little chargers of the Turkish cavalry are dozing away the hours between morning and evening feed.

The troopers themselves are smoking or sleeping in their tents, save here and there where a more devout Mussulman than ordinary lay almost prostrate on his little square piece of prayer-carpet, his face turned towards Mecca, and his thoughts wholly abstracted from all worldly considerations.

The tents were as white as snow, all save one, and that was green—the colour of the Prophet.

It was the tent of the Commander-in-Chief.

The tent of the great Omar Pasha—an Hungarian by birth, but a Turk by adoption, and the Sultan's far most able general.

I had taken leave of my rough cohort of Bashi-Bazouks close to the outer lines.

A solitary aide-de-camp conducted me through the siesta-wrapped army to the tent of the Commander-in-Chief.

When I entered it I found Omar Pasha, seated on a camp-stool before a small camp-table, in deep converse with a couple of officers, evidently high in rank—one of whom wears the British uniform, the other a nondescript Asiatic one.

He was a spare, sinewy-looking man, above the middle height, with figure developed and toughened by constant exercise.

An excellent horseman, a practised shot, and an adept in all field sports, Omar Pasha looked as if no labour would tire him, no hardships affect his vigour or his health.

His small head was set on his shoulders in the peculiar manner that always denotes physical strength, and his well-cut features would have been handsome had it not been for a severe and somewhat caustic expression, which marred the beauty of his countenance.

His deep-set eyes were very bright and keen, and their glance seemed accustomed to command, and also to detect falsehood under a threefold mask.

He wore his beard and moustache short and close, and grizzled here and there—but more with toil than age—and they added much to his soldier-like exterior.

His dress was simple enough, consisting of a close-fitting, dark green frock coat, adorned only with the order of the Medjidie, riding boots, and a crimson fez with a blue silk tassel.

A carved Turkish scimitar hung from his belt and a double-barrelled gun, of English workmanship, was balanced across his knees.

As I entered his tent he looked up from the map he had been studying, and, perceiving me, exclaimed suddenly in French—

"An English officer, as I live!"

"Yes, general," I replied. "An English officer from Kars and the top of Mount Ararat."

"The top of Mount Ararat?" said Omar Pasha. The other officers stared at me inquiringly.

"Yes," I answered calmly. "I escaped from Kars by balloon, but the balloon deposited me on the top of Mount Ararat, and I rolled down the greater part of the way on to the hut of some charcoal burners, who, taking me for either Shem, Ham, or Japhet, conducted me in safety to Bayazid, where I fell in with some Bashi-Bazouks."

"Your story is a very remarkable one, sir," said the English officer, surveying me through his eyeglass, whilst Omar Pasha told his beads, like a true Mussulman, exclaiming—

"'Tis said that no human being has ever reached the summit of Mount Ararat since Noah and his family came down from thence."

"It is very probable," I rejoined; "but here are my despatches, general," and I handed them to him.

He took them from my hands and read them attentively.

Then his face brightened up—

"Gentlemen," he said, "we are saved. This news is of the most vital importance, and had it arrived twenty-four hours later it would have been too late to be of service to us."

"Yes," I remarked, "I ate—or at all events helped to eat—the last cat in the city nearly a week ago. The inhabitants must be by this time devouring each other."

"Then we will march to the relief of Kars before the sun is an hour lower in the heavens," said Omar Pasha, decisively. "Sir William Williams is a gallant officer. In three days he shall see the green flag of the most holy Prophet advancing to his succour."

"It is well," I said. "General Williams expected such chivalrous conduct at your hands. But he is very hardly pressed."

"I can't help that," said Omar Pasha. "I will do my best, and no man can do more."

He turned to his maps again, and I took this as a polite intimation that it was time for me to be gone, and that the conference was over.

But I had still another point to gain.

"General," I said, "I wish to reach the lines before Sebastopol as soon as possible. Can you pass me on at once?"

"Yes," said Omar Pasha. "I am going to send a special messenger to the Allied Generals to-morrow at daybreak, and you can accompany him. Will that content you?"

"Yes," I said. "So that I arrive there in time to see the fall of the city, I am content."

"Fear not, you will see that," replied Omar Pasha. "This gentleman, Captain Armstrong, of the English Dragoons, is your travelling companion."

I bowed to the English officer, and he bowed to me.

Then we shook hands, and he said, with a very pleasant smile—

"As we are to be travelling companions, we had better be tent companions whilst in camp as well. Come, the commander-in-chief is busy."

Of course I at once accepted his invitation, and away we went.

I found him a very genial companion, and his tent full of good things.

He produced champagne and caviare, patês-de-foies-gras, and Perigord pies, with many other good things, and I made a heartier meal than I had done for many a long day.

Then we strolled through the camp together, and saw all the curiosities thereof, and the next morning we saw it strike its tents and march, ourselves setting out Sebastopol-wards at the same time.

CHAPTER LXIII.

ONCE MORE AT SEA.

OUR journey from Erzeroum to the Crimea was a long and tedious one.

On the second day we crossed the Euphrates, and on the seventh reached Kumbah.

From thence we proceeded by way of Niksar-Bogha Hissai and Vezin Kopri to Batra, a Turkish port on the Black Sea, whence we took ship direct for Balaclava.

We had no choice of vessels, or, at all events, a very bad one, for the best we could find was a craft that seemed a kind of cross breed between a Genoese felucca and a Turkish caïque, manned by as rascally looking a crew as it would have been easy to find in a day's march.

The master, though he insisted upon being a good Turk, and a good Mussulman, too, looked far more like a Greek or a Suliote than either, and his crew resembled him in features and style as closely as Beelzebub resembles Lucifer.

Still he was profuse in his protestations of devotion to our service, and his ability to carry us in safety across that most treacherous of all seas, the Pontus Euxinus.

And then we had but one option, either to go with him, or stay behind altogether.

So, of the two evils, we chose the lesser.

It was on a cold, bleak, wretched morning that we sailed out of Batra, and entrusted ourselves to the tender mercies of wind and ocean.

But anything was better than the filth, fleas, and food at the establishment, misnamed an hotel, where we had resided for the past forty-eight hours, and so we were, at first, thankful for the change.

Our stomachs, in fact, rebelled before our hearts, for the short, chopping waves of the great inland sea were too much for them, and our Turkish breakfast was soon food for fishes.

Yet still the Long Snake—for such was the name of the craft we had shipped aboard, and a beastlier name vessel surely never bore—bounded steadily forward, sailing so close up to the wind that she seemed to be eating her way into its very teeth; and still her master and crew attended to their several duties, bestowing occasionally a cringing salaam, or oily smile upon us, as they passed to and fro the decks.

"Are you a physiognomist?" I asked my companion, when, after the lapse of an hour or two, and the imbibing of sundry sips of brandy, I became more accustomed to the movements of our volatile craft.

"Not much of an one," was the reply, "but it needs not an adept in the art to read the faces that are passing up and down before us."

"And how do you interpret them?" I asked.

"Why, that we shall have a safe voyage," he replied, with a dry laugh.

"That's a very strange reading," I remarked.

"On the contrary, I think it a very clear one."

"Translate it, please, to my ordinary comprehension," I said, rather petulantly.

"Well, then, they look such unmitigated rascals, every man Jack of them, that I'm sure the ocean will never cheat the gallows of its due; and if they escape, why so shall we."

This reply was perfectly comprehensible.

"I believe you are quite right," I said; "but there are other dangers attending a voyage with such rascals, besides those dependent upon wind and wave."

"Of what kind, pray?" asked my companion.

"Why, the rascals may cut our throats."

"Oh, yes, so they may," said my fellow voyageur, as he shrugged his shoulders; "but I think the odds are a hundred to one against it."

"How so?" I asked, with some surprise.

"Because they are such awful cowards."

"Cowards! How on earth do you know that?"

"By instinct, as dogs know the smell of a fox, or a cat the proximity of a mouse."

"Umph! I doubt instinct in such matters; but even if they are cowards, they are nine to two, and surely it would require very little courage on their part to attack us."

Oh, yes it would, of the quality they are possessed of. They'd make sure we should kill two or three of them first; and then each man would fancy that he might be one of the victims, and that would cause all to hold aloof."

"But what do the fellows carry their curved scimitars, long daggers, and pistols for, if not for use," I asked, rather petulantly.

"For show more than anything else; the two former weapons, perhaps, for giving anyone a sly thrust through the back with, when they were paid well to kill."

"I'll be shot if I'll turn my back to one of them whilst on board, then," I said.

"Nor will I," replied the English officer, with a laugh; "and so nothing will be lost on the score of politeness, eh?"

"Nothing; but I wonder what they will give us for dinner. An empty stomach re-acting on itself is no joke, and if I must continue to proffer tribute unto Neptune, I would prefer giving him a meat-offering to one of wind and nothingness," I said.

"Well, and I think so could I," replied my friend the captain. I generally called him captain, though knowing that it was not strict etiquette so to do. "By Jove, and so would I, by a long way."

We didn't talk any more for a long time.

One reason perhaps was, that at this juncture it grew rougher.

Another might have been, that we were thinking about our dinners. I say might have been advisedly, for I don't for an instant fancy that it was.

The shores of Asiatic Turkey had by this time receded from our view, and all around was sea.

A sea of ink lashed into creamy foam.

There are writers—and experienced writers too— who assert that the waters of the Pontus Euxinus are as blue as those of any other sea.

I deny the statement in toto.

True, when a bright sun is shining, an unclouded sky may in a greater or a less degree lend its colour to the sullen waves.

But when the heavens become overcast, and the wind gets up, then, instead of that pale grey-green sickly hue that distinguishes other seas, the waves of the Pontus Euxinus become literally black, and gleam like ebony, in contrast with the snowy fleecy foam that tops each onrolling billow.

Over those billows the Long Snake seemed to alternately glide and wriggle, for all the world like the uncanny reptile she was named after.

Sometimes she would plunge right through a sea, and at others she would bound over one as though scorning so puny a barrier to her course.

Her sails were wetted and drew well—so well, that often her long tapering mast, formed of a single pine, as elastic as a fencing foil, bent like a fishing rod under the great weight of canvas that it carried.

And still the sea rose, and no canvas was taken in.

The Turkish sailors evidently knew the powers of their craft.

If they were cowards in other matters, they at all events feared not the wrath of the great deep or the stormy gale.

"Those fellows are good sailors, but very bad Mohammedans," said the captain, after he had smoked two pipes of cut cavendish.

"How know you that?" I asked.

"Because, were they so, they would once in every hour turn their faces towards Mecca and pray. Now, I've kept my eyes upon them for something very like three hours, and never once have they done so."

"Well, and what do you argue from that?"

"Why, if they are not Mussulmen, they are not Turks."

"And, then?" I asked, curiously.

"Why, then they are Greeks, and Greeks, beside being most of them villanous cut-throats, are all heart and soul devoted to Russia," he said.

"Then you think they meditate treachery?"

"Rather. I hope you have a good revolver?"

"I have; loaded in every chamber too."

"It's well. If they attack us we can rid the world of the knaves in double quick time."

"But, though they dare shoot us, we dare not shoot them," I said; "because you know we could not ourselves navigate the vessel into port."

"Ah, true," said the captain. "Now, I call that a nuisance—a great nuisance. Well, never mind, if the occasion arises we must frighten the beggars by shooting one or two, and threatening the rest."

"Yes, that we could do," I replied; "but look those two fellows are carrying something savoury down into the cabin. I think it's the dinner, and my sickness seems to have passed quite away."

"And so has mine," said the captain. "Come along."

Down we went into the close, stifling, stinking hold, and took our seats at an uncloth-covered table.

Two or three tin dishes were laid thereon, one holding a kind of curry, a second, plain boiled rice, and the third, something that looked like yams or sweet potatoes.

We had pewter plates and wooden spoons to eat with, and two of the crew stood up with their heads bent (for the cabin was too low in the roof for a full grown man to stand upright in), to wait on us.

Despite the plainness of the fare and the dirtiness of our dining room I felt hungry; my Neptune-votive stomach yearned to be refilled, even at the cost of another sacrifice to the sea god, and I regarded the curry particularly with longing eyes, for I knew that it was a dish at which even the meanest of Oriental cooks excelled.

The waiters handed us the yams and the rice, but not the curry.

I pointed to the dish, but they seemed not to notice me.

I perceived that thereupon the captain chuckled grimly, and helped himself to the yams and rice most liberally.

I was indignant, however, and, half rising from my bench, I drew the curry dish towards me and filled my plate with the golden food.

I was about to put a good spoonful into my mouth, when my companion drew my plate away from me and pitched its contents upon the floor.

"Stick to the rice and the yams," he said.

"Wherefore?" I asked, anything but amiably.

"Because, you may depend upon it that that curry is poisoned," explained the captain.

"The devil it is!" I ejaculated. "Yet I don't see what reason you have for coming to such a conclusion. Besides, the yams and rice that you are making such havoc with may be poisoned too."

"No, they are all right, I'm convinced."

"Then I'm equally convinced regarding the curry," I answered, giving myself another helping.

"Stop, listen to reason," said the captain, this time merely laying a hand upon my arm. "I am more acquainted with Oriental rules than you are. They didn't hand us that dish of which you are so desirous to partake, for one of two reasons."

"And what are those two reasons, pray?"

"Well, firstly they may have refrained from handing it to us in order to take away all our suspicion, and make us the more eager to partake of it. But I think the other reason is nearer the truth, and that is, that they fancy that if they do not hand it to us, and we eat thereof, the crime of murder will not rest upon their shoulders."

"You are a casuist," I said, still with a longing eye upon the curry; "but I believe that in the present instance your suspicions are altogether unfounded."

"Very well, then, refill your plate, do not raise your first spoonful to your mouth too quickly, and I promise that if nothing arises to renew my suspicions before the savoury mess is between your teeth I will raise no further objections to your making a hearty meal thereon."

"All right," I said. "Now you talk sensibly."

I refilled my plate, and then my spoon, and the latter was at my very lips when a back-hander from the captain sent the spoon flying across the cabin, and the curry all over my vest and trousers.

"Hang it, this is too much," I cried, springing to my feet, and in the act striking my head against the deck above with such force that I dropped into it again considerably more than half stunned.

Had it not been for this, I think I should have tried to have knocked the captain down, but as it was I could only ruefully rub the summit of my pericranium and watch his further movements with a dreamy interest.

The Turks or Greeks, or whatever they were, were laughing at the captain's treatment of me until the tears rolled down their cheeks, and this kindled my anger afresh.

The captain, however, dropped his spoon into my plate of curry in place of his own, took it in his left hand, and rising from his chair, first closed and fastened the cabin door on the inside, and then walking up to the still grinning Orientals, he held the plate towards them, and said sternly—

"Grecco veda!"

They stopped grinning then, and stared at each other.

I began to stare too.

My travelling companion was evidently trying to reduce theories to practice.

"Grecco veda!" he exclaimed again.

The men shook their heads irresolutely.

Then the captain with his right hand whipped a revolver from his belt, and again addressing them in what I knew to be modern Greek, yet, nevertheless could not translate into plain English, he evidently gave them to understand that they must choose between curry and lead.

But the contents of the dish appeared to be as unpalatable to the rascals as the contents of the pistol.

They excused themselves, with many shruggings and pantomimic expostulations, from taking the curry.

By the same means the captain intimated sardonically to them how good it was.

But whilst he did so he played with the trigger of his revolver most meaningly.

Then the wretches fell upon their knees.

They begged piteously for mercy.

But, as they did so, the captain's smiling face turned into one of iron.

"Seven men are sufficient to manage the vessel," he said, addressing me, but with his eyes still fixed on the two kneeling tremblers, "and these villains shall eat curry or lead."

Then he spoke to them sharper and sterner than before; but his words had no effect, save to make their cheeks of bronze turn into a sickly green hue.

But when my fellow voyageur put on a mighty scowl, and held the muzzle of his pistol right against the brow of one of the sallow knaves, he seized the tin dish out of his grasp with a wild cry and began greedily to devour its contents.

But the other still moaned, protested, and prayed for forgiveness.

In vain, however, for directly the plate was cleared, the captain literally piled it up anew for the other rascal.

And he towered as a Nemesis over him, until he had cleared the plattern.

Then he opened the cabin door and politely bowed the two Greeks up on deck.

"Well, what do you think of matters, now?" he then said, turning to me.

"I think that I'm a fool, and I owe you my life," I answered, grasping his hand and wringing it fervently.

"Well, I certainly think that the curry is better in their stomachs than in yours," he replied. "But if you are still hungry, come pitch into the rice and yams; the beggars would not have taken the trouble to poison more than one dish."

And I did pitch into the yams and rice. Although they were nearly cold I somehow enjoyed them, and, making a hearty meal thereon felt all sensation of sea sickness utterly depart.

Then I said to my companion—

"Let us go on deck again. It is close and stifling down here."

He agreed with me, and up we went.

CHAPTER LXIV.
STILL ABOARD THE LONG SNAKE.

WHEN we reached the deck, we found that the storm had increased into a gale.

The Long Snake was driving through the yeasty, angry waters, instead of rising over them, and consequently her decks were flooded.

But still the air was fresh and bracing, and the conflict of the elements was grand.

It seemed to nerve me for whatever might come to pass during the voyage.

I noticed, and so did my fellow voyageur, that only seven sailors were on duty.

What had become of the eighth and ninth?

Had the curry disagreed with them?

Anyhow, they were nowhere to be seen.

Doubtless they were in the forecastle.

The rest of the crew, I thought, looked at us from under their bushy brows menacingly.

The captain had the same opinion, and he read my ideas as he looked at me.

"Never mind," he said, in answer to my thoughts, "we have fried a couple of the rascals in their own fat, and with our revolvers we are more than a match for the other seven."

"In fair stand-up fight," I rejoined; "but the rascals will try to overcome us by treachery."

"Let them," was the reply; "we will beat them even at that game, or I'm much mistaken."

"You forget the old proverb—cheat a Greek, and there's only one more to cheat—the devil," I ventured to suggest.

"I don't mind about that," was the reply; "we are more than a match anyway for these petticoated, balloon-breeched sons of the foul fiend. Return their scowls with interest, and the slightest insolence with a bullet. We can yet afford to shoot two more of them."

His words gave me courage.

Besides, I had been in far worse scrapes than this even, when alone.

It was child's play compared with my balloon voyage with a madman.

So I chatted with my compagnon de voyage on a variety of subjects, and held the seven Greeks in the most profound contempt.

We smoked and conversed, seated on two coils of rope right in the stern of the vessel, our feet just clear of the wave-washed deck.

And whilst talking, we could not but admire the way in which that single-masted, single-sailed craft walked the angry waters like a thing of life

She looked more like a graceful sea-gull, or stormy-petrel now, than the hideous reptile she was named after; and though the wind whistled through the cordage, and the mast swayed like a graceful willow-wand, whilst clouds of snowy spray poured over her bow, she seemed to make very light of it all.

The Greek sailors—for we knew them to be Greeks now—had nothing to do but play cards, all, at least, save the man at the wheel, who managed her as a skilful jockey manages a high-metalled racer, keeping her close up to the wind, and never suffering her to fall off an inch from her proper course.

"How very easily these fellows might run us right into Sebastopol Harbour, instead of Balaclava Bay," said my companion, presently.

"If we approach the shore in the night, yes," I replied; "but if we near it in the day-time, we could force them to steer whichever way we listed, by the forcible persuasion of a revolver at their heads."

"Yes—yes—so we might, of course," was the response, and for awhile we spoke no more.

It was a most unpleasant voyage that, for we did not know for an instant what devilish device the crew might not be up to.

We were afraid to go down into the cabin, for fear that they would somehow or other get us into their power.

And yet, when it began to rain, and we got drenched to the skin, we would each have given a good deal to have crept into some place of shelter, had it been only a dog-kennel.

Just as it grew so dark that the bow loomed indistinct in the distance, we saw the sailors bring out of the little forecastle, two somethings sewn up in sacks, and with some difficulty launch them over the bows.

"I'll bet ten to one those sacks contain the bodies of the sallow rascals who dined upon curry," observed my companion.

I did not reply, but walked to the side with the intention of catching a glance at one as it drifted astern, and giving a guess at its contents.

They both sank as if they had been loaded with lead, and the helmsman chuckled as he saw me return to my seat on the coil of rope.

He had evidently read my actions and my thoughts.

I looked at the captain, and he looked at me.

"I believe you are right," I said. "It must have been."

"Quite right, sir," said the helmsman, in very good English. "They ate something that disagreed with them, and in turn the fishes may now eat something that will disagree with them. Good."

"You rascal," said the captain; "when we took our passages aboard your ship you pretended not to understand one word of any other language than Turkish. What is the meaning of this?"

"I will tell you," replied the fellow, perfectly unabashed. "Have you not in your language a proverb that a still tongue makes a wise head? Well, that was the case with me."

"And why with you?" I asked.

"Well, firstly to get your passage money, and secondly, to get you. I knew at once that you were people of some consequence, and I thought that you might sell well to the authorities at Sebastopol."

"That's where you make the mistake, however," I said; "for we will force you to take us into Balaclava Bay, whether you will or not."

"That remains to be seen," replied the Greek, with one of his invariable chuckles. "I guess you'll have to go where I and the Long Snake choose to take you."

"We will see about that, my fine fellow," said the captain; "we will see about that when we get close in shore. I believe we have both as good steering tackle in our pockets when the time comes as you have in your hands."

The man at the wheel, who was the master and owner of the craft, smiled grimly, but made no answer.

I saw that at all events he didn't fear us.

And this want of fear gave me uneasiness.

Then, hour after hour, we continued to sit on our coils of rope, the gale apparently increasing in violence all the while, and at last, the bitter, biting cold seemed to eat into our very marrows, whilst we were drenched to the skin with the salt ocean spray.

"I can stand this no longer," exclaimed the captain, at length, in a half whisper. "If I remain up here five minutes longer I shall be frozen, and a frozen man is no good in the world. Let us go below, Dunbar."

I willingly assented to this suggestion, for I was myself so benumbed that I could no more have pulled a trigger with correct aim than have flown.

Below we went, therefore, staggering across the decks hatchwayward, like two drunken men, and pursued, as I thought, by the invariable chuckle of the Greek master.

"Now," said the captain, when we had reached the cabin, "we must draw the shutters over this skylight, or the beggars may shoot us down like pigeons in a trap, without our even catching a single glance at their ugly mugs, and that would not be pleasant you know. Come, bear a hand, comrade, and that quickly."

I shook off my torpor, and helped him as well as I could.

The shutters were hard to close, perhaps they had not been shut for years; but at last we did it, and then the captain said—

"Now for the door."

This was very easy, and when 'twas done we were in a measure fortified against all attack and intrusion.

"Well," said the captain; "now I call this snug and comfortable, and if we can't see the villains, the villains can't see us. And now I propose that we try to sleep by turns, for it would not do for us to go off together."

"No, for we should assuredly wake up with our throats cut," I made answer. "Therefore, you take the first turn, and I will take the second. We will have a spell of three hours each."

"Yes," said the captain; "but aren't these sofas jolly hard, and the air, isn't it stifling? I hope we sha'n't be suffocated outright down here, like the poor fellows in the Black Hole of Calcutta."

"No fear of that whilst one of us keeps awake," I made answer. "Now go to sleep as quickly as ever you can, for in three hours to the minute I shall awake you."

"All right," said the captain, and we spoke no more.

Hour after hour passed by, each one seeming a century, for it was as much as I could do to keep from sea-sickness and at the same time keep good watch and guard.

The air was not only stifling, but stunk with something of a garlicky smell, and the vessel rolled and pitched heavily—so heavily, that often I had to hold on to my seat to prevent being richochetted across the floor to the opposite side of the cabin.

This was by no means agreeable, and I ardently longed for the expiration of the three hours when my watch would be up.

But how was I to tell when it was up? I knew when it commenced, because the ship's bell rang, but it had never sounded since, and yet at last I felt that the time must be nearly expired.

I could not see my watch, it was so dark, and though I opened the glass case I could not feel the hands with any certainty.

I was reduced to guess-work, therefore, and had just made up my mind to wait another supposititious half-hour before I aroused the captain when he awoke of his own accord and exclaimed abruptly—

"You should have aroused me before, I have had more than my fair share of slumber. It must be near eight bells."

"No one has struck the ship's bell during my watch," I said, "I can't make it out at all."

"Nor can I," replied the captain. "Perhaps there is some devilry up of which we know nothing about. Never mind, my boy, where ignorance is bliss, &c. They can't harm us down here, unless they poison us with their noxious fumes, so tumble in, and I'll tumble up."

I did so with pleasure and alacrity, and steadying myself on my back by working my arms and digging my elbows into the interstices of the sofa, I thus effectually prevented myself from being pitched off it on to the floor.

I was sound asleep in five minutes, and did not awake until some one shook me by the shoulder.

It was the captain.

"There's something very strange going on," he said; "your spell is'nt up, but I thought it best to wake you and tell you that something's wrong."

"What do you think it is?" I asked.

"Well, I hardly know. Don't you fancy the vessel is pitching very strangely?"

"Yes, that she certainly is," I rejoined; "she seems to be plunging about to all the points of the compass at once. There cannot be a man at the wheel, or else he must be dead drunk."

As I finished speaking a lurch sent me flying to the other end of the cabin.

I picked myself up, sorely contused, and instinctively essayed to open the cabin door.

But as I fumbled with bolt and bar a monstrous wave saved me all trouble by bursting it in, and sending me spinning to the floor again by its inherent force.

The captain picked me up, and set me on my feet again.

The cabin was half full of water.

The ship was still lurching heavily.

"I believe she is a wreck," said the captain.

"She certainly seems to be at the mercy of wind and waves. What the deuce can her crew be about?" I said, somewhat indignantly.

"Let us go on deck and see," was the rejoinder.

We went on deck, and as we gained it another great wave breaking over the starboard bow dashed against our faces and chests with such force as to wash us into the lee scuppers.

'Twas a wonder that it did not wash us overboard, for the decks were full of water—so full that casks and tubs were afloat.

But we regained our feet, and, staggering towards the hatchway, grasped it with the tenacity of despair, to save ourselves from another catastrophe of a like nature.

Then we cast our eyes around, and to our horror and dismay perceived that the mast was gone, that the Long Snake was tossing helplessly upon the sea, and that the crew were gone.

The rudder was lashed, all the boats were gone, and so was hope from our hearts.

The wind was blowing violently, screaming madly like a leviathan in anguish, lashing the sea into a white fury, and driving huge armies of ink-black clouds with terrible rapidity across the overhanging heavens.

It was all I could do to hold on to the hatchway, and so save myself from being washed overboard, and in time it was the same with my companion.

The vessel, too, lay so deep down in the water that I felt sure she had sprung a leak, for she shipped heavy seas every time she rolled to leeward, and sometimes, I thought, seemed inclined to dive bodily under.

"This is what I call a pretty considerable mess," said the captain, as he witnessed the waves rising in towers above the vessel's sides, only to break and thunder down upon her with crushing violence every instant.

"I don't know what on earth we are to do?" I replied. "Do you understand navigation?"

"Not a bit," was the reply; "and if I did I don't

think it would matter much, for my firm belief is that she is settling down."

"Stop," I said; "I will be back presently."

I crept down the ladder again, and discovered that in the cabin the water was over a table.

Returning upon deck, I told the captain the state of affairs.

"Then," he said, 'as we are out of sight of land, and don't know which way to steer, we may as well give ourselves up for lost."

"No—no," I made reply; "whilst there is life, there is hope. I'll steer the vessel somewhere."

"You'll steer her to the bottom," said the captain, "and nowhere else, take my word for it."

"Well, I'll try;" and I cut the lashings and seized the helm as I spoke.

I found that I could keep her bow to the wind; without mast or sail I could not force her to bound over the waters.

Every sea made a complete breach over her, sweeping the deck from stem to stern.

After great portions of the bulwarks were swept away bodily, and from my station at the tiller I witnessed one gigantic roller break aboard and shatter the windlass to pieces.

The complete submerging and sinking of the Long Snake and ourselves aboard of her seemed certain and imminent.

I could not doubt but that my last hour on earth had come.

But at the moment of my darkest despair (my companion seemed to feel more) there came a sudden lull in the hurricane.

The storm had apparently exhausted itself.

The worst was over, or at all events seemed to be so to me.

Yet what hope of real safety did it leave us?

Was not the leak gaining upon us at a fearful rate?

Did not the Long Snake lie like a log in the trough of the sea at the mercy of every wave?

The force of the wind had certainly much diminished, and the sea now broke over us less angrily and at longer intervals.

But the leak was gaining upon us fearfully.

I was wet to the skin, and buffetted by the fierce and angry waters; but still I clutched the helm tightly, and did my very best to keep the ship's head to the wind.

The captain presently came up and helped me.

"I don't see the good of it," he said. "'Twill only prolong our misery a very little."

"Whilst there's life there's hope, you know," I rejoined. "We must do our best, and leave the result to Providence."

"Very well, all right, I'm willing; but it's a mere matter of time, you know," said my companion, with a bitter laugh.

He assisted me as much as he could; but that much was very little indeed.

At last, when I was tired, he took the helm in my place; but he did not manage it so well as I did, and so I soon relieved him again.

CHAPTER LXV.

SAFE ABOARD THE TIGER.

IT was a long and a weary time of it. Often we hoped, and often we despaired again. The water was but too surely gaining on us.

Happily, however, it was gaining slowly now; so slowly as to be scarcely perceptible.

And, alas, not a vessel was in sight—nor sand, nor rock, nor cliff, nor shore.

The gale was, however, abating.

Of that there could not be the shadow of a doubt.

Yet we derived little hope from the knowledge, for we were forging our way through the black and seething waters at the rate of a furlong an hour, and we were out of the track of all ships.

My companion, therefore, was right in saying and thinking that all our efforts to preserve our lives would be futile and in vain.

We didn't talk now, but we smoked and we thought. Smoking is conducive to thought, and our horrible position was not at all conducive to conversation.

I remember that I thought of the most strange things, too. How that I had read of the great depth of the Black Sea. I shuddered at the thought of sleeping four miles down under the water—never reflecting that a paltry six feet would have drowned just as effectually.

What the captain thought about I really cannot tell. He smoked, and he smiled at intervals. He evidently had not the slightest fear of death, or of any other danger whatever.

At last, however, his face lighted up all of a sudden, and he indulged in a long whistle.

"What is the matter?" I asked, anxiously.

"Oh, nothing; au contraire, I begin to feel an intense respect for your 'never say die' and 'put trust in Providence' theories," was the reply.

"For heaven's sake speak clearly," I said.

"Well, then, look yonder—straight over the weather cat-head, as I think they call it. Do you see nothing?" he said.

"No," I replied, after dashing the salt spray from my eyes with the back of my hand. "No; I don't see anything. But tell me what you see?"

"I don't wonder at your not seeing her, because you have let the Long Snake fall off at least three points, so that she now lies over the weather quarter. Now do you see anything?"

"No," I replied, petulantly; "I certainly don't."

"Ay, that is because, withdrawing your left hand again from the tiller to shade your eyes, you have let her off a point or two. Don't you see?"

"For heaven's sake tell me what you see yourself!" I responded. "Don't keep a fellow on thorns, when you can lift him off them."

But, before the captain could reply, I exclaimed, while a thrill of joy ran through my frame—

"Why, gracious powers, it is a steamer; and she is coming directly towards us!"

"Why, of course, she is," said the captain; "I knew that you couldn't help seeing her if you gazed in the right direction."

My heart was too full to make any reply.

The steamer was certainly far, far away, but we could see that her bow was towards us. The smoke and her great white paddle-boxes were distinctly visible.

"We are saved! we are saved!" I shouted.

"Make not too sure of that yet," replied my companion. "We are very low down in the water, and as we have no masts standing, they will not see us until they are very close by, and then they may change their course at any instant."

"Well, you're a wretched Job's comforter," I replied, "but I'm not going to despair. You've a red pocket-handkerchief, I notice. Wave it like a madman when she comes a little nearer; and then, when she is well within sound, we will fire our revolvers off together."

The captain thought this advice good, and we lost no time in putting it into practice.

Then a most anxious quarter of an hour followed, for we feared every instant that the Long Snake would founder beneath us; but, at last, the approaching steamer returned our signals, and then was soon alongside.

She turned out to be H. M.'s War-steamer Tiger, and, when she had taken us aboard, she steamed straight away for the Crimea.

CHAPTER LXVI.
ONCE MORE AT THE FRONT.

BALACLAVA one more; Balaclava with its cold grey rocks frowning down on its cold grey sea; Balaclava with its ruined convent perched high upon the summit of its northern bluff, and its harbour choked with vessels of every rig and tonnage.

Stately ships of the line, huge unwieldy transports, dashing rakish frigates, long wicked-looking steamers, dirty colliers, snorting, snobbish, officious tugs, and sullen, bull-dogish gunboats by the score.

Amongst these various craft we held our way, until at last finding a clear enough space to swing round in, without coming in collision with a neighbour, we dropped our anchor; and made all snug.

Whilst we were doing so, I could not help thinking of my last landing at Balaclava, and my subsequent capture by, and escape from the Cossacks, with the battle that followed, et cetera.

Nor could I help devoutly hoping that no such adventures might be in store for me now, for again I had despatches for the British Commander-in-Chief—this time from Omar Pasha—and I did not wish to be delayed on my way to the front.

Besides, although naturally fond of adventures, I had had quite enough during the last few weeks to satisfy my craving therefore for a considerable time.

I began to yearn for a quiet life again—for my mornings at my club, my afternoon's ride in the Row, and my evenings at the opera.

And so I looked at the trailing ensigns of England and France that hung over every stern, with a kind of dissatisfied feeling, and more discontented still I grew as, the wind chopping a little round, the boom, boom, boom of the heavy siege guns smote upon my ears as they had done months, months ago.

I landed as soon as I possibly could, and as soon as I possibly could also I gathered intelligence of what was going on at the front.

When I did obtain it, it was far from satisfactory.

The English had attempted to take the Redan, and had egregiously failed, whilst the French had made an equally futile and disastrous attempt to capture the Mamelon, suffering enormous loss for nothing.

"And are we no nearer taking the accursed place than we were a couple of months ago?" I asked of my informant, a sergeant of infantry, who looked clean and soldier-like despite his long beard and faded and patched uniform.

"Well, I cannot tell, sir. Sebastopol's a very hard nut to crack, and the crackers are getting very feeble. We are losing more men by disease than ever the Russian balls and bullets dispose of," was the reply.

And wherever I went I heard the same sad tale.

"There was another sortie yesterday, and no end of our fellows were killed," said one.

"The muddleheads at home are suffering us to die off like rotten sheep for want of food and clothing," ejaculated another, bitterly.

"They say that thirty thousand fresh troops have entered Sebastopol from the north harbour, and that General Liprandi swears he will drive us all into the sea within a week," observed a third.

And so on ad infinitum.

I had some difficulty in getting a horse, and when at last I did procure one at almost a fabulous price, I found that his bones came nearly through his skin, and that I was expected to ride him barebacked, and with a halter in lieu of bridle.

I remonstrated, but it was of no avail.

Once on my Rosinante, and I lost no time in setting out.

Remembering my previous difficulties in finding the way, I had at first asked for a guide to the front, but everyone laughed at me, declaring that I should find quite enough guide in the road itself, which I could not possibly miss.

Once clear of the town, I found this to be indeed the case.

Road indeed! It might more truly have been termed a river of mud, for my sorry nag sank knee deep at every step, and often I thought that he was stuck so firm that he would never be able to extricate himself from the Slough of Despond.

And it had been a Slough of Despond to many a weary man and beast, for skeletons of both were plentiful enough on either side of the way.

The poor brutes had perished from sheer starvation, their more unfortunate riders or drivers from sudden attacks of cholera, or more frequently perhaps from that intense weakness caused by dysentery.

It was a melancholy and a ghastly ride that seven miles' jog trot from Balaclava to the front.

Sometimes I would pass a train of mules, guided by a motley crew, apparently composed of every nation under heaven; but commanded in every case by an officer in the neat blue uniform of the Land Transport Corps.

Occasionally I would meet, or be passed, by an officer of the Commissariat department—red faced and blustering, and generally robust and portly, and no wonder, for the rascals feasted whilst better men starved.

Never surely was there such a vile commissariat as that which undertook to clothe and feed the brave British army throughout that awful war, and suffered thousands to die of cold, disease, and hunger.

When, after an hour's ride, literally at a snail's pace—and I'm not sure that I don't villanously libel the snail in saying it—my bag of bones, misnamed a horse, reached the lower plateaux of the camp.

Here the scene grew more lively.

On my right, the vast plain was dotted with the tents, clustering waggons, and piquetted horses, of the Land Transport and Army Service Corps, whilst on my left stretched the lines of the Light Cavalry; a forest of tents, with a scarlet or blue coated sentry pacing up and down here and there, with the morning sun glistening on his drawn sword and burnished epaulettes.

Horses are being groomed in all directions, grey and brown and black, in clusters.

By their colours I knew to what regiments they belong.

The Queen's Bays are nearest to me, and to the left the Second Dragoon Guards (Scots Greys of Waterloo renown), and further away on the slopes of the Kadikoi Valley, Cardigan's gallant Hussars and the Death-or-Glory Lancers.

These men were the comrades of those who had immortalized themselves in the Light Cavalry charge at Balaclava; and many, very many, had taken part therein. Oh, wondrous exploit, that had made every man a hero, surpassing even those of Thermopylæ or Marathon, of Marengo or the Borodino, for every man of the Light Brigade knew that he was riding to almost certain death, and yet never dreamed for a moment of craven flight, or of disobeying orders.

I thought of all this as I jogged along on my sorry razor-backed nag; but presently my thoughts were diverted by other sights.

I passed the great camp of the Guards, a perfect town of tented streets on the left, and the camp of the Highland Brigade on the right, and then all of a sudden I found myself on the crest of the hill, and down at the very base of its opposite declivity stood Sebastopol, a city of marble, standing upon the brink of an ocean of glass, and all around it to landward trenches and parallels and mounds of

newly thrown up earth, fortified heights, enormous batteries and siege trains, and around all a wondrous city of tents and huts of at least nine miles in circuit, and in many places nearly as many in depth.

I noticed that the firing was very slack on both sides, but that for every gun discharged from either the French or the English batteries the Russians sent back a sullen response from one of their great forts.

I perceived, however, that the embrasures of these forts were in a very different state to what they were when I had looked upon them last.

In many places two had been knocked into one, and within the orifices I thought I could see dismounted cannon, whilst the stonework every where was chipped and scarred by ball and shell.

Within the city many of the buildings seemed to be mere heaps of ruins, and in some places whole rows of houses had gone down together.

Churches had lost their domes and cupolas, and theatres their roofs, vast walls were perforated by balls until they looked like kitchen collanders, and even some of the trees in the public gardens had fallen victims to the hostile fire.

I had no great difficulty in finding the tent of the Commander-in-Chief, and Lord Raglan received me with his usual courtly affability.

But if I had been surprised at the change in the aspect of Sebastopol since I had last looked down upon it, the change in the countenance of the old Commander-in-Chief was far more apparent.

The rosy flush of health had gone, and his countenance was cadaverously pale.

His form, too, had shrunk until his uniform hung around him as it were; the expression of his face was very sad.

He read Omar Pasha's despatch in silence, and then he asked me if I was not hungry.

I truly declared that I was famishing, and at his command his two regimental servants placed before me boiled salt pork, biscuits, and oh, wondrous treat, a bottle of Bass's pale ale.

What a feast I made; and after I had done, Lord Raglan began to question me on the adventures I had had since I had seen him last.

I amused him therewith for more than an hour, though I noticed that never a smile rested on his lips.

I did not know then, as I did afterwards, that the sufferings the criminal stupidity of the Home Government had entailed upon his gallant army had broken the old general's heart.

At last he said to me—

"I have no return despatches to give you for anyone, so I suppose your labours are accomplished, and that you may return home as soon as ever you like."

"My lord," I replied, "I would like to delay my departure until I could take home full, true, and particular accounts of the fall of Sebastopol."

"I dare not promise you when that will take place," said his lordship, very sadly.

"Then," replied I, gaily, "as I am off duty, and my own master, I cannot say when I shall leave the Crimea. I think I deserve a long holiday."

"That you indeed do," said Raglan, "and in the despatch that I write home to-night I shall speak in the very highest terms of your courage, hardihood, and devotion; but if you wish to profit by that report, I advise you to return to old England at as early a date as you possibly can."

"My lord, I thank you for your kindly advice," I replied, "but I would sooner return as a joyful courier in advance of yourself and your victorious army, who cannot but conquer in the end."

"I hope—I believe so," said Lord Raglan, "but I shall never live to see it. The fall of Sebastopol will be another's glory. My race will be run in less than a week; and although we make an important movement to-morrow at dawn, I have reason for believing that at all events the city will hold out for another fortnight."

"And what are to-morrow's operations, my lord?" I asked, forgetting in my excitement, the beginning of the old general's sentence.

"Well, I will tell you—in strict confidence, of course. With the first gleam of dawn, we attempt to seize the quarries and the Redan, and the French try to obtain possession of the Malakoff. If these formidable works fall into our hands, we can turn all the guns therein down upon the lesser line of forts that gird the city, and crush them utterly with a heavier weight of metal. Then the possession of Sebastopol will only be a matter of days," was the reply.

"I hope to goodness the affair will be a success," I rejoined. "I shall serve as a volunteer, anyhow. I've been in Sebastopol once, strongly against my wish, and I want to enter it again strongly against the desire of its inhabitants."

"I see you are a regular fire-eater," said the general; "and as I have no control over you, and you won't take my advice, go, and may you return in safety from the expedition."

And after a little further conversation, I quitted the general's tent and repaired to that of an old friend, an officer in the Grenadier Guards, who I knew would give me a warm welcome.

CHAPTER LXVII.

THE NIGHT BEFORE THE ASSAULT.

THE whole of that day nothing was talked about in camp, but the expedition of the morrow.

Everyone thought that success was certain, and everyone wanted to take part in the enterprise.

Cavalrymen were particularly wrath, as no share of the glory could by any possibility accrue to them; and, but for stringent general orders to the contrary, many would have volunteered and taken part in the attack, along with the more fortunate infantry.

As a sort of prologue to the events of the morrow, the allied batteries opened a fearful fire upon the doomed city at sunset.

For hours and hours they had been comparatively silent; but active preparations had been making in them nevertheless, damaged guns being replaced by new ones, and light pieces by those of heavier calibre.

Exactly as the orb of day sank behind the distant mountain peaks, the comparative silence of the long, close, sultry day was rudely broken by the loud boom of a gun from the French battery on Mount Saponne.

This signal shot was followed in quick succession by other cannon, the shots being evidently discharged against the Kamtchatka redoubt on the Mamelon Vert.

The Russian redoubts east of Careening Bay promptly replied, and then the guns on the left French line of attack took up the fire, those on the British left line of attack quickly following suit, and, lastly, those on our right line of attack, until at last full five hundred pieces of heavy ordnance were hurling a tempest of iron into the beleaguered city at once.

The horrible roar I cannot even attempt to describe.

In fact, such a thing is indescribable.

None can imagine it save such as have heard it, and many that did so hear it were deaf ever after.

There was a crescent of scathing, running, gushing fire for nine miles in extent, with a halo of white ghostly smoke above, whilst the air seemed to be full of writhing, quivering, hissing rockets, rising and descending shells, and red-hot cannonballs that tore straight away on their mission of

death, instead of describing brilliant parabolas in their course.

And then the crash of falling buildings, of exploding powder, of roaring flames where houses had been fired by the descending missiles, the shouts of the Russian soldiery, and the answering roar of the Russian cannon, made the Babel-like confusion more confounded still.

The fire of the allies was kept up for the first three hours with excessive rapidity, the Muscovites answering by no means on an equal scale, though with considerable warmth.

On our side the predominance of shells was very manifest, and the superiority of our fire over that of the enemy became apparent at various points as the night wore on, especially of the battery in front of the Redan, which was manned by the Naval Brigade.

The Russians displayed, however, plenty of determination and bravado.

They fired frequent salvos at intervals of four or six guns at once, and also, by way of further reprisals, threw heavy shot up to the camp of our Light Division, and also on to Picket-house Hill.

But shortly after midnight the Russian fire sensibly slackened, and at last it ceased altogether, but the allies kept up an incessant firing hour after hour, to prevent the enemy from repairing damages, but so silent continued the Russian works that many "knowing ones" declared a belief that "they had withdrawn their guns from the embrasures, placing them behind the parapets, and themselves retiring to places of shelter.

"Now, Dunbar, if you like I can give you a treat," said my friend, as, after we had been watching the grand and awful sight that I have so feebly attempted to describe for four hours, he threw away the stump of his last cigar, and tightened his sword-belt with a sudden jerk.

"What kind of a treat, Chomondley?" I asked.

"Why, a stroll in the advanced trenches, just at the base of that grim old Redan, which will be christened with some of the noblest blood in England before the Union Jack takes the place of the double-headed Eagle that now floats so doggedly and so defiantly before it," was the reply.

"The very spot I would like to visit," I rejoined, my prudence evaporating, and my old love of excitement and danger returning in full force.

"Come in and have a glass of brandy, then, and we will be off. I command the relief, and I expect it up every minute now," said my friend, consulting a valuable gold repeater.

I went inside with him and drank about half-a-quartern of the pure spirit out of a broken gallipot, Chomondley losing no time in following my example.

Then, seeing some cigars lying about, I proposed that we should take a few, to keep the damp night air out of our mouths.

"No, no, that will never do. We must not smoke in the trenches, not at least in the trench that we are going to visit. Egad, our smoke would draw upon us smoke of quite another description."

"What do you mean?" I asked, thoroughly bewildered.

"Why, that the spot I am going to take you to is so close up to the great Russian earthwork, that the defenders thereof would be as sure to smell our tobacco, as we are sure to hear them chatting and conversing," was the reply.

"And if they did smell our tobacco?" I queried.

"Why, then we should have our pipes put out, or, in other words, be dead men before we could exclaim 'Jack Robinson.' We are never more than half-a-dozen of us in that trench at once, and at least five hundred Russian infantry man the Redan," replied Chomondley.

Of course, all my longing for a cigar vanished

upon my receiving this explanation, and I looked to my sword and pistols instead.

Then the measured tramp of men was heard outside the tent, and Chomondley exclaimed—

"Here are my bull-dogs. Come along, old fellow."

We went out together, and there was the relief standing at attention in front of the tent.

The brigade-major on duty galloped to and fro and saw to everything with his own eyes.

Company officers in rags and tatters, with swords, long sheathless, in worn white belts, and wicker-covered bottles slung over a cord on the right hip to balance the six-barrelled revolver on the fall into their proper places on the flanks of the men; and then Chomondley put himself at their head (I sticking close to his side), and calmly gave the word—

"By the left. Quick march!"

The column was instantly in motion, not an accoutrement jingling adown the whole line, and the men as silent as spectres.

Naught was to be heard save the soft muffled tramp of their many feet, proceeding purposely out of step, and in this manner the column wound quietly down into the Valley of Death.

CHAPTER LXVIII.

I START ON A DESPERATE ENTERPRISE.

THE Valley of Death indeed, for every square foot of dry arid soil they marched over had been watered at some time or other during the preceding two years by English or French blood.

And perhaps the separate units of that long, tortuous, purple-black, ragged column, themselves in all human probability marching straight into the jaws of death, thought of this, as they wound down and down and down, their braids floating in the chilly night breeze, and a scowl of fixed determination upon all their faces, but never a smile—no, never a smile on one of them.

The only things bright about them are their eyes, their musket-barrels, and their bayonets, and if some of the latter are not as straight as they should be, they have been bent in doing England good service.

Good service indeed, for which their country gives them in return for their heroism, their patriotism, and the best years of their manhood, a retiring pension of sixpence a day; and if they cannot exist on a very small loaf every twenty-four hours, why then—the workhouse.

And every miserable petty tradesman in the realm—every butcher, baker, tinker, and tailor, ay, and candlestick-maker too, not counting those estimable individuals who make a living by keeping a shop in the hardware line—would feel it as a keen disgrace were a daughter of theirs to be seen walking in company with a common soldier.

Common soldier? Heaven save the mark! Is there such a thing as a common soldier in existence? Men who will fight and endure as the soldiers of the British army fight and endure have nothing common about them.

There are great rascals in every regiment, but take a thousand men from any given trade or profession and you will find quite as great an abundance of black sheep amongst them.

Every officer will tell you that nine out of every dozen soldiers are steady, well-conducted, and christian men, and patient into the bargain.

Let us then have common Members of Parliament, common lawyers, parsons, authors, et cetera, but not common soldiers.

Because, if our soldiers were common, we should all of us, long before now, have been very common people indeed—slaves to a common conqueror.

But to return to our marching relief.

We soon reached the well-trodden covered way of the first parallel, and then everything was shut from our view, save the six-foot high walls of earth on either side, and we knew that naught could hurt us here, save a perpendicularly falling shell or rocket.

And now we thread the zig-zag maze of semi-subterraneans, the starlight overhead and the reflected glow of the bombardment lighting our way so clearly that no lanterns are needed.

Every here and there we come across half-a-dozen men, in charge of an officer (either commissioned or non-commissioned), one of their numbers pacing up and down as a sentry.

These we relieve, dropping half-a-dozen similar men in their place, and they march back the way we have just come to their cantonment.

This sort of thing goes on until, out of the hundred men or so with whom we started, we have but a dozen left, and with these we at last come to another halt, not to relieve living men, but dead.

A sentinel was pacing up and down alone.

At one end of his short line of march lay a confused heap of strangely huddled-up forms.

On seeing us, the sentry came to a halt, and, standing stiff and upright at the attention, presented arms, and waited to be questioned.

"You've had a mishap here, sentry," says Captain Chomondley, nodding his head at the heap.

"Ensign Clarke, Lance-Corporal Prime, and Privates Benson, Virgo, and Jones, killed by the fall and bursting of a shell, sir," was the reply.

I glanced at the remains whilst the sentry was making his report, but the aspect of the dead men was so horrible that I could not look again.

The poor ensign (I knew his rank by his epaulettes) had his head blown to pieces, one of the soldiers was disembowelled, and the wounds of the others were almost equally frightful.

"Bear a hand here; we must lay them along one side of the trench, head to head—the permanent way must not be blocked up," said Captain Chomondley, as calmly as possible.

I thought him hard hearted at first, but quickly came to the conclusion that he spoke so because he had become accustomed to such sights, and such was indeed the case.

"Now," he said to the relief directly they had performed his bidding, "you may take up ground a little to the right, and be sure to show no light, or speak above a whisper. Sentry, your name."

"Private John Cramp, of the Thirty-sixth."

"I will report your conduct favourably in the morning — if I am spared till then," replied Chomondley, and we once more moved on.

Very cautiously and warily now, for we are just entering the advanced trench of all, and Chomondley tells me that the roar of heavy cannon that seems to be bursting our very heads asunder, and makes the solid earth quake like jelly beneath our feet, comes from the Redan, and not from our own batteries.

"And how near are we to the Redan, now?" I asked with some curiosity.

"Let me post my men, and I will show you," was the reply, and as he spoke we came to the last piquet.

"Privates Trotter and Rudge wounded slightly, and Sergeant Mason killed," was the report we received here from a beardless subaltern of eighteen.

"Let their comrades carry the wounded men to the rear—the dead sergeant must wait for his burial until after the Redan has fallen," said Chomondley.

And away went the beardless ensign, with his four unwounded soldiers carrying their maimed comrades on stretchers, and leaving the dead sergeant wrapped in his cloak at the bottom of the trench.

AS HARRY DUNBAR CLOSED THE PAPER BOTH HE AND THE TARTAR CHIEF WERE SEIZED FROM BEHIND.

"And here we are at the end of our journey," said Chomondley, after he had posted his men and made his every arrangement in his usual calm, leisurely way. "We have nothing to do now but make ourselves thoroughly comfortable, and enjoy ourselves—with the dexter eye wide open, of course, all the while. I have a dark lantern in one pocket and a pack of cards in the other; what do you say to a quiet game of ecarté, at, say, a guinea the rub."

"I don't feel exactly up for cards," I rejoined; the situation is altogether too novel for me to pay any attention to the game. Besides, you promised me that you would show me the far famed Redan."

"You can show it to yourself if you will place your hands on the upper ledge of the trench and lift yourself up a couple of feet by them. Be careful though, and don't let any earth or loose stones rattle down."

"All right," I answered; "I will be very careful."

I did as he had advised, and in another instant was hanging by my hands and chin to the edge of the trench. The spade-battered earth was as hard as baked bricks, so there was little fear of any of it becoming detached and falling.

Certainly not more than three hundred yards in front of me yawned the deadly batteries of the Redan, which was not a stone fort, but a re-markably ugly earthwork, encircling the top of a steep hill.

I could clearly see the eagle-topped helmets of the Russian sentries, as, with shouldered muskets, they passed the deadly embrasures from which the wide-mouthed cannon peeped threateningly forth.

But those cannon were silent now, for the sudden cessation of the Russian fire before spoken of had just taken place.

The night breeze whistled shrilly around the great hill, which in a few hours' time was to be sprinkled as thickly with corpses as it was now with big stones, boulders, exploded shells and cannon balls; and ever and anon I felt sure that I could hear the Russians talking and laughing within their great earthen fortress, above which waved a grim black eagle.

"Better not tempt a bullet by keeping your head exposed too long," came Chomondley's whispered warning, presently. "They've got some fine sharp-shooters within the Redan, who'd hit an orange with ease, were it placed where your chin now reposes."

This information was by no means agreeable, and so, having seen all that was worth seeing and all that I cared to see, I dropped lightly into the trench again.

"Now do you feel more inclined for ecarté?" asked Chomondley, with a dry chuckle.

"Well, I think I do," I made answer; "but will not a lighted lantern be dangerous down here?"

"Not my dark lantern, because it will throw no upward rays, but only a light down upon the cards."

"Very well; then let us play by all means."

We sat down on the hard earth, our backs against one earth wall, and our feet nearly touching the opposite one.

Chomondley lighted his lantern, and placed it between us.

Then he pulled forth his cards.

"The last time I played ecarté was at the Army and Navy, in Waterloo Place," he remarked, as he shuffled the pack. "Deucedly comfortable Club House is the Army and Navy; much better accommodation than the trenches."

"I should say so," I replied, as I cut for deal, and lost it, as was my inevitable fate; "but I should think that this infernal sewer—for that's what it looks like—must be really unbearable in wet weather."

"Oh, I don't know," was the reply, delivered with the utmost sang froid "Wet mud makes a precious deal softer bed than baked earth, and when we have rain we have, at all events, no dust. Ah! a king. Je marque le roi. Do you propose?"

"Oui, certes," I replied, and I went on proposing and changing cards, but without bettering my hand.

Chomondley won every trick, and marked a rôle, which, with his king, made him three, and in the second deal he increased this score to five, with another king and a single, and so won the game.

Whilst I was shuffling the cards for a fresh deal, I thought I heard a strange noise, as though men were at work close by with muffled pickaxes.

I told my companion, and he listened in turn.

"I believe it is the stroke of pickaxes that we hear," remarked Chomondley, after a pause. "It is very strange. I know to a positive certainty that we are neither enlarging nor making fresh trenches. We are in the last 'sap' in this direction now, and the French approaches are far away on our right. By George, Dunbar," he added, suddenly, "it must be the Russians who are at work!"

"Yes, I think it must be the Russians," I re-joined; "the sound seems to come from behind our backs, and our backs are certainly towards the Redan. Let us clap our ears to the earthen wall and listen."

"A good idea," said Chomondley; "we will do so."

With our ears pressed hard against that side of the trench that was against the Redan, we could hear the measured pick strokes very plainly. On removing them to the opposite side, we could hear nothing at all.

This convinced us.

"They are driving a parallel to meet ours. They are preparing a great battle of the trenches," said Chomondley, clasping his hands in excitement.

"What would they gain by such a move?" I asked.

"Well, I hardly know. Only a transient advantage at the most, for we should soon drive them out again," replied Chomondley.

"Do you know what I think they are doing?" I said, rather nervously, for I did not like to air my opinions before an old soldier.

"No—that I don't," was the reply, delivered in a tone which showed me that the speaker put quite as low an opinion upon my thoughts as I did myself.

"Why, I think that they are undermining all this side of the Redan hill, in order to blow our poor fellows up as they charge over the ground."

I brought the opinion out in the tone, and with the nervousness with which a school-boy attempts to elucidate a problem in Euclid, in which he feels himself all at sea and utterly mistaken.

But, to my astonishment, Captain Chomondley grasped my arm, exclaiming in an excited whisper—

"I believe you are right! On my soul I do! But how are we to convince ourselves of the fact? If we could do so, and then obtain an interview with the Commander-in-Chief, we might not only advance our own interests, but save hundreds of poor fellows from death, and the expedition against the Redan from a most disastrous failure."

"I wonder if any good could be gained from a little prying and eavesdropping?" I asked.

"Prying and eavesdropping! What do you mean?"

"Why, with my head above the trenches just now I could plainly hear voices within the Redan, and I was thinking that if I clambered out and up the steep hill-side to the very walls of the earth-work, I might creep around it, and at some point or other succeed in picking up some very valuable information," I said.

"But surely you aren't serious when you speak of doing such a thing yourself?" said Chomondley.

"Indeed, I am. I will go alone," I rejoined.

My unfortunate love of peril and adventure was getting the upper hand of my common sense once more, egregious ass that I was.

"I don't like to say anything to deter you," quoth Chomondley, "and confound it all, I would go with you myself did not stern and inexorable duty chain me to my post; and, by George, unless you are really tired of life, I think here you had far better remain with me."

"No, no—I would, indeed, far sooner go," I retorted. "Dangers met half way are well nigh overcome, you know. I will be very careful."

"But the sharp-shooters within the Redan are ever on the alert. I can tell you this from a long experience of them, and they are armed with rifles, not with regulation muskets, mind."

"I don't mind what they are armed with, or how Argus-eyed they are. I feel an insane desire to go, and unless you actually command me not to, why go I will," I said.

"I cannot command you not to go, because you are not under my orders, but I most strongly advise you to stay where you are, though I own, at the same time, that by going you might obtain information that might be of almost fabulous value, always provided that you got back with it alive, which I fear you wouldn't do."

"Oh, I must take my chance of that—I think I shall."

"Are you still resolved then?" asked Chomondley.

"Yes," I answered, "I am quite resolved."

"Then take this revolver, in addition to your own, and leave your sword behind. The gleaming steel would be sure to attract attention."

I thought this good advice, and followed it.

"Have you any big nails about you?" I asked.

"I have a few of the ordinary spiking nails."

"Give them to me, then," I said, excitedly.

"Why, what do you want them for?" quoth Chomondley.

"Why, if I fail to get the information I am going in quest of, I shall revenge myself by spiking some of the Russian guns," I said.

"Nonsense. Then you will be sure to be found out."

"That remains to be seen. I think not."

Chomondley offered no further opposition.

I think he fancied that, for some reason or other, I wanted to be quit of the world, and desired the Russians to save me from the sin of suicide.

Be that as it may, he gave me a few short bits of advice, and then "a leg," by which means I was out of the trench in a twinkling.

For the success of my most perilous enterprise, heavy clouds had by this time obscured the heavens, and the English and French fire had also considerably slackened.

I could scarcely see the gloomy form of the great Redan under these awkward circumstances, but I knew that it was very near, and that if I kept climbing upwards I must presently reach it.

So I kept crawling and crawling on, upon my hands and knees, taking care not to dislodge any stones in my upward progress.

Often I stopped and listened, my nervousness sometimes causing me to imagine that I heard the rattling of ramrods in rifle barrels in my front.

But each time I was wrong, and at last I found the outer wall of the Redan, by the simple process of running my head against it.

Then I rubbed my head and listened.

I could hear the "tramp—tramp—tramp" of a Russian sentry on duty, distinctly; but I soon got tired of that. One does not learn much by being left alone with a man's footsteps.

So I crept, crept, crept, around the formidable redoubt, getting past every embrasure on my belly, with a particularly snake-like wriggle.

At last, just as I thought I must almost have described a complete circuit of the redoubt, a light suddenly flashed almost on my face, just as I was gliding past an embrasure.

I crouched just behind an angle of the encampment, and opened my eyes and my ears as I saw two Russian officers (one of whom carried the lantern whose light had startled me) meet and shake hands, just within the embrasure.

"Now they will begin to talk," I thought to myself, "and I can hear every word they say."

Then suddenly the idea occurred to me, "Of course they will talk in Russian—a language I don't understand."

I ought not to have forgotten that educated Russians always converse in French.

"All goes well," said one presently, in that language; "the men have made tremendous progress since yesterday."

"And when will the trains be laid," asked the other.

"Oh, before seven o'clock in the morning, and then, if the red coats assail the Redan, not one will ever reach its walls. There will be twenty-five mines all ready for firing beneath their feet. Twenty-five volcanoes will burst and destroy them."

"But I don't believe that the English will attempt to storm the redoubt—they would never be so insanely daring—and so all your volcanoes will be useless," said the other, with a shrug of the shoulders.

"If they do not, I will hang the deserter who brought the intelligence, as an example to all other false tale-bearers," replied the first speaker, with an oath; "but at present I believe his report, and that a grand attack will be made on the Redan at nine o'clock to-morrow morning."

"In that case, it is of course best to be prepared," was the retort, and then the officers separated.

I had heard quite enough, and what I had heard was too important to permit of my risking my suddenly valuable life by the attempted spiking of any cannon.

No, it was my duty to get back to the trench as quickly as ever I could.

But suddenly a cold sweat burst out upon my brow, at the thought of "Should I be able to find it?"

In creeping round the Redan, with all my thoughts bent upon gleaning whatever information I could, I had never taken any bearings in order to enable me to find my way back.

And now, for the very life of me, I could not think in what direction the English trenches lay.

The darkness had increased to such an extent as to be almost palpable.

I could not see Sebastopol or the English lines.

I could not even see my hand before me.

True, I could see watch-fires all around me, but I could not tell which were the French or which the English, or which those of the Russians, away on the heights of St. Nicholas.

I was in an awful dilemma.

CHAPTER LXIX.

WHEREIN I REACH THE FRENCH CAMP.

FOR some time I felt perfectly stunned by the horror of my position, from which there seemed to be no way of escape until it grew lighter.

And then, if I was on the Sebastopol side of the Redan, what chance had I of successfully running the gauntlet of all the sharp-shooters within the great fort, and reaching our lines alive? whilst, if instead of being shot I was captured by the Russians, my being caught in the rear of their defences would insure my being shot as a spy.

These were the risks of waiting until the intense darkness passed away, and the danger of moving during that intense darkness seemed just as great.

The hill was nearly equally steep on all sides, and the French, English, and Russian camps seemed to form the three points of a great triangle.

Could I have seen the sea or the outline of a single fort or building I should have known pretty well how to steer my course; but I could not, for the city was unlighted, the troops having long ago drunk up all the lamp oil, so that if I moved I was just as likely to stumble down into the town and there get shot or captured as not, whilst even if by rare good luck I bent my steps towards the English trenches, from all but that particular one where Chomondley was without doubt anxiously awaiting my return, I should stand a very good chance of being shot down as a prowling foe before I could make them understand I was a friend.

What was to be done, then?

Again and again, and each time vainly I asked myself the question.

What made it worse was that I had not particularly noticed our watchword and countersign.

I remembered that both were very common-place sentences, but that was all that I could recollect.

Suddenly I thought of the wind.

It might aid me.

I remembered that when I had been climbing up the steep hill towards the Redan it blew in my face.

Well, then, surely I had only to keep it at my back in order to return to my starting point.

I felt quite elated for an instant or two, but then I remembered that the wind all the evening and night had been chopping round to different points of the compass, and that therefore by now it might be blowing from quite a different quarter.

I determined to try it, however, for it seemed to be my only chance of escape—a rotten reed to lean on at least; but then, a rotten reed was better than nothing.

But when I looked around for the wind I found it not.

It seemed to have utterly subsided.

I wetted my finger and held it up, knowing that if the faintest breath of wind did stir that part of my finger which was towards it would feel the coldest.

But even this test failed.

The breeze had evidently died right out.

It was a dead calm everywhere.

And so was my last hope gone; but yet of the two deadly perils it struck me that remaining where I was until some kind of light dawned to enable me to guess a way to safety would be the least.

How long I did so wait I cannot tell.

Time like that is to be measured by mental centuries, not by the ordinary computation of hours.

At length, however, I became aware, as I lay crouched up under a huge boulder, that blackness was giving place to greyness, and then I knew that the dawn was slowly breaking.

At all events my agony would not be drawn out much longer.

How I strained my eyes to catch the first gleam of surrounding objects, and yet, though the light continued to increase, it came not!

What could it all mean?

But suddenly I became cognisant of the fact that darkness was only giving place to fog.

Doubtless a genuine Black Sea fog that it is almost possible to cut with a knife, and which is well-nigh as opaque as a brick wall.

And such a fog it turned out to be.

From blackness to whiteness I had gained nothing, since each were equally dense and impenetrable.

Yet the fog, unlike the darkness, might rise almost in an instant, like the drop scene of a theatre, for Crimean fogs frequently do, and then I should stand revealed to no doubt a hundred eager sharp-shooters.

The fog, therefore, was far more dangerous than the darkness, and I soon came to the conclusion that it would be far wiser to move in almost any direction, than to remain where I was, just under the frowning embrasures of the great Redan.

I began to shamble away, therefore, my legs being next to useless from having been cramped so long in one position under the big boulder.

And as I proceeded I listened for a very possible challenge, for I knew that about this time the English, the French, and the Russians alike relieve guards at the different outposts, and the language in which the watchwords and countersigns were given would tell me unmistakably whether I was approaching friend or foe.

But I heard no challenge, nor the measured tramp of sentries' feet, and I became more and more uneasy.

I knew that hundreds of thousands of men were all around me, everyone ready to shoot me as a foe should I come near him without knowing four or five little simple words, and yet was I as one alone upon a mountain top lost in a dense fog.

Still I went on and on, treading gingerly over the stones, for even a dislodged pebble might bring half-a-dozen musket bullets humming in the direction of the sound, and one might take my life.

I soon felt convinced that whether in the right direction or not, I had got a great deal farther away from the crown of the Redan than Chomondley's trench, and this discovery made me more uneasy still.

'Twas no good coming to a halt, however.

I was like the tempest-tossed bark midway between Scylla and Charybdis.

My only chance of safety lay in a bold onward course.

And so onward I went.

I was traversing almost level ground now, and presently I was ascending a slight rise.

Where could I be?

Not going towards Sebastopol I knew, because, from frequent observations through a field glass, I was aware that from the Redan to the city was all down hill.

I was crossing the debateable land, probably between the British army and the Russian advanced forts.

The Valley of the Shadow of Death was a large one, and presently I knew that I was crossing it from the many great globes of iron I kept knocking my toes against, and the numberless mounds (graves every one of them) that I kept stumbling over.

Once or twice I fell amidst a horrid crashing of dry bones, and found by touch, more than by sight, that I had come to grief through charging full tilt the vulture-picked skeleton of a dead charger.

Oh, it was a dismal walk in a fog that, all earthly peril set apart, and I cannot tell how glad I was when, at last, after what seemed to me like the Wandering Jew's circuit of the entire globe, I heard the cheery blare of trumpets and warble of bugles only a little way on my right.

Those joyous flourishes put new life in me, and I hastened my pace, steering in the direction of the sound, for I knew the trumpet calls to be French.

On and on and on, until I saw a dim glow, as of a camp fire, right before me, though I could not be certain.

But when I heard a hoarse shout of " Qui va la ?" and the rattle of a musket, as it was brought to the present, I knew that I was close to a picquet.

" Halté la ! Avancez et je feu !" cried the sentry again, and now I could see his towering form and his high bearskin cap through the fog.

As may readily be imagined, I halted at once.

What's more, I shouted, " Un ami !" as loud as I could.

"Ou est la consign ? " cried the sentinel, without even lowering his levelled musket.

Here was a predicament.

If I didn't know the watchword, he was quite authorised to shoot me, and I had no more idea of it than I had of the family patronymic of the Man in the Moon.

"Je ne sais pas, mais je suis un ami—un Anglais," I made reply, in a very faint voice.

In sober truth, I expected my explanation to be answered with a bullet through my head.

Great was my delight therefore to see the sentry recover arms, and hear him order me to approach the fire.

I did so jauntily and joyfully, for I felt that all dangers and disagreeables were over, and as I reached it, my friend the sentry was pacing up and down at his post as stoically and unconcernedly as ever.

But just as I came up to the fire, I was pounced upon by two soldiers, who held me firmly by either arm, whilst a third, whom, by the superior richness of his uniform, I perceived to be an officer, stepped up to interrogate me about how I came there.

Although I spoke French as fluently as he did himself, I could not make this officer understand me at all; that is to say, not understand my explanations.

He could not comprehend why I wore a lancer's uniform, if I wasn't a lancer, or how I came to be in the Crimea, if I was unattached to any regiment in the British army.

When at last I begged his permission to depart at once for the British lines, he gave a peremptory refusal, and when I told him the reason of my haste, and of my discovery that the whole of the Redan hill was undermined, he shook his head, saying—

"I am very sorry, monsieur, that I cannot give credit to all you say. Your tale seems to me a very lame one. I will not declare it to be untrue, but it is my duty whilst there remains any doubts of your being a Russian spy to detain you a prisoner until at all events your escape can do us no harm. We are on the point of executing a very important movement against Sebastopol. The instant that it is crowned with success I will send you on a fast horse, with a well-mounted cavalry escort, to the British Commander-in-Chief. I can do no more."

"Alas ! then it will be too late," I groaned.

"I cannot help that, monsieur," was the polite reply. "You have to thank your really inexplicable explanations. I merely do what I conceive to be my duty."

And no words of mine could move him.

CHAPTER LXX.
THE ATTACK ON THE MALAKOFF.

I CEASED after a while to entreat at all, and resigned myself sullenly to the inevitable.

The warmth of the watch-fire was at all events very comforting after my long exposure on the chilly slopes of the Redan, and presently the French soldiers made some coffee, and gave me a large tin pannikin full, which further comforted me.

Then all at once a rocket shot upwards through the foggy atmosphere, with a rush, a roar, and a bang.

Half-a-dozen more followed in quick succession, and then, as though these rockets had been a preconcerted signal, the fog suddenly rolled upwards, and Sebastopol, the ocean beyond, the intervening valley, and the allied camps all shone gloriously forth beneath one of the brightest summer suns that ever gleamed from a southern sky.

But though my most ardent thoughts and aspirations were with my own beloved red-coats, my attention was mainly and irresistibly attracted towards the movements of our gallant allies, who were mustering in great force on a plateau on my right, and exactly opposite to a monstrous Russian fort, crowning the hill top just as did the Redan, and which I knew, from instinct as it were, must be the Malakoff, that far-famed Malakoff, which so many Russian despatches had declared to be irresistible.

'Twas evident, however, that the French columns that were to march against it took a very different view of the matter; that is to say, if smiling faces and joyous mien meant anything.

The men were evidently straining, like hounds in the leash, to be let loose against the steep height and the frowning cannon at its top, with nobody knew how many Russian artillerymen and infantry hidden behind the formidable earthwork.

There were the Zouaves, in their bright oriental garb, thorough gamins of the Paris streets nevertheless, with kittens and monkeys on their knapsacks, and the brilliant reputation of the Alma encircling them with a halo of invisible glory.

And on their right the Algerian regiment of Turkos, with white turbans surrounding the scarlet fez, their blue open jackets and blue vests covered with yellow embroidery, their trousers in ample folds of the same cerulean hue, contracted at the waist and at the knee, where they were met by the yellow leathern greaves and white gaitered feet; their bare necks and light elastic tread presenting in all respects a perfect picture of manly ease and grace.

Their swarthy, and in many instances jet black, countenances, beamed with excitement and delight, and, as they grasped their muskets, the veins could be seen swelling out on their half-bare arms like whipcord, whilst many in their rage gnashed their white teeth until they foamed at the mouth.

These warriors of Northern Africa, in company with the equally wild and excitable Zouaves, were evidently intended to bear the first brunt of the fray, but the Zouaves were flanked by three battalions of the Fiftieth Regiment of the Line, and the Turkos by three battalions of the Seventh Regiment.

A strong regiment of Chasseurs-à-pied were apparently intended to act as a covering force, making in all five thousand men.

Gaily again the bugles warbled forth, and the little brass drums beat a hoarse accompaniment.

French soldiers can do nothing without noise, but, with drums and trumpets playing, they will march against the gates of ——, or any other place.

They know no fear in such a case; no, not if they are outnumbered by ten to one.

And now a brilliant staff sweeps down the hill side.

It is Marshal Pelissier, with quite a bevy of generals and other officers of high rank around him.

He rides along the front of the attacking column, addressing a few words to each regiment in turn, and raising his cocked hat ere he rides on to the next.

Then, with his staff, he takes up a position a little to the right, and another rocket shoots almost perpendicularly upwards from the French battery opposite Careening Bay.

That rocket is evidently the preconcerted signal for the advance; for, ere it has had time to burst and fall, drums again crash and bugles blow, the eagle-crowned standards bend forward, and the whole attacking force is in motion.

I request permission to stand up, and am allowed to do so, the French following my example, but apparently not sharing half my excitement, for *they* are grenadiers of the Imperial Guard, the descendants of the conquerors of Marengo, Austerlitz, Jena, Leipsic, Wagram, and a score of other great battles, and they evidently consider it "bad form " to show concern at "a small matter," such as they would doubtless pretend to consider this.

Luckily, I am no Imperial guardsman, and so I can look on and admire the heroism of the line, and I do look on and admire it amazingly.

Forward they go, at the French double-quick of a hundred and eighty steps a minute, throwing out skirmishers to the right and the left as they advance.

As they approach the Russian trenches, the great guns of the Malakoff open upon them, but are answered in an instant by the counter roar of the French batteries on Mount Saponne.

Meanwhile, Turkos and Zouaves, although the Russian cannoneers are playing at skittles with them, rush on as regardless of the gap that each well-directed missile makes in their ranks, as though the hurtling iron spheres were mere cricket balls, and the game of war was a right jovial and merry one.

Trench after trench they jump into, and clamber out of the other side, after bayonetting all therein, and then I behold them swarming up the steep hill-side beyond, in three columns.

I beg the loan of a field-glass from the French officer, who has not once condescended to raise it to his eyes, and he hands it to me with a bow.

Through it I can see that both Zouaves and Turkos are still pushing on in good form, and in a thorough, workman-like manner, though the Russian cannon balls are bowling them over quicker than ever during their upward rush.

The Chasseurs-à-pied are marching in open order in their rear as steadily as a wall of iron too, whilst still the drums beat and the bugles warble, and the golden eagles flap their wings above the field of slaughter.

And I can still see, for my glass is a very good one, the Zouaves dumb pets crouching half-frightened on the tops of their masters' knapsacks, all save one grim old monkey, who has mounted to the summit of its owner's turban, where it squats grinning and mouthing, and waving its own little cap in the air defiantly.

And now comes the hottest part of the fray, for Turkos and Zouaves are within rifle range, and the rattle of the fusillade rises for a minute or two even above the roar of the cannon.

But it is all one to the gallant French stormers, who regard the leaden hail no more than if it had been a snowstorm.

The Zouaves sweep round towards the western face of the formidable earthwork, the Turkos towards its eastern face, whilst the Chasseurs-à-pied dash straight up the slope.

The whole surface of the hill is, however, at this moment covered with skirmishers, formed of the best shots in the three regiments, and these creep and dart and writhe upwards, apparently along the ground, using every boulder or bush for a momentary cover, and from behind it picking off every Russian sharpshooter who ventures to show his head above the walls or at the embrasures.

And those walls and embrasures are at last reached, though not until the numbers of the attacking force have been reduced one-half.

For a moment, and a moment only, the front ranks of the Turkos and Zouaves waver and recoil, as a musketry fire, from upwards of a thousand wall-protected men, rolls on their very breasts.

Then, with a wild yell, they dash over the parapets, and through the embrasures—just for all the world as a pack of hounds overtops and crashes through a stiff Leicestershire bull-finch.

For a minute I saw the sword bayonets at work, and heard the clash of steel on steel, and then the roaring guns of the Malakoff suddenly ceased to vomit forth flame and smoke and iron messengers of death, for the gunners had quite enough to do to defend their own lives, nor were they successful even in that.

A minute more and the Chasseurs-à-pied were over the parapets and into the embrasures likewise, and all the skirmishers after them, whereupon the whole of the attacking force was lost to my sight.

But the din within the Malakoff was tremendous, and I still kept the field-glass to my eyes, not knowing at any instant but that the French might be driven out far more quickly even than they had got in.

But suddenly a shot from the hitherto unmoved Grenadiers caused me to alter the direction of my glass a little, and above the pale wreaths of smoke that floated like a halo around the summit of the terrible earthwork, I saw the French tricolor floating proudly where the Russian eagle had been, and, on looking to the right, I also saw a long line of green-coated, helmetted Russian infantry flying in the utmost confusion from the rear of the great fort towards the town.

The Malakoff had unmistakeably fallen into the hands of our gallant allies; but the Redan—ah! my heart began to bleed as my thoughts reverted to it.

———

CHAPTER LXXI.
THE ATTACK ON THE REDAN.

"NOW, monsieur," said the French officer. "If you are a Russian you can do us no harm, and if you are, as you affirm, an Englishman, you may be able to do your countrymen much good by the information you say you have obtained. Whilst you have been looking at the attack and capture of the Malakoff, I have obtained you a horse and an escort to the British camp. There they are."

I looked round, and saw a couple of dashing looking Chasseurs d'Afric mounted on wiry, hardy Arabians, one of them holding the reins of a third charger.

"A thousand thanks," I said to the French officer. "If quick riding will save my countrymen, it shall not be wanting, I promise you;" and we shook hands.

Then I flung myself into the saddle, and spurred the grey Arab to a gallop, a speed that he maintained all the way to the British lines.

But when we reached them I saw that I was too late.

The Grenadier and the Coldstream Guards were marching down in serried battalions into the Valley of the Shadow of Death, and the Highland Brigade, composed of the 45th (the old Black Watch) and the 93rd, were moving up towards the neck of the Dockyard Creek, and I knew that such regiments would not be used except to cover and support some important movement, and what could that important movement be but the attack upon the Redan?

Yes—I was assuredly too late!

I rode up to the spot, however, where I saw Lord Raglan and his staff drawn up, and my sudden appearance, escorted by two French Chasseurs-à-cheval, seemed to create considerable surprise.

But, unabashed by this, I made my report to the general, who thanked me, and then declared sorrowfully that my information had come too late.

"Ere an aide-de-camp could reach the head of the column, it will be half way up the glacis," he said. "But it seems, from your report, that the one Russian officer told the other that everything would be ready to blow up the attacking forces before nine o'clock, and as it is now only a quarter past six, we must hope that we are too early for them."

"We are—we assuredly are," I replied joyfully. "I had never thought of that. However, I shall know all about it in ten minutes, for I will join the attacking column."

"If you return alive, come and dine with me this evening," said his lordship, while I was dismounting.

I accepted the invitation with a laugh, as I surrendered my horse to the two Chasseurs, and tipped them half a sovereign each to drink to the fall of the Redan, which I have no doubt they did right heartily.

Then I asked for the loan of a sword, and had at least a dozen proffered for my acceptance at once.

I chose the largest and the strongest looking, irrespective of embossing and adornment, and, buckling it around my waist, I raised my hat to the staff generally, and ran down the steep hillside.

How our cannon were thundering out from the heights as I crossed the valley at the double, and the guns of the Redan answering vigorously and defiantly, though the Russians seemed to be trying more to get the range of the Guards and the Highland Brigades, and knock those stalwart troopers over at long bowls, than to wage a deadly duel with the smoke and flame-belching monsters of the Flagstaff and Naval batteries!

But the regiments of Guards and Highlanders were so admirably manœuvred, that they suffered but trifling loss, and before I was half way to the front, they had got under shelter of a gentle rise, from which their tall bearskins and plumed bonnets were alone in danger.

It was more than a mile from the staff to the front, and over such ground it was not to be done at a run the whole way, for trenches had to be rounded or leapt over, and more than once I accomplished the latter feat, much to the surprise of the men who were packed therein three abreast, waiting for the advance to be sounded, and upon whose bayonets I might have fallen.

They were never more than nine feet wide however, and I was always estimated a famous leaper at school and college, and as I could get a moderately fair run each time, I preferred this way of advancing to a more circumbendibus one.

I was close up to the last sap, when I heard the drums suddenly beat and the bugles burst forth into ripples of joyous melody.

Then, instantly as it were, I saw the dark green riflemen leap out of the advanced trench, and with inconceivable rapidity spread themselves out fanlike over the steep hill until every little hollow and big boulder acted as a shield for some crouching, or flat lying sharp shooters to take aim over.

Then the instant these hundred men opened fire upon every helmet and bearded face that showed but for a moment at the embrasures, or above the parapets of the Redan, the 34th Light Infantry rose up out of the trench like a blood-red wave bursting over a dyke, and went straight at the hill.

On their left are fifty strong fellows bearing woolpacks to bridge over the ditches, and on their right half a hundred sailors of the Naval Brigade carrying scaling ladders, wherewith to mount the earthworks.

This is the forlorn hope as it were.

If that regiment of a thousand strong can show a hundred bayonets at the close of the glorious struggle, it will be as much as they have any right to expect.

And yet they are going into the mêlée as fearlessly as though they were marching forth for a review in Hyde Park, and, what is more, the men of the 77th and 88th Regiments, who are in reserve, keenly envy them the post of honour, though they are well aware of the price that will be paid for it.

Even I, as non-combatant, enter into their feelings so fully that I resolve to join the storming party at all risks, and I rush on perfectly breathless, taking everything in my course, until at last I come up with it at the same instant as the 77th and 88th sweep out of other trenches on the right and left lines of attack, forming two sides of a triangle, of which the storming party is the apex.

An apex that is apparently melting away as fast as it ascends, for the Russian fire is stern and deadly.

A tempest of grape and cannister from the depressed muzzles of the great grey cannon sweeps the steep sides of the glacis, and our gallant red coats are falling as quickly as fall the crimson poppies of a cornfield before the sweeping sickles of the reapers.

"Steady, my men!" shouts Colonel Yea, the gallant leader of the forlorn hope; and he turns round, faces his men, and waves his shako in the air, to animate them. "This is too hot to last. We will turn the beggars out of it with the bayonet in less than five minutes."

He is answered by a cheer, and the advance becomes a rush.

Comrade encourages comrade, and side by side, and shoulder to shoulder, with hearts throbbing wild and fierce, a blood lust that has no mercy in it in all their eyes, and grips of iron upon their trusty muskets, that will not be relaxed even in death, the doomed men rush on.

I have not been able to get further forward than the rear of the column, for the pace is killing.

Each man knows that the quicker he is inside the redoubt, the better for himself, and for all.

Yet still down go the front ranks, like nine pins, before the well-played cannon balls, and the column melts away like a column of mist.

Down goes the gallant colonel, with a bullet through his heart.

The senior captain takes his place, and is cut in twain by a round shot, which furthermore makes a long lane in the solid column behind.

The second captain then dashes to the front, clutching the colours out of the hand of a falling ensign in his course.

He waves them frantically, and dashes up the hill-side at a run, knowing that the men will follow their flag, if they will not follow him.

But one cannon ball cuts the flagstaff in twain, and another carries away the head of the gallant bearer, who falls prone to earth.

Then the yelling, upward rushing, powder blackened, rage maddened remnant of the 34th are met, when within pistol range of the dark walls that they are doomed never to cross, by such a withering discharge of grape, that they break, waver, and give way, flying in confusion upon their supports, whom they slightly disorganise.

At this juncture I had my schapska carried away by a round shot, which so dazed, and nearly stunned me, that I hardly knew what I was about, until I found myself advancing to the attack again with the 88th, just as I had done with the unfortunate 34th.

All that I remember experiencing was a dogged resolution to get inside the Redan, in whose company I did not seem to care a bit.

War has the same effect upon some temperaments as champagne. I think on me it had more the effect of a strong dose of British brandy, with a dash of opium in it, for I felt determination without enthusiasm, mixed with a growing somnolency.

I could see that the awful glacis over which I was again advancing was strewn with dead and dying. I could hear around me, on all sides, the most piteous supplications for water, mingled with the curses, groans, and shrieks of those who were writhing in mortal agony, or raving in wild delirium.

But again the roar of the cannon drowned all other sounds, and the 88th began to melt away as rapidly as the 34th had done.

I could see nothing now of ladder-carrying sailors, or sack-bearing Land Transport men.

They had been stricken down long ago, so that, provided we ever reached the formidable earthworks, we should have to clamber over them as best we could.

But there seemed to me to be no chance of our

ever reaching them, for the Russian fire was as scathing and vigorous as ever.

Besides, not only now had we to deal with the natural inequalities of the ground, but we had to advance over our own dead and wounded—to trample writhing, shrieking men under our feet—and this seemed to be more horrible than all.

"We *must* have the place, lads," cried Colonel Windham, who led the 88th; and his voice sounded shrill and clear, even above the roar of the artillery. "We *must* have it, though only a dozen men out of the three thousand survive to hold it. The French flag floats over the Malakoff, and shall it be told at home that we couldn't place the Union Jack on the Redan? No, never. You won't let it be!"

The cheer that answered this appeal to our valour and our patriotism was more like that of infuriated demons than of mortal men, and the 77th, being now almost up with us, we resolved that they at least should not carry off all the glory.

I hardly know what followed, but I do know that men continued to fall on all sides, and that the onward rush was not for one instant stayed, that the cries and groans continued to mingle painfully with wild and ferocious cheers, the trampling of feet, and the thunder of the Russian guns.

Then through the columns of smoke that curled, low and white, along the ground, veiling half the horrors of the carnage, I saw a British officer upon the ramparts, waving his shako in one hand, and his sword in the other.

He wasn't there long alone, for never did wasps dance quicker up a window pane, than the gallant soldiers of the 88th swarmed up the walls of the Redan to support their colonel.

And up after them, mounting on each others shoulders like skilled acrobats and dispensing with ladders, the 77th followed them.

In through the embrasures they also swept, half of them falling in the attempt; but the remainder bayonetting the Russian gunners where they stood, and neither giving nor asking for quarter.

Oh, it was an awful sight whilst it lasted. Hell itself could not have given birth to more horrors; for men were transformed into demons, and hacked and thrust until swords were broken and bayonets were bent and bloody.

The Muscovites were stubborn foes, and hardly knew when they were beaten.

They fought until their dead cumbered the ground in heaps, until they choked up every embrasure with their bodies, until the inside of the Redan was almost ankle-deep in blood.

Then at last they gave way, and were driven out of the earthwork; and a great cheer went up to the smoke-canopied heavens, as the large trianglar blue and black flag of Russia was lowered, and the gay Union Jack run up in its place.

CHAPTER LXXII.

THE HOLDING OF THE REDAN.

AND now Colonel Windham had a brief moment of leisure in which to calculate the British loss, and, to his inconceivable dismay, discovered that the wreck of the three noble regiments of a thousand men each, numbered barely three hundred and fifty unwounded warriors.

How was he to hold a huge earthwork like the Redan, with so small a force? And he looked out anxiously from an embrasure less full of dead than the rest, to see if the Foot Guards or the Highlanders were marching to his assistance.

But no, there were no signs of any reinforcements moving upon the Redan, and whilst he still looked with gathering impatience, the roar of cannon commenced again, and we one and all made the very unpleasant discovery that the Russian forts in the rear, known as the Woronzoff and Little Redan batteries, were playing upon us.

Now this was most unfortunate, for the Great Redan and these forts formed the three points of a triangle, the Great Redan being the apex, and thus we were placed under an awkward cross fire from which we soon began to suffer considerabl loss.

The cannon balls tore their way in through th embrasures, first of all knocking out of the way th dead and wounded men, and then bowling over th living with just as much unconcern.

The Redan was weak towards its own lines of circumvallation, for there existed no need of its being strong; and so the balls came crashing in a very different manner to what they would have done had they been fired at its front.

Colonel Windham drew forth a short, well-coloured meerschaum pipe from his pocket, filled it with tobacco, and lighted it.

After a few vigorous puffs, during which quite as many soldiers fell dead around him, he turned to a young officer who stood at his elbow, and said—

"Ensign Irving, you will try to reach General Sir E. Codrington, and, if you do so reach him, you will tell him that I am in urgent need of reinforcements."

The subaltern saluted and departed on his mission, but, before he had run half-way down the hill, a bullet found his heart, and he fell over dead.

"Now, Ensign Fletcher, it is your turn—the odds are against two men of the same rank being killed whilst on the same service in the same way," said Colonel Windham, turning to another young officer.

This one saluted his superior, as the first had done, and, equally undaunted, went forth upon his mission.

But, almost in the same spot where his brother ensign had fallen, he also fell dead.

"It is my turn now, colonel," said a gay young lieutenant, stepping up. "There's luck in odd numbers, you know, and so I volunteer for the service."

"Thank you," said Windham, proffering him a cigar, which he at once accepted, and forthwith proceeded to light at his colonel's pipe. "If there is luck in odd numbers, tell Sir Edward Codrington that, if he doesn't wish to lose the Redan again, he must send me powerful reinforcements at once, and some good gunners with them, so that we may turn these cannon upon the lesser forts that are so annoying us."

"Yes, colonel, I will tell him all."

"Be sure to tell him, too, that should only a thousand Russians attack us in the rear, before the reinforcements arrive, tired and worn out as we are, they could not help dislodging us."

"Yes, colonel, I will remember."

"Get you gone, then, and may God be with you."

The young lieutenant saluted his colonel, and raised his shako at the name of the Almighty.

Then, puffing his cigar into a red glow, he departed on his mission.

He ran well, he had nearly reached the trenches, we all hoped that he at last had escaped, when we saw him stagger and reel, recover himself, press his hand to his left side, run on a little way further, and then fall over on his face.

Colonel Windham removed his pipe from his mouth, and gave vent to his feelings by spitting fiercely through an embrasure.

Then he fixed his pipe between his teeth again, and looked round at the remnant of his garrison.

Perhaps he expected another volunteer.

If so, he didn't find one, and the danger was so deadly that he did not seem to like to command another officer to attempt the dangerous crossing of the plain.

But suddenly his eyes rested on me.

"You are not one of us," he said, calmly.

"No, colonel—I am only a volunteer," I answered.

"Well, Mr. Volunteer, I want you to bear witness that I am no coward," and he looked at me keenly.

"No one who has seen you to-day will ever think that, colonel," I ventured to answer.

"But I want you to vindicate my character to those who have not seen me to-day. It is an old saying, that what you want to have done thoroughly you must do yourself, and I'm not going to send others where it may be said I was afraid to go. I don't see an officer of the three regiments left, but I've watched you fight, and can see that you've a little of the general, and a good deal of the devil in you. I'm going to Sir Edward Codrington for reinforcements. If I get there he'll attend to me, and send them precious quick too; but as lots of fellows will see me running from the Redan, if I chance to get knocked over, be sure and tell them that I ran away with the firm resolve of coming back again."

"But, colonel," I exclaimed, "let me go."

"Not a bit of it," was the reply, and the speaker knocked the ashes from his pipe. "I'm not sure that the general would listen to you, and, egad, he shall to me;" and away he went without another word.

I saw him halt for a moment at the corner of the salient to relight his pipe, which had gone out, and then I saw him cross the parapet, and drop over it.

The men wanted to give him a cheer, which I repressed with difficulty, for the thoughtless enthusiasm would have been sure to have drawn the Russian fire upon him.

A minute later we saw him descending the hill-side towards the trenches, amidst such a deadly cross fire of grape shot and musket bullets, that the ground was ploughed and furrowed up all around him.

But he seemed to bear a charmed life. He ran the fiery gauntlet in safety, he reached the first trench, and paused for an instant to turn round and wave his shako to us. Then he leaped down, and was altogether lost to our sight.*

Then there was no repressing the cheers that would burst forth, even though many cheerers were struck to earth ere their shout was over.

But this spontaneous enthusiasm was quickly put an end to by some one exclaiming that a heavy column of Russian infantry was coming up from the town directly towards us.

We surveyed them through the embrasures, and soon came to the conclusion that they were 2,000 strong.

They would be up with us in five minutes, too, and we had not 200 unwounded men to oppose them.

Colonel Windham could not return with any reinforcements under a quarter of an hour.

Could we hold the place until he returned?

That was a question very difficult to answer.

CHAPTER LXXIII.
THE LOSS OF THE REDAN.

ON came the Russians, in that dogged, unhurried manner that distinguished them on all occasions.

They feel no enthusiasm in war or patriotism either, but they fight because they are told to fight, and would as soon do that as anything else, and when they are worsted they are slow to run away, because they have a dread of a musketry fire upon their backs.

Strange fellows are the Russians, with a keen admiration of courage in others, and a complete ignorance that they possess the same quality in a large degree themselves.

Were they quicker in their movements, and prompter to see and take advantage of the errors made by their foes, they would be the best soldiers in Europe.

But whilst I am thus moralising, I should be describing.

The grey great-coated, black helmetted legions came on, not at the double, but at a long striding march, that covered a lot of ground in very little time, and singing a hymn, like the Scotch Covenanters of old, as they surged up, as it were, towards the Redan.

As yet, nothing in the nature of a support was visible; but then Colonel Windham could hardly by this time have reached the brigadier general's staff.

It was plainly our duty, however, to hold the Redan to the loss of the last man, and I resolved to do it if possible, even if that last man were myself.

I had been left in charge, as it were, by Colonel Windham, and I was determined to be true to my trust.

The soldiers, after all, never guessed that I was a civilian, and my rich uniform and my ardour won their respect.

They were quite ready to obey me in all things.

Therefore, though the cannon balls continued to plunge in upon us from the Woronzoff and the Little Redan, everyone taking a life or two, and, though the Russian column of infantry drew nearer every moment, not a British soldier faltered, or thought of retreat.

They merely bit their cartridges viciously, and rammed them home with a little more energy than usual, whilst determination flashed in their eyes.

No bugle blared, and no drum beat to sustain their steady courage.

Buglers and drummers were all dead long ago.

No officer harangued them with fiery words, for they were all dead too.

And I felt so confused and nervous with the sudden and unexpected responsibility thrown upon me, that I hardly knew what I did.

The rattle of the Russian rifle balls recalled me to myself.

"Return their fire, my lads, whilst you have a charge left in your cartouche boxes; aid will surely come by that time," I shouted.

The survivors of the 34th, 88th, and 77th, obeyed me, with cool and deliberate aim too.

The Russian advance was staggered for a moment, but then once more it rolled on, the front ranks returning our fire with such precision that several of our men fell before it.

Thereafter it was nothing but a musketry duel until the Russians were within bayonet thrust of us over the parapet, which, however, we for a considerable while prevented them from crossing.

But a cannon was brought up, and half a dozen Russians tore down a gabion at the angle of the salient to run the muzzle through.

In vain our best sharp shooters brought down man after man as they were loading this grim monster with grape.

There were plenty more to take their places, and at last it was discharged point blank at us within pistol range, killing half a dozen men and wounding ever so many more.

Again and again that infernal cannon opened upon us, each time with deadlier aim.

Then the Russian infantry swept over the parapets and in at the embrasures, and another discharge of grape settled us.

No troops on earth could have stood—reduced in numbers and bleeding at every pore as were our poor fellows, an onset such as this.

One frantic glance was cast round for the long-expected supports, but they were still nowhere to

---

* True in every particular.

be seen, and then, with a yell of mingled rage and fear, we fled from the earthwork we had so gloriously won, and which we might easily have held and secured, if only one more fresh regiment had been sent up in time to our assistance.

Yes, out we went far quicker than we got in, unable even to take our flag with us, and the great cannon belched forth upon our rear, and the Russian infantry, leaping on to the parapet and filling the embrasures, discharged their muskets at us as fast as ever they could fire, reload, and fire again.

Colonel Windham had left about three hundred and fifty fighting men in the Redan.

We had held it until that force was diminished below a hundred, and then we gave way before two thousand fresh forces, aided by the cross fire of two batteries, and a cannon that belched forth grape shot upon us at pistol range.

There was no disgrace, therefore, in our flight, and yet, as whilst rushing down the hill-side along with the other fugitives, I saw Colonel Windham coming up it, bareheaded and smoke-begrimed, at the head of a regiment of fresh infantry, I felt ashamed to meet him, and rushed off to the right, towards where I saw a fierce fight going on in the cemetery.

I need not have taken the trouble to have thus gone out of my way, for Windham, seeing that all was over, and the Russian eagle once more resume its wonted position, in place of the Union Jack, sorrowfully turned his back on the Redan, and the 18th (Royal) were marched against the Barrack batteries.

CHAPTER LXXIV.

WE FIGHT OUR WAY INTO SEBASTOPOL.

BUT though the Redan was lost, the great battle was not half over, and when I reached the cemetery, I saw that there was very hot work going on even there, for the 9th, 19th, 28th, and 38th regiments were striving to drive an immense number of Russians thereout at the point of the bayonet, and as these used every tombstone and monument for a cover from whence to fire upon their assailants, the combat was a protracted and stubborn one.

I joined myself to a regiment of infantry, whom I knew to be Irish from their green facings.

They had not yet been engaged, but they were burning to be under fire, and 'twas as much as their officers could do to prevent their double-quick step from deteriorating into a run and a rush.

"Steady men, steady," roared their colonel, with a strong Hibernian accent. "It's fair and aisy that wins the game, and this day we are going to do something that will make every cabin in Connaught ring again."

I bethought me now of looking at the numbers on the shoulder-straps of the men I had got amongst, and found, with a thrill of pleasure, that I was about to take part in a charge of the gallant Connaught Rangers, who have a higher reputation for the handling of the bayonet than any regiment in the British army.

And "Picton's pets" did not seem to have at all deteriorated by the forty years' peace.

They were still the "Up, and at them boys!" of the old Peninsular campaigns, with a weakness for close quarters and cold steel, in place of long shots at a distance.

And they had what they thirsted for quite soon enough, for the Russians occupied the cemetery in strong force; and, with the tombstones for shields, and the guns of the Greenhill battery playing upon us over their heads, ours was no child's-play.

Yet, for all that, it was very different work from the capture of the Redan, for we were four strong regiments, two of which had not long arrived from England, and were, consequently, not enfeebled by the wear and tear of long weary months, sans clothing, food, and any kind of comfort.

Having outflanked the Russians on the right, our colonel pointed to a little battery just beyond us, whose defenders were peppering the 44th and 28th with grape, whilst the Russian infantry continued to play hide-and-seek with them in the cemetery, and said, briefly—

"We must have that, my lads!"

He was answered by a genuine Irish yell, which is as unlike a British cheer as it is possible to conceive, and, almost ere the echo thereof had died away, we had carried the battery, and the men had spiked the guns, with a thrust and a vigorous wrench of their bayonets, thus breaking the points off in the touch-holes.

We received a deafening cheer from the other regiments for this, for it was done in their full sight, and, elated thereby, we looked round for fresh obstacles to overcome, for our appetite was by no means satiated.

"Connaught Rangers," shouted the colonel, suddenly waving his sword, "through the smoke in our front, I see the commencement of a street. We are close to one of the suburbs of the city. Let it be our proud boast that we were the first to enter Sebastopol."

Again a yell, a tossing aloft, and catching as they fell, of numberless shakos, the brandishing of muskets, and other demonstrations of delight.

"Come on, me boys—I see that ye all agree with me," responded the colonel then. "There's an awkward cross fire from two batteries to be stemmed, and a Russian rifle pit or two to be carried, but a divil a bit you care about that, I know. On then, for the glory of old Ireland!"

He waved his sword again—bloody enough from point to hilt it was by this time—and away we went.

We crossed the murderous fire of the Wasp and Barrack batteries.

We leapt down into one rifle pit after another, and bayonetted every Russian therein.

And then, at the double-quick, we advanced upon the suburb that seemed so near to us.

All went well till we came abreast of a great yellow stone building, which somehow or other we never guessed to be a barrack, until in an instant, as it were, every window was filled with Russian soldiers.

From this building a perfect hail of bullets descended upon the head of our column, accompanied with such a rattle of musketry as I had never before heard.

From loopholes, from windows, from doors, and from across the stone wall that surrounded, as I suppose, the drill ground, a fusillade came flashing upon us that was absolutely blinding.

Our men fell in heaps, but the officers all kept waving their swords and shouting the while.

"On—on for Sebastopol! Our comrades will avenge us on these fellows. We can't stay for such a purpose."

"Forward! forward!" cried the colonel, in a voice louder than the rest, and forward we went, still at the double, and knocking over every Russian whom we overtook with our musket-stocks.

And then at last we reached the first houses; but, instead of being inhabited by harmless civilians, as we had expected them to be, they were evidently in the possession of Russian soldiers, for a fresh fusillade was opened upon us from every window as well as from the corners of the streets.

Our colonel, I think, saw that he had made a mistake then; but it was too late to retrieve it.

I don't think the men would have retreated, even had they been commanded.

Anyhow, had he ordered it, the colonel would have made himself an unpopular man amongst them for ever, and that would have been a terrible thing for him.

Not but what he was as averse to a backward movement as any of his officers and men, but I think duty was fighting in his breast with inclination, and, whilst the latter urged him on, the former whispered to him that it would be prudent to retreat.

Be that as it might, however, when at this juncture he looked round and saw that a British regiment had just mastered the Barrack battery, and were turning its guns upon the town, the men grew so excited that the officers saw clearly enough that their hot Irish blood was getting too strong for them, and that if they did not lead they would have to follow.

"Forward! we must have these houses!" they therefore began to shout, and then at them we went.

The bullets flew around us like hail, and every kind of missile was, furthermore, thrown from the upstairs windows upon us.

But the men went to work with their musket-stocks and broke in the doors, whilst others stood more in the middle of the street, and returned the fire from the windows, with interest.

The doors did not hold out long, and directly they gave way, in rushed the soldiers, and it was all bayonet and sword work after, the Russians fighting like demons, because they knew that they could not get away, and because they feared that if they surrendered they would, nevertheless, be slain.

I, with some half dozen more, rushed into a house, the ground floor of which was dark as pitch.

It was by reason of the window being filled with sacks of earth, the roar of the great guns having long ago broken all the glass therein.

Whilst we were groping about, however, a lantern was let down from above at the end of a rope, and the instant that its light fell upon us, musket shots rang out, and other missiles were sent crashing down, the result being that three or four of us were shot and stricken to the floor.

I immediately sprang forward and cut down the lantern, trampling it to pieces under my feet.

Then having, during its temporary gleam, noticed where the staircase was, I dashed up it, sword in hand, with a tingling pain in my left shoulder, as if it had been bored by a bullet.

I know that my temper was up, and that I felt a match for any number of Russians who might be upstairs.

I found plenty of them—eight in one room, and they all turned upon me as I entered.

Luckily they had expended all their ammunition, or they would doubtless have riddled me with balls, and have done with me.

But they had only cold steel to rely on, and so I got with my back against a wall, and for a minute or two parried every bayonet thrust with my sword, calling loudly for succour the while.

It came in the nick of time, for just as one of the rascals passed my guard, and was on the point of burying his bayonet in my chest, a Connaught Ranger gave him a knock on the side of the head with the butt-end of his piece, and placed him effectually hors de combat, whilst half a dozen more red-coats rushing in in his rear, the Russians were quickly overcome, and thrown out of the windows.

Then we visited house after house—sometimes finding that others had been before us, sometimes that a fierce fight was still going on, the staircase dripping with blood, and the Rangers forcing their way up, whilst the Russians at the top were striving their very utmost to beat them back.

Then, on other occasions, we were the first in, and 'twas our blood that had to christen the possession.

Oh! it was all terrible work.

Luckily there were no women or children about, or I believe that, in our soldiers' insatiable blood-lust, they would have been bayonetted along with the rest, for no one can tell, except such as have beheld it, how the brutal game of war turns men into demons.

And so we fought our way through the suburb, taking care to leave no house unvisited, and generally setting fire to each as we quitted it.

Then at last we got to a square with a brick church on one side of it, and here a great fight was going on on every side.

Hundreds of muskets were going off at once, mingled with the sharper noise of pistol shots, and the crash of steel on steel, as every here and there bayonets were crossed.

For a minute or two we thought that it was our own fellows that were engaged; but then we perceived by the regimental colours, that in spite of all opposition seemed to be steadily pressing on, that it was the 18th Royal Irish, who had entered the town from a different direction.

The Russians fought well here, as they had done everywhere, but the dash of the Irish was too much for them.

They gave way, and whilst some fled in one direction, hundreds more burst open the doors of the church, and rushed therein for shelter.

Perhaps they thought that such a sanctuary would not be violated; but if they did, they should not have taken the extra precaution of closing, bolting, and barring the great doors in their rear.

They should have surrendered, too, when called upon to do so, when their lives would assuredly all have been spared.

But instead of that their officer gave taunting replies, and so a couple of captured field-pieces were rolled up, loaded with grape, and the doors blown inwards, falling with a crash.

Then the Royals rushed in with levelled bayonets, and I could see no more until, five minutes later, from the window of another captured house, I perceived fugitive Russians hiding on the leads, and being pursued round, and pitched over the parapets of the tower, their last place of refuge.

There we beheld a red-coat climbing up, up, up the bright green steeple, with something in his mouth, and when, at a giddy height indeed, he threw his left arm around the weathercock, that something flaunted out, and was secured thereto, and a tremendous cheer rose to the cloud-canopied heavens, when we saw that it was the Union Jack.

"Come, my lads, this will never do," then said our colonel lustily. "I'm glad an Irishman has done that gallant deed, but the Connaught Rangers mustn't be given the go-by by any regiment in the service. So come on, and at the double. By St. Patrick, the green flag of Erin shall this day float nearer the centre of Sebastopol than any other! I have said it. Shall I break my word, boys?"

His words were received with perfect howls of delight.

The little drummer boys rub-a-dubbed with a will, those that were inside houses rushed out, and we had a compact column in almost less than no time, ready for anything.

Off we went at the double, looking out for nothing but a yet taller church spire nearer the centre of the city, from which to suspend our regimental flag, with its green ground and great yellow harp.

Muskets crackled around us, and, from the occasional shaking of the ground and the crash of falling houses, we were aware that mines were being sprung every here and there.

But the Connaught Rangers never halted once.

We narrowly missed running into a great column of Russian infantry that was marching down a main thoroughfare, and which would have annihilated us in five minutes had we dared to have attacked them.

But we did not debouch from our side

HARRY DUNBAR MEETS WITH A FRIEND IN THE HOUR OF NEED.

until they had gone by, and then we crossed the main thoroughfare at a rush, not knowing but what cavalry, or even field artillery, might be coming down it next, and they would have made very short work of us.

Then our colonel suddenly exclaimed—

"That is the sort of church we want! Gemini, what a fine spire! It seems to rise into the very clouds. But it's at the very summit that the flag of the regiment will have to float."

We received this speech with a cheer.

In fact, we were ready to cheer anything and everything.

The excitement of war makes men hysterical.

I know they would scorn the epithet, yet no other word will express the feelings they experience.

We pressed on towards the church, still fired at now and then from either side of the way.

As we swept on we heard vigorous file-firing, too, between us and the British lines.

It was like the pattering of falling hail upon window panes, only a thousand times louder.

It told us that a strong body of foes cut us off from our friends.

We had arrived where we were by rare good (or bad) fortune.

We had just cleared another main street when a noise like thunder in our rear caused many of us to glance over our shoulders, and we saw a Russian field battery sweeping down it at a gallop, the drivers lashing the horses, who foamed and shook their heads—ay, and actually shrieked as they tore along; while every now and then guns and tumbrels crushed and scrunched together—wounded artillerymen falling from their seats with the shock, the next instant to be flattened out of all human shape beneath the ponderous wheels.

We knew this was a flight.

It cheered us, and the men struck up a song.

I could not hear them though I marched in their midst, the roar of the cannon and the rattle of the musketry was still so great; but I knew that it was a song, from the way they opened their mouths, and shook their heads about.

Well, it did no harm, and I suppose they were bound to let the steam off somehow.

I don't think they stopped singing until we reached the great open space wherein the second church was situated, and here, to our chagrin, we beheld strong and apparently intact regiments of Russians drawn up.

They looked like reserve troops.

They certainly had as yet had no share of the fighting, for their uniforms were neat and spotless and their arms burnished as for a review.

There were infantry, cavalry, and artillery too.

To have attacked them with our slender force, now scarcely more than five hundred men, would have been nothing short of insanity.

And yet, without attacking them, and thrashing them too, we could not get near the church.

"We will take possession of this fine old mansion and fortify ourselves therein until they are gone," said the colonel, and he tried the front door as he spoke.

It was locked on the inside, but this was but a trifling impediment, for the colonel with his pistol shivered the lock to fragments, and opened the door.

"Hadn't some of us better seize upon the house opposite? They all seem to be deserted hereabouts, but, for all that, foes might take possession of it, and then it would be a case of point blank firing at each other across the street," said a captain.

"You are right, O'Hara," answered the colonel. "Do you seize hold of that house as you advise. I'd sooner have you for an opposite neighbour than the Russians, by a very long way."

The two officers laughed and shook hands, and then some of us followed the colonel into the house, the door of which he had already opened, and others followed Captain O'Hara, and helped him to break into, and take possession of the opposite one.

CHAPTER LXXV.
WE STAND A SIEGE.

I FOLLOWED the colonel, and we closed and barricaded the door and lower windows directly we got in, to keep any Russians from entering after us.

Then we went upstairs to post ourselves at the upper windows, and everywhere else from whence we could get a good shot at the enemy, did they offer to molest us or become in any way troublesome.

But when we got on the first floor a terrible sight met our gaze—a sight that I shall never forget as long as I have life.

On the carpet of the richly-furnished room lay a woman headless, and with her body mangled in a frightful manner; whilst around her lay the bodies of two children, also dead and terribly mutilated.

A hole in the wall, so large that I could have thrust my head through, the broken mirrors, the shattered furniture, and the fragments of iron that were strewn here, there, and everywhere, showed plainly enough how she and her children had met their deaths.

A shell from an English or French battery had done it all in the twinkling of an eye.

We threw table-cloths, hearth-rugs, and antimacassars over the remains, for we had no time to remove them.

Their fate might be ours at any instant.

But presently we heard British cheers, and saw the 18th Royal Irish coming down the street, with drums beating and colours flying.

They clearly thought that they had it all their own way.

That the Russians had evacuated that portion of the town altogether.

We threw up our windows and roared to them a warning, telling them that the great square just beyond was full of Russian troops.

They waved their caps to us and cheered us, but 'twas evident that the continuous roar of cannon and rattle of musketry, mingled with the explosion of mines and fall of houses, must have prevented their hearing what we said.

They still marched on in their false confidence, and our colonel could not help growling from under his grey, wiry moustachios—

"Well, there are no fools like the Irish after all!"

But they soon awakened from their folly at any rate, for their front ranks had hardly turned the corner of the street, into the great square beyond, when we heard three rapid, but distinct crashes, as of musketry, and then the rush of countless iron-shod hoofs over the stone pavement.

"They have let loose the cavalry upon them," said some one, as he reloaded his musket.

"I believe those three crashes were not musketry, but grape shot," responded another.

Scarcely had the words escaped his lips, when we saw the 18th rushing back in the utmost confusion—drummers, soldiers, and officers all mixed up together.

It had been grape that had so shattered them, and now a regiment of Russian dragoons were hard at their heels, riding them down, and sabreing them without mercy.

But still they rushed on—nobody looking behind.

Those who fell were lost men, and those who didn't fall weren't much better off.

"Hang it—we can't see our comrades perish, whilst we can do the slightest thing to aid them," said the colonel. "I dare say we shall bring down destruction upon ourselves by interfering; but for all that, my boys, just shoot as many of those brass helmetted, red-cloaked dragoons as you can."

The Rangers were only too ready to obey him, and, as the pursuing cavalry thundered along on flank and rear of the panic-stricken British foot, we emptied many a saddle for them from both sides of the way, though, at the time, the survivors paid us no attention, and discharged not a single pistol shot in return.

But they hoarded their revenge up in their hearts for all that, and when some ten minutes later they rode back, looking as though, at least, the 18th had turned upon them, and given them somewhat of a drubbing, they brandished their blood reeking sabres menacingly at us as they galloped past.

We would have treated them to another volley or two for that, but our colonel sternly forbade us.

"They will send the infantry down upon us presently," he said, "and then we shall want all our powder, and every bullet in our cartouche boxes."

And he was right in his prophecy, too, for presently we heard the measured tramp of feet, and there were the Russian infantry sure enough, coming down the street at a run, and looking up at our windows maliciously as they advanced.

They mean mischief and no mistake, and we were but a handful compared to them.

It would be a case of retiring from drawing-room to upper floor, and from upper floor to attic, defending every inch of the way, and being bayonetted at the last when we could retreat no further.

This was what we expected, for we never anticipated that our countrymen or our allies would come to our rescue.

We remembered now a general order of the day forbidding the troops, if successful, to advance too far into Sebastopol for fear of the explosion of mines, which deserters had told us were here, there, and everywhere, the Russians intending to leave their city a heap of ruins rather than let it fall into our hands.

And even the military and the engineer authorities believed these reports, for they remembered Moscow.

We were in a tremendous scrape evidently, and would have to fight it out alone.

Our only desire was, therefore, to kill as many of our foes as we could before they succeeded in annihilating us.

Directly they were well within range we let fly therefore, and laid at least a score of them in the dust.

The Rangers possessed some capital marksmen.

They gave way for a moment—but a moment only.

A regiment of a thousand strong could afford to lose many a score without fear as to the ultimate issue.

But the loss enraged and maddened them, and when half a minute later we doubled, and, in a minute, trebled it, their anger knew no bounds.

They returned our fire with interest, shouting out guttural oaths the while, and the leaden hail was so terrible that the colonel withdrew us from all the windows.

Then we heard the blows of their musket butts on the house doors and windows, and our colonel shouted—

"We will barricade the top of the staircase with this furniture. We aren't conquered yet."

A hundred willing hands were ready to help, and in less than five minutes—the exact time that the Russians took to effect an entrance—a cottage piano, two cabinets, a massive cheffonier, two card tables, a loo table, a heavy couch, and eight or ten heavy chairs made a most respectable barricade on the first landing.

The Russians howled with rage when they saw what preparations we had made for their reception, and then they fired desultory volleys at us.

But though some of our men were hit, and hit badly, too, it was only by chance that they were stricken down, for the foe could not see us, whereas our shots all told, and with terrible effect.

But suddenly a Russian officer shouted something, and everyone who heard him began to cheer.

Nothing fresh occurred, however, for four or five minutes, when the cheering began again, and we perceived that our foes were throwing with their hands what looked like powder balls at us.

"They won't do much damage," I thought to myself; and some of the Rangers laughed at them.

But a few old soldiers shouted out, "They are hand grenades," and as they spoke a couple of them burst, one killing three of our men and injuring a lot more, and the other setting fire to our barricade, which flared up as if every article of furniture had been tar-soaked.

The Russians cheered again now, and I could hear their officers shouting out to them, "No prisoners!"—that is to say, we were to be all slain, and no quarter given.

Our present position was untenable, for the flames from the blazing furniture were blown back in our faces by the wind that rushed in through the smashed-in doors and windows below, and the hand grenades continued to fall and burst amongst us.

"We must ascend higher," said our colonel.

"We shall be rushing to the summit of a burning house," suggested a subaltern. "How are we to cheat the pursuing flames? We can't shoot or bayonet them."

"Obey my commands, sir, unquestioningly," said the colonel, "or by —— I will court martial you."

"Wish to heaven you could," was the muttered retort; but the subaltern asked no more questions, and we retreated up the second flight of stairs, losing many a man in the passage upwards, for we were fully exposed to the Russian fire during the ascent.

Then the colonel instructed us to make a second barricade of the furniture of the bedrooms, anticipating that the Russians, directly the flames had sufficiently subsided, would dash through and over our first, and pursue us to the upper story.

But we presently perceived that, instead of trying to crush the flames out, they were feeding them, and throwing their grenades all over the house.

Then we knew that they meant to burn the house down, and us with it.

We were powerless to prevent them.

To charge down and endeavour to break our way through them would have been madness.

We were only 140 men now, all told; and the Russians in the house and thronging the street outside could not have been fewer than 1,500 men.

Doubtless Captain O'Hara and his brave fellows were in as desperate a strait as ourselves.

It was no good making barricades now that we saw the Russians had no intention of following us.

"My lads," said the colonel, "it is plain that we can't go down; therefore we will go up. We have bayonets enough to lift off the roof of the house, or at all events a portion of it; and then we will try, by hook or by crook, to force our way down through the roof of another, and so make good our escape."

This plan seemed a very feasible one, and we would have cheered the colonel for it had he not frowned, and cautioned us to silence with a finger on his lips.

'Twas evident that in no other way had we the slightest chance of escape; for the flames were roaring up the great wide wooden staircase in pursuit of us, and we could hear the Russians laughing at the idea of us being roasted alive like crabs in their shells.

We could not see them, nor could they see us, on account of the flames and smoke that intervened ; and perhaps it was as well that it was so.

When we got nearly to the top of the house, we found that a common step ladder led up to the attics.

Up this we could only mount one at a time ; but those who got up first set to work at once, so that when the last man ascended and very prudently pulled up the ladder after him, a great hole had already been knocked in the roof.

The men then scrambled on to the tiles by mounting on to each others shoulders, the colonel first of all warning them not to stand upright thereon, lest they should be seen by the Russians in the street.

I was one of the last to scramble through the hole in the roof, and by that time the attic was so full of smoke as to be almost suffocating, and by the heat and horrid roar I could tell that the flames had reached the rooms immediately below, and were feeding on the furniture therein.

The man who came forth last told me in a whisper that his feet were scorched with the heat of the floor he had just quitted, and almost as the words escaped his lips there was a great explosion from the opposite side of the street, and tiles, stones, bricks, and charred pieces of wood came raining down upon us, killing and maiming more than a dozen.

Amongst other things came down, too, a couple of dead bodies clad in scarlet coats, and then we knew that these were Connaught Rangers, and that it must have been the house held by Captain O'Hara and his brave fellows that had been blown up.

But we had no time to grieve for them, for we were still in deadly peril ourselves.

The roof was getting warm, soon it would be hot, and then at any moment it might fall in, burying us in the midst of a fiery volcano.

Then there was just as great a risk of the walls caving in, in which case the roof must fall too, and we with it.

Oh ! there was assuredly no time to be lost.

Our colonel and the officers knew that, and they were prompt to lead the way.

Luckily the roof was flat, and it seemed to run continuously from house to house.

We crawled along on our hands and knees therefore, and had really no difficulties to encounter.

CHAPTER LXXVI.

WE CHANGE OUR QUARTERS.

WE had now quitted the roof of the burning house, and put the roofs of three or four more between us as well.

But then we wished to get into another street, for we could tell that the one beneath us was still invaded with Russian soldiery from the noise they made.

It would never do to descend amongst them from any house, or we should be immediately massacred.

But, to our intense joy, we presently came to a long line of roofs that ran off from the others at right angles, forming the perpendicular stroke of a capital T, of which we had been hitherto crawling along the horizontal.

Well, this was a grand discovery, and, rising to our feet, but still maintaining a stooping attitude, we ran down the transverse line of roofs until we got nearly to the end, and they must have been a quarter of a mile long.

"Here we will descend," said the colonel, "for see, there is a skylight ; and glass is more easily broken through than tiles, lath, and plaster."

There was no gainsaying this, but someone moved as an amendment, "that perhaps the skylight was set as a window, and would open."

This, upon examination, we found that it would do, so we opened it very noiselessly.

"Now," said the colonel, "we've had enough of cutting throats, except in our own defence, so that, if we find that this house is inhabited by civilians only, we will lock them up in one room to prevent them giving a premature alarm, and do them no further injury."

There was a murmur of assent to this proposition.

We then went down into the house two by two, but on searching it over, we found it perfectly empty.

"Fasten securely all the doors and the lower windows," said the colonel. "We had far better stay here until darkness sets in, for then we shall have a better chance of returning to the camp without molestation. We will see what we can find in the place fit to eat and drink too, for fighting is hungry work."

We all agreed with him on that point, and we were not long in quietly securing and barricading inside all the doors and windows that were on a level with the street without.

Then we began a rigid search for food and drink.

We had been commanded to spread all that we could find on the great dining-room table, so that the food might be fairly apportioned, and no one was to taste of his discoveries before the general division.

This was quite fair ; in fact, nothing could have been fairer, and we all set hunting with a will.

While doing so, we found out why the house had been abandoned.

Shells and cannon balls had in some places riddled it.

Such visitors were formidable enough to frighten away any person, especially if he was the owner of wife and children as well.

We discovered, to our great joy, a pretty extensive larder, though everything in the nature of meat had long ago grown putrid and uneatable.

There was an enormous cheese, however, and bags of hard sea biscuits, a cask of butter, tins of sardines, and innumerable pots of jam ; and in the cellar we found quite as many bottles of wine as we were men, so that we were in a rare good humour.

After we had feasted—for us, right royally—the colonel posted sentries here and there inside the house, and told the rest of us we might go to sleep.

Every bed, couch, sofa and arm chair in the house was immediately utilized ; those who couldn't get them, being quite content to lie in rows on the soft carpets with their knapsacks for pillows.

We were all very tired, and 'tis a wonder that our united snoring did not bring the old shot-riddled house down around our ears.

I daresay most of the gallant fellows were too worn out even to dream ; but I was not, and I *had* a dream which I don't think I shall ever forget.

I dreamt that I was a French Zouave, and that, in company with another French Zouave, I had strolled into conquered Sebastopol for loot.

We had filled our pockets with all sorts of valuables, consisting mainly of gold, silver and precious stones ; and had just entered another house, which we intended should be the last for that day, when in one of the rooms we were encountered by another Zouave, a gigantic fellow, who declared all there was his own.

Hot words ensued ; but, seizing my companion by his left wrist, he plunged his sword into his heart.

Then he sprang upon me, tore my weapon from my grasp, flung it out of the window, and dragging me across the room, vowed he would first choke and then send me after it.

In vain I struggled, and in my struggles pulled from my captor's face a sort of mask, leaving bare the mocking cynical visage of my evil genius, Louis Foucarte!

He was all too strong for me.

He cast me forth, and presently I felt myself falling through innumerable glass roofs, each one apparently a mile beneath the other; when I was awakened by a horrible fusillade, and opening my eyes, I saw that the street without was lighted up as by a rolling fire, whilst cannons thundered in the distance!

CHAPTER LXXVII.

WE ARE RESCUED BY THE FIFTIETH.

ALL the soldiers now seemed to wake up at once, and load their muskets instinctively.

They evidently thought that the end was at hand.

And they boldly advanced to the windows, to look the worst in the face at once.

They were not afraid to die—not one whit.

At all events, not if, while dying, they could kill.

The street below was full of Russians.

But they did not seem to be intent on mischief.

On the contrary, they appeared to be panic-stricken.

They were running as fast as they could run.

And, in the distance, we heard a cheer.

A real, genuine British "Hip-hip-hurrah!"

"What is all this?" we asked ourselves.

It could mean but one thing—that friends were at hand.

That they were coming to rescue us.

And it was so; for a minute later, the head of a scarlet column debouched into the street—the British colours, all riven and torn, bullet-pierced and sabre-slit, floating above the black shakos.

The Russians now and then turned upon their pursuers, but the well-plied bayonets were too much for them, and each time they wheeled round and fled more precipitately than before.

Their cries, and the roar of the cannonade, were mingled together.

It would soon all be over now, for the shades of evening were just beginning to veil the scene.

When the gallant 50th were fairly abreast of us, we rushed down to join them, but we could only just open the doors in time to get out, and close in upon their rear.

We marched on, over a heap of dead men, whose half coagulated blood we splashed up like liquid mud as we tramped along.

But we did not look down to see where we trod.

Had we done so, the slain and the wounded were so numerous that we could not have picked our way.

So, over chests, and limbs, and hands, and feet—ay, and faces too—we marched onwards.

Then again we came to a place where the Russians treated us to a fusillade from the windows on either side of a long street.

And again it was a case of carrying house after house, massacring all therein, and then giving each building to the flames.

I was glad to perceive, however, that we were gradually working our way out of the city instead of deeper into it.

But still death was all around us in every form of horror that it is possible to conceive.

Many sat propped up against the walls of the houses on either side of the way.

These were those who had had the strength and the presence of mind left to drag themselves out of the way of trampling infantry and charging cavalry, and to die quietly from loss of blood.

Some of them had pipes in their mouths, the tobacco in which had gradually burned out like their own lives.

The faces of these were very peaceful, but the bullet of poor old Brown Bess gave peace—a painless passing away of life. Would that as much could be said for the conical rifle ball, which often inflicts the most acute torture.

And some of the dead stood up—merely leaning against a wall, or a closed door, which they had been striving to open to seek shelter within, when the leaden messenger of death overtook them.

But the majority still lay in little heaps about the street. English here, Russians there, and in other places English and Russians together—some with the death grip still fastened upon each others throats, and their eyes glaring with hate.

In some places, too, we could see poor wretches crushed almost out of shape, beneath fallen houses, with beams, or masses of masonry lying across their bodies.

Many of these were as black as ink.

Sights like these, seen when the blood was getting cool, and the excitement of battle was over, were far more terrible than the taking part in the more desperate charge.

Now one could perceive what a curse war was, and how hellish it looked when divested of all its barbaric pomp and glitter.

We had long ago given up the pursuit of the Russians.

The 50th had only entered Sebastopol to find us, and bring us forth alive.

The Royal Irish had taken the news back of how we were situated, and hence this chivalric incursion to our rescue.

They had had some difficulty in finding us, for, as it will be remembered, we had changed streets; but at last they had succeeded, and they were carrying us back with them in triumph.

Not that many more than a hundred of us remained alive; but then, had they not come, we should doubtless all have been killed.

And we marched on until we came to that suburb of the city which was nearest to the British camp.

We saw the great barrack, the continued fusillade from which had killed so many of our men at an earlier hour of the day.

It was a heap of ruins now.

The guns in the captured Barrack battery had been turned against it, and in an hour had battered it to the ground.

When in view of this point, but before we reached it, we, however, wheeled to the left, and marched into a suburb I had not before visited.

CHAPTER LXXVIII.

WE FIND COMFORTABLE QUARTERS.

I FOUND that here the 50th had pitched their quarters, from which I knew that we must have obtained real possession of a portion of the city, a possession that we felt sure we should be able to keep.

Doubtless this suburb was protected and covered by some of our own heavy batteries on the heights; anyhow, I could see that it was well out of the range of the Redan—now, as it will be remembered, once again in possession of the Russians.

We all of us thanked our preservers when we had come to a halt, and the soldiers had fallen out—and our thanks, if blunt, were at all events sincere, for we felt that we owed our lives to these brave men.

They received them very lightly however, declaring that one good turn deserves another; and that perhaps the time would come when we should be equally useful to them.

Then we were told that out of the dozens of empty houses that stood around, we might quarter ourselves in whichsoever we liked; an officer, a sergeant or corporal, and a dozen privates to each house.

With this arrangement we were very well contented, and I was just looking around to see upon what officer I should like best to fasten myself—for as I was not attached to any regiment I should have to accept the hospitality of one or another—when I felt a slap on the shoulder, and looking round, saw that it was Chomondley.

I had quite forgotten that he was in the 50th.

But that was a time to forget everything.

He seemed equally surprised to see me.

"I'm deucedly glad to find you still in the land of the living," he remarked; "I thought that some sharpshooter in the Redan had settled you long ago."

"Oh, I escaped the Redan, and have had a host of adventures since. I've seen more fighting to-day than I hope to see again in all my life. But where are you quartered?" I asked.

"Well, I hav'n't picked out a town residence yet," he replied, with a shrug of the shoulders, and a sharp glance around.

Then he quickly added, "What do you say to that tall old mansion, just back in that side street there? It looks ancient and respectable; the kind of place that will be sure to have a family ghost. Do you know, I should like to see a Russian family ghost, wouldn't you?"

"Well, I don't know; it strikes me that, under the circumstances, I should prefer a sound night's sleep. But if you fancy the house, take possession of it, by all means; and I will be your guest."

"You may be my companion—I won't call you a guest; for that relationship would entail the exercise of some hospitality on my part, which can hardly happen, because that infernal commissariat is very likely to forget all about us down here Out of sight, out of mind, you know."

"Oh, but most likely that old house is well stocked with provisions," I remarked.

"In that case it will be all right, and we will go in for an good supper; for which a previous six hours' hard fighting is the best sauce extant. I will gather my chickens together, and then we will proceed to take possession."

Chomondley's gathering his chickens together was a mere brusque order to a lance-corporal to bring a dozen men along at once, and instal them in the house we had taken a fancy too.

He carefully pointed it out to the non-commissioned officer, and then he took my arm, and we sauntered leisurely towards it, smoking.

We found the front door ajar; but this was nothing unusual under the circumstances.

We entered the house.

The lower stories were as dark as the grave, save where here and there a ray of light was let in through a cannon shot-hole, so we ascended to the upper.

In going up the steep stairs, I—who was in advance—fell over something. I put my hand down and felt that it was deathly cold.

I called out to Chomondley, and, coming up, he burnt some priming, and discovered it to be a dead man.

"Let us choose some other house," I said.

"Nonsense," laughed Chomondley; "the same objection would doubtless apply to all. I believe the 40th had some hot work here, and turned the original birds out of their nest. Dead foes at the close of a long day's fight are far more satisfactory than living ones."

I said not a word further, and we reached the drawing-room floor.

Here, on the carpet, lay three or four Russians, and three or four English, stretched in all kinds of attitudes, but all dead, and their faces white as wax.

"When the men come, they shall remove all these poor fellows into one room," said Chomondley. "These are too comfortable quarters to surrender their possession to those who cannot appreciate them.'

I couldn't understand his joking upon such a subject; but then he was an old campaigner, and campaigning sadly hardens the heart.

I felt that hardening myself very preceptibly, though I was so new to the bloody work.

Not but what there was no denying that the apartments were very comfortable—as comfortable as velvet-pile carpets and the most luxurious furniture could make them.

And when the lance-corporal and his men had removed the dead and mopped up all traces of their blood; when, moreover, the coal-cellar and the wood-cupboard had been laid under contribution, and a cheerful fire blazed in the grate of polished steel, we should hardly have known—if we had not glanced at our faded, patched, and war-worn uniform—that we were not in some Belgravian or Parisian drawing-room.

Yet, at a second glance, there were other trifles that destroyed the illusion also.

The plate glass of the windows was, here and there, ventilated and starred by intruding bullets, and on one side of the room there was a hole through the solid masonry, marking the track by which an uninvited round shot had entered.

We stuffed up this hole with sofa cushions, for it admitted a most disagreeable draught, and then Chomondley ordered the corporal to lay the table with every luxury that he could find in the place, paying fully as much attention to liquids as to solids.

We never expected, when the order was given, what that corporal could do, for not only did he find edibles and drinkables, but the whitest of napkinry, the brightest and most massive of plate, and the cleanest of glass, to make the repast look tempting.

And on the well laid out board he placed a cold roast turkey, a brace of ducks, a fine ham, cavaire, bread by no means stale, a vast tankard of foaming ale, and half a dozen bottles of champagne.

"Hallo! we seem to have got into fairy-land here, and you appear to be the presiding genius, worthy corporal," laughed Chomondley. "I hope you have similar good things for your own table, because, if not——"

"I assure you, sir, our feast is as luxurious as your own, barring the fact that we have port and sherry instead of champagne, and plain roast and boiled instead of the poultry," replied the corporal, with a salute.

"A merry evening to you, then," said Chomondley, with a laugh. "But I say, corporal, see that your men do not indulge too freely. We are in a still unconquered city, recollect—a Russian city, too; so just remember Moscow, and be as vigilant as if you were still in camp, or more so. I shall hold you personally responsible for whatever goes wrong."

"I will keep the men sober, sir, and they shall sleep with their eyes skinned. A sentry inside and out, sir, as usual?"

"Inside and out, yes, to be relieved every four hours; and I say, corporal, call me at midnight. I am on duty to-night, out piquet duty."

"Yes, sir," and the corporal saluted and withdrew.

When he had done so, we kicked off our boots, and undid our tight tunics.

We went in for luxurious ease in fact.

And as the cheery fire burnt and crackled, throwing a warm light over the rich furniture and the well-laid table, we were fain to confess that there was a bright side even to campaigning.

By George, what a meal we made! Turkeys and ducks disappeared as though by magic, and the wine went faster still, for it was prime.

In default of a corkscrew, which our clever caterer had forgotten to provide us with, or else had been unable to find, we knocked off the necks of the champagne bottles with the backs of our sabres; but we were adepts at that.

And when our hunger and thirst were quenched, Chomondley said, "Now we only want some good cigars to complete our happiness."

"And a good yarn teller," I remarked.

"Oh, well, if you will find the cigars I will spin you a yarn," laughed Chomondley; "one that I had from a French Cuirassier the other night."

CHAPTER LXXIX.

CHOMONDLEY SPINS A YARN.

NOW, as I have as great a dislike to telling a tale as I have a *penchant* for hearing a good one, I at once rose from my chair, stretched myself, and set out on my cigar hunt.

I made no doubt but that I should find some, for in this strange house one had really but to wish for a thing, to discover it at one's elbow.

"Here are a couple of chandeliers on the mantel-piece with a round dozen of wax candles in each," said Chomondley with a yawn.

"Oh, the fire gives sufficient light, and I've a notion that I shall find what I want without quitting the room," I made answer.

"What! in a drawing-room?" asked Chomondley.

"Yes, in a drawing-room," I responded.

I opened every drawer, but found no signs, nor did I discover any in an elegant little lady's work-table; but when I came to a richly carved walnut wood davenport, I felt that I was "warm," as the children say in hunt-the-slipper.

I searched each of the five drawers, however, but still no cigars.

I then broke open the top with my sword blade, for it was locked, and in a little pigeon-hole I found, not bundles of cigars, but three boxes of what turned out upon examination to be the most exquisitely flavoured cigarettes.

"The finest Turkish, by Jove!" exclaimed Chomondley, as he lighted one.

"Yes," I replied, throwing myself in my cozy arm chair again, and losing no time in following his example; "and now I expect a tale just as fine."

"Nay, I won't promise—I'll give you one for what 'tis worth, and in the poet's words, 'I'll tell the tale as 'twas told to me,' but on the express condition that when I have done you will give me a full, true, and particular account of everything that befel you from the time of your leaving me in the advanced sap in front of the Redan until we met in the streets below."

"Oh, I'll do that right willingly," I answered; "and I'll bet you, blindfold as it were, that my tale will have more incident in it than yours."

"Well, I don't mind. What shall the wager be?"

"An even five-pound note, if you like."

"Done; and if we can't agree we will toss."

"Yes; if we can't agree we will toss, and now fire away."

"Let me see. I told you that the yarn was spun to me by a French Cuirassier. It was on the night after the battle of the Alma, if I recollect rightly; and he declared to me that the affair had really happened to some officers of his regiment half a century before in the Peninsular war."

"Come, a true tale is worth half a dozen imaginary ones," I remarked; "so commence."

"Well, it was during the exterminating warfare which characterised the invasion of Spain by the French (I am speaking in my own words, not in those of my informant) that a small body of Cuirassiers, detached from the main division, had halted for the night at Figuieras.

"The appearance of this company was to the poor inhabitants of the village a source of disagreeable anticipations, actuated as they were by natural antipathy to a domineering foe, and by a very natural anxiety for the safety of a little property acquired by the toil of congregated years.

"'What, ho!'" cried the leader of the soldiery as he stopped before the gates of the monastery, the only building in the hamlet that appeared capable of rendering any tolerable accommodation.

"'Open your gates! or by the great emperor—your master as well as ours—your aves shall not profit you in saving your heads.'

"And, as he spoke, he struck the portal with his drawn sword, as though to hint that his threats would speedily be enforced if a ready acquiescence were not accorded to his commands.

"There was silence for a time, as though the monks were deliberating on what course to pursue.

"Then the figure of an aged man became apparent, as, with trembling hands, he loosened the bolts and bars and threw open the door.

"He bore a torch, whose gleam threw a murky glare upon the helmets and breastplates of the Cuirassiers, and served also, though indistinctly, to illumine the gloomy court and gloomier building.

"'Save you, good father,' said the French colonel, ironically, at the same time making a low bow, 'I bear my brigadier-general's greetings to your holy brotherhood, and expect the best that your larder and cellar contains for myself and my troopers. Both are well stored, no doubt.'

"A crimson glow for a moment flushed the pallid cheek of the venerable monk as La Rivière—I think that was the colonel's name—concluded his address, but it passed instantly away, and he returned no response, save by a strange smile and an inclination of the head.

"La Rivière regarded not his momentary emotion, but ordering his soldiers to dismount and piquet their chargers in the spacious courtyard, he entered the holy and solemn pile accompanied by his light-hearted brother officers.

"The clang of their spurs and sword scabbards as they tramped along the vaulted corridors, escorted and preceded by their aged guide, too plainly announced to the monks the propinquity of their enemies, those profane scoffers of all the sacred ordinances of religion, for such a character had the French troops acquired, though my informant declared unjustly so, the misrepresentations being started and inculcated by those who were well aware how much such a belief would kindle patriotic zeal and Spanish bigotry against the invader.

"As the soldiers entered the refectory, the assembled brethren rose from their oaken stalls and calmly gazed upon their haughty intruders.

"'Excuse me, reverend sirs,' exclaimed La Rivière, awed into respect by their dignified demeanour, 'but my men require repose, and in these troublous times, as little courtesy is needed, I have that plea to warrant my intrusion. My men must be provided with good cheer, or else (and here he touched the hilt of his sabre significantly) there may arise an occasion of proceeding to extremities, and I think the odds are too much in our favour for you to dare to provoke us to that.'

"'Sir,' replied the abbot, 'you speak truly. Your wishes shall be obeyed, no matter how little may be our desire to serve you.'

"'I imagine that if we relied on that, our entertainment would be poor indeed,' laughed the colonel.

"'That is an unkind opinion,' replied the reverend superior; 'deeds will convince you of its fallacy.'

"So saying, he motioned the officers to sit down, and commanded the lay brothers to load the table with the best the monastery could afford.

"The table soon groaned beneath the weight of the delicacies, and cordiality usurped the place where distrust had so lately reigned.

"The abbot left the apartment for a brief inter rat, but speedily returned, followed by two attendants bearing immense silver vessels filled with cool and sparkling wine.

"'Now, tell me candidly,' exclaimed a young officer but six months joined from the military college of St. Cyr, 'tell me if you have got some pretty damsel here—you understand me, a novice, or something of that kind—to benefit her by your example and pious admonitions.'

"The eyes of the abbot shone with a wrathful glare at the impertinent speaker, and then a bitter smile passed across his stern features.

"'Fear not,' he replied; 'for this night's entertainment shall be better and more complete than any which you shall hereafter enjoy.'

"'Bravo!' retorted La Rivière; 'I knew that we should find something better here—sub rosa, of course—than even the sparkling wine. You must teach us irreligious laymen, who know not how to temper our love suits with pious sighings for the great iniquity of our frail nature, the quickest way to the hearts of women, for thou knowest it, I'll be bound,' and the Cuirassier laughed immoderately.

"'A truce to raillery, colonel. Let us confine ourselves to the wine, for it is prime, and nothing so much promotes good fellowship,' said another officer.

"'But, good father,' ejaculated a third, as he filled a goblet with the amber liquid, 'you must pledge your guests in a full bumper first.'

"'The rules of our order forbid our indulging in wine, and therefore you must excuse me and my brethren from drinking with you,' said the abbot.

"La Rivière smiled ironically at this, as though he thought it only hypocrisy on the holy father's part in refusing openly to drink anything stronger than limpid water.

"He raised his goblet to his lips, but a sudden idea seemed to strike him, and he replaced it on the table, shuddering slightly the while.

"The monks regarded this movement with apparent surprise, as though they could not understand the hitherto volatile Frenchman's conduct.

"'Comrades,' cried La Rivière then, 'a sudden suspicion has seized hold of me with well-nigh irresistible force, and if it turn out to have some foundation, we will leave these monks minus their heads. Taste not the wine on your lives, until we know that it is not poisoned. Such deeds have been performed before in Spain, and by monkish hands.

"As the colonel concluded his impassioned address, every eye was turned on the tall and stately abbot, but he blanched not, and the calmness of his countenance afforded no credit to the Cuirassier colonel's suspicion.

"But he was not convinced thereby, and rising to his feet, he held out his goblet, saying—

"'Drink of the wine first, you and your brethren as well, and then we will drink also.'

"The abbot thereupon raised his eyes to heaven, and seemed for a moment to be buried either in meditation or devotion.

"Then, taking the proffered cup, he slowly drank its contents, even to the dregs.

"The other monks filled up their horn cups with the wine instead of water, and also drank it.

"'Now are you satisfied?' inquired the abbot of the colonel. "Now are all your doubts dissolved?'

"'Fill me up another goblet and try me?' laughed La Rivière; and when this was done he held it above his head, shouting, 'We pledge you, holy fathers, and hope that you may always have as good wine in your cellars to feast the great emperor's soldiers upon.'

"'I trust that we may, my son,' replied the abbot; 'for they would ever be welcome.'

"Cup succeeded cup, as the elated Cuirassiers, delighted with their superior and wholly unexpected entertainment, sought to make the best of their present comfortable quarters.

"'By St. Denis!' stammered out a jovial and more than half-drunken lieutenant, 'we will ever prove grateful for the kindness we have this night experienced; and, egad, if the old boy will produce his pretty niece I'll carry her away with me, and send him in exchange a girl of my own, of whom I am somewhat weary, the fair and beauteous Louise.'

"'Hang the fair and beauteous Louise, and all other women, too,' hiccoughed another reveller. 'Man has only two staunch friends worth caring for, and they are wine and steel.'

"'And the last is the best, for it will obtain us the first,' laughed a third.

"'Silence, gentlemen,' roared La Rivière; 'I am about to make a speech. When our golden eagles flap their wings over the entire land, and a Buonaparte is firmly seated on the throne of Spain, the brethren of this monastery shall be amply rewarded for their hospitality.'

"'They are already rewarded, for through them that day you, at all events, will never behold,' said the abbot, suddenly changing his voice and manner. 'Base tools of a usurper,' he continued, 'hear me, and shudder at my words. Know, that in spite of all your precaution, the wine that you have drank is poisoned, and that you nor we have an hour to live. Of us Spain claimed the sacrifice, and for our beloved country we willingly made it; and though the pangs of death are fast approaching, yet the thought that you, our enemies, our persecutors, must die with us, is balm to our fire-racked chests. Does not the venom even now rankle in your veins? Speak, slaves, speak!'

"Consternation and horror had prevented the French from interrupting the abbot in his speech, but even as they listened to his awful declaration the agonising throbs they endured declared how true were his words.

"Madly, then, they rushed on their betrayers, but death was already in the act of laying his cold hands upon them, and their swords dropped from their relaxed and nerveless fingers.

"Then they fell upon the floor, and the smothered groan, the frightful swearing, the mingled prayer and curse, rose on the silent air of night.

"When the morning came, not a soul awoke within those grim monastic walls. The monks were dead, the soldiers dead; they lay about the floor in all directions, their swords and wine-cups all scattered around.

"And the private soldiers buried their officers and rode back into France with only their sous officers to command them; but deadly was the hatred they bore the Spaniards from that day—so deadly, that the regiment retains it even now."

CHAPTER LXXX.
I AM LEFT, BUT NOT ALONE.

"WELL, that *is* a strange tale," I remarked, when Chomondley had concluded, "and I've no doubt a true one. I've read of such cases of Spanish vengeance, and I wouldn't be at all surprised if Russians, on emergency, behaved in much the same way. I believe they have many failings in common—I do, indeed."

"Well, never mind about that now. The evening draws on, and by the time you have narrated your own adventures it will be time for me to visit my sentries," said Chomondley.

Thus urged, I could no longer refuse, and I forthwith proceeded to narrate the incidents that have occupied nearly a dozen chapters of this narrative, but as concisely as I could.

When I had done, Chomondley said—

"By George, you must have as many lives as a cat, or rather double pussy's natural complement. I own that you have won the wager, and I'll pay it you the day that Sebastopol falls, being at present preciously short of the ready; and now it is time for me to be off."

"Surely it cannot be nearly midnight already."

"It is, though; a quarter to twelve exactly, and in confirmation strong of the accuracy of my repeater, here comes the corporal upstairs to call me," said Chomondley.

'Twas even so. "Rap, rap, rap," came to the door, and then a gruff "Quarter to midnight, sir."

"All right," shouted out Chomondley, and the corporal strode away again, whistling.

"I will go with you," I said, rising.

"I'll be hanged if you do! What, after all you have gone through during the last four-and-twenty hours? You must have the strength of a lion and the constitution of a rhinoceros, not to have been sound asleep in that chair long ago," said Chomondley, pulling on his boots.

"But it looks so dashed unfriendly to let you go forth alone on such a night as this."

"Never mind what it looks as long as it isn't," replied my companion; "I had four hours' good sound sleep this morning whilst you were fighting like the Grand Turk, and my work all through the day has been mere child's play compared with yours. Therefore, just find yourself out a sumptuous boudoir and get between the sheets, or else curl yourself up on that comfortable lounge beside the fire, and sleep until I return."

This was a long speech for the prosaic Chomondley, but it contained a good deal of sound advice; and so, as I was dead beat, and no mistake about it, I did not press my company upon him further, but curled myself up upon the roomy, well-springed couch with a fresh cigarette between my teeth, and in an already half somnolent state watched him button up his uniform and buckle on his sword, don his long military cloak and shako, and then, with a smile and a nod to me, quit the room.

I believe that I was sound asleep before he was out of the room; but, be that as it may, my nap was not a very prolonged one, for when I woke up the fire was not out in the grate, though it had certainly sunk very low therein.

I think that it was the feeling very cold that awoke me.

I know that I was trembling violently.

I sprang to my feet, and seeing the brandy decanter standing on the very edge of the table, I took a hearty drain thereat, and then seizing the poker, set to work to stir up a genial blaze.

The fire had happily not sunk beyond that, and it was soon flaring merrily again.

It was at this juncture that I looked in the great mirror that surmounted the broad marble mantelpiece.

It was to see, I think, whether my face was not in need of an application of soap and water; well, it did, for I was almost as black as a nigger.

But it was not the chimney-sweep aspect of my own face that startled me, and caused me to give utterance to an exclamation of surprise; it was the reflection of another face, and, what was more, of a young and good-looking one.

It had peered forth for an instant from behind the voluminous folds of one of the window curtains, and then was immediately withdrawn.

But at the very instant of its appearance I had caught its reflection in the glass, and wheeling round I said, as gently as I could—

"Pray come forth, whoever you are. Don't be afraid of me; I will do you no harm."

No reply was vouchsafed to this civil speech.

But I suddenly reflected that I had spoken in English, a language with which the fair owner of the head was doubtless unacquainted.

I repeated my friendly assurances in French, therefore, advancing half way towards the curtain the while, and this time they were responded to, the owner of the head revealing herself.

I was glad the firelight was so bright, for it helped to reveal to me her dazzling loveliness.

She could not have been more than eighteen years of age, but her figure was tall and at the same time well-proportioned.

The face was very fair, too, for a Russian maiden's, and surrounded apparently by a perfect halo of short, golden hair; whilst her eyes, of the darkest violet, and her lips of the most cherry redness, fixed upon me one of the sweetest smiles imaginable.

Yes, she did smile with her eyes as well as with her mouth, that I could vouch for; and oh, they were all-conquering!

"To what fortunate incident am I indebted for the honour of this visit?" I asked, again in French, as I advanced and took her hand.

"I might in turn ask to what I am indebted for the honour, if it be one, of your visit?" she replied archly, "seeing that this is my, or rather my father's house."

I now noticed for the first time that the young lady was in indoor costume, a most captivating dress of rich, blue velvet, trimmed with fur of the most snowy whiteness.

As may readily be imagined, I felt rather awkward on hearing this declaration.

I had made up my mind to show her, in the most brotherly manner, that she was in no way intruding, but she had suddenly thrown on me the onus of proving that I wasn't, and that with her father's emptied champagne bottles and demolished turkey on the table, and her father's broken-up kitchen table and chairs burning away for firewood.

The position was evidently quite untenable.

"I really am most awfully grieved," I began; and then I stuck in the mud, for not one word would come.

"I suppose you want to say that you are grieved that the chances of war necessitate your being here, but that really you can't help it. That your colonel put you in this house, and that it would be as much as your head was worth to leave it without his permission, or to refuse to eat and drink whatever it contained," observed the young lady, smilingly.

Oh, how I inwardly blessed her for coming to my rescue in such a genial manner!

"I am afraid it is very much as you affirm," I said; "but, for all that, I am very much concerned at putting you out of the way. I will have all these things cleared away, and give you up the possession of the drawing-room at once, and any bedroom that you will mark on the outside of the door as your own. I will guarantee that no soldier shall enter."

"Oh, how very kind of you!" said the young lady; "and we have always been told that you black soldiers are so very blood-thirsty and ferocious."

"Black soldiers!" I didn't understand her for a moment, but then I recollected the colour of my face when I surveyed myself in the glass a minute or two before, and I felt maddened as I thought, "She thinks it real. No doubt she takes me for a Turk, or something of that kind."

But I wasn't going to leave her under that impression, and I took care to assure her how that I owed the dark hue of my skin to gunpowder and the smoke of explosions.

She listened to my explanations with a smile, and when I had ended them, she said—

"Well, you are a brave soldier, anyhow; and, though a foe, I am sure you will grant me a favour."

"Only put me to the test," I said, rapturously; and I think I squeezed her hand a little.

"Well, then, my dear father is upstairs, oh so very ill! and I fear he will die if he does not see a doctor soon; and yet where are we to find one? I dare not go forth to find one, with hostile soldiers all around the house and neighbourhood; and if I did, not one would come back with me, for fear of being made a prisoner."

"All this is very sad," I said.

"Yes," was the tearful response, "and all the more so, because my poor father is not a man of war, but a peaceful civilian. A rich, a very rich merchant, in fact, and I am his only child ; " and here a lace kerchief was brought into use.

Now, a pretty girl's tears are things that no fellow, with an ounce of feeling, can successfully withstand.

I think my right arm found its way around her waist then, and I'm sure I murmured—

"Do tell me what you would have me do for you and for your father, and I give you my word of honour, as a gentleman, that if it can be done, why, it shall."

I fancy I pressed her to my side then.

"Then you will let me take him away from here. You will give me a pass through the British troops. Oh, I'm sure he will die before morning, if he does not see Doctor Olgoriki, the only really skilful medical man in Sebastopol. Oh, he could be so easily carried to the doctor's house, but I'm sure the doctor would never be induced to come here ; " and as she spoke she clasped my hands, and looked up into my face in a way that would have tempted even the good Saint Anthony to have broken his vows.

"I'm sure I don't know about that," I stammered. "I am not in authority here. I really possess no power whatever to give safe conducts."

"Oh, I see, you are afraid of your colonel—a surly old bear, no doubt. They all are ; but will you not run the risk of a reprimand for me ?"

She looked archer than ever at me now, and seeing that I didn't speak, she continued—

"My poor father is all that is left to me. My mother has long since been dead, and my three brothers have all been killed in this cruel war. If I lose my father I shall be alone and friendless in the world ; and there's only one man in Sebastopol who can preserve him to me, and that's Dr. Olgoriki."

"Let me see your father," I said, desperately.

The fact is I thought it would be easier to say "No" to her before an uninteresting-looking old man, with a night-cap on, than down in that luxuriously furnished drawing-room, with my arm around her waist, her little tiny hands on mine, and her beautiful voilet eyes up-raised to my face.

Besides, I hoped that by temporising for awhile, Chomondley would return, and lift the whole weight of responsibility from off my shoulders.

She at once consented to my seeing her father, saying—

"When you perceive how really ill he is, I'm sure you'll grant my request."

Then, seizing my right arm, she dragged, rather than led, me, out of the room, and up a softly carpetted staircase ; at last rising one little taper rosy finger to her lips as we approached the door of the sick room.

CHAPTER LXXXI.

WOMEN ARE DECEIVERS EVER.

SHE then softly opened the door, and we entered.

"Father," she said, walking on tip-toe over to a great four-post bedstead, and drawing back the curtains, "I have brought with me a brave young English officer, who will allow you to be taken straight away to Doctor Olgoriki's. I have told him that otherwise you must die, dear father."

"Hang it, I have never promised anything of the kind," I growled to myself ; and then I walked across the room to have a look—and a good look, too, I resolved it should be—at the sick man.

He certainly did look very ill.

His face was as white as that of a corpse, his eyelids were half closed, and his form seemed to be as attenuated as that of a skeleton.

He shook, too, as one palsy-stricken, so much so indeed that the great bedstead shook with him.

Very evidently his daughter had not exaggerated the danger that he was in.

And what a handsome old man he was, too—what splendid features, what a majestic forehead, what a handsome iron grey moustache, what a high military bearing altogether, in spite of his night-cap and the bed clothes being up to his chin !

"I hope you are not as ill as your daughter seems to apprehend, sir," I remarked in French, feeling constrained, under the circumstances, to say something to the poor invalid.

"Oh, I'm very ill," retorted the old man. "Ah, if I could only see Doctor Olgoriki—he understands my constitution so well. He might save me."

"If that's the case, I will send for Doctor Olgoriki ; assuring him that if he will only come to visit you his person shall be respected, and that he shall depart as free as he comes," I said, making sure that I had hit the right nail on the head, and that the invalid would jump at this offer.

Therein I was mistaken, though.

"Oh, Doctor Olgoriki would never come here ; he wouldn't risk his liberty, whatever you promised. A suspicious man—a most suspicious man—sir ; but, oh, so clever ! He was about to perform an operation upon me when your troops broke into this quarter—a most critical operation—but one which I am sure he, and he only, could have brought to a successful issue ; but at the sight of the foe in the distance he beat a precipitate retreat, and I don't believe that all the gold in Sebastopol would induce him to set foot in this quarter until you are all gone."

A long speech this for a dying man, but he delivered it in so many gasps, and with such evident difficulty, that I could not but believe every word of it ; and so I said—

"Really, I am very sorry. I wish I was in authority here, for I would give you leave to depart at once ; but I assure you I am not. You must, at all events, wait until my friend, Colonel Chomondley returns. I've no doubt he will permit of your departure directly I have represented the case to him."

"But if he is your friend, and you are so sure that he will let us depart, why lose precious time—for every instant is precious, I do assure you. Why not let us go on your own responsibility ? " pleaded the gentle voice of the daughter. And once more her hands were on my arm, and her deep violet eyes were looking up into mine.

"Well, I really don't know why I shouldn't," I began, speaking very confusedly ; "but——"

Ere I could get out another word I was stopped by a kiss, followed by the joyful exclamation of—

"Oh, papa, he has given us permission, and I will give us a safe conduct in his friend's name. You are saved ! You are saved ! "

And then, before I could blurt out a half-denial, she slipped a valuable diamond ring from the middle finger of her left hand on to my little one, saying—

"Receive this as an earnest of my deep gratitude. After this unhappy war is over, should you think it worth your while to renew our acquaintance, my father and myself will ever esteem you as a dear and a valued friend."

What could I say after that?

I couldn't have the heart to tell her that she had thoroughly misunderstood me.

No, I was won over. Another poor man was gone wrong, and all through a pair of violet eyes, cherry lips, and tiny white hands.

"Have you pens, ink, and paper ? " I asked.

They were forthcoming almost instantly.

I then wrote in a clear, bold hand—

"Permit Nicholas Orloff, and Marie, his daughter, with litter bearers, to pass all piquets and outposts, and enter Sebastopol."

Here I paused.

I didn't like to sign Chomondley's name, and yet I knew that my own would be of no use whatever.

"Hadn't you better put 'merchant' after my father's name?" asked Marie, at this juncture.

I did so, as an interlineation, at once, but I still hesitated to append my friend's signature.

"What is your friend's name, and what regiment is he colonel of?" asked Marie.

"John Prendergast Chomondley, 50th Regiment," I made reply; still, however, not writing it down.

"And how do you spell his name?"

I at once told her.

There could be no harm in that.

But directly I had done so, she seized another pen, and in a bold, clear hand, for all the world like a man's, and a soldier's, too, she signed the safe conduct herself.

"There," she said, "no one now can accuse you of having forged your friend's name. I thank you for the little document very much; may we go? I do not wish to delay an instant."

"Oh, yes, you may go," I said. "Six of our soldiers shall carry your father as far as you own outposts. I shall only insult you by asking that they may be allowed to return in safety."

"We do not need them, dear friend. Six of our serving women are still in the house, and they will be able to carry my dear father, so emaciated is he by disease, very easily."

As she spoke, she crossed the room and unlocked a door at its opposite end, when upon her calling to them, six tall, strapping—but, as I thought, very ugly women—in Russian costume, and with the greater part of their faces hidden by the hideous covering which all females of the lower order wear, entered the room curtseying.

I thought that these good souls need not have hidden themselves so very carefully away from our soldiers, for their faces would have been quite a sufficient protection from all harm.

But in other ways I was glad that they had turned up, for I should have shrunk from ordering any of the 50th who were in the house to carry the Russian merchant into Sebastopol, though I might have asked them as a favour.

The women, by Marie's directions, returned into the room they had emerged from, and presently came out again with the sacking of a bed.

It was evidently to form a litter, and with some skill they had made three handles on either side.

On to this Marie and I lifted the merchant, with all his bed-clothes rolled around him.

His daughter placed three pillows beneath his head, and then held out her hand to me.

"May I accompany you as far as your own lines?" I asked. "I may, perhaps, be useful."

A gracious assent was given, the invalid not speaking.

His eyes indeed were closed, and he appeared to be in too great pain to care to converse.

Marie looked at him, and I saw the tears swell up into her eyes.

It was no time wherein to distress her with words, so I drew her arm within my own, and pressing it, we went out of the room first, the invalid and his bearers following us.

And so down the staircase, across the great hall, and out of the front door into the street.

The lance corporal and his privates were still feasting down below in the kitchen.

We could hear their laughter as we quitted the house.

But on the very doorstep we were stopped by the sentry, though only for a moment, for I knew the watchword and countersign, and the safe conduct, with his own colonel's signature thereto, took away all suspicion from the rest.

Neither did any difficulty assail us on the road.

Five times the safe conduct was glanced over, and five times we were permitted to resume our course with a simple "Pass friends."

And at length, when we had come to our last out-piquet, and I saw the advanced sentry of the nearest Russian out-piquet pacing up and down at the head of an opposite street, I bid Marie and her father adieu, but not before I had made the former tell me where I could find her after the great struggle was at an end.

She told me, she pressed my hand, and allowed me to kiss her; her father gasped his thanks; and I then watched them until they were out of sight. Then I returned to my quarters with the feeling of a man who had done a good action, and thereby won, perhaps, a lady-love.

When I got upstairs, I found that someone had replenished my fire with the legs of a chair and the flaps of a table, and I believe that I went over and kissed that portion of the window curtain which I thought her soft cheek must have passed as she glanced forth at me from behind it.

After this, feeling chilly, I drank a glass of brandy, and then, feeling meditative, I lighted a cigarette, and it was whilst I was puffing away at this that I heard the clash of arms in the street, and a minute later Chomondley ascending the stairs with apparently half a dozen men at his heels.

He entered the room with his drawn sword in his hand, and a glance of triumph and exultation in his eyes.

I couldn't understand it at all.

"What on earth is up now?" I asked.

"Everything; the most splendid stroke of fortune in the world," was the excited reply. "I have it on reliable authority that the Grand Duke Michael, the son of the Emperor, you know, with Prince Radetski, a youth of sixteen, and six officers of the highest rank, all members of his staff, are at this moment concealed in this house. Come, draw your sword, and let us hunt them out—we shall have all the credit of their capture. We shall make our fortunes. We shall put an end to the war."

"Oh, there must be some terrible mistake," I cried, pulling my hair out by handsful, at the thought of the egregious folly I had been guilty of in making love to a young prince in mistake for a girl, and allowing a Grand Duke to escape in the guise of a dying merchant. "Oh, there must be a horrible mistake. Who was your informant?"

"A Polish deserter. He swore that the Grand Duke and his staff were in this house, and that our fellows swooped down upon the neighbourhood, and carried the surrounding streets at the bayonet's point too quickly for them to make an escape. The Poles hate the Russians, and this one showed such a fierce joy in betraying them to us, that I could not but believe him. So come along," and Chomondley seized my arm.

"Oh, God!" I exclaimed, in reply; "they are gone, and I am the most confounded fool under the sun."

CHAPTER LXXXII.

CHOMONDLEY RELATES AN EXPERIENCE.

WHEN I had fully explained to my friend the way in which I had been deceived, his anger and mortification knew no bounds.

He stamped on the floor, swore, paced up and down the room like one distraught, and then commenced to smash all the china and glass that he could lay his hands on.

I own that I was in just as great a rage, with

LOUIS FOUCARTE RESCUES HARRY DUNBAR FROM THE MURDEROUS HANDS OF THE DANCING DERVISHES, AND THUS WINS HIS WAGER.

the mortification added thereto, that I had made an egregious blockhead of myself. Egad, if the story got about the camp that my brain had been turned by the bright eyes of a youth of sixteen, who I had mistaken for a girl, and that through that I allowed the Grand Duke Michael and suite to get clear away, I should be laughed out of every club in London; nor should I dare to show my nose west of Trafalgar Square for a deuce of a time to come.

I was in fully as great a rage, therefore, as Chomondley; though I only showed it by biting my lips, contracting my brows, digging my heels into the hearth-rug, swearing internally and infernally, and roasting that portion of my frame which a free-born Briton often presents sans coat-tails to a good fire, though he ever scorns to turn it towards a foe.

In fact, so thoroughly did I roast myself, that when at last I threw myself into a chair, I sprang out of it with a yell which caused Chomondley to turn round with—

"What the devil's the matter now?"

"Oh, nothing," I replied, rubbing the part affected.

"By George! I thought 'twas a Russian war-whoop or a Cossack yell. What made you jump out of your chair so quickly? Has an idea struck you?"

"No," I rejoined, fiercely, "the devil a bit of one."

"Well, this is a deuced bad matter, isn't it?"

"That's hardly an original remark," I replied.

"Well, we look two precious fools, don't we?"

"I assure you, I feel like one; but I don't see what reason you have to claim alliance in this asinine affair. It is all my doing, every bit of it," and I believe that I could have cried out of very spite.

"Never mind," rejoined Chomondley, seeing how thoroughly I was put about. "It is no good crying over spilt milk, you know. Smashing those things up has done me a lot of good. I go down now, and tell the fellows that I've brought with me that it was all a confounded mistake. It won't do to let the tale get abroad, you know."

I quite agreed with this view of the case—it would not do to let it get abroad, indeed. I should have been driven to resign my appointment in the Foreign Office. I should have been laughed out of London—ay, and England too. I felt very grateful to Chomondley for the way in which he was going to treat the matter, and I watched his scarlet coat-tails flying out of the room with the intensest satisfaction.

I heard the soldiers he had brought with him go tramping forth. I saw them debouch into the great square, the moonlight glistening on the points of their bayonets. Then, presently, I heard Chomondley reascending the stairs.

When he entered the room his face was smiling.

"After all, it is a good joke," he said. "Excuse the violence of my temper. It is a way I have when excited."

"I am happy to say it is a way with a method," I rejoined. "You have only broken the empty glasses and decanters, and mercifully spared all of the latter that have anything left in them. Here is even a full champagne, and I vote that we crack it in a more legitimate manner than you have been practising of late."

"With all my heart," said Chomondley, "and in it we will drink total oblivion to the little incident that has caused us such annoyance and uneasiness."

"It's very good of you to say so, old fellow."

"Not a bit of it—a pair of bright eyes might have bewitched me in a precisely similar manner. Many boys don't make bad looking girls when dressed up in the proper togs. In fact, I was once taken in quite as thoroughly as you were to-

night, and in order that you may have as great a laugh over me as, I think, I have over you, I'll tell you how it happened, if you like."

"Oh, do!" I rejoined with a laugh of gratitude.

"All right—wait till I've cut up this chair; it's rather a handsome one, but then it will burn as well as any other, and it would be a pity to disturb the corporal at such an hour to bring us fuel;" and, as he spoke, Chomondley drew a beautiful carved occasional chair towards him, hacked it up into firewood and with it fed the dying flames.

"Now take a cigarette, pass over the box, refill your glass, and I will begin," he said gaily.

I did all that I was bidden to do, and then, crossing my legs and turning my feet to the cheery blaze, I prepared to listen to Chomondley's yarn.

"You remember the wonderful Mademoiselle Ella, whose bold, daring, and brilliant horsemanship delighted all the frequenters of Astley's Amphitheatre, in the year of the Fifty-one Exhibition?"

"Yes, perfectly," I rejoined; "a very pretty dark girl of fifteen—with the brightest and largest of oriental eyes, and glossy black ringlets. I remember her very well."

"Then perhaps, having seen her, you won't feel very surprised when I tell you that I saw her also, and, what is more, fell in love with her."

"Oh, a young fellow of twenty-one, as you must have been then, often falls in love with a pretty girl in a different station in life to himself," I said.

"Very well, then, I fell in love over head and ears. I wrote my inamorata love verses; I sent her bouquets; in fact, I made a very ass of myself."

"Not at all an unusual thing at such a time, and she was certainly a very pretty girl," I remarked.

"Just so. Well, from letters and bouquets, I went on to valuable presents; but they were all returned to me."

"That was very odd," I exclaimed, and so it was.

"But, undeterred by this, I made her an offer of marriage, promising her three hundred a year pin money."

"At which, of course, she jumped," I hazarded.

"Not a bit of it—she returned my letter."

"What? Did you tell her that you were an only son, the possessor of three thousand a year from your mother, and the heir to one of the finest free-hold estates in Yorkshire on the death of your father?"

"Yes, I told the young lady all that, old boy."

"But she was a foreigner, wasn't she?—a Spaniard or a Creole, by name Loyara? Perhaps she could not read your writing, and others, whose interest it was to retain her in her then mode of life, might have read it and made gibberish of your proposal."

"Alas, she could talk and speak English fluently."

"Well, then, I can't make out where her sense or philosophy lay. Surely she was not enamoured with her life."

"Perhaps she was. Yet listen to the end, and you will be able to draw correct conclusions as to her conduct. Seeing that my letters produced no results, and that all my presents came back to me, I followed her home one night, and poured out all my love on the cold doorstep of her house."

"What, wouldn't she let you enter, even?"

"No, she only laughed, and told me to go home to my mother. You know, I was a raw ensign then."

"If you were, she was extremely rude."

"Just so rude that I lost my temper, and swore to her that I was an officer bearing the Queen's commission, and had never had a mother in my life."

"That was rather stretching it?" I exclaimed, oracularly.

"Well, you see, I was in such a passion, owing

partly to her words and partly to having knelt in a puddle, which had formed in a hollow of one of the steps, that I didn't know what I said. However, I seized her hand and covered it with kisses, and then offered her a valuable diamond ring that I wore, if she would only let me salute her lips," said Chomondley.

"Which, of course, she let you do?" I exclaimed.

"Oh, yes, and the ring fitted the same finger on her hand that it did on mine. I didn't like that, I own; but I liked much less the way in which she said—'Now, go away, you silly fool, or my husband will come out and thrash you to within an inch of your life.'"

"You don't mean that she said that? But could that pretty young creature of fifteen—I vow she wasn't a day more when I saw her—really have a husband?" I exclaimed, as I lighted another cigarette.

"Ha! ha! ha!—he! he! he!—ha! ha! ha!—haw! haw! haw! Had a wife, maybe. She was like your princess, merely a—good looking young fellow."

"The deuce she was?" I ejaculated, bursting out laughing too—and, I'm ashamed to own it—intensely delighted that my friend had in times past made as absurd a faux pas as I had done in times present. "But how did you find all that out?"

"Not until a month or two before I came out to the Crimea, when a cousin, who knew of the incident, sent me a newspaper from Melbourne with the full account of the bankruptcy of the firm of Cook, Lizard, and Wilson, circus-proprietors. It seems that my young lady could not go through the court and get properly whitewashed under her assumed sex and name, and therefore did so as plain William Jones."

"Let me see, that was nearly four years after her first appearance in England. Did he keep up the deception all that time?" I asked.

"Yes, he did; and was so good-looking, too, that no one ever thought him to be a young man until the grand smash-up came. Oh, he made fools of others, I can tell you, besides me; and had he not been too honourable to receive presents from his admirers, he might have retired on the contents of his jewel casket. Now what do you think of that little narrative?"

"I think that your experiences are a fair set-off to mine," I rejoined. "We will neither of us speak of either again."

"I told you merely to put your mind at ease by placing ourselves equally in each other's power. But, now, what do you say, after what has occurred to-night, to taking a midnight walk? It's not at all cold outside, and there's a strange old church well within my outer line of piquets that I should like to explore."

"Oh! I'm your man for anything of that kind," I rejoined, "and I'm no more sleepy than you are."

"Drink up your champagne, then, pop a box of those cigarettes into your pocket, and away we go," said Chomondley, setting the example as he spoke.

Five minutes later we were in the streets.

CHAPTER LXXXIII.

THE CATACOMBS OF ST. VLADIMER.

IT was a beautiful night—the moon shed a silvery radiance over everything, and it was not so very cold.

Not a cannon thundered, not a mortar boomed; a dead silence reigned around. It was as if both sides were so thoroughly exhausted that they were bound to take rest, and, doubtless, it was so.

We walked along the battered streets, occasionally passing a watch-fire, whereat all the soldiers were fast asleep save the grey great-coated sentry, who was ever pacing slowly up and down with shouldered arms.

At last we reached the church which had somehow or other excited Chomondley's interest, and somehow or other aroused his curiosity.

Its exterior was certainly very handsome, even though much of the carved work and the pillars of the portico had been chipped and knocked about by cannon balls and exploding shells.

The bright green copper dome of vast proportions, and surmounted by a great gilt cross, shone brightly in the moonlight, and by the rays of this same queen of night, we could see that we should experience no difficulty in effecting an entrance, as the great doors were lying full length across the broad flight of marble steps.

"The place has been sacked, I fancy," I said.

"Never mind; I wasn't going in quest of the gold altar plate, or of any jewels that may, or might have studded the Madonna's crown," replied my companion. "It struck me, as I was returning home just now, that there were strange discoveries to be made, or strange adventures to be met with inside that old pile. We shall soon see if I was right."

We had entered the sacred building almost ere the last words were out of my companion's mouth, but I made him no reply, for there was something in the rapt stillness that surrounded us, that turned my thoughts suddenly into another channel.

The clear, pale moonlight shone in through the great western window, bathing nave, and aisle and altar in a flood of subdued light.

Our footsteps sounded hollowly on the marble pavement, every stride marking a tomb, and, as we approached the high altar, we noticed the six tall wax candles—three burning on each side of the golden crucifix, as well as the eternal fire that glowed within the silver lamp of the inner sanctuary.

"It is a fine old church," said Chomondley, at length.

"Yes," I replied, "and we seem somewhat out of place here. I would sooner come into a sacred place like this, fasting, than with a couple of bottles of champagne under my belt, and my pockets laden with cigarettes instead of missals and hymn-books."

"I don't think anyone can enter the house of God, especially of a night, without leaving it both a wiser and a better man," said Chomondley; "but I came here to explore, and not to moralise."

He looked around, and I looked around too.

Strange to say, our gaze at the same moment rested upon a large black door, on either side of which stood a gigantic marble angel with wings and eyelids drooped, and leaning upon a trumpet.

"That doorway leads to the vaults, and the vaults lead to—to—to—perhaps somewhere else," said Chomondley. "Those gigantic figures typify the angels of doom leaning on their trumpets, which shall be used at the last dread day."

"They are marvellous works of art," I rejoined; "but what propose you now to do, my friend?"

"Well, we will explore the vaults," he said; "a couple of those long altar candles will show us the way."

"I will not allow the altar lights to be touched," I said, sharply; "no, nor the precincts of the altar to be trodden by our irreverent feet."

"Very well, then," quoth Chomondley; "you stay here for a few minutes, and I'll warrant me I'll find candles and matches—ay, and perhaps keys, too, without invading any holy of holies whatever."

"All right," I responded; "go and see."

But he was gone before the words were well out of my mouth, and I wandered uneasily about, looking at the marble tablets, the delicate carving of the pillars, the light spring of the arches, and the many other beauties of the old church, architectural and otherwise, until his return, which did not happen for some little time.

When eventually he did turn up I noticed that he had two enormous wax-candles tucked under his left arm, and a bunch of equally enormous and very rusty keys dangling from a finger of his right hand.

"I've been overhauling what in England, I suppose, we should call the vestry," he said, "and here is the result. Take you one candle and light it with a fusee; I know you have a box about you."

I did as he bade me without reply. In fact, I had a horror of conversing of secular matters in a church, so I bottled up my speech until we should reach the vaults.

Chomondley was a long time finding the particular key that fitted the great, black, unvarnished door, but at last he did so, and then, though not without the vigorous application of a shoulder and a knee, it rolled slowly open.

A gust of cold damp air came rushing up.

An air that seemed to be impregnated with the mouldering effluvia of dead men's bones.

The candle that I carried was instantly blown out.

But my box of fusees soon re-lighted it.

And then Chomondley lit his from mine.

We passed through the door and locked it behind us.

We then noticed for the first time that we were at the head of a long flight of green, slimy, stone steps.

Down them we went, step by step and side by side, holding our tall candles high above our heads.

Pshaw, what a smell! 'Twas rank and foul enough to poison a legion of carrion crows or vultures.

"I vote that we go back," I said, coming to a halt.

"Do, old fellow, if you fear contagion; but in that case, as I am of a most inquisitive turn of mind, I shall go on alone," was the decided reply.

Of course after that I could back out no longer.

"Oh, as for that matter, I'm possessed of as much curiosity as you, and I only wish I'd brought some of our late host's very excellent French brandy down with us," I said.

"Never mind, my boy, we'll have a good drain when we get back," replied Chomondley, and down we went again; down, down, down, as it seemed, into the very bowls of the earth, the smell getting more nauseous at every step.

At last we reached a level subterranean, where our lamps burned dim and blue. Yet they gave enough light to show us that we were traversing a veritable Golgotha, or place of skulls. On either side, these ghastly relics of mortality were nailed up in the forms of crosses, hour-glasses, scythes, or gigantic deaths heads.

"Deaths heads playing at deaths heads! How horrible!

But our attention was soon distracted from dead to living horrors. We stepped on things that caused us to shudder, we knew not why. We heard croakings and hissings, we knew not from what or whom.

And when we did look down on the wet, greasy, slimy floor, we saw huge bloated toads—some as large as hedgehogs—looking up at us with swelling throats and filmy eyes; and hideous newts, great fat white worms, and little bright green snakes; all wriggling and writhing along, and crowding so thickly upon each other, that it was difficult to step free of them.

"This is disgusting and horrible," I could not help exclaiming. "Have you not yet seen enough?"

"No," replied Chomondley; "for I have an idea that these subterraneans have another exit; and if so, they might be of great service to our troops, you know."

"Oh, in that case," replied I, brightening up,

"let us go on, by all means. I won't raise another word of objection."

On we went—our candles burnt better now; but the stench was more overpowering than ever.

We passed openings on our right and on our left continually, and whenever we did pass the mouths of such openings, the faint, sickly, foetid smell intensified, until I could scarcely forbear from vomiting.

For a long while, however, Chomondley took no notice of these, bending all his thoughts upon, and proceeding straight along the main subterranean.

We must have got quite a quarter of a mile away from the great black door in the church, through which we had entered these labyrinthine passages, when these side opening seemed first to attract his attention; and then he came to suddenly and abruptly, took a couple of strides down one of them, slipped, recovered his feet with difficulty, and then, holding his great tall candle above his head, peered into the cavernous recess before him.

I heard him utter a cry of horror. I saw his face turn pale as monumental marble, his jaw fall, his eyes dilate, and I sprang to his side.

"Good God, what is it?" I exclaimed anxiously.

"There! there! Merciful heavens, are we in hell, or where?" was the agonised and disjointed reply; and he pointed with a trembling finger to a heaving undulating something before him.

Then I advanced my candle, and saw with a thrill of horror that I can't attempt to describe, that that heaving something was waves upon waves of human corruption—a battle field of a hundred yards in depth, fifty in breadth, and in some places at least a dozen in depth, in the hollows of the waves, wherein countless legions of the all-conquering worms were celebrating their great victory over man.

Now we knew whence arose the horrible stench—now, too, we knew how the Russians all though that long weary two years' seige had disposed of their dead thousands. We were surrounded by a putrid sea, without a hope of leaving it death untainted!

CHAPTER LXXXIV.

CAPTURED BY THE RUSSIANS.

PUTRID sea indeed! It was a living, rolling sea of putridity, on the billows of which dank helmets, ragged epaulettes, mildewed boots, and scraps of cloth were perpetually bobbing up and down as the twining, twisting, writhing, intercircling waves of worms, and great fat maggots—now in many places preying upon each other—chose to toss them.

For a full minute we could not avert our eyes from the horrific and loathsome spectacle.

Then arm in arm and reeling like drunken men, we staggered back into the main passage.

"Rather a dozen forlorn hopes than a scene like that again," I said, with a shudder I could not repress.

"I don't suppose we shall ever live to take part in another forlorn hope or battle either. We must have death already in our throats, after inhaling air poisoned with human corruption like this. Bah! I feel as if I could spit up foetid lumps of it now."

"Let us hurry on," I said, dragging him forward; "and if we get into a purer atmosphere, as pray God we may, then be as sick as ever you can."

"Yes, yes; but not that way, not that way," he gasped, seeing that I was taking a backward course, "On, on—I know we shall find an exit that way the soonest."

"No, no," I replied, "we will return. In going on we may be rushing upon other evils and perils that we know not of—in going back we, at all events, know that soon, very soon, we shall be amongst friends."

Yes, yes; but I can't mount those terrible stairs, my legs give way beneath me, a terrible burning is rising from my throat into my brain. On, on, Dunbar. I feel a cool draught from in front. On, on, I say."

I could resist no longer. I, too, began to fancy now that a fresher air was coming up the subterranean that we were traversing. I held my candle out steadily; the flame blew backwards, I was convinced.

"Come on, you are right—there is hope," I gasped.

"Tramp, tramp, tramp," how hollowly our footsteps sounded whenever they did not inadvertently squish, or squash, or squab upon some loathsome reptile.

These, happily, grew less frequent as we progressed, and I presently noticed that the grinning skulls that still formed quaint devices on either side of the gloomy way, were no longer a ghastly green with foetid grease and mildew, but hard, brown, and nearly dry.

Still, however, from the lateral passages, the vilest of stenches continued to pour forth as we passed them by, and it was not until I had counted six of these on either side, that it began sensibly to abate.

By that time I knew that we were approaching some kind of an opening into the outer world, for frequent whiffs of pure air alternated with a burning smell, and every minute I could see a glow in the dim distance as of the reflection of fires.

"Come on, Chomondley, old fellow," I said; "you are right after all. We will soon be out of this."

"You may. I—shall—never—get—out," he gasped, in accents that with difficulty escaped his lips.

I looked round. I saw that his mouth would only open a very little way. I noticed that his lips were black, that his face had broken out in dull, leaden-coloured spots, that his eyes were nearly leaping out of his head.

And as I gazed he seemed to slip away from me. I tried to hold him up, but no, he fell with a dull thud upon the foul earthen floor.

I stooped over him and tried to lift him up.

But I could not, for he was as heavy as lead.

"Come, old fellow, try to rise," I said. "We are close to an exit now. You can surely drag yourself a little farther."

He tried to make me a reply. I could see his painful effort to articulate—then his jaws suddenly snapped asunder, a swollen, black, pustuled tongue came lolling out, the single word "Dead" came gurgling up out of his throat, and with it the horrid stench of putridity.

I rose to my feet. I staggered back against the wall, dislodging two skulls that fell with a hollow rattle to the ground. I felt giddy, faint, stupified with despair.

But at that moment I heard a tramp, tramp, tramp of feet in front and some way down the passage.

I looked up, and saw a torchlight procession coming towards us, and oh, such a procession.

They were men in uniform, Russian uniform, and they wore black masks. They formed a long, long line, each two men carrying a corpse upon a stretcher, whilst in advance of every dozenth stretcher, marched a man, also masked, holding aloft in either hand a resinous torch that emitted a strong fragrance.

They were evidently a detachment come to bury the dead that had been killed in the fighting of the previous day.

It was a solemn sight—no doubt the masks were worn to protect the bearers from contagion, and without doubt the torches were so strongly perfumed to overcome in some measure the horrid stench of putridity.

As they came nearer I could distinguish the long grey great coats and spiked helmets. I could see, also, from the stripes on their arms, that the torchbearers were all non-commissioned officers of the Russian line.

"Tramp, tramp, tramp," nearer and nearer still, with steps regular and slow, and I could see the pale faces and blood-stained uniforms of the dead.

Was I glad to see them approach, or was I sorry?

I could hardly answer the question. I did not know what they would do with us. I feared (and as the thought occurred to me my very hair stood erect upon my head) that they would throw us two Englishman, the living and the dead, both into the same horrible slough of putrid decay, as food for the worm and the maggot.

I could not run away, however, for I was losing the use of my legs, they felt as though they were reeling and rocking beneath me, every instant I expected to fall, and I clutched a couple of skulls at my back with both hands so as to maintain my perpendicular.

At length the head of the procession reached us.

The bearers of the first stretcher came to a halt.

The non-commissioned officer held his torch aloft.

He uttered an expression of disgust, and turned away.

I spoke to him in English, in French, in German. In all three languages I besought mercy and pity.

But 'twas evident that he didn't understand either.

In my despair I clutched hold of his sleeve.

Then he drew his pistol and pointed it at me.

I let go of him at once and fell on my knees, for I could no more have drawn my own weapons than I could have flown. Then he returned the pistol to his belt.

I pointed to the body of my friend, and the sergeant shrugged his shoulders and turned him over with his foot.

"Vocsa!" he growled, and I knew that vocsa meant dead. "Vocsa," I repeated, and then I pointed to the recess opposite, now rapidly kindling up with the glow of the torches, and shook my head, intimating thus that ●would not have him thrown therein.

The sergeant laughed within his mask, and growled something in Turkish, which from my now slight acquaintance with that language I knew meant "If such a place is good enough for comrades it is for enemies."

Then he turned, and by the light of a dozen great flambeaux that now penetrated far into the mysterious depths of the great branching side passage that opened exactly opposite to me, I saw therein just such a scene of horror as poor Chomondley and I had looked in upon not a quarter of an hour before.

Into this horrible slough, with a splash and a hollow booming echo, the dead Russian soldiery were pitched one by one. When the last had sunk out of sight the stretchers were clattered down one a-top of the other, and all the masked faces turned towards me.

I think that was the most horrible moment of my life. Happily the terrible strain did not last long, or then and there I should have become a hopeless maniac.

A sergeant pointed to the body of Chomondley, and instantly half a dozen strong hands pounced down upon it. Vain was my feeble clutch at the tails of the scarlet coat, my friend was raised aloft on their burly shoulders, carried forward a few yards, and then launched into the very centre of the putrid horde.

I could see a broad splatch of red amidst the blended hues of blue, green, and grey, that was all.

The next instant I was seized upon and raised aloft in turn. In vain I screeched in every language that I could think of for mercy, or at all events, to be shot first.

But laughter greeted my prayers and ravings, and then madness seemed to come to my aid, and I stared my fate in the face—stared at it, and thought that the seething mass of corruption had changed into millions and millions of dead, glaring, phosphorescent fishes' eyes, that winked and blinked at me, dilating and contracting by turns.

One swing, three swings, and the next instant I should have been sinking deep, deep into that horrid slough of decaying mortality, when I heard a hoarse voice shout something, and I was placed again on my feet.

A masked sergeant then advanced, whether it was the same as the one with whom I had held converse before I could not tell, and lifted up my gold albert watch guard and inspected a maltese cross that depended as a charm from one end.

At first I imagined that my execution had only been delayed to permit of his appropriating as lawful spoil my watch and chain, but I soon saw that it was the cross alone that rivetted his attention.

"Grecco!" he exclaimed, looking me full in the face, "Grecco Catollico?" and he touched the trinket meaningly.

"Bono Grecco Catollico!" I rejoined eagerly.

He patted me on the shoulder then, and ordered a couple of privates to lay me on a stretcher.

The little cross had saved me. Catching sight of it, the honest non-commissioned officer had taken me for a co-religionist, and a fellow feeling had made him wondrous kind, as the proverb hath it.

I was laid gently on the stretcher indicated, and an instant later was being borne at a jog trot down the main subterranean, towards where the occasional glow of fire, and puffs of pure air came from.

And at each step the air seemed to get purer still, until at last the pale moonlight streamed in and struggled for mastery with the glare of the torches.

We were soon out of the horrid subterranean, then four immense gates were presently opened, and we emerged into a kind of square, into which the moonlight was pouring down, passing between enormous fires that were lighted all around the mouth of the catacombs—no doubt, to prevent the deadly fumes from coming forth and spreading a plague or a black death through the besieged city.

And when I had observed all these things, reason left me, and I fainted dead away on my stretcher.

CHAPTER LXXXV.

NOT BAD TREATMENT FOR A PRISONER.

WHEN I came to, I found myself the occupant of a very roomy easy chair, propped up with pillows, in a well-furnished room that was nearly full of Russian officers.

These were drinking and smoking and laughing and talking with extreme volubility.

Directly I was observed to have my eyes open, however, one or two of them came up to my chair and asked me very kindly, in French, how I did.

Well, I replied, that I did very well, and would very much like to know where I was, how long I had been ill, and one of the officers answered me in French, which he spoke very fluently, that I had been ill for more than a week, and that I was in Sebastopol.

"I am sure I am awfully obliged for all the kindness that I have received then," I made reply; "but is it possible that Sebastopol still remains in Russian hands?"

"It does indeed, and is likely long to remain so," was the answer. "Though you English took the Redan, and the French the Malakoff, we had both places back before night; and though one northern suburb is in the hands of the Allies, they are no nearer the heart of the place than before."

"And cholera and dysentery are sweeping off a thousand men a day in the three camps, we hear," said another Russian officer, coming to the front.

"And General Liprandi, with thirty-five thousand fresh troops, is within three days' march of us, and will assuredly raise the siege," quoth another.

"Hang it!" I exclaimed, "this is no very cheering news, but what is to be will be, as the Turks say, and however matters turn out, I'm willing to pledge you in champagne, 'May the bravest get the final victory.'"

"A very good toast, which no soldier can refuse to drink," said one of my hospitable hosts, and forthwith glasses were filled up, and every one shouted in French ere they tossed them off, 'May the bravest win the day.'"

Then they all gathered round me and told me many anecdotes of the siege, and spoke highly of the gallantry with which both the English and the French had fought, keeping my glass well filled with champagne the while, and pressing me to partake of every luxury in the way of dessert that was on the table.

They informed of Lord Raglan's death from cholera; but one Russian officer declared that he had died of a broken heart, occasioned by the non-success of the allied attack upon the Malakoff and the Redan, and the loss therein of two thousand of his best troops.

And in that supposition he was right, for there can be no doubt that that was the real cause of his death.

They told me also that Sir James Simpson was now the Commander-in-Chief of the British army, or what was left of it, for that in numbers it was but a fraction of what it had been a month before.

"A month ago," I ejaculated. "How long then have I been ill?"

"It is four weeks to-morrow since you were discovered in the catacombs of St. Vladimer," was the reply. "When you were brought here, you were down with putrid fever. It was a bad case, indeed, but care and attention have brought you successfully round."

"I am sure I am deeply indebted to you for your great kindness," I said; "and pray who is my particular host?"

"Well, the house belongs to the Grand Duke Michael, but he is with General Barclay de Tolly at the camp on the northern shore. We are members of his staff, and he bade us show you every care and attention during his absence, declaring that he lay under a great obligation to you."

I looked around at their faces to see whether any of them were laughing with mouth or eyes, but they evidently were not conversant with any joke connected with the matter.

I was glad of this, and very grateful to the Grand Duke for not letting the cat out of the bag, though how he could have kept the whole animal in, and so many in the secret, was more than I could tell.

However, so that I did not meet the dark eyed young princess to whom I had made such passionate love, I didn't much mind. Encountering him would certainly have been the last straw on the tired camel's back.

The roar of the bombardment could be heard in the distance, for Russians and Allies were still pounding at each other as hard as they could, but we seemed to be far away from any danger, for the Russian officers laughed and chatted and smoked, carefully refraining from uttering anything that could by any possibility hurt my feelings; and at last, when all subjects of converse seemed to be exhausted, they took to story telling.

"Ah, I remember the last siege of Prague," said an old grizzled officer; "a curious affair was that."

"Tell us about it, colonel," replied some one.

"Yes, tell us, tell us," shouted the other officers.

Thus pressed, the veteran lighted a cigar, and tossing off a glass of wine, commenced as follows :—

"Prague, as you are all well aware, is the ancient seat of Bohemian royalty, and as the traveller pauses when passing over its picturesque bridge, which has a character of higher antiquity, ot more regal and imposing grandeur than any other metropolis or city in Germany or Russia, to the admirer of Gothic architecture of the middle ages, the aspect of Prague is more impressive than that of Rome herself.

"This remarkable city, which rises from both sides of its broad and noble river and covers the flanks and summits of several hills, occupies so large a surface as to be indefensible except by an army.

"On the right bank of the Moldav is an eminence called the Wissherad, on which once stood the castellated palace of the ancient kings and dukes of Bohemia, razed to the ground in the great rebellion by the fierce disciples of John Huss.

"On this side also are the two large divisions of Prague, called the Old City and the New, both of considerable extent and surmounted by the towers, domes, and spires of innumerable churches and convents.

"The Hradschin, or Castle Hill, and the contiguous hills of Stravôo and Savrentius are on the left hand of the Moldav, and that portion of Prague called the Lesser City covers the slopes of these hills down to the river, which is here spanned by the most picturesque bridge in Europe, strongly built of square hewn stones, stained with the rich hues of antiquity, and adorned with eight and twenty large statues of saints' time-worn and rudely chiselled.

"These venerable looking images stand on the battlements, while a lofty crucifix rises in the centre of this truly majestic structure.

"At each end of the bridge, which connects the Lesser with the Old and New Cities, is a strong tower with an arch, through which is the carriage entrance.

"These towers aae adorned with the city arms and with the elaborate carvings of the remote period when they were built, and are strongly fortified to defend or impede the passage over the broad waters of the Moldav.

"The Lesser City is distinguished by the vast and stately royal palace which rises on the summit of the Hradschin, but is overtopped by the tower and dome of the fine old Gothic cathedral of St. Veil.

"Most of the huge and decaying edifices of the ancient Bohemian nobles are in the Lesser City, and amongst them the forsaken but still magnificent palace of the ambitious and princely Wallenstein, who purchased and destroyed a hundred dwellings to obtain a site for his house and gardens.

"Here, within lofty walls which precluded all view of the grounds from the adjacent buildings, he erected with royal taste and splendour the famed garden-saloon ; an immense hall, with one end resting upon a colonnade, and the other extremity opening to the garden of fountains. The walls he adorned with paintings in fresco.

"Here, too, he planned and completed an immense aviary, consisting of columns connected by iron network, and enclosing birds of all kinds, colours, and zones, that were obtainable at that period.

"This aviary was planted with trees, refreshed by fountains, and the pillars and adjacent wall were adorned with artificial stalactites in imitation of the grottoes of Italy.

"The immense saloon in the palace occupies an elevation of two floors. Fresco paintings, still wonderfully bright, enrich the lofty ceiling, and in the time of Wallenstein the walls of this vast saloon glittered with gold.

"This ambitious Duke of Friedland was attended by sixty pages in state apparel of blue and red (his family colours) superbly embroidered, while countless attendants, numerous officers of his guard, and even chamberlains, wearing gold keys like those of the emperor, thronged the endless range of richly decorated apartments through which visitors were ushered to the audience chamber of the powerful chief.

"Such is the present appearance of this extraordinary city, and such in every prominent feature was its aspect during the great war of the Reformation, which began in Bohemia and desolated Germany for thirty years.

"This protracted and terrible contest had ceased to be a war of religious opinion long before its termination.

"It had degenerated into an ordinary struggle of mercenary chieftains for power and plunder.

"The Swedes, who under the immortal Gustavus were esteemed the saviours of the purified religion of Luther, had become common robbers and oppressors under the reckless generals of Christina, who established military colonies in the heart of Germany, and enriched themselves by the systematic and barbarous spoiliation of the unfortunate inhabitants. But enough of the past.

CHAPTER LXXXVI.

WHICH TREATS OF THE SIEGE OF PRAGUE.

"IN the year 1799, a considerable Russian force had taken root in Bohemia, under the command of General Count Orloff, and a strong detachment from his corps d'armée had penetrated far into the kingdom, under Brigadier General Wrangel, who established himself at Egen, after having ravaged and plundered the adjacent country.

"Whilst they were in their winter cantonments, a disappointed and vindictive Bohemian nobleman, named Odowalski, who had attained the rank of Colonel in the Austrian army, and had then been discharged in consequence of a severe wound in his sword arm, which rendered him unfit for further service, proposed to Count Orloff to attempt the capture of Prague by a sudden attack during the night.

"He was a man of brilliant courage, of consummate address, and well acquainted with the approaches, the localities, and the resources of the city.

"His description of the palaces and wealth of the Bohemian nobles tempted the cupidity of Count Orloff, who, after some distrustful consideration, entered into his views, and promised him high rank and reward should the plan to surprise the important capital of Bohemia succeed through his agency.

"Odowalski now assumed the German name of Streitberg, and appeared in the Russian camp, and in Russian uniform, while from Egen he made excursions in various disguises to Prague, where he endeavoured to gain over to the Russian party the Protestant malcontents who were rather oppressed by Catholic rule.

"While Odowalski was thus employed in maturing plans for the capture and devastation of the metropolis of his native country, Count Orloff changed his head quarters to the fortress of Pilsen, where he waited only the arrival of a reinforcement from Egen of two regiment of cavalry to make the proposed attempt.

"It was a fine night in the last week of November that the aged Count Martinitz, High-Burg-Graf, of Bohemia, gave a princely entertainment in the Hradschin palace, to all the nobility of Prague.

"A sumptuous banquet ushered in the festivities of the evening. Then followed a splendid ball, and the grand old hall seemed to rejoice in the presence of the brave and the beautiful, whose elastic steps scarcely invaded the slumber of its echoes, and whose gay and many coloured drapery imparted a picturesque relief to the solemn devices of Gothic architecture.

"The whole was terminated by a brilliant display of fireworks.

"The aristocracy of half a century ago did not prolong their carousals to the mature hours of their modern representatives, and Count Martinitz and his guests separated about midnight; he, prodigal of thanks for the honour they had conferred, they all smiles and acknowledgments for the pleasure they had received.

"And amidst these parting salutations of the noble host and his friends, you may be sure others were exchanged of a less formal character; the whispered adieus of young and ardent lovers, who lightened the regrets of separation by many and many a vow to meet upon the snow.

"But there were engines at work to produce within the walls of the sleeping city scenes far different from those that had given so much contentment to the visitors of the High-Burg-Graf, for this was the night appointed by General Count Orloff for his attack on Prague.

"He had been apprised of the intended festivities by Odowalski, and concluded that on such an occasion the nobles and the military were likely to revel in security, and to leave the fortified approaches to the city in comparative defencelessness.

"The music had ceased, the company had retired, the countless lamps and tapers were extinguished, the pleasure-wearied inmates of the High-Burg-Graf palace, as well as the inhabitants of the adjacent Lesser City, were all buried in profound repose, and it was advancing towards the first hour of the morning, when the Russians, who had so timed their march, reached the environs of the Hradschin.

"There the cavalry halted, while the infantry, under the command of Odowalski and a Russian Colonel, silently approached a breach in the wall which was guarded by a detachment of soldiers already corrupted by the traitorous Bohemian.

"Admitted through this opening, they gained undetected the Hradschin square, and hastened to obtain possession of the Stravoo gate, for the purpose of admitting the cavalry.

"The guard at this important fort were faithful to their trust, and fired on the Russians when they gave no answer to their challenge.

"But this slender band was soon cut to pieces by the assailants, with the exception of two persons, one of whom, a young ensign of eighteen, named Przichowski, hurried towards the bridge, as far as a dangerous wound would permit, with a view to rouse the old city to a sense of its imminent and terrible peril.

"In the meantime, the Stravoo gate was hewn and battered into fragments, and General Count Orloff, with his troops, entered and drew up in the palace square.

"Hence, he instantly despatched Odowalski and a body of picked troops with orders to occupy the bridge, and secure a passage into the Old City for the soldiers then engaged in making a lodgment in the royal palace, and firing at such of the alarmed population as ventured to show themselves even at a window.

"Odowalski and his men promptly obeyed these instructions, and pushed forward, dealing death to those terrified citizens who happened to appear in their onward course, whether they were armed or no.

"But their career was arrested for a time in the open place called the Ring of the Lesser City.

"Here a party of brave Bohemians had rallied, and although much inferior in numerical force to their foes, maintained an obstinate defence that reasonably favoured the project of young Ensign Przichowski, who continued to stagger on, though almost fainting from loss of blood.

"At length he gained the bridge tower, but as he passed through the archway, he heard the Russian infantry marching in double-quick time down the street of the Jesuits, leading directly to the tête-du-pont.

"With redoubled efforts, and a fervent invocation of the stone saints, he rushed upon the battlements and gained the centre of the bridge just as the enemy arrived at the first tower.

"Bullets whistled around him, the tramp of the foe sounded nearer and nearer. Feeling that in a single moment more all would be lost or gained, he summoned his whole remaining energies, sprang forward, reached the archway, tottered into the guard house, called out to the sentinels and the soldiers of the main guard, "Save the old city—the Russians are on the bridge!" and fell senseless at their feet.

"The city guards had heard the firing in the Hradschin and the Lesser City, but had attributed the reports to the discharges of fireworks at the palace.

"The tower gate was now closed, well manned, and so ably defended, that Odowalski was obliged to retreat, nor during the siege of many months could the Russians, though superior in artillery, discipline, and numbers, prevail against the heroic resolution displayed by the nobles, garrison, and citizens of Prague, in defence of their ancient metropolis.

"The gallant High-Burg-Graf, though a veteran of seventy years, fought with youthful courage against an overwhelming force. He was eventually wounded and taken prisoner in the Hradschin palace.

"The Lesser City, and the royal and other palaces on that side of the river, were ransacked and plundered.

"The Russian leaders occupied the most distinguished houses during the term of several months employed in besieging the Old and New Cities, which, but for Ensign Przichowski, would have been carried by surprise in as many minutes, but which now both sustained and repulsed various desperate attacks.

"Affairs at last, indeed, began to look unfavourably for the besiegers. Odowalski was shot in leading a storming party, and severely wounded. A report also began to get about that Bohemian troops were approaching in considerable force to raise the siege, so that General Count Orloff, perceiving that his soldiers were wearied and harassed by the indefatigable hardiness of the citizens, and disheartened by this intelligence, was half inclined to draw off his forces.

"On hearing, however, that a large Russian army was advancing to his support, he altered his mind, and when that army and the Bohemian forces met, a great battle took place on the plains, in which the latter were routed with immense slaughter. What girl in her teens, of any European nationality, if she has never otherwise heard of this great engagement, yet knows of it from the popular piece of music of the same name, wherein the booming of cannon, the brattle of drums, flourish of trumpets, charging of horses, ay, and even the very groans of the dying, are to some exten[t] successfully imitated.

"Well, the Old City capitulated the day after th[e] and a war, which had lasted for three years, w[as] brought to a close, though at a cost of blottin[g] Bohemia forever out of the map of Europe."

The old man ceased, and after a momentary pause one of the younger officers asked—

"And what became of the renegade, Odowalski?"

"Oh! he met his deserts. The day after the surrender of Prague, he was hanged, by order of Count Orloff."

"Hanged?" exclaimed nearly everyone. "What for?"

"Well," replied the old officer, gravely, "it was

discovered that he only betrayed the city in order to get into his power the lovely grand-daughter of the High-Burg-Graf, who, it seems, had scorned and rejected his addresses. He got her into his power, too, and the poor young creature was discovered by four of the Secret Police—who, on hearing that she was missing, Count Orloff instructed to investigate the whole affair to the bottom—lying bound hand and foot, and apparently dead, in the cellar of a house that had been occupied by him in the Lower City. On a closer investigation, they found that a dagger was buried in her heart, and that she was dead. As the dagger hilt bore the arms, crest, and motto of Odowalski, the evidence was deemed conclusive, and he was hung without any humbug of judge or jury."

"And serve him right," was the unanimous verdict of the listeners. "And the brave Przichowski, the gallant ensign who saved the city, what became of him?"

"On the death of his country, his allegiance to her was buried, and being a son of the sword, he offered his services to the most warlike nation in Europe. He was accepted, and in her armies he has fought his way upward to the rank of colonel. In other words, gentlemen, I was once Ensign Przichowski. I changed my name to what it is, because the former appellation so puzzled both soldiers and officers to pronounce it aright."

Of course the old officer's health was drank after this, and equally, of course, his conduct was extolled.

Then there were other yarns spun, but not any particularly worthy of narration, and at last the party broke up, the officers having to go on duty, and I was left to amuse myself with books and papers, some of the latter, to my great joy, being English, and of rather a recent date, too.

CHAPTER LXXXVII.

A VISIT FROM THE GRAND DUKE.

ABOUT a week after the events recorded in my last chapter, I received a visit from the Grand Duke Michael.

I recognised him immediately as the interesting cat whom I had let out of the bag on the night of our capture of the north-east suburb of Sebastopol—at the solicitation of a pair of bright eyes that I fancied had belonged to a loving girl, instead of a handsome boy.

I felt rather confused when I saw the merry twinkle of his dark eyes, and noticed that his lips curled in a smile underneath his heavy moustaches.

"I am delighted to see you an inmate of my house," said the Grand Duke, grasping my hand warmly; "I trust that you have been made comfortable."

"Most particularly so, your highness," I rejoined, "and how to express my gratitude, I'm sure I cannot tell."

"Do it as I do then, by saying nothing about it. Had not it been for you, you know, I might not have been alive now. I was desperately ill, you know, almost at my last gasp indeed, when you allowed me the inestimable benefit of consulting with my family physician, Doctor Olgoriki," and the Grand Duke laughed at the remembrance most heartily.

"Ah, your highness," I responded. "That was hardly a fair ruse de guerre, and yet I'm almost glad that it happened so for very many reasons."

"For the sake of the bright eyes that won the boon?"

"No, your highness—confound the bright eyes—but he would have made a dashed pretty girl, notwithstanding. Other men might have been deceived as well as I. He made up, too, uncommonly well."

"He'll never make up or deceive again, poor boy!" said the Grand Duke, with a touch of sorrow.

"How?" I asked eagerly. "Has anything happened to him?"

"Yes, poor lad, he fell yesterday in the battle of the Tchernaya. He was a cornet in the White Cuirassiers of the empress. Somehow or other those French Chasseurs d'Afric rode them down, though I had fancied they were the finest cavalry regiment in Europe, made mincemeat of them in fact, and the boy prince perished gallantly in defence of his standard."

"I am very, very sorry," I rejoined, "the more so as I can hardly divest myself of the idea of his being a girl. He was very young to die, but then he died a heroic death, and that in some measure atones for it."

"Yes," responded the Grand Duke. "His father fell just as gallantly in arms against Russia, as his son has fallen in her defence. It is very strange, but some of our greatest leaders owe their birth to nations that we have conquered—such nations as Circassia, Georgia, Bohemia, Poland, and the like—but this poor boy was my peculiar protegée. I was warmly attached to him, and I feel his loss very much."

Tears rose in the Grand Duke's eyes. I pretended not to notice them. I turned over the pages of a book.

But a soldier's emotions are short lived, for I was presently startled by a merry laugh and the exclamation—

"And did I really look the dying man on that particular night. I know I felt inclined to burst out once or twice, but that would have spoilt the little game. I wanted to see my own face in a glass, but they wouldn't let me. I think they feared that I should have given way to boisterous and unconstrained laughter, and that might have been disastrous."

"Yes, dying men don't often indulge in unconstrained laughter," I replied, with a smile that I couldn't repress; "but I assure your highness that you looked a very handsome old gentleman of seventy, and almost in articulu mortis as well. I feared that the flame of life would have been extinct before you reached Doctor Olgoriki's."

"And didn't the sudden appearance of those six strapping wenches, my bearers, arouse your suspicions?"

"For a minute—but a minute only," I made reply.

"Then an Englishman cannot be so shrewd as a Russian after all," laughed the Grand Duke. "I was ready to bet on the whole thing being a dashed failure, but it was the bright eyes that effected it all."

"Assuredly it was, backed up by the artful tale and abundant tears to wash it down my too susceptible throat. But how was such a bewitching toilet at hand in the very moment of need?" I asked with interest.

"Oh, well, the togs, the chignon, &c., belonged to a daughter of Prince Gortschakoff, and, may I confess it, the padding and false etceteras, as well? The lady has been twenty-seven for the past nine years, and so has of a necessity called in art to the assistance of nature. However, art was really essential in our dilemma, to give a little extra fulness where required, to tint the cheeks and lips, brighten the eyes, soften down the complexion, and raise a wonderful excrescence on the human head. Ah, it was grand!"

"Very grand," I retorted, feeing rather riled.

I think the Grand Duke saw the change in my expression, for he changed the subject with—

"By-the-by, you ask me no questions about the grand battle of the Tchernaya. We lost the day."

I could not say that I was sorry to hear it, and of course I was too polite to say that I was glad.

"Was it an important engagement?" I asked.

"Well, there were fully a hundred thousand men engaged on both sides, and the struggle lasted some hours."

"It must have been quite a second Inkerman!"

"It was a second Inkerman, with the difference that we had for foes the French and Sardinians, instead of the British. But, egad, the frog eaters fought like devils incarnate, and our grey coats could not in a single place make head against them."

"That is a very generous admission, your highness," I remarked. "But were the English not engaged at all?"

"Not a man of them. It is true the British cavalry were all mounted and drawn up in order of battle, ready to take instant advantage of us did our retreat once become a rout, but we did not give them an opportunity. Russians never retreat except in good order."

"The Russians are good soldiers," I rejoined. "Like the English, they do not know when they are beaten, and as you say, they never seem to give way to panic, but they are slow and laborious in their evolutions, and not quick enough to take advantage of any mistake of the enemy. Am I not right, your highness?"

"You have hit upon their failings, and described their merits exactly," was the reply. "The failings lost us the battle of the Tchernaya, with six thousand dead, and six hundred prisoners; the merits saved our every cannon, and prevented the retreat from degenerating into a rout, when the British cavalry would assuredly have chopped us into mincemeat. Well, we have less mouths to feed, that is one consolation."

"Is your food supply becoming very low?" I asked.

"What a disingenuous question," laughed the duke. "Well, as a prisoner to whom the information will be of no practical service, I will answer you candidly that we have too little food to be at all agreeable, but quite sufficient to maintain life for a considerable time longer. Sebastopol happily swarms with cats and rats, so we are not likely to be so bad off as they are in Kars, where, I hear, a staff officer offered a private soldier the other day half a guinea for one rat, and was refused."

"The devil!" I ejaculated. "Is Kars so badly off as that?"

"Worse—the soldiers are dying off from sheer starvation at the rate of a hundred a day, the hospitals are crowded, the troops on duty often drop their muskets from sheer weakness, and General Mouravieffe expects the capitulation of the place hourly," said the Grand Duke.

"Alas! poor Kars," I sighed. "Well, the defence, at all events, come what will, has been an heroic one."

"One of the most heroic in the annals of history," assented the Grand Duke; "but it is Sir William Williams and his four heroic British officers who alone have made it so. We should have had Kars months ago but for them. They are foes in every way worthy of our steel, which the Turks are not. I should like to join you in drinking their healths in champagne."

Of course I readily assented to this, and on the quiet I drank to them success as well as health.

Then the Grand Duke turned the conversation into a personal channel, and asked me if I felt any stronger.

"Oh, yes," I replied. "I walked across the room to-day. I shall be fit for anything in a week to come."

CHAPTER LXXXVIII.
I TAKE PART AT A WEDDING.

"IF I hadn't chanced to meet the litter whereon you lay, just after it had emerged from the catacombs of St. Vladimer, and recognised you, despite your blotched and spotted face, you would have been food for worms before now," laughed the Grand Duke.

"However," he continued, "get strong as soon as you can, and when sufficiently convalescent, I will do for you what you did for me under similar circumstances, send you amongst your own people —on board one of the British ships-of-war outside the harbour I mean, for of course I shall expect you to be a non-combatant during the remainder of the campaign."

I willingly promised this, for I had seen quite enough of the " pomp and circumstance of glorious war," to last me for the remainder of my life.

The Grand Duke, a little later, took his leave.

*　　*　　*　　*

From the date of the Grand Duke's visit I began to rapidly grow better, and at the expiration of a week therefrom I was well enough not only to go out, but also to walk a matter of a mile or so without fatigue.

I daresay I should have been sent aboard one of our men-of-war had not the equinoctial gales just begun to set in, and blow with immense force and fury, as they almost invariably do in the Black Sea.

Consequently, both the English and the French fleet had to give the shore and the fort-girt islands a wide berth, to avoid the possibility of being dashed to pieces thereon, and for a fortnight naught was seen of them.

With the Grand Duke's express permission therefor, and with a safe conduct under his hand and seal always about me, I spent a portion of every day in wandering about the beleaguered city, taking notes of everything that turned up worthy of comment, with the ulterior motive of one day incorporating it in this veracious, and, I fondly hope, amusing history.

The bombardment still continued, but by no means briskly, and I own that this fact made me often fear that the Allies were growing dispirited, and were contemplating a raising of the siege.

After events proved that I was quite mistaken in this.

I took good care to get into no danger, however, or, at all events, not more than was absolutely necessary for the prosecution of my researches.

I had seen enough of war and glory in every shade and form to care to dabble in it further, when, as a civilian, I could win neither rank nor decoration thereby.

I longed to get home to old England, too, and the society of a sweetly pretty little girl, to whom I now recollected I was engaged to be married; but still I was determined obstinately to adhere to my resolution not to start before Sebastopol had fallen.

Very likely it was the thinking of the pretty little girl aforesaid, and of the nuptial knot that I still hoped would be tied before Christmas, that made me one day, while walking down the Rue de Perekoff (Russian streets have generally French names), gaze, with some interest, at the progress of a two-wheeled cart, driven by a stolid Russian boor, and whose cargo consisted of an extremely comely young woman, a few large bundles, a great wooden bedstead, and a bed, and by this I know that she was on her way to her lover's house, and to be married on the morrow.

What made me follow that cart I know not, but I did, and at last I saw it stop before a door in a side street, and a young man in uniform come out of the house, lift the young girl to the ground, carry her indoors, and then return to superintend the unpacking.

As I walked leisurely past the house I heard a sudden exclamation, and the young soldier came running after me and clapped me on the shoulder, asking me, in Russian, how I did.

I knew enough of the language now to make reply, and recognising in him the sergeant who had saved me, a couple of months back, from being thrown into the waves of loathsome putridity that rolled and surged in the dark catacombs of the church of St. Vladimer, I grasped his hand, and poured forth my thanks for his magnanimous conduct on that occasion.

"Oh, don't talk about that," he said. "I did but my duty. If you would repay me for such a trifle, do me the honour of coming to my wedding to-morrow."

"I will, with pleasure," I rejoined. "Tell me the time and place, and I will be with you to the moment."

"Well, sir, you see that little church round the corner. It is the church of St. Ivan. There the ceremony will take place at ten in the morning exactly."

"Then, at five minutes to ten, I will be there," I said.

We parted, and on my way home, I bought, at one of the very few jewellers shops that were open, a gold watch and a diamond ring. The two only cost me a matter of seventeen guineas, and I was glad that an opportunity had arisen for me to show my gratitude to the gallant sergeant, other than by words.

Strange to say, I looked forward with considerable interest to this wedding; doubtless, the very novelty of the thing, in such a place and at such a time, begot the feeling, for every incident during the past few months had been so intimately connected with blood and slaughter, that it was a wondrous relief to turn the thoughts, if only for a time, on any other subject.

And yet it might never come off. The bridegroom might be killed in a sortie or at the embrazures long before morning; and the bride—well, a bomb-shell might enter her chamber at any moment during the night, and blow her to shreds and ribands.

These are the disagreeable contingencies that ever attend love, courtship, and marriage, in a beleaguered city.

Happily, none were in the present instance destined to occur, however, and the following morning I was in the church porch of St. Ivan betimes.

Presently I heard the clattering of hoofs coming up the deserted street, in the centre of which grass and weeds now grew, though it had evidently once, and that not very long ago, been a main thoroughfare.

I thought that they must be a body of cavalry, but a minute later, I saw to my surprise that it was the bridal party, and I then remembered that the very poorest classes ride to church on such an occasion in Russia, and that even when they live only a few doors therefrom.

It was a truly picturesque procession, though the half-starved artillery horses could hardly keep their feet, so weak were they. I did not know at the time that a joint from one of them was to form the pièce de résistance at the marriage feast.

The gallant sergeant, in full uniform of dark grey, with green facings, rode first, by the side of his bride, who wore a kind of white knitted hood that enveloped her entire head and body to the waist, as effectually concealing her face as if it had been a Turkish yashmac.

Behind them rode the parents, brothers and sisters, and friends of the young people—the women all cross-legged, whilst some had no saddles, and others no reins.

Some knew how to ride and some didn't, consequently some of the women were very pale, and a faint little cry would now and then issue from their lips.

Nor did many of the cavaliers seem to know how to manage their horses one whit better, and had any of the poor beasts had one grain of spirit left in them, there would, it forcibly struck me, have been many an ignominious fall in the dust.

Their days of rearing, kicking, prancing and curvetting, were for ever past, however, and thus it was that the whole party reached the church in safety, and dismounting, left their sorry nags to wait their coming out, with the rank weeds and a few dandelions to amuse them in the interim.

I waited in the porch, and went into the church in the rear of the procession, for I wanted to stand where I should not be a conspicuous figure, and where I could take my cue as to behaviour from others.

The ceremony was a very impressive one, and fully as long as it was impressive. At its conclusion, the bridegroom took the bride's hand, and with her, walked thrice around the altar, bending the knee each time.

Then, when he had let her go, she plumped down on her knees at his feet, and knocked her forehead three times on his right shoe, with no gentle thumps either.

He next waved the tail of his coat over her head, and then a great black loaf appeared, from I know not where, and the officiating priest, after carefully counting us all twice, so that there should be no mistake, I suppose, cut it into as many pieces as we were people present, and then a hideous old female party, whom I conjectured to be the bride's mother, handed it round, and I had perforce to accept a piece.

It was quite a quarter of a pound slice, and apparently as dry and hard as though it had been manufactured of sawdust, sand and pebbles.

Horror of horrors! I saw everybody begin to munge and devour this strange edible, which they did with apparent gusto and keen appreciation of its goodness.

I essayed to do the same, for I perceived by sundry furtive side-long glances that it was expected of me.

Poof! what horrible stuff it was. I had made a more hearty breakfast at the Prince's table, washing down sundry choice comestibles with champagne and hock.

I had never dreamed that my mastication and digestive faculties would have been called into request so soon again, or in such a truly trying manner, or I would either have fasted for three days previously, or have shirked the wedding altogether—most probably the latter.

However, there I was, and so I nibbled and tried to swallow, but oh, would not a sawdust cake have been easier to get down than that abominable piece of bread?

I choked down two mouthfuls and looked hopelessly round.

My neighbours had almost finished theirs.

One or two had quite finished, and were smacking their lips as though they would very much like another lump.

I bit off another piece and tried a gulp.

It stuck in my throat—I was choking.

I believe I began to turn black in the face, for a herculean Russian began to thump my back, and while he was at it, I surreptitiously slipped what remained of my abhorred crust into my pocket.

But the very instant that I could see through my tears, caused by the choking, I saw a huge, and by no means cleanly paw, holding something before my eyes.

I blinked then, and saw that it was my piece of bread. The holder thereof grunted and frowned, making me clearly understand by dumb pantomime that he had been watching me, and would not let me insult the newly married couple by breaking through a ceremony.

Very likely it was a very important one, but I couldn't get down the hideous morsel now, after it had been fished out of my pocket and otherwise fingered by his oily fried-fishy looking fingers.

I cast around me for a way of escape, but could see none.

The priest was pattering a sort of exhortation to the bride and bridegroom—instructive, and full of

SHE WAS BOUND HAND AND FOOT, AND APPARENTLY DEAD.

good advice doubtless—and the church doors were closed.

Suddenly a brilliant idea struck me.

I twitched the sleeve of my right-hand neighbour, he who had thumped my back so lustily, and whispered, in the Russian that I'd been studying so hard for the past few weeks—

"That man wants me to eat his piece of bread as well as my own. Look at him!"

By Jove, I never guessed the thunderstorm in a tea-pot that would follow this, my lying confession.

'Twas evident that the big Russian believed me, and there was the other fellow's outstretched arm with the piece of bread between his finger and thumb to bear witness to the truth of my assertion.

He stepped between us, and not to disturb the pious exhortations of the priest, merely shook his head from side to side, grinned, mouthed, pointed alternately to the piece of bread and the holder's mouth, and lastly tapped the hilt of his long knife significantly.

In vain the other expostulated back again in equally elegant dumb show. The dagger of my champion got tapped and tapped again, harder each time, while his facial contortions grew more and more, and, at last, he half drew the weapon from its sheath.

This final pantomime sufficed—my piece of bread was promptly gulped by alien jaws, and quiet was restored.

At this juncture, everybody appeared to bow to everybody else, and then the procession was re-formed.

But in the church porch there was another halt.

"What on earth is going to happen now?" I thought.

It seemed to me as if new personages were appearing upon the scene, and trying to drive us back into the church.

"Another wedding, I suppose," I thought, to myself; "and neither party will give way to the ther."

But now I saw the shimmering, and heard the jingling of pots and cups. Surely they weren't going to hold the wedding feast in the church porch.

I saw the bridegroom take a great cup in his right hand, and the bride's right hand in his left.

Then I heard him mutter something, I knew not what. And next I saw him bow to her and raise the cup to his lips, seemingly taking a deep draught.

Then he handed her the cup—first releasing her right hand and taking her left—and she pushed the cup up under her veil, and I suppose drank also of its contents, for there ensued a pretty little gurgle in her throat.

Next, pots and cups seemed to fly around to everyone, and I had one forced upon me as the bread had been, nolens volens.

I took it and looked at its contents, dubiously at first, for it was rather thick, and very yellow; but much more resignedly when I thought I smelt honey.

Anyhow, it is much more easy to drink nasty things, than to eat them—viz., a black draught and a Gregory's powder, and so I tossed it right off.

By George, it was awfully nice, a kind of mead strengthened with brandy, I took it to be.

I began to wish that I had taken it by sips, instead of gulping it all down at once, so as to have enjoyed it, and appreciated the flavour the more. "But, never mind," thought I; "the way in which I tossed it off will find me favour in the eyes of these Russians, at all events."

Did it though? Not a bit of it. My left hand neighbour relieved me very politely, as I thought, of the empty cup; but when he looked into it, an expression of unutterable disgust passed over his stolid countenance.

"Hang it," thought I, "I hope I haven't left any heel-taps. I expect that I must have, he glowers so."

I was about to ask for the cup back again, as I could have remedied anything in that way—it was very different to the bread when he passed it on to someone else — and watching his countenance narrowly, I saw that he began to look more disgusted than the other.

"What a glutton!" exclaimed he, in Russe.

"What a greedy guts!" retorted the other.

"Hasn't left us a drop," quoth the first.

"Has drank treble his share," was the grunted reply.

"Such fellows would drink the Neva dry."

"Or swallow up all the water in the harbour."

I now perceived, on looking around, that every three people had one cup between them, out of which they sipped and sipped in turn, and so I had in reality drank off treble my share at a single draught.

Before I could apologise, however, we were all in motion. The two who should have been my fellow-drinkers were away in the front, and I found by my side the brawny fellow who had been my champion inside the church.

He seemed to have taken a great fancy to me, for he proceeded to link his arm within mine, and when we reached the street he insisted that I should bestride the same horse.

Had not the strong draught I had indulged in by this time got up in my head and rather obscured my intellect, I should have declined this polite offer, for to any ordinary capacity it was as clear as the sun at noonday that not one of those poor, wretched, half-starved animals could bear a double burthen for a score of yards without coming to total grief.

Up got my friend and up I got behind him. The procession was formed and away we jogged in the most sorry amble that ever was got out of horse-flesh.

"Horse-flesh?" said I, "horse-bone rather—it was like riding on the edge of a sabre. Every instant I expected that I should fall on either side of the way divided in twain by the sharp, bony ridge that I was bestriding.

I did not fall on both sides of the way, but I pretty soon fell on one of them, and that of course, the hardest.

On rounding a corner both the sorry Rosinante's fore legs gave way, and down he went on his nose.

As a natural sequence, over went my Russian acquaintance too, the spike of his helmet penetrating the hard earth between two stones and holding him perpendicular for a moment, but vice versâ from what he ought to have been, and then it snapped short off, and he went beautifully over on the broad of his back.

I fell against a lamp-post, an iron one, battering in my busby and skinning my nose.

I got up and tried to shrink away, feeling that I had had quite enough of Russian weddings, but the attempt was futile: my tall friend was on his feet as soon as me, and had linked his arm again within mine before I could as much as take one step in a homeward direction.

And in this way we marched in the rear of the riders, accommodating our pace to theirs until the whole cavalcade came to a halt in front of the residence of the bridegroom.

Clearly there was no way of getting away. Evidently I must resign myself to the force of circumstances.

I had just made up my mind to this, when, "rattle, rattle, rattle," down came a perfect cloud of corn or some other kind of grain from the upper windows, and even the house roof right over us.

If 'twas wheat, 'twas bearded wheat, that I am ready to swear, but I fancy it must have been barley or oats, for it went down inside my collar and into my ears, and got mixed up with my hair, and tickled and made me itch wherever it touched, most distractingly.

Then we went inside the house, but that day was doomed to be naught but a chapter of accidents.

The wedding feast was, as might have been expected from the position of the parties, a very humble affair.

But yet I was expected to eat from every dish and drink of every liquid, some of which were nauseous and others as fiery as cayenne pepper and capsicum.

These tortures came from being the honoured guest of the day, for my friend the sergeant had found out that I was a British officer (how, heaven alone knows, for I'm sure my uniform was worn and patched enough for one of the Ragged Brigades), and insisted on calling me "Excellency," and informing his acquaintances, sotto voce, that I was a guest and a great favourite of the Grand Duke.

Of course, whilst thus blowing my trumpet he was also blowing his own, for all this was as good as saying, "See what grand acquaintances I have."

His friends evidently all swallowed it in like treacle (like oil would perhaps be a better synonym where Russians are concerned), and we were both of us very great men forthwith.

I almost fell into a similar error, for hearing the bride and bridegroom frequently spoken of as moloday knegay and moloday kneg (young duchess and young duke), I began to wonder whether they might not have some right to those titles, for many Russians of high rank are reduced by gambling and what not, to serve as private soldiers in the army.

But I was afterwards told by the Grand Duke that all newly-married people are called young duke and young duchess until the honeymoon is over.

What surprised me most was that the bride never raised her veil nor spoke. This was a disappointment, for I wanted to see her pretty face again—pretty faces being as rare in Sebastopol at that time as plum puddings.

"At all events," thought I, "when I present her with her diamond ring she is sure to raise her veil, and speak too."

Directly the feast was over and I had considerably more than half poisoned myself with the different viands and beverages which I dared not refuse for fear of giving offence, I presented the gallant sergeant to whom I owed my preservation from a horrible death, the watch.

He was mightily pleased therewith and turned it round and round, but didn't know how to open it, which was no great wonder, as it was a hunter.

I did so for him and showed him the face and the works, finally instructing him how to wind it up.

When he had done so he stood with it open in his hand listening intently, and presently he exclaimed in Russe—

"Why it don't play. No music comes from it."

The poor fellow didn't know what a watch was! I had to explain it all to him, and then he seemed very pleased again, and said it would be a grand thing when he was on sentry duty, for he should know whether the reliefs were to their time, and be fine company.

With her ring the bride was in ecstacies, but her husband thanked me in her name, and she only kept curtseying without once raising her veil.

I learnt afterwards that the whole of the first day and night a bride may not speak (for that charge she receiveth by tradition from her mother and aunt), nor for three days after may she be heard to speak save a few words at table in set form to her husband, and even they must be uttered with great humility and reverence.

After I had given the presents I got away on the plea of a promise to the Grand Duke, and, as the reader may imagine, very glad to get away I was, for I had seen quite enough now even of Russian weddings.

CHAPTER LXXXIX.

ILL-BRE(A)D DISLIKE—A RUSSIAN'S REVENGE.

THE Grand Duke Michael was very much amused when at breakfast the next morning I told him of my experiences of a Russian wedding.

"You will be able to write a book about us when you return to your native land," he said. "Well, I don't think you will have much longer to study Crimean life and character; but the gale is abating fast, and we shall soon have the allied fleets back, when, aboard one of the ships, you go under the protection of a flag of truce."

"I am sure my gratitude to your highness will live for ever. I am even afraid that the kindness, attention, and hospitality of friends will compare unfavourably with that of foes—surpass them they cannot," I made reply; and I felt every word I said, for it was the truth.

"Well," answered the Grand Duke, "we are glad to be able to do anything to ameliorate the horrors of war; but I have news for you, the defence of Kars is over."

"What!" I exclaimed, "has General Williams surrendered?"

"Conquered by starvation more than Russian arms, he has. General Mouravieffe allowed the garrison to march out with all the honours of war; but scores of the poor soldiers dropped down from sheer weakness whilst on their way to the Russian camp."

He proceeded to give me the full particulars of the surrender of Kars, from which it appeared that the sufferings of the citizens and the garrison when I left it, per balloon, for the summit of Mount Ararat, in company with a madman, were small indeed compared to what they reached prior to the final surrender.

"General William's, Colonel Lake's, and Captain Thompson's journey to St. Petersburg will be a triumphal march rather than aught else," said the Grand Duke. "We Russians appreciate courage and heroism even in our foes, and are ever ready to do homage to it. The Czar will load them with favours and honours, and send them unransomed home to their own country."

"I can quite believe his majesty capable of any generosity, from the conduct of his son," I made reply; "and I hope that our generals will exhibit the same degree of chivalrous courtesy when Sebastopol at last yields."

"I am glad you say at last," laughed the Grand Duke, "for Sebastopol will never yield. Neither in men nor in guns are the allied armies equal to the task. Four nations against one, they will yet have to draw off their forces before the world is a month older. A third Crimean winter would annihilate them."

"That remains to be proved; they would all be comfortably hutted this winter, and be well clothed and well fed also. I fancy you'll find the Allies stick as close to Sebastopol as do moths to a sealskin jacket."

And so we continued to converse for more than an hour, until, in fact, the Grand Duke took his departure.

That day passed slowly enough, as days generally do when you are expecting a sudden change of any kind.

After dinner I sauntered forth again, for I was at perfect liberty to wander through the town in any direction, and at any hour, so long as I did not approach the north-eastern suburb that was still in possession of the English, and to the south and south-west of which great earthworks had been thrown up and fortified with heavy guns, ever grape-loaded to prevent a further incursion from that direction.

It was a windy, cheerless night, and Sebastopol, with its battered buildings and deserted streets, looked inexpressibly dreary and miserable.

The cannonade was less lively on this particular evening than I had ever heard it before.

It seemed to me as though the allied armies were only firing minute guns in mourning for their approaching enforced departure, and every sullen boom was promptly replied to by a couple of short spirited reports from one of the great Russian forts, which at length began to sound to me like an impudent and constant refrain of "Two to one you won't get in!" "Two to one we keep you out!"

"And hang it, they will too; I'm sure of it," I muttered to myself, and such was really my conviction.

I did not imagine that my gallant countrymen, and the equally gallant French, were husbanding their energies and resources, after so many reverses, for one supreme effort, and that that final effort would be magnificently successful.

No, I began to despair, and to think that the grim, black, double-headed eagle of old Russia was, after all, invulnerable; and in this unhappy frame of mind I wandered on and on, and I scarce knew whither, until I found myself in a portion of the town which I saw at once that I had never visited before.

I immediately turned to retrace my steps upon making this discovery, and for a long time steered in what I imagined was the right direction homewards, until, at last, I came to a bubbling, foaming creek, far too wide to leap, and far too deep to wade.

I looked up and down for a bridge but could see none, whilst the stench that came from the pent-up mass of rushing waters told me that 'twas little better than an open sewer that barred my course.

I turned to retrace my steps when, to my surprise, I found myself face to face with a Russian soldier.

"I've been following you about like your shadow, and I've brought you to bay at last," he said, with a nod.

"What the deuce do you want with me?" I asked.

"What the deuce do I want with you?" he replied, mimicking me. "Why, I have been laying in wait for you all day long, and following you ever since you left the prince's house. That's what I've been doing."

"That's no answer to my question. I asked you what you wanted with me," I replied sharply, very much regretting the while that I had left my sword at home, which it was, however, my custom to do now that I was a prisoner of war, as I found from experience that I was less likely to be stopped and questioned when without it.

"And do you want an answer to your question?" asked the man impudently, leering into my face the while.

"You will either answer me or take yourself off, I don't care which you do," I answered hotly.

"I'll answer you, then; answer you to the point, too," and the soldier, with a big Russian oath, which I did not understand the meaning of, and am quite incapable of spelling. "You bull-headed Englishman, you lied in the church before the priest, you made me eat your bread as well as my own, you fixed big disgrace on me, and your life pays the forfeit."

"Hold, fool!" I shouted, seeing him draw his bayonet; "why did you put your hand in my pocket, and, drawing the dry crust out, hold it up before my nose? You tried to make me eat, and I tried to make you. You're the most to blame, because you began."

"But" (another oath) "it was your place to eat it."

"But" (interjection) "it was so dry I couldn't get it down."

"That's" (string of oaths) "humbug. It was the best black bread. You insulted everyone by not eating it, and you made them think that I insulted them instead. Drouksvitch told them after you left. It was he who forced me to swallow it, and not one of them has spoken to me since. No more wedding feasts for me. Not one."

"I'm awfully sorry," I said; "I will go with you to the sergeant's. I will explain to him and his bride how the matter really occurred. I never knew the thing was so important."

But the soldier would not listen to my well-meant overtures. He gnashed his teeth and advanced upon me.

He evidently intended to stab me with his bayonet, or to force me back into the foul river.

"Ain't you going to listen to reason?" I asked, dodging him.

"No, I want your life," was the reply.

He was a great, powerful, hulking fellow, and his bayonet was keen and bright, and quite long enough to skewer me upon.

I saw that he was in deadly earnest, and that I had but one chance; so, springing suddenly forward, I clutched his bayonet wrist with my left hand, just as he was about to lunge forward, and sent my right fist crashing against his teeth.

I must have hit pretty hard, for down he went like a shot, I taking care to fall on him and not release my grasp on his bayonet wrist for an instant.

And then we had a pretty rough-and-tumble struggle, he trying to use his bayonet with all his might.

But presently I wrenched it from him, and sent it shimmering away into the rushing river.

Then gathering my strength for a final effort, I shouted in Russian, "Quick! huzza! this way, friends, this way!" and as the fellow glanced over his left shoulder, I exerted all my remaining strength, swung him round, freed my right hand with a jerk, and gave him a smashing blow in the face and a vigorous kick in the bread-basket, almost at one and the same instant.

That was too much for him. He went bang into the rushing stream as though he had been shot from a catapult, and the next instant was swept away from my sight by the angry waters.

CHAPTER XC.
WHICH IS STRICTLY MERCANTILE.

I PAUSED to rest a minute after this unexpected and unwonted exertion, and then I suddenly recollected that I had lost my way.

The only resource open to me by which to find it was, in hunting parlance, to try back.

I did so, but for a long while sought in vain for a clue to a right direction, and presently a second incident occurred which made me as oblivious of my whereabouts as I was before.

I had got into an inhabited portion of the city, and, as I imagined from the style of houses and the presence of a huge synagogue, the Jewish portion.

Within one of these houses—which was a good deal larger than the rest—a great row was being kicked up.

Somehow, I felt a great desire to enter the house and see what was going on therein.

The door was ajar, so that there was nothing to check my intrusion except the darkness that seemed to envelop the whole interior; but then I was never afraid of darkness even when a child, so in I went.

A long, narrow passage opened into a room of some kind that absolutely blazed with light.

I entered the room, and I found it to be in possession of a crowd of Jews and Tartars, and on a kind of platform at one end stood a horrible looking old wretch, with a beard reaching to below his waist, and a beautiful young girl of eighteen years of age in the costume of a vivandière.

I discovered, a minute later, that she was put up for sale.

The bearded old Jew was evidently owner and auctioneer as well, and in one hand he held a heavy whip which answered all the purposes of a hammer.

"Now then, who's going to bid?" he roared. "The girl's young and comely enough for the harem of the sultan. She was taken prisoner at the battle of the Tchernaya, and she fell into my hands, no matter how, for that's neither here nor there. She is worth five hundred thalers of anyone's money, but as she is to be sold under the rose I don't expect nearly so much as that. She has her faults, too, and I ain't the man to hide them. She has never been accustomed to hard work, and she can't speak a word of Russian. You see I don't hide anything. Daniel Levi ain't the man to take an unfair advantage of anyone;" and "crack" went the whip, by way of final peroration to this speech.

"Never had such a pretty little bit of merchandise in my possession," said Daniel Levi, with another crack of his long whip. "She should be treated like a pretty flower, and only kept for looking at and kissing, and that's what would be her fate if I could smuggle her over the other side the water, which, being war time, is out of the question; so she shall go at a sacrifice—at a great sacrifice—no fair offer shall be refused."

"Twenty"—"Thirty"—"Forty"—"Fifty," were cried from different parts of the hall. Then there was a pause.

"Sixty," growled a Cossack chief, "and not a thaler more."

"Sixty thalers!" exclaimed the auctioneer, in accents of disgust; "sixty thalers for a lovely young creature like that, why I've had as much for toothless hags of sixty. Sixty thalers—oh, no, I can't sell at that price."

"A hundred thalers!" exclaimed a voice, and another Cossack, a high and mighty chief this time, to judge from the magnificence of his attire, ascended the platform, and at his frown the former bidder slunk away.

He spun the slave girl round, examined the quality of her hair, opened her mouth and looked at her teeth, and then surveyed her as critically as an English jockey would examine a mettled racer.

"She seems all right," he then said; "so, to make a short job of it, and at once to silence all other bidders, I'll give you a hundred and fifty thalers for her, Daniel Ben Levi. Come, money down."

The old Jew's eyes glistened; but he looked eagerly around the circle in the faint hope of getting a higher bid. He saw nothing to encourage him, however, and so he said, with a shrug of the shoulders—

"The girl is yours, excellency—the girl is yours."

The Cossack chief laughed, and then said to the trader—

"Lend me your whip, Levi, that I may show her, as she understands not our language, who is her master."

"The cash down first, your excellency," said the sly Jew.

The Cossack chief frowned at his word for an instant being called in question, and then, plucking from his girdle a purse, he counted the gold pieces one by one into the Jew's hand, who soon transferred them to his pocket.

Then he handed to the Cossack chief his whip.

The barbaric warrior took it, drew the long lash between the finger and thumb of his left hand, whilst he grasped the stock firmly in his right, and the next instant there was a simultaneous crash and

shriek, and its snake-like coils flew around the young girl's neck.

Then it uncurled, leaving a thin crimson ring where it had embraced her. I could see her flesh quiver with the agony of the blow.

Without a weapon, weak from my late illness, and surrounded by nearly a hundred armed rascals, who were evidently accustomed to such scenes, and who would have thought no more of slitting my throat than of eating their dinner, I had been puzzling my head all this while for a plan whereby to stop this nefarious traffic in beautiful humanity, and to deliver the sweet maiden from her perilous and painful position.

But until this last crowning outrage on the part of her purchaser, no plausible scheme had occurred to me.

But simultaneous with her shriek and the uncurling of the accursed whip, one did, and, though it was of desperate nature, I did not hesitate for an instant about putting it into practice, for no time was clearly to be lost.

"Your sword and pistols, in the name of the Grand Duke, whose slave you are," I said sternly in Russian to a tall warrior who stood next me.

The man looked round in my face amazed, but I repeated my command, with even more of hauteur in my tone, and then he cringingly gave the weapons up.

"Make way in the name of the Grand Duke, whose slaves you are," I now continued to growl, as I pushed my way through the crowd, a curved scimitar in one hand and a long single barrelled pistol in the other.

Everyone did make way for me, pretty quickly too, so quickly indeed that the Cossack chief had only time to give his crouching, terrified victim one slash, before I sprang upon the platform and confronted him.

"Drop your whip and give me your name," I cried.

The Cossack chief turned pale, and hesitated.

I saw this, and perceived that I was on the right tack.

"Your name, and rank in the imperial army of our father the Czar? Answer, or it will be the worse for you," I roared, stamping my foot upon the platform.

"Haluf Blidah Metidja, colonel of the tenth regiment of the Cossacks of the Orenburg, excellency" was the reply, delivered as cringingly as can well be imagined.

"Then, Colonel Haluf Blidah Metidja, you will present yourself before his imperial highness, the Grand Duke Michael, at ten o'clock to-morrow morning, at his head quarters in the Rue de Pera, and stand the consequences of encouraging illegal slave traffic within the domains of the Czar."

"Oh! mercy, mercy!" exclaimed the Cossack chief, falling on his knees. "Mercy, mercy, excellency!"

"It is not in my power to show mercy. I am a slave of our father the Czar, even as thou art. I was sent here in disguise this night, in order to watch the proceedings; for know, oh, Colonel Haluf Blidah Metidja, that the eyes of the Grand Duke are everywhere, and he has, besides, ever sure and secret information of all that happens, or is about to happen, within Sebastopol," I replied.

"Let me then, not be the only one," yelled the Cossack colonel." "Arrest the Jew thief. Daniel Ben Levi; arrest Captain Milianal, whom I outbid; arrest some of those rascals who are slinking out of the bazaar like whipped curs, with their tails between their legs."

I looked round, and saw that sure enough the crowd were making themselves very scarce—their retreat was a flight. The Jew auctioneer was gone.

I did not care a fig for all this, but, to comfort the Cossack colonel, who evidently had an invincible dislike to suffering alone, I told him that governme spies were in all the surrounding streets, who would take note of everyone who left the bazaar, and doubtless follow everyone whom they supposed to be the leaders to their houses or their quarters.

This seemed to give the Cossack chieftain great satisfaction, but I made him surrender his weapons ere I suffered him to depart in peace.

Then I and the trembling girl had the bazaar entirely to ourselves.

I went up to her, and raising her to her feet, told her not to be afraid, for that I was ready and willing, if need be, to shed the last drop of my blood in her defence.

"I am a vivandière of the Chasseurs of the French Imperial Guard, monsieur, by name Naomie L'Estrange," she said, with a fascinating curtsey, by way of introduction. "I was taken prisoner by the Jew Levi, and other robbers and death hunters, whilst tending the wounded the night after the battle of the Tchernaya. Oh, God! what I have gone through since!"

"Poor child, I hope your troubles are nearly over," I said. "Tell me, do you know how to fire a pistol?"

"I am a dead shot, and can use a sword equally well," she replied, with a truly charming smile and shrug of the shoulders.

"Bravo! Take the rascally Cossack's sword and pistols that I deprived him of, for I see that they have deprived you of your own weapons. We may have need of them ere we gain our quarters, for we are in a bad part of the city, and are only two to many."

"Oh, with you I shall not be one bit afraid," she responded.

Nor was she, for we left the bazaar, and traversed a lot of miserable, dark, and dirty streets, before I hit upon the correct route back to my quarters, in the residence of the Grand Duke Michael.

By Jove! weren't the Russian officers astonished when I introduced to them my gay and beautiful charge.

The Grand Duke praised me warmly for the manner in which I had acted, and declared that Colonel Haluf Blidah Metidja should be degraded to the ranks, when he showed up on the morrow, and have a score of strokes as well.

Naomie L'Estrange's health was drank n champagne, the best room in the house was given to her for the night, and on the morrow, the little soldier-of-fortune was inundated with presents, and sent, under a flag of truce, back to French camp.

On the morrow, too, the English and the French fleets were observed to be close in shore, and I was sent aboard the Terrible; not, however, before I had seen Colonel Haluf Blidah Metidja undergo his punishment, and had been assured that the Jew, Daniel Ben Levi, had been arrested and shot.

From my kind hosts I was very sorry to part.

CHAPTER XCI.

ABOARD THE "TERRIBLE."

AND now my lengthened narrative is drawing to a close. In ten minutes I have left the land of the Czar for British territory, for the deck of a British man-of-war is British territory to all intents and purposes.

But as I have described how the British and the French were driven out of the Malakoff and the Redan, and how, for a lengthened time the Russians seemed to be getting the best, it will not be out of place here to describe how the gallant Allies turned the tables on the besieged, and carried everything before them.

Some of the scenes that I am about to endeavour to describe I saw with my own eyes, from the decks of the Terrible, as the fleet assisted the land forces, by tackling the seaward forts or throwing red-hot shells into the doomed town, whilst others were described at our mess table by officers in every branch of the service, after the tremendous struggle was over, and feasting and idleness were the order of the day.

The bombardment of the town, which, as I have before said, had been kept up with less vigour for a week or two, broke out at daybreak the morning succeeding the one in which I had taken up my quarters on board the Terrible, into a complete fire from end to end of the allied lines.

It burst over every part of the Russian works with the fury of a tornado, sending up clouds of dust and smoke, which were driven back by a cold north wind, blinding the men whose duty called them to the trenches, and filling the air so densely as to render objects indistinct a short way off.

As the bombardment commenced preparations for the assault were made in the English and French camps, and numerous regiments were drawn up under arms.

It had been considered proper to forward the men in detachments, and not in columns, so as to keep the enemy as much as possible ignorant of our intentions.

The storming was entrusted to the Second and Light Divisions, portions of which were to form immediate supports, whilst the rear was to be kept by the Third Division, supported by the Fourth Division, which included the Guards and the Highlanders.

At ten minutes past twelve the signal for the storm on the Malakoff was given by the explosion of two mines close to the counter scarp, and in the confusion caused by the smoke and the uproar the Zouaves and Chasseurs rushed on.

They made their way over ground ploughed up by the explosion of shells, and full of holes, and elevations of jagged and irregular formation.

Their speed, however, was scarcely impeded by these obstacles, and they jumped down into the ditch, and up the other sides of the work, without even using their scaling-ladders.

The Russians, who were completely taken by surprise, were driven out of the redoubt or killed, and left the French perfect masters of it; the short distance of twenty five yards which separated the ditch of the Malakoff from the French parallel contributing not a little to the fortunate issue of the attack.

In the meantime, two other attacks had been made upon the Russians, with far less fortunate results.

General Codrington, hearing the signal for assault on the Malakoff, after a short pause, gave the order to storm the Redan.

The ladder parties of the 3rd and 95th at once dashed out, and, favoured by tolerably even ground, passed the abattis, which was no sensible obstacle to their progress, and planted their ladders on the salient angle of the work.

The stormers, less active than they had been, were delayed by their inability to issue from the parallel except by one aperture, and when they succeeded in reaching the scarp of the Redan, the ladder party had already mounted to the assault.

The stormers followed, mounting on each side by the salient angle, and fought their way into the Redan, killing the Russians within the first traverse.

But in their eagerness to outstrip each other, the parties on the left pressed across the work to join those on the right, and, in doing so, fell into the concentrated fire of the enemy, whose supports, upwards of two thousand in number, were rapidly coming up.

A hand-to-hand conflict followed, desperate in its nature, the Russians fighting for the hold with the tenacity of bears, and using every sort of missile, in addition to their arms, to repel the assailants.

Our generals saw that they must bring up their supports, or that the stormers must perish.

But, as usual, the forward movement was delayed, and the remnant of our men gave way in disorder, as they had once done before, and retreated headlong from the parapets and embrazures they had so gallantly stormed and carried.

At this time there were several regiments in the 3rd, fourth, and fifth parallels, which, if they had been moved up sufficiently quick, would have been in time to have saved the stormers, and secure the position.

The Redan was thus won and lost a second time.

The French attack on the Little Redan and the works upon the Careening Bay side were failures for other reasons.

The troops moved resolutely on, rapidly crossing a broad space which lay between them and the Russian redoubt.

They were thrown into considerable confusion, however, by rows of holes called trous a loup, into which the men stumbled in the midst of the darkness caused by the dust and smoke, and thus their attack was deprived of its firmness, and was repulsed by the enemy. The struggle was, however, maintained doubtfully for a considerable time.

Then fresh supports came up and struggled to gain the summit of the scarp. But at every fresh attempt they fell back discomfited into the ditch, covering the ground with the dead and dying.

The Russians had not only the advantage of position, but they had been materially assisted in this portion of the attack by the fire of their steamers inside the harbour, which continued to fire broadsides upon the Malakoff and the counter scarps of the Little Redan.

These broadsides committed dreadful havoc, and threw the ranks of the assaulting columns into great confusion.

Notwithstanding every adverse circumstance, however, the French maintained their ground at the foot of the scarp and in the ditch of the Little Redan and Black Batteries, firing resolutely at every Russian who showed himself over the parapet, whilst the Russians, on their part, were equally quick in returning shot for shot, when a Frenchman raised his head higher than usual.

This part of the fight partook, indeed, at last of a sort of Indian character, the struggle from cover to cover resembling those of which we have all read in the glowing pages of Cooper, Mayne Reid, and Gustave Aimard.

These painful phases of the combined assault proceeded, whilst the main attack on the Malakoff rapidly lost its early characteristics.

The Russians did not passively allow their enemy to enjoy his new possession.

They had no sooner been driven out, than they attacked the French with the energy of despair, and the Zouaves and Chasseurs then found themselves the defenders, instead of the assaulters, of the Malakoff.

The Russians trusted more to stones and missiles of that nature than to their muskets, and from the summit of the traverses they heaved all kinds of miscellaneous articles, such as stones, beams, buckets, old grape shot, and muskets.

The French, short of ammunition, replied with the same weapons, varying this resistance by rushes at the point of the bayonet.

They were giving way, however, before the advancing Russians, discouraged by intelligence of impending failure at the Redan and Black works, but at the critical moment the supports of the division marched up, and entered the works on all sides.

The Imperial Guard, consisting of Grenadiers and Zouaves, swarmed into the Malakoff, and commenced a desperate conflict with the stubborn Muscovites.

Hand to hand amongst the labyrinthine windings of the redoubt, amongst shell holes, broken gabions, and irregular elevations, each side fought and bled.

They fell side by side, and in many instances above each other.

The ground was strewed with them, so as to be completely invisible.

To add to the horror of the moment, the shells from the Redan and steamers fell in great number upon the portion of the work in the possession of the French, and added to the heaviness of their losses.

But the Russians were unable to regain the Malakoff.

CHAPTER XCII.

THE FALL OF SEBASTOPOL.

AS the French poured in fresh supports every moment and brought in field artillery over a hasty bridge into the redoubt, the Russians slowly yielded and commenced a retreat, which ended in a rout.

Darkness now supervened, and the Russians, under its cover, withdrew from the works of the Karabalnaia, the Little Redan, and the Black Battery.

The capture of the Malakoff and failure of the attacks on the Redan and works of Careening Bay were not the only episodes of the day on which the Allies finally established a footing in the heart of Russian defences.

General Palissier had combined his attack in such a manner as to prevent the enemy from concentrating heavy masses against any point of British approach.

It had been previously concerted that, whilst the Black Batteries, Malakoff, and Redan were assaulted at noon, storming columns should be moved against the Central Bastion and the Flagstaff Redoubt on the eastern side of Sebastopol.

Had all these attacks been simultaneous, success would probably have crowned the efforts of the Allies on more than one point, and the French might have established a firm footing on the west, whilst the English effected a lodgment on the Redan.

The operations were not taken simultaneously, perhaps because the commanders were unwilling to risk the loss of life consequent upon failure, had we been repulsed at all points.

The Malakoff was, therefore, stormed first, and the attacks on the other points undertaken afterwards.

The consequence was that time was given to the Russians to make preparations which rendered their resistance effectual on all but the first point, spiritedly carried and maintained by the French.

One grand result compensated the Allies for the carnage which had marked the operations of the day.

The Malakoff taken, gave them such a hold over the remainder of the town that it was at once obvious that the Russians could not remain there.

Gradually, as the gloom of night spread its dark mantle over the town, a mournful silence succeeded to the roar of battle, and songs of victory alone broke the stillness of the atmosphere, as the wind moaned against the innumerable tents of the allied camps, and swiftly drove heavy lowering clouds over the dark-grey sky.

A hum, as of marching legions moving through Sebastopol, was then heard, and presently portentous clouds of smoke were seen to arise from the houses which lay clustered along the sides of the harbour.

From the base of these columns of smoke flames then began to issue, and as midnight came, glaring masses of flame burst out from all parts of the town, and proclaimed the Russians vanquished and retreating.

Undisturbed in their work of destruction, the enemy were allowed to proceed, and as the forked fire illumined the horizon, spreading from house to house and obscuring the sky with dense masses of smoke and vapour, we clearly witnessed from the decks of the Terrible the scene of a burning city destroyed by its defenders.

Moscow had, in fact, repeated itself.

Long before the Russian columns began to cross the long bridge of rafts on their way from the town to the northern shore, the Redan had been occupied by the Highland Brigade in charge of the trenches.

Volunteers from several regiments entered the works shortly after midnight, and found them deserted of defenders.

Shortly after daybreak the last straggler of the Russian army had abandoned the south side, and then the bridge of rafts was cut adrift, taken in tow by the steamers, and scattered in all directions.

The only Russians left in the town were convicts, whose task it was to keep up the fires in all directions.

* * * *

Thus ended the great siege of Sebastopol, which had been in progress for more than a year.

It had involved the construction of seventy miles of trenches and the employment sixty thousand fascines, eighty thousand gabions, and a million of sand bags, and during its continuance more than one million five hundred thousand shells and cannon balls had been fired at or into the town from the mortars and heavy siege guns of the allied forces.

We captured in the city 4,000 cannon and 50 brass field pieces, 100,000 projectiles, and 200,000 milogrammes of gunpowder. Our total loss was under 10,000 men.

CHAPTER XCIII.
I GO ASHORE AND GATHER INCIDENTS.

THE sinking of the Russian three-deckers across the mouth of the harbour had prevented more effectually any of our ships getting in, and on two prior occasions they had had quite enough of opposing their wooden walls to the granite sides of the great Russian forts.

They could only, therefore, anchored at a respectful distance, pour shell and shot into certain portions of the city, which they did with great effect.

Then Balaclava was to come, however, at a later date.

After the fall of the city I very naturally expected that the war would be brought to a close, or at all events the fleet be ordered home, but such was not the case.

The Russians threw up earthworks and made an entrenched camp on the northern shore, and the Allies refortified the city to some extent and kept their old cantonments on the heights around as well.

Thus the foes still stood regarding each other like two battered prize-fighters who had fought many a hard round, but were quite ready for as many more.

I was annoyed, but there was no help for it.

I was now of course able to go ashore when I liked—Sebastopol being, so to speak, British (and French) property.

Burning with a very natural curiosity, I did so for the first time the day succeeding the one on which the city had been evacuated, and on landing I bent my steps at once in the direction of the Malakoff.

CHAPTER XCIV.
A WELL DESERVED THRASHING.

ON arriving at the Malakoff I found the French burying their dead.

They had plenty of work on their hands, for their red epauletted dead strewed the hill-side as thickly as poppies stud a field of ripe corn, whilst inside the great wall they lay like those same poppies cut down in rows by the sickle of the reaper in golden August.

Whilst I was surveying the scene with much of sorrow and meditation combined, I started at beholding amongst the dead a beautiful female face.

A face, too, that seemed strangely familiar to me.

I bent down and saw that the owner thereof was a vivandière, clad in the gay and dashing uniform of the Chasseurs de la Garde. I knew the now pale, cold face, half veiled by its wreath of golden hair. The beautiful dead had been Naomie L'Estrange.

She was dead beyond a doubt. There was a black, round bullet-hole in her ivory throat, and there was a large spatch of blood on the breast of her light-blue uniform. I put my fingers on her pulse and heart—both had ceased to beat. She was as cold as marble.

"A pity that a mere rat of the camp should have so pretty a face, isn't it?" said a voice behind me.

I looked round and saw that the speaker was the second lieutenant of the Terrible.

"Rat of the camp, indeed!" I retorted, hotly; "allow me to inform you, if you do not know already, that French soldiers entertain a most chivalrous and almost sacred regard for the vivandières of their regiments That poor dead lamb died, I have no doubt, as pure and spotless as an English princess could do."

"Oh! man of much faith!" laughed the lieutenant, "I would wager very heavily to the contrary, very heavily indeed; and you must be a chivalrous—well, fool—to defend a wretched camp follower in such language as you have done. Bah! they are all tarred with the same brush."

"Will you kindly keep your evil thoughts to yourself, and avoid my company as much as you can?" I said, scarcely able to keep my fists out of his eyes.

"Oh, come, Dunbar, don't let us quarrel over a bit of French corruption like that," was the retort, accompanied by a taunting laugh.

"You dare fling such epithets at one who never can have wronged you, and whom you can by no possibility know anything about," I said, and as I spoke I drew my sword and smote him slightly across the chest with the flat of the blade.

Of course, I expected that he would at once draw his own and defend himself like a man.

But he turned black-red with passion, that was all

"You have not left your weapon behind you," I said, "I hope you have not forgotten how to use it."

"I never draw it except against a foe of my country," he said, sententiously, but biting his lips the while.

I sheathed my sword with a clash. I looked around in search of something, I knew not what.

But when I saw a drum-major's rattan lying on the ground, I knew what I wanted well enough.

I picked it up and half a dozen strides sufficed to bring me up with poor Naomie L'Estrange's insulter.

Before he well knew what I was going to do, I had grasped him by the collar, and then I thrashed him like the foul libeller that he was, until I broke the drum-major's rattan in fragments over his back.

"Now," I said, flinging the fragment away, and giving him a releasing push that caused him to measure his length upon the blood-sodden turf, "when you speak of any class of women in the future that you know nothing about, speak respectfully, or may you on every occasion receive just such another lesson as I have given you now."

"I will remember," was the reply, accompanied with such a look of deep and deadly animosity as I shall never forget, but I walked away without answering him, leaving him like a scotched snake amidst the tall rank grass.

I then got a burying party to dig a deep solitary grave for poor Naomie, and with my own hands I arranged her hair (first cutting off one long tress for a remembrance), wrapped her in the voluminous folds of a dead officer's scarlet cloak, and lowered her into her cold dark bed, waiting on its brink until her earthen coverlet was filled in to the surface.

I then gave the four soldiers (they did not belong to her regiment, or they would have made it a labour of love) a sovereign each, and watched them pile, as a worthy tombstone, a pyramid of cannon-balls above he grave.

This done, I sorrowfully returned to my ship.

CHAPTER XCV.

BACKBITING ALMOST LEADS TO BACKSHAVING.

THE very next morning, to my great surprise, I found when I got up that we were under weigh.

"Are we homeward bound?" I very naturally asked. The reply did not console me, for it was that we were bound northwards, to bombard the important Russian sea port of Kinburne.

It was a two hundred mile voyage, and would, doubtless, take us, with the then light baffling winds, two or three days to get there, and when there—well, then we should be just those two or three days further away from Old England than we were when lying off Sebastopol.

I was not very delighted, as may well be imagined, for I had seen more than enough of fighting in every shape, and I knew that Kinburne was a strongly fortified place, and that it would be a case of wooden walls against stone forts again, with all the advantage on the side of the atter.

But there were far greater disagreeables in store for me.

I noticed a great coolness on the part even of those who hitherto had been the most friendly with me, and their coolness seemed to increase with every succeeding hour of the day.

Half guessing, yet determined fully to know the way and wherefore of all this, I, after dinner, called the ship's surgeon, who had been a particular crony of mine, into my cabin, and asked him what the deuce was up.

He hesitated for a minute or two, but I pressed him closer and closer, for I saw by his manner that he knew, and so presently he burst out with—

"Well, I have told everybody that perhaps there's something to say on both sides, though the majority won't have it. Right or wrong, however, I certainly think you should have challenged Hayward for the thrashing he gave you. Of course, some people conscientiously disapprove of duelling, but in cases like this a man must challenge or become a laughing-stock."

"What the deuce are you talking about?" I asked.

"Why, he says that he caught you the other day attempting to foully use a pretty little French vivandière in the ruins of the Malakoff. That having a stick in his hand, he sprang upon you and thrashed you to within an inch of your life. That afterwards he had offered you satisfaction, where, when, and with what weapons you liked, and that you had replied that you had conscientious scruples against duelling," and the doctor looked me very hard in the face.

It was plain that he half believed Lieutenant Hayward's tale.

I was naturally in a great rage, but I replied—

"Wait till supper time, doctor, and you'll see some fun."

A brilliant idea had, in fact, come into my head.

Supper time at last came, and we were seated once more round the gleaming mahogany.

It was the first lieutenant's watch, and so both the captain and the second lieutenant were at the table.

So was the doctor and many other officers in both branches of the service. It was quite a brilliant sight.

Brilliant as ice to me, for whereas everyone had been cool in the morning, cold at noon, freezing in the afternoon, they were now a very long way below zero.

Nobody spoke to me, nobody offered to take wine with me, but toward Lieutenant Hayward they were extra polite, and he seemed to glory in his position.

I waited until everyone had made a good feed, for I neither wanted to spoil their appetites nor my own, and then I said, fixing Hayward with my glass—

"How does your back feel? Still rather stiff with the welting I gave you the other day, eh?"

Hayward flushed crimson to the very roots of his hair.

"I ought to ask you that question," he said, with a sneer.

"Oh," I replied, "have you been informing this worshipful company that you broke a stick over my back the other day, because you caught me insulting a little French girl within the ruins of the Malakoff?"

"If I have, it is the truth," he rejoined, sullenly

"Liar!" I retorted, tossing a glass of wine in his face. "You know that 'twas I who thrashed you for insulting the dead, and that you took the thrashing like a cowardly cur."

"Liar in your teeth," replied Lieutenant Hayward. "I swear by my hopes of heaven, and my honour as an English gentleman, that my tale is true and yours utterly false. Most of these gentlemen, who have known me for years, will have no hesitation which of us to believe."

"Well, then, to convince them who is right, I challenge you," quoth I, rising to my feet, and facing him.

"That chance is gone by," sneered Hayward; "you refused my challenge, and now I won't condescend to accept yours."

"But I don't mean a challenge to swords or pistols," said I. "I challenge you to show your back, and you dare not, you poor, miserable, branded whelp. Has it healed from the music staves I gave it with the French drum-major's rattan yesterday. I'm quite willing to peal, and show that mine is free from any marks of your fictitious hiding."

"Bravo!" shouted my friend the doctor. "I'll bet fifty to one that Hayward bears the brand."

But Lieutenant Hayward growled that, "If people didn't choose to accept his bare word, he'd be hanged if he'd take the trouble to convince them in any other way," and forthwith slunk out of the cabin.

Then the company thawed, and I could tell by their almost instantaneous change of manner that my bold challenge and its refusal had carried conviction with it and that my version of the thrashing in the ruins of the Malakoff was accepted as the true one.

Twenty-four hours later we were nearly lost on the Kosa Tendra, or Great Tongue Reef, so called from its shape, but a change of wind saved us, and very soon after Kinburne Head rose to view.

We were off the town about midnight.

CHAPTER XCVI.

THE BOMBARDMENT OF KINBURN.

WE should have commenced the bombardment forthwith, had not the wind rose and blown us off the shore.

The weather continued so squally that operations could not be commenced for two more days, during which the forts fired upon every vessel that approached near enough for the bullets to tell on, though without doing very much damage.

Wednesday, the 17th October, the anniversary of the first great naval attack upon Sebastopol, was fine enough to permit the allied fleets to attack.

The wind was blowing off shore. The swell had subsided.

This was indispensable, because many of the line-of-battle ships were drawing twenty-six feet of water, and they were to anchor and attack with only two or three feet of water under their keels.

This was a ticklish job, in a narrow difficult channel hitherto almost unknown to us.

Well, at eight a.m. the sand batteries opened at a steamer and a gunboat, which had forced their way inside the spit. The French floating batteries were making up, preparing to go in, and at 9.30 they opened a tremendous fire at five hundred yards from twelve long guns on each broadside.

At ten, the mortar-boats opened fire, and three French gunboats were working along from the southward by the shore where the troops had been landed.

The boats of the Firebrand, Furious, and Leopard had been digging out their own paddle-box boats and flats, which had been swamped in the surf and then half buried in the sand.

At 10.30, however, these steamers weighed, and proceeded to the flagship.

At this moment fifteen gunboats were blazing away over the mortar-boats and batteries.

Some heavily armed French steamers and the Odin were also firing, and shells were from every direction bursting over the Russian forts, which returned the terrible fire rapidly and boldly.

The Russian gunners could be seen standing bravely up on the ramparts, sponge and rammer in hand, loading and firing away as if they were at practice.

When one was knocked over another jumped up.

Three of them were enough to work each gun—one to work the elevating screw and let the gun slip down the incline to run it out, another to lay and fire (the recoil sent the gun in again), and a third to sponge, &c.; and this is how so few were killed.

At 11.30 a.m., signal was made to the Valorous to weigh immediately; to the Sidon, Curacoa, and Gladiator to follow; also to the Firebrand to go in at once and engage the batteries to right and left.

The two earth and sand batteries on the spit were spitting away merrily out of their ugly mouths.

It was not a pleasant thing to look at their square, black embrazures, looking like five or six old, black, tobacco-stained teeth stuck in a Fury's upper gums, and to know that they were only waiting to get you in a favourable position to open fire upon you at five hundred yards point blank range.

The Curacoa went in at them in a business-like way; the Dauntless very gingerly and circumspectly indeed; but the Terrible dashed on, and was now hammering at them so hard as almost to bury them in a heap of stony sand.

She did her work admirably, and nearly shut them up.

It was a brilliant sight, too, to see the Valorous, Sidon, Firebrand, and Gladiator run up to within eight hundred yards engaging north shore batteries, then run down to within five hundred yards of the sand battery, engaging that, and lastly float into the calm waters at the Dnieper's mouth, where, perhaps, no British ships had ever floated before.

Noon. The liners go in to work, and the barracks in the fort burn fiercely, especially around where the Russian colours are hoisted. Their guns are firing rapidly still.

12.30. The line-of-battle ships open fire all at once, the Hannibal alone bestowing her attentions at too respectful a distance upon the land batteries.

The brave Admiral (Stewart) had gone into the Valorous. But even this was not peril enough, so he forthwith hoisted his pretty white ensign aboard a small steam gun-boat, the little Pilot Fish, pushed her in front of all, and led in his little squadron, like the gallant dashing commander that he is.

2.30. A flag of truce was hoisted, and the whole Russian garrison marched out under arms.

The gunners from the sand forts marched in, bearing on stretchers their wounded; one dead.

They buried him, stretcher and all, in the sand, stuck up a rude cross at his head, and marched on.

The allied troops then marched into the fort and the union of British ensign and tricolor was seen on high.

The general and officers of the Russian battalion were made to pile their arms outside the fort.

Their muskets seemed new and in first-rate condition.

They walked on, bearing the banners and ornaments of their church, and were placed under a French guard at the headquarters, about three miles north of the town.

They formed one complete battalion, two colonels, four majors, four captains, and about twelve hundred men.

Their loss was reported at one man killed and ninety-eight wounded, some very severely.

The English lost two men by the bursting of a sixty-eight pounder gun on board the Arrow gun-boat, and Lieutenant Hayward, of the Terrible, slain by the fragment of a shell, with three wounded.

The French lost twenty-seven in killed and wounded in their floating batteries.

This was the last port blockaded. Soon after its fall Russia sued for peace, and the allied fleets were at once ordered home.

I returned in the Terrible, and very glad was I to see the shores of old England after so long an absence.